Dear ~~Kimberly~~,

# A CLOUD
of **WITNESSES**

Hope you
enjoy it !

Emily
Hanlon

A MARTHA AND MARYA MYSTERY

# A CLOUD
*of* WITNESSES

# EMILY HANLON

CHRISM
PRESS

This is a work of fiction. All characters and events portrayed in this novel are either fictitious or used fictitiously.

A CLOUD OF WITNESSES

Chrism Press, a division of WhiteFire Publishing
13607 Bedford Rd NE
Cumberland, MD 21502

ISBNs:  979-8-88709-059-7 (print)
        979-8-88709-060-3 (digital)

For Edith

and

Mark

# MURDER SUSPECTS
## IN ORDER OF APPEARANCE

FATHER THADDEUS MARTIN, a fire-and-brimstone priest from the Legionnaires of Dies Irae, who will do anything to win his spiritual war against the evil one and his minions.

MICHAEL WARD, the handsomest man in the parish of Saint John of the Cross, whose mousy wife, Lisa Ward, recently died.

DR. STEVEN IANELLI, the doctor of most of the Saint John's parishioners.

BITSY IANELLI, looks like a model and dresses to kill, hails from a family as rich and classy as they come.

ISABELLA BONINO, a fiery beauty who came from Italy as the teen bride of a man decades older than she.

JOHNNY BONINO, the much older husband of Isabella Bonino and lawyer to most of the Saint John's parishioners.

ALDO TODI, as unattractive as his good friend Michael Ward is handsome. He grew up in Pequot Bays, then left for a long time, but won't speak about what happened in those missing years.

GERTRUDE DOPPELDECKER, a woman of vague appearance and indeterminate age, a newcomer who has managed to learn everything about everyone, yet no one knows anything about her.

KEN VANCE, Father Thaddeus's right hand man and treasurer of Dies Irae, out to recruit the richest members of the community into the organization.

BARBARA VANCE, Ken Vance's long-suffering wife, who will do anything he asks of her.

LUZ FLORES, Father Thaddeus's most devoted follower.

# CHAPTER 1

The 26th Week in Ordinary Time
Tuesday, September 27

BANG. THE DOOR TO FATHER SEAMUS'S OFFICE slammed open, and a sonorous voice rang out. "Suicide is a mortal sin. I will have no part of it."

*Buzz.* Martha Collins's phone lit up, announcing a call from Marya Cook.

*Bam.* Martha dropped a carton filled with stuffed and sealed envelopes for the Bishop's Annual Appeal on the outgoing mail pile.

All three happened at the same moment, but Martha prioritized and acted on each of them in her usual efficient manner.

First, she checked off *Bishop's Annual Appeal mailing* from her to-do list.

Next, she went to the door of the office and observed a cassock-clad cleric in his forties, skinny to the point of appearing emaciated, whose piercing eyes glared out from under a sharp brow topped with stringy black hair. He strode out of Father Seamus's office, nose in the air, not acknowledging Martha's presence although he walked within two feet of her.

She let the call from Marya go to voicemail.

Father Seamus, the pastor of Saint John of the Cross Parish, stood sputtering at the door of his office. Tall and slim with a mop of white hair and dark, shaggy eyebrows drawn together as he glared at the exiting priest, he looked as Irish as his accent proved him to be. He shook his head. "What an eejit." He glanced at Martha. "What are you doing here?"

"And good day to you too, Seamus. I'm finishing up the mailings for the Bishop's Annual Appeal. In a couple of days, we're meeting to report on our progress, and the bishop will be there to thank us for our hard work. So I figured I should have it done."

Father Seamus's eyes narrowed. "The bishop. It's all his fault." He gazed at Martha, head tilted. Then his eyes lit up. "Of course. The bishop. And you're going to see him. You're in good with him. You're sort of his diocesan liaison, right?"

"Sort of."

"He likes you."

"I guess."

"He doesn't like *me*."

"No?"

"No. Do you have time for a chat?"

They walked past Lena, the church secretary, who scowled at Martha as she began to feed the hundreds of Bishop's Annual Appeal envelopes into a postage meter. As she entered Father Seamus's office, Martha fought her urge to neaten the heaps of papers strewn over his large walnut desk. But she could not stop herself from closing one of the open drawers of the putty-colored file cabinets that lined the walls. She sat down across the desk from Father Seamus.

"Well now, Martha, have you met that eej—that priest who just walked out of my office?"

"No, can't say I've had the pleasure. Who is he?"

Father Seamus shook his head, and his face took on the same thundercloud expression it had worn as he watched the eejit leave. "His name is Father Thaddeus Martin. He's a priest of the Legionnaires of Dies Irae."

"Never heard of them."

"More the luck on you. I hadn't either, until the Bishop said the— Father Thaddeus was to stay here while he organized a group of lay members of Dies Irae from around the area. Unfriendly fellow. He didn't want to stay with us in the rectory, so I gave him an office and living quarters on the second floor of the parish center. I still don't know what his group actually does. He talks a bit about homeless shelters, and a lot about fear and trembling, the day of wrath, and a war against the devil. It's bad enough he's snatched away a nice-sized group of my parishioners, active ones at that, who are now exclusively devoted to his cause, but now, but now…" He sputtered again. "A follower of his, one of my parishioners, and a lovely and faithful woman at that, has died, and he's washing his hands of her."

"I heard him. Said it was a suicide. Are you going to do the funeral? Is it allowed?"

"Of course it's allowed. We leave final judgement to God's mercy, not to that…that…Father Thaddeus. And yes, I'm doing the funeral in…" He glanced at the grandfather clock by the office door. "Forty-five minutes. It's Lisa Ward. Did you know her?"

*Oh no. Lisa Ward. How sad.* She was young, maybe in her forties, not much older than Martha. Mousy brown hair, small build, with great big eyes, always looking about, blinking. "No, not really. I mean, I knew her well enough to say hello. You know, from church."

Father Seamus locked eyes with Martha. "Martha, I need your help."

Martha raised an eyebrow. *By the gunny sack of Saint Caesarius, the last time Seamus asked for help, it was to investigate the murder of a parishioner. Could he think that Lisa Ward was murdered?*

Martha had a lot on her plate at the moment, but if Seamus needed her help to solve another murder, how could she refuse? She felt a thrill of anticipation run down her spine.

"Well, Seamus, she *did* look her usual self last Sunday in church. Quiet as always, but friendly enough. And after all, why should she commit suicide? She was married to the best-looking guy at Saint John's. From my mailings, I know she lived on Pequot Island. So she was rich. But who could have killed her? And why?" Martha grabbed a notepad from under a pile of papers on the desk and took a pen from a ceramic pot serving as a pen holder. It had no ink, so she reached over and took another, then another, until she found one that worked. She made a neat line down the middle of the paper and wrote *Suspects* on one side and *Motivation* on the other. "Let's start with suspects." She looked up at the priest, pen at the ready.

He stared at her, mouth agape. "Suspects? What are you talking about? I'm talking about Father Thaddeus."

Martha felt her cheeks redden. "What about Father Thaddeus?"

"I need your help to get rid of him." He chuckled. "And I *don't* mean by murdering him. You're to see the bishop in a couple of days. And you'll have an opportunity to talk to him, right?"

"Well, just a few of us will be there, and there's a luncheon."

"Perfect. So you can explain to him that Father Thaddeus is a disruptive influence here."

"But I don't know anything about him."

"Well, now, that's not exactly true. I just told you about him. He's an unfriendly, unforgiving, off-putting fanatic, and we don't want him around our friendly, forgiving, welcoming parish. Will you do it?"

"Well, I'll tell him that's what you said."

"No, you can't do that. You can't mention me."

"Why not?"

"I told you. He doesn't like me."

"Why doesn't he like you?"

"That's a tale for another time." Father Seamus looked down as his already ruddy complexion turned ruddier.

Martha understood wanting to keep quiet about some things that had happened in the past.

"Well then, Martha, maybe you could learn yourself what an, um, *disruptive influence* he is. Go to Lisa's funeral. She was one of his greatest supporters. Her husband Michael too. Some of the others will be there, I'm sure. You can talk to them. Get an idea of how he operates. He seems to brainwash my parishioners into joining, like a cult. The bishop won't like that. Give me that notepad, and I'll make a list of his followers from Saint John's. They call themselves," he rolled his eyes, "the guardians of the good."

She gave him the notepad. He looked down at the first page, gave another little chuckle, tore it off, and began to write.

Martha glanced at her watch. She had hoped to get in at least two more fares in the next hour. Money had been tight since the maintenance on her condo skyrocketed. Plus, her car's suspension system had broken, and she'd needed a new boiler. Her Uber work wasn't keeping up with expenses, even with the extra hours. She'd have to dig into savings again this month. Martha liked the freedom of her Uber work and didn't want to have to take a nine-to-five job. She would have to come up with a plan to take care of herself, as she had since she was nineteen years old. She had no time for this territorial war between two priests.

She looked up and met Father Seamus's gaze, wide-eyed, with his shaggy eyebrows raised in hope. She stared back, eyes narrowed in what she hoped was a determined "no" look. They stared at each other for about ten seconds. Then she shook her head and blinked.

"Oh, all right, Seamus, I'll check out the situation and come to my own conclusions. If they match yours, I'll talk to the bishop."

Father Seamus's features broke into a grin. "I knew I could rely on you, Martha. Together we'll take care of that eejit." He handed her the list of parishioners. "Got to get ready now. See you at the funeral."

Father Seamus walked out of the office toward the sacristy. Martha eyed her watch again and checked her to-do list, which had a total of seventeen items remaining. She added, *18. Go to funeral* just so she could have the pleasure of putting a check mark next to it when it was done.

*Oh well. At least this time it doesn't involve a murder.*

M&M

Martha entered the church through the side chapel and looked out from the front of the nave. She had never seen a funeral with so few in attendance. It had not been posted on the bulletin board, and she guessed that Lisa's relatives had been quiet about it.

The organ music began, and the sweet strains of "Ave Maria" accompanied the principal mourners—Lisa Ward's husband, Michael Ward, and their son Justin—who led a small group that preceded the casket down the center aisle. Justin was about twenty, but his face had transformed with the contortions of a crying child. In contrast, Michael's handsome, strong features, olive skin, and green eyes appeared to be carved in marble, one black curl falling over a brow lined in sorrow. With his athletic build and movie-star looks, Michael had always outshone his wife Lisa, who had seemed a timid, mousy presence at his side.

Justin reached out and touched his father's arm but received no response. The son slowed his pace and dropped back to walk next to an older woman and gripped her hand. Michael led the sorrowful procession alone, his steps slow and heavy, at odds with the tempo and rhythm of the organ music.

Martha looked away from the grieving husband and glanced around the church. The sun streamed through the stained-glass saints in the windows that lined both sides of the nave, and shimmered its multicolored beams of light on the few mourners in attendance.

As Martha looked around for the members of Dies Irae Father Seamus had noted on the pad, her doctor, Steven Ianelli, gave her a friendly smile. She gave him a small wave back. A ray of blue light hit his kindly features, bringing out the grey in his short, salt-and-pepper hair, making him appear older than his mid-fifties. He wore the same old-fashioned, well-fitting, three-piece gray suit, blue and red striped tie, French-cuffed white shirt, with cufflinks and matching tie tack, that he wore every day. He sometimes joked that he did not have time to choose his clothes in the morning, so he owned five identical suits, shirts, and ties. Martha thought it was good of him to take the time to come to the funeral of one of his patients. She knew he had just returned yesterday from a month in Europe because her annual checkup had been rescheduled to accommodate the vacation. His face reflected more than the measured sadness he usually showed at his patients' funerals. Martha remembered that Lisa had been his receptionist before she married.

The blue light from the stained-glass window added drama to the photogenic features of Dr. Ianelli's wife, Bitsy, as she acknowledged Martha with a slight nod. Bitsy had mentioned more than once that had it not been for her diminutive height, she could have had a successful career as a runway model, and her high cheek bones, poreless skin, and slim, toned figure still justified that claim. She carried herself with an air of superiority, of looking down on the "little people"—though not literally, considering her short stature. She was a purebred, a Boston Brahmin from a family of the highest status. Someone had once joked that Bitsy's people were just below the Lowells, who spoke only to Cabots, and the Cabots spoke only to God.

Neither Bitsy nor Dr. Ianelli were on Father Seamus's barely legible list of the Dies Irae followers. But Isabella Bonino was.

A yellow sunbeam spotlighted Isabella Bonino and her family in the pew behind the Ianellis. A curvy woman with a Roman nose and soft lips, she appeared a bit too young to be the mother of her teenage son, Luca, seated on one side of her, and far too young to be the wife of her husband, Johnny Bonino, who was seated on the other side. She wore a black silk blouse with an alarming number of upper buttons unbuttoned. Isabella looked up at Michael Ward with lips parted and bright eyes as he passed. He met her glance, then looked away.

*Now if Lisa had been killed…* But Martha was not here to investigate a murder. She looked down at the list of Dies Irae members.

Aldo Todi. Martha squinted in an effort to decipher Father

Seamus's handwriting. It looked like he'd made a note that Aldo had been a member of Dies Irae and then quit. A swath of red light bathed the sickly pallor of Aldo's pockmarked skin. Martha didn't know whether Todi meant "toad" in Italian or not, but it would have been an appropriate name for him. His appearance could not have been in greater contrast to that of his good friend, the grieving husband, Michael Ward. Aldo's eyes met Martha's, and the corners of his mouth turned up in a way that Martha would not have described as a smile. No way would she strike up a conversation with him to ask why he left the group. But if Lisa *had* been murdered, he would be her principal suspect.

No other Dies Irae members were present. Father Thaddeus must have discouraged his flock from attending. Only one other person sat in the front pews. She was a member of the funeral committee, but while the other committee members sat together in the back, she had chosen to sit behind Aldo Todi. But then, she could sit wherever she wanted and no one would notice. Her only distinguishing feature was the name on the funeral committee tag pinned to the loose beige cardigan she wore over a pair of loose beige pants: Gertrude Doppeldecker. That name was not on Father Seamus's list. She sat in shadow, no sun ray illuminating her presence.

Martha heard a tap-tap-tap and followed a soft beam of lavender light from one of the stained-glass windows down to the rear of the center aisle, where she saw Marya Cook. The light turned Marya's fuzzy white hair to a Goth girl's purple tint. A mauve hat with a lilac veil and purple grapes perched precariously on the old woman's head. It must have slipped in her hurry to make it to the funeral on time. Her lavender raincoat draped with an eggplant shawl was unbuttoned, disclosing a neon orchid button-down shirt with a plum and white striped scarf tied in a bow at the collar. A violet and amethyst checked sweater vest completed the visible part of Marya's apparel. Martha had never thought that purples could clash until she met Marya.

A pang of guilt flashed through Martha, like the shadow of a passing cloud on an autumn day. It had been quite a while since she had driven Marya to the doctor or to church. And then Marya always wanted her to stay, have a cup of tea, chat. Martha had been busy working lately, trying to make up the deficit in her finances. She would call her tomorrow.

The bright timbres of "Ave Maria" floated away. Father Seamus stood up, his vestments a bit short, and walked over to the lectern. Martha loved the opening prayer that he always used for funerals—the same prayer used at her parents' funeral, filled with hope and faith in the resurrection.

"Almighty God and Father, it is our certain faith that your servant, Lisa Louise Guardino Ward, whom you called out of this world, will be carried safely home to heaven and come to enjoy your eternal reward."

The Mass proceeded quickly. The brief homily gave no hint of the manner of Lisa's death, and there were no words of remembrance by a member of the family. Martha checked her watch. She might be able to get in at least one extra Uber fare after all.

The organ began the uplifting measures of "Be Not Afraid," and the family followed the casket down the aisle. There was no receiving line, and they continued to their cars to drive behind the hearse to the cemetery.

In the parking lot, Father Seamus caught Martha's eye and gestured with his head toward Isabella Bonino, who stood nearby. Martha gave him a slight nod and turned to begin her investigation.

If Bitsy Ianelli could have been a model, Isabella Bonino could have been a star in the 1960s Italian cinema. Long, wavy black hair and thick, perfectly-formed eyebrows framed her smoky hazel eyes. She had moved to Pequot Bays from Italy only fifteen years ago as a new bride. She still retained the accent from her country of birth and a wealth of Italian expressions that enlivened her speech. Isabella wore a slight smile as she watched the grieving family walking toward their cars.

"Hello, Isabella."

Isabella jumped. "Oh! Martha. *Scusa*. I was daydreaming." She shook her dark waves away from her face and gave Martha a big smile. "So sad about Lisa."

Martha nodded.

"They were my nextdoor neighbors. Well, they still are. Michael and Justin, that is. It will take time for Justin to get over the loss of *la sua madre*. Look at him. The image of *il suo padre*."

Martha followed Isabella's gaze. Justin did indeed look like a taller, skinnier version of his father, down to the stray curl falling onto his forehead. He had finally stopped crying. His eyes, glinting green even from this distance, were focused on Marya Cook, who rested both hands on her cane as she arched her neck to look up at the young man. He nodded as she spoke. She gave him her cane to hold and began rummaging through the neon orange and lavender plaid tote on her right shoulder.

"Justin." Michael Ward called from the black limo.

"Just a sec, dad. It's Marya Cook. Remember her?" He turned back to Marya, who handed him one of her laminated notecards inscribed with a Bible quote in her immaculate purple script. Martha wondered which quote she had chosen for Justin on this occasion. They were always remarkably apt, as Father Seamus had put it. Justin took the card, read it, and started crying again. He enclosed Marya in a big hug, then released her and gave back her cane. He walked to the limo, his eyes on the card.

Martha turned to Isabella, who was waving at Michael Ward as the limo passed by. Michael did not respond. Martha studied Michael's impenetrable expression, pondering the possibilities. By the time she turned back to ask about Father Thaddeus, Isabella had already hurried away to join her husband and son.

*But if this were murder…*

# CHAPTER 2

Wednesday, September 28

THE NEXT MORNING, MARTHA WOKE UP EARLY FOR Mass. She had never really been a daily Mass goer, but Father Seamus had issued a desperate plea for new eucharistic ministers when the usual volunteers began to retire. Martha felt that her talents were more organizational than spiritual, so she had not answered the call until Father Seamus made a personal, direct appeal. Someone had to do it. She recalled a saying on a card that Marya had given her.

> *God loves a cheerful giver.*
> *2 Corinthians 9:7.*

Martha wondered how He felt about reluctant givers.

She poured her first cup of coffee and looked around her home with approval. It was a corner unit with an open floor plan and large windows that illuminated the space, even in the early morning light. Glass-paned doors opened onto the deck and backyard, which extended into a side yard. She congratulated herself for the umpteenth time for her foresight in buying the best unit in the condominium after her parents had died. Even at nineteen years old, after discovering that her deluxe life had been built on hopes, dreams, and debt, she'd had the wisdom and practical sense to buy this apartment on spec at a low price with part of her limited inheritance.

After she bought the condo, she'd invested the remaining monies, which allowed her a quiet middle-class life as long as she supplemented it with a side job. She had worked in a bookstore until the owner, who'd also served as Pequot Bays Civilian Police Commissioner, had decided to move to Florida. She had encouraged Martha to run for commissioner in her place. With her support, Martha had won. But she'd lost her last bid for reelection thanks to her own version of "the eejit," Police Lieutenant Michael O'Hara. She'd had to begin driving for Uber to make up the lost income, but it paid less and had no benefits. The condo's maintenance costs had doubled since she bought it and were set to rise again at the end of the year. She had to come up with a plan, and soon.

Bookshelves lined one wall of the dining area, the paperbacks separate from the hardcover books, all arranged by color. The four dining room chairs were pulled out a precise, equal distance from the round table, with each placed directly across from its mate. Two matching tweedy armchairs stood at ninety-degree angles on either side of the chocolate brown couch, which faced the TV. The chocolate brown blankets covering the couch were the only messy thing in the room. Martha looked fondly at Quincy, her chocolate brown Labrador Retriever, asleep on the couch. Quincy was as finicky as Martha, and religiously replaced her doggie toys in the doggie toy box in the corner of the room.

Martha finished her coffee and drove to church. She was disappointed to see Father Seamus preparing for Mass. Martha had signed up to be eucharistic minister on Wednesdays because Father Peanuts usually presided, and she appreciated his pace. His daily Mass homilies were invariably based on a joke he attributed to Charlie Brown, and lasted no more than two minutes. Father Seamus spoke longer, but at least he was not as bad as Father Damien, the priest who used to visit Father Jim until they were both charged with murder. After Martha and Marya tracked down the true killer, Father Damien had decided his real mission was to serve jailed convicts. She felt sorry for the prisoners who had to sit through his one-and-a-half-hour Masses.

Father Seamus waylaid Martha as she entered. He whispered, "Did Isabella give you the lowdown on Thaddeus? Will you talk to the bishop for me?"

She avoided his eyes. "Um. Talking to more people today."

Mass began promptly at 8:30. Martha glanced at her watch before and after the homily. Only five minutes and twenty-seven seconds. Not bad. The petitions would be a bit longer than usual though. At daily Mass, Father Seamus allowed the congregation to call out their personal intentions.

When the time came, a squeaky voice piped up, "For my sister who's going to have an operation this morning. Let us pray to the Lord."

Heads turned in the direction of the voice. "Lord, hear our prayer."

"For all those who have no one to pray for them, let us pray to the Lord."

"Lord, hear our prayer."

"For the repose of the soul of Lisa Ward, let us pray to the Lord."

All heads, including Martha's, swiveled toward Gertie Doppeldecker, who had called out that petition.

"Lord, hear our prayer."

The Mass proceeded. Martha gave Communion to the attendees, including Marya, who had made it to church just in time. Martha could not look Marya in the eye as she said, "The Body of Christ," before placing the Eucharist into her outstretched hands.

After Mass, a group of people gathered around Gertie Doppeldecker. She was a small woman, neither old nor young. Her hair was an indeterminate beige cut to an indeterminate length, her eyes a lusterless brown. Even her expression was vague. She always seemed to be lurking in the shadows of Saint John's, and if the church's old walls did not have ears, Gertie certainly did. And a mouth too! Martha slowed down. Maybe after everyone left, she could get some information about Dies Irae from Gertie.

"...the funeral, I heard one of the relatives say she overdosed on sleeping pills. It was the same night as the Italian Festival. She looked just fine when I saw her eating spaghetti and meatballs at the Knights of Columbus tent. But Lisa—"

"Amazing meatballs!" someone said.

"The best," someone responded. "They make twenty-five hundred every year and still run out."

"And the sauce, so spicy. I tried to get the recipe but—"

"Ahem." Gertie looked pointedly at the sources of the interruption. "But Lisa must have gone home, and, well… She had a prescription for sleeping pills. At first they thought she'd accidentally ODed. But after the autopsy, they said no one could take that many pills accidentally."

*Hmmm. Sleeping pills.* Sleeping pills had played a part in their last murder investigation. She glanced at Marya, who stood at the edge of the group huddled around Gertie. *Wonder if she's thinking the same thing I am.*

Gertie shook her head. "So sad." But she did not look sad.

"God have mercy on her soul," someone said.

"Lisa was such a devoted Catholic," someone else offered.

"She and Michael were going on Father Seamus's pilgrimage to the Holy Land."

"So am I," said another. "Lisa was really looking forward to that trip. She'd just put down the full payment. It's $7500 this year. That's $500 more than the last one."

Over murmurs of disapproval about making a profit on such a holy experience, Gertie piped up, "Isn't that nice they were planning to take a vacation together? They must have worked things out at their counseling session with Father Seamus."

The murmurs died away, and heads snapped back to Gertie. "I didn't hear what they were saying, but I bet I know what it was about. Sara Jane Paulsen came in just then and asked me to help her clean up the wax on the altar. You know," Gertie glanced around and whispered, "she was having an affair with Ken Vance! I—"

"Sara Jane Paulsen was having an affair with Ken Vance?"

"No. Lisa Ward," Gertie said. "Sara Jane doesn't even like him. Why she was saying just the other day that he was on the Pastoral Counsel with her, and at the last—"

"Lisa Ward was having an affair with Ken Vance?"

"Yes," Gertie answered. "I saw them in a coffee shop. Not in—"

"Who's Ken Vance?"

"The guy who looks like The Hulk. He's married to Barbara Vance. Barbie and Ken. Like the dolls," someone else supplied.

"Oh, yes. I know who they are. But she's no Barbie—"

"As I was saying," Gertie interrupted, "I saw them. Together. In a coffee shop in Millerton. I looked in the window and there they were, hidden away in a back booth, but I couldn't help seeing he was holding her hand. I think she was crying."

Ken and Barbara Vance were on Father Seamus's list. Those Dies Irae members certainly seemed to flaunt the sixth commandment. The bishop wouldn't like that.

The door to the rectory opened, and Father Seamus walked in with a repairman. The group scattered. Martha heard a loud whisper.

"Did you hear? Sara Jane is having an affair with Ken Vance."

Gertie walked toward the door, still chatting. Martha glanced at Marya, who smiled and waved at her. Martha waved back, but she had no time to talk now. To assuage her guilt, Martha added *23. Call Marya* to her to-do list as she followed Gertie onto the portico of the church.

The sky had darkened, and it threatened rain. Martha waited for Gertie's conversation to end, but it went on and on. She took a deep breath and tried to relax. She did not have time for this. She needed to rustle up some Uber fares. Seamus would have to get someone else to do his dirty work—someone who wasn't in danger of losing her savings or her condo. She'd call him this afternoon and tell him.

As she turned to go, she caught a glimpse of Father Thaddeus striding toward the parish center, his cassock flapping in the wind.

She'd give it one last try. Go straight to the horse's mouth. She caught up with him in the middle of the parking lot. "Father Thaddeus, may I talk to you?"

He turned around. He was impressive up close. Tall and gaunt with sharp features, he wore a large metal crucifix, the vertical post of the cross sharp like a spear, hanging from a heavy chain around his neck. His lank hair and eyes were as dark as his black cassock, his skin pale. His eyes darted everywhere. In a guttural, harsh voice, he said, "What do you want?"

Martha opened her mouth and then shut it. She had not thought of what she would say. "Um. Well. I was thinking that…uh…"

"I understand, my daughter."

"You do?"

"Yes, you are afraid."

"I am?"

"But you have come to the right place."

"I have?"

"We can protect you here."

"You can?"

At that moment there was a clap of thunder, and it began to rain. The priest looked at the sky and then at Martha. "You and your friend can follow me inside to continue our discussion."

"My friend?" Martha turned and saw the top of a violet umbrella with white polka dots. She had no need to look underneath to see who it was. She and Marya followed the priest past the thrift shop, Marya chattering away.

"My goodness, what a shame. It appears that the thrift shop is closed. The weather is becoming colder, and I had hoped to purchase an extra layer or two to wear under my raincoat. This is where I found that paisley scarf I gave you, my dear. Perhaps you could find another colorful scarf to brighten up your outfits. Or a nice dress. I think a lavender floral print would suit you very well…"

The three continued toward a red brick three story building, formerly the convent for the Immaculate Heart of Mary sisters who had taught at Saint John's elementary school. The sisters had, one by one, been reassigned or retired back to their mother house, and shortly after the last one, a dynamo of a principal, had left, the school closed. The first floor of the convent had been renovated to serve as a parish center and offices, but the sisters' living quarters on the second and third floors had remained untouched. A statue of Mary holding out her arms in welcome was set into an apse next to the door. Marya touched Mary's hand as they went by, and Martha noticed that the fingers of the statue were worn from years of such loving gestures.

They followed Father Thaddeus up a set of stairs to the second floor, where Father Seamus had assigned him several rooms as his living quarters and office space.

Marya nattered on, "Oh my. We were never allowed to enter the sisters' private living space. I recall that once, as a joke…"

The priest unlocked the door and stepped through. It banged shut behind Marya, closing off any illumination from the stairwell, leaving only a few bare lightbulbs that cast a harsh glow along the high ceilings of the hallway. A strong synthetic citrus fragrance met Martha's nose, some type of cleaning solution. But the sanitary smell could not overcome the ancient spirits that still inhabited the rooms. The aura that overhung the premises silenced even Marya.

The gloomy corridor ended in a pair of double doors with stained-glass medallions through which a dim light flickered. Father Thaddeus ushered the two women into a wood-paneled chapel, the stained-glass windows so covered with grime that the saintly figures were barely discernable. The only lights in the room were candles set on the windowsills.

A figure stood next to the altar at a lectern, clad in a monk's robe with large sleeves and a hood that left the face in shadows. A similar figure knelt on the floor in front of the lectern, not taking advantage of the kneelers in the pews. Another sat in the front pew, legs crossed, perusing a cell phone. Martha heard singsong chanting.

*...day of wrath, that day will break up the world into ash. As testified by David and the Sybil. How much trembling will there be when the judge comes...*

Father Thaddeus joined in, *"How much trembling will there be when the judge comes and strictly examines all things."*

At the sound of Father Thaddeus's voice, the figure sitting in the pew dropped to its knees.

"I must interrupt your prayers for a few minutes, my children."

The three robed figures turned toward the priest and lowered their hoods. Martha knew them, and they were all on Father Seamus's list. Barbara Vance had been the kneeling supplicant. Luz Flores had led the chant. And it had been Ken Vance thumbing through his cell phone. All three wore smaller versions of Father Thaddeus's spear crucifix.

Ken stood up. Tall, with a heavily muscled upper body, he could barely fit in in the robe, which should have swished gracefully along the ground. Instead, it showed at least five inches of chartreuse jogging pant with matching Nike sneakers. His usual immaculate, brown, Ken-doll-style hair had been mussed by the hood. Ken clenched his jaw, which made his devil-like goatee more prominent, and his eyes narrowed into a fierce glare. "What are they doing here?"

Barbara Vance pushed herself up from her knees. She glanced at Martha and Marya, then turned her gaze to her husband. Short, pasty, soft, and pudgy, Barbara looked nothing like a Barbie doll. The bow of the high-necked blouse she always wore peeked out of the monkish robe. Her thinning, mid-length hair showed too much scalp, the strands failing in their meager attempt to curl. Only her large brown eyes, focused intently on her husband, could have been called pretty. She clasped and unclasped her hands.

Luz Flores's eyes never left Father Thaddeus. Her robe fell like a sack over her skinny body. She had amber brown skin and sharp, bony features framed by short, jet-black hair with a shocking line of white running Mohawk-like down the middle. Her thick, dark eyebrows emphasized her oval, light green eyes. She followed Father Thaddeus's every move and seemed unaware that anyone other than the priest had entered the room.

How different she was from the Luz that Martha had once known. She used to run into Luz while walking Quincy. Luz always had one hand in her husband's and the other holding onto the leash of a lively and friendly Basset Hound, Merrie. At that time, Luz had had a trim, fit body and short, dark, wash-and-wear hair, and she always wore jeans, sneakers, and a T-shirt. They used to chat about Luz's adventures. She dragged her husband along to hike the Himalayas or helicopter ski in the Bugaboos. Whatever she did, he said, she did to the extreme. He would have preferred to spend all his time sailing, which they did a great deal of too, cruising to Bermuda and the Caribbean.

Five years ago, after Luz's husband died, she began to speak more and more about a religious organization, until eventually it was all she talked about. When Martha repeatedly refused Luz's invitations to the meetings, each began to drift to the opposite side of the street when their paths crossed while walking their dogs. The odd white streak had developed in Luz's hair soon after.

So, Dies Irae had replaced skiing and trekking. Now, having witnessed the intense stare and commanding ways of Father Thaddeus, Martha understood how Luz had come under his spell in her search to fill the void left by the death of her husband.

"Sit," the priest said to Martha. She sat in the front pew on the opposite side from Ken. Marya settled in next to her.

Father Thaddeus turned to Ken Vance. "These two women have come to us like lost lambs. They wish to join."

*By the little horse of Saint Nestor! He thinks we want to join this crazy group!* "Well, we don't exactly want to join, Father, but maybe you could tell us a little about yourself."

He turned back to Martha and Marya and held them in his gaze. "I will explain our mission and give you the choice to join..." His voice dropped an octave. "Or not."

Martha glanced at her watch as the priest moved toward the altar. She hoped this wouldn't take too long. He clasped his hands on top of the lectern and looked down, silently moving his lips. As he raised his head, Martha's glance shifted to the agonized face of Christ on the crucifix behind him. Both faces were lit by the eerie, flickering candlelight, and she could not decide whose expression was more tortured.

He spoke in measured phrases. "I am a priest of the Legionnaires of Dies Irae. Our mission is to educate and evangelize. We provide shelters to protect the homeless not only from cold and hunger but also from the powers of the dark and the spiritual forces of evil. I have been assigned the task of serving the Guardians, the lay members of our organization. God has been good, and there has been a large increase in our membership here and in the surrounding towns. Father Seamus has consented to allow me to lodge here when I am in the area to do our work." Father Thaddeus's eyes narrowed as he mentioned Father Seamus.

He stared at Martha. His jaw tightened, and he almost growled, "The devil prowls like a lion. He is a deceiver, and his greatest trick is to convince those who live in the world that he does not exist. Most are blinded by his lies, but I have been granted the grace to see through his disguises. A spiritual war is raging. I am equipped for battle and prepared to engage in it, no matter what the cost. It is my personal mission. My soldiers are the lay members of Dies Irae. Are you with us?" His eyes had not left Martha's, and she felt herself being drawn into his gaze.

She was about to nod her head yes when Marya spoke.

"That is so very kind of you to invite us, Father, but I am afraid that I must refuse. My champion is Mary, who is the strongest of all against the snares of the devil." She unwound a lilac and mauve striped scarf from around her neck, fumbled with the knot of a violet fringed shawl, and unbuttoned the top buttons of her lavender raincoat and the periwinkle sweater underneath it. She reached into the neck of her purple polka dotted blouse and pulled out a rectangular square of cloth. Her expression became as fierce as the priest's. "I wear our Lady's armor, you know. Our Lady of Mount Carmel scapular. Most people think of Mary as the gentle woman cradling Jesus. But she can also march into hell and snatch a sinner from the clutches of the evil one. I would advise you to place yourself under the protection of the Blessed Mother and trust her with the work of interceding to save souls."

The priest turned to Luz. "The brochure."

Luz ran over to a box in the corner of the chapel, removed two pamphlets, brought them to the priest, and then stood at attention at his side. Her almond eyes, large in the confines of her thin face, remained focused on Father Thaddeus until he nodded in the direction of the pews. She returned to her seat.

Father Thaddeus stepped away from the lectern and brought the pamphlets to Martha and Marya. "Read these before you decide." His eyes narrowed. "Whoever is not with us is against us."

Marya pulled out an index card covered with lavender writing from her bag and offered it to the priest. "Permit me to give you this in exchange." She turned to Martha. "Shall we go, my dear?"

Martha nodded.

"Wait," he ordered. "Bow your heads." He placed one hand on top of Marya's head and the other on Martha's. He closed his eyes and bowed. "Lord Jesus, the divine exorcist, protect these women from the evil spirit. In the name of the Father, of the Son and of the Holy Spirit. Amen."

He made the sign of the cross over their heads. Then with his head still lowered and his eyes still shut, he bent his elbows and entwined his fingers in an attitude of prayer. His lips moved silently. The two women left, and Martha shut the door behind them.

The rain had let up but still threatened, and once back down in the parking lot, Martha inhaled the fresh smell of ozone, which helped clear away the effects of her close encounter with Father Thaddeus.

"By the stepmother of Saint Edward the Martyr, I nearly enlisted back there, Marya. He's crazy, but he's convincing."

"Indeed. He is a mesmerizing and dangerous man, my dear. I must make up some new notecards to respond to him."

Martha checked her watch. 9:42. She'd lost track of time up there. Something she never did. She had to get working.

A voice called Martha's name. She turned around to see Aldo Todi walking toward her. He was short and barrel-chested, and the flat nose and angles on his gray face looked like they had been formed by a hasty potter with no time to smooth over his thumb marks. His lip was curled in its perpetual sneer.

He stopped in front of her, shoulders hunched, coughing. "Sorry. Breathing problem. Emphysema, they tell me." He slipped a cigarette between bluish lips, lit it, and took a deep drag. "Hello, Martha, how are you?" He nodded to Marya. "I don't believe I have ever had the pleasure of meeting your friend."

Martha thought there was a little sarcastic emphasis on "your friend."

"This is Marya Cook. I'm fine. Got to go, though."

"I'm not bad, not bad at all," he answered a question she had not asked, and not very truthfully at that, considering the hacking cough and the emphysema. "So, I see you've met the newest member of our parish family, Thaddeus, Guardian of the Guardians, hah! Thinking of joining Dies Irae?"

"No."

He nodded at Marya. "How about your friend here? Is she interested?"

"No, I am not, sir. I have found that Mary is a much more effective advocate against—"

"Stay away from them."

"Why?" Martha asked.

"I was a member. Once. Dies Irae is more controlling than our Holy Mother Church," he sneered, tracing a sign of the cross in the air. "Father Thaddeus and his minion, Ken Vance, they get a kick out of dominating the members. Once the two of them dupe someone into joining, they control how they act, what they say, even what they wear. But I know how to stop them." Aldo took another drag of his cigarette and coughed a few times.

Martha said, "Got to get go—"

Aldo talked over her. "Like the Bible says, you can't serve God and money—and money always wins. If I see anyone interested in Dies Irae, I let them know that members have to tithe ten percent of their earnings and change their wills to leave one tenth of their estate to Dies Irae. Ken is trying to up it to fifteen percent! I don't know why. They're raking it in. Of course, our holy Father Thaddeus doesn't let anyone know about the ten percent rule until they're under his spell. Then it's *pizzo*. A protection racket. You give us ten percent, we'll get you into heaven. But when I tell a chump up front, it stops them in their tracks. I just need to figure out how to convince the members he's already brainwashed that Thaddeus's 'mission' is just a scam. You two should steer clear of him. He doesn't take no for an answer."

Aldo turned, walked over to a white Mercedes SUV, revved the engine, and careened out of the parking lot, tires squealing.

Martha checked off 3. *Find out about Father Thaddeus*. She had plenty to talk about with the bishop.

She took a quick glance at Marya, who was rearranging the bags on her shoulders. Martha opened her mouth to ask Marya if she wanted a ride home but then closed it. A ride would lead to tea. And tea would lead to a conversation about the old days in Pequot Bays, and who knew where it would meander from there. Her whole morning would be gone, and she'd have no time for any Uber work. Martha's muscles tensed, and she rubbed the back of her neck as she felt a pang of conscience. "Marya, would you like a ride?"

"How very nice of you to ask, my dear. But I would not want to keep you from your work." She smiled and then shuffled off toward church. Sometimes Marya could just read a person's mind.

Martha was free to drive for the rest of the day, but somehow she didn't feel as pleased as she'd expected.

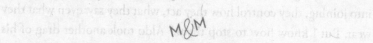

After several profitable fares, Martha returned to Saint John's in the late afternoon to grab the records for the Bishop's Annual Appeal luncheon. A group was gathered just outside church, with tall, sharp-featured Father Thaddeus and his "top lieutenants," the Vances and wispy Luz Flores, at its center. She recognized Michael Ward and Isabella Bonino in the group, but the rest were not Saint John's parishioners. The "soldiers" of Dies Irae were having a council of war with their general. Martha ducked into the rectory to avoid them.

Ten minutes later, she emerged. The war council was gone except for Ken Vance, Michael Ward, and Isabella Bonino, but it looked like the three of them were engaged in a skirmish. Isabella and Michael stood next to each other. They made an attractive couple, both with olive skin and dark, wavy hair, Isabella shapely and sensuous, Michael firm and fit. But of course, they were not a couple. Isabella's husband, Johnny, was nowhere to be seen, and Michael's wife had been buried only yesterday. Isabella, hands on hips, faced Ken. She was dwarfed by his massive, musclebound physique, yet something in their stances intimated that Isabella was getting the best of him. She tossed her dark hair out of her face, her eyes flashing with fury. "*Basta. Statazit.*"

Ken took a stride toward Isabella. Michael stepped between them and shoved him back. "Try fighting a man for once."

Ken threw a roundhouse punch at Michael, who moved aside. Ken tried again. And missed again. Michael threw a short left hook that connected, hard, with the left side of Ken's face. Ken staggered back, and his hulking body hit the ground. He scrambled to his feet, glared at Michael, and slunk away. Isabella and Michael looked at each other, then around the parking lot, where several people were staring at the scene. They walked to their separate cars and drove away.

Martha stared after them, thinking that if they *were* a couple, how convenient Lisa's death had been. A car door slammed, and Ken revved the engine of his white SUV, tires squealing as he released the brakes.

Michael Ward had won a battle, but would he win the war?

# CHAPTER 3

29th Week in Ordinary Time
Saturday, October 22

MARTHA WALKED AROUND THE SIDE OF THE PEQUOT
Bays Yacht and Country Club to the wide back porch. The Georgian-style building was perched higher than the surrounding area, so it had a breathtaking view of the bay. The lawn, as perfectly manicured as one of the greens at the golf club, sloped down to the water. Martha remembered rolling around on the grass when she was a little girl while her parents sat in Adirondack chairs drinking gin and tonics on the deck, watching the sunset. Nowadays, the only way she could even get on the property was to buy a ticket to the Knights of Columbus annual golf outing. She walked down a path, past a mast-like flagpole with a large American flag flying from the gaff with a red and blue striped yacht club burgee, and came to a dock with seventy- and eighty-foot sail and motor yachts, the halyards of the sailboats tinkling in a sudden puff of wind. Sleek racing sloops danced at their moorings. She took a deep breath of the fresh, salty breeze.

The wind blew her skirt so that she had to hold it down. Martha never wore dresses, and certainly not lavender floral prints, but on impulse that morning she had taken an outfit from the back of her closet. She had probably last worn it when she was eighteen, maybe even to a yacht club party. The dress, a classic and always in style, still fit and even flattered, making her appear slimmer, taller. And she did have good legs. Not that it mattered, of course.

The breeze whipped up the water, creating wavelets, then white-caps, turning the bay from silver to deep blue. Boats under sail began to heel over. Thunderheads rose in the distance.

Martha retraced her path, opened the door, and walked into the hum and buzz of the crowd attending the golf outing, the biggest fundraiser for the charities supported by the Knights of Columbus. As she scanned the room, she recognized a woman whose last name graced the newest addition to a New York City hospital chatting with the founder of the largest home improvement center in the US. The CEO of a prestigious hotel chain looked on. She caught a glimpse of a purple feather in the middle of the room that reminded her of…but no, it couldn't be. Even for those who skipped the golf tournament with its $2000 per person fee, the Bay Fest Brunch that followed cost $150. She was sure that was too expensive for…

She looked at the purple feather bobbing its way through the crowd. Glitter and purple sequins glinted in the sunlight. She'd grab a drink and then go say hi to Marya.

She bumped into Lena, the church secretary, a four-foot-nine-inch powerhouse who dictated to Father Seamus where and with whom he should spend his non-liturgical working hours. At work, she usually dressed in tailored suits and skirts with her hair in a neat bun, but today she had let her straight blond hair down and wore a revealing polka dotted sun dress. She eyed Martha up and down. "You look… *good*!"

The woman standing next to Lena, whom Martha saw every Sunday at 10:00 a.m. Mass, said, "Martha? I didn't recognize you at first!"

Martha nodded, not sure whether to say thanks or take offense. As she made her way toward the open bar, she heard several more comments: "Martha?" and "How nice you look!" She decided to accept them as compliments as she ordered a cosmo.

"Martha? Martha Collins?" a voice from behind her said.

She turned around. "Yes?"

"Remember me?"

Martha looked up into a rugged, lined face and blue eyes framed by curly blond hair pulled up into a man-bun. A tattoo peeked out above the neckline of the dark gray T-shirt he wore under a sports jacket that hung from wire-hanger shoulders on a slender frame. In Martha's mind's eye, though, he transformed back into a chubby adolescent with a face surrounded by sun-bleached ringlets. "Christopher?"

"Yup, it's me."

"You've changed."

"You haven't."

Martha smiled.

"Good to see a friendly face, Martha. It's been a while. I never came home after college. I'm sure you heard why... It's hard to keep a secret around here." He smiled.

She nodded. "Yes, it is." He still had the same aquamarine eyes.

"I'm visiting for a couple of weeks. Maybe we could have a cup of coffee and talk."

"Sure. That'd be nice." They exchanged phone numbers.

"I heard about your parents. I'm sorry. That must have been—"

Suddenly, Christopher's mother appeared on one side and his father on the other, each grasping an arm. "Come with us, Christopher dear," his mother said, "We want you to meet Amanda Lombardi. I'm sure you've heard of the Lombardis. They recently had a hospital wing named after them." The mother gave Martha a cold nod as she led her son away.

Martha took a swig of the cosmo and surveyed the scene, trying to catch sight of the purple feather that would lead her to Marya. It was nowhere to be seen, so she moved toward the buffet trays. She looked forward to the Bay Fest Brunch every year. It featured local delicacies pulled from the bay—lobster, crab, scallops, clams, oysters, and flounder—and carafes of red and white wine from local vineyards on each table, which were much better than anything Martha bought for herself. The buffet line had shortened, and most of the attendees had taken their plates to the tables scattered around the spacious, sun-filled room. Each table held a floral centerpiece in the shape of a three-masted schooner, with leaves for the sails and a tall gladiolus for the bowsprit.

Martha scanned the room, considering where she could find a seat. She was surprised to see Michael Ward here, only three weeks after he had buried his wife. Isabella Bonino sat next to him, their chairs nearly touching. She tossed back her luxurious hair and gestured as she spoke. Did Isabella just push back the little black curl that was always falling over Michael's forehead? No sign of Isabella's husband. Martha's eyes narrowed. She would not interrupt that tête-à-tête.

Nor would she sit at the next table, where that Dies Irae priest sat surrounded by his three most devoted followers. She had spoken to the bishop about him. He had thanked her, and she had no idea whether he considered her a concerned parishioner or an interfering gossip. Father Thaddeus's cadaverous, black-cassocked frame and disapproving demeanor were out of place in the midst of gaily colored frocks, golf shirts, and happy chatter. Ken Vance sat next to the priest, his swollen pecs and delts on display in a skintight polo shirt. Ken pointed out someone to Father Thaddeus, then whispered in his ear. Ken's wife Barbara, pale and plump, sat next to him, her eyes never leaving his face. She wore a white version of her usual loose, long-sleeved blouse, buttoned all the way up, with a floppy bow at the collar.

Luz Flores, easily identifiable by the bright white streak in her short black hair, sat on the other side of Father Thaddeus, talking to that unpleasant, unattractive man, Aldo Todi. Luz wore a black jumper, white shirt, and black sweater that hung loosely on her thin frame, resembling the habit of a nun. Aldo stood next to Luz, plate in hand. He leaned over, listening, but had to turn his head away to cough into his napkin. He wore a black beret with a Knights of

Columbus badge canted over his left eye, the right side folded downward over the left ear. Gray trousers and a blue blazer with a Knights of Columbus crest and emblem over a sash completed the look. The outfit as well as the animated expression on his face as he listened to Luz made him look…well…dapper, which was a term Martha had never expected to apply to Aldo. Similarly-dressed Knights, who had opened the Bay Fest Brunch by leading in Father Seamus, the winners of the golf tournament, and the honorees of the fundraiser, stood scattered around the room.

As she surveyed the other tables, her eye landed on her childhood friend, Christopher, who was waving at her. He motioned to an empty seat next to him. She gave him a thumbs up.

She walked toward the buffet tables, the rich odors of butter and garlic tantalizing her senses. Embossed cards in fish-shaped card holders proclaimed the contents of each dish. Lobster tails, seared scallops with truffle butter. Martha plotted how to make room on her plate for every dish in the long line of shiny metal trays.

The third tray had no card, but it looked tasty. As she reached over to take a spoonful of the poached eggs with hollandaise sauce atop a seafood salad, she heard a crash. One of the seven-foot potted palm trees in front of the hallway leading to the bathrooms swayed, leaned, and then tumbled over, hitting another, which hit a third in a domino effect. A man stumbled around the trees into the buffet area and fell down not six feet from Martha. He tried to push himself up but could not, and lay with his back against one of the clay pots.

He pulled out his right hand from his pants pocket and reached out with a tightly closed fist as though offering something to the crowd that was now gathering around him. There was something odd about the fingers on the hand. They were swollen, almost sausage-like. Outstretched fingers on the other, equally swollen hand inched toward a crucifix around his neck, the spear-like crucifix of Dies Irae. His cheeks flushed, his lips and throat swelled, his eyes bulged, and his tongue protruded from his mouth. He thrashed and came to rest on his back, struggling to breathe. Martha looked away from the face that was so contorted it was unrecognizable. He was trying to say something. "Ga, ga." God? No. Garden? Then he said it very clearly.

"The guardian."

Someone yelled for a doctor. Steven Ianelli rushed over carrying his black leather medical bag, and the crowd parted to let him through. His wife, Bitsy, dressed to kill in a designer dress with an asymmetric neckline, followed. She was surprisingly agile despite her six-inch heels.

Ken Vance followed in Bitsy's wake. "Back off, everybody. Back off. Let us through." His voice squeaked a little.

Martha backed up into one of the toppled potted palms. She turned around to see Gertie Doppeldecker watching from the shadow of the fan-like leaves. Rising above the palm fronds, a glittery royal purple feather attached to a lavender straw hat with an amethyst and violet striped ribbon around the brim sat on the head of Marya Cook.

Martha heard radio static and then Ken Vance's voice. "I need an ambulance, stat." She recalled that he volunteered for the local ambulance service. Ken started to kneel down, but Dr. Ianelli pushed him away.

"I'll take care of this." Dr. Ianelli knelt next to the man. "Anaphylactic shock." He reached into his bag, came out with a plastic EpiPen, and jammed it down hard onto the thigh of the fallen man, whose pleading eyes darted amongst the people now gathered around him. Dr. Ianelli held the EpiPen on the thigh for several seconds and watched his patient, then shook his head. He threw the plastic tube back into his bag, removed another, and repeated the process. Again, he waited.

The stricken man's eyes closed. He gasped for air every few seconds. Dr. Ianelli began CPR.

Ken held back the crowd. He cleared out the immediate area,

putting the palms back in their spots, brushing away the dirt that had fallen out of them with his foot. He pulled out a box from his own bag and said to Dr. Ianelli, "Why don't we try one more EpiPen?"

Dr. Ianelli shook his head. "It's too late. Could you take over CPR, Ken? I'm getting a bit tired." Dr. Ianelli stood up and brushed off the pants of his three piece suit. He neatened his jacket and pulled down his French cuffs so the gold cufflinks faced out. Bitsy came up next to him and straightened his tie. He put his arm around her.

The crowd parted to let Isabella Bonino through. She stopped short when she saw the man lying on the floor and pushed her luxurious hair back from her face. She whispered, "Johnny." She knelt down and took one of the swollen hands in her own.

Only then did Martha realize the grotesque shape on the ground was Johnny Bonino.

Ken ripped open his box, removed an EpiPen, and stabbed the thigh with it. The body jerked and then went flaccid. The crowd was quiet. Only Isabella Bonino's sobbing was audible over Ken's grunts as he continued CPR. Father Seamus stepped forward through the crowd, approached Johnny, and made the sign of the cross.

A black-cassocked priest brushed against Martha.

"I'll do it," Father Thaddeus said harshly. Father Seamus stared at Father Thaddeus but did not move. The Dies Irae priest met his gaze, and his eyes narrowed into slits as he said, "He's mine." He bumped into Father Seamus as he moved closer to Mr. Bonino. Father Seamus stepped away, his jaw tightening.

Father Thaddeus placed a brown leather briefcase on the floor. He knelt and removed a narrow purple stole trimmed in gold, which he kissed and put around his neck. He withdrew several other items from the briefcase and then clicked it closed. He covered it with a white, embroidered cloth on which he placed a Bible, a gold pyx for the Eucharist, a glass bottle of blessed oil of the sick, and a small box. Last, he placed an upright wooden crucifix on the cloth. He paused, observed the display, and then made the sign of the cross.

Ken continued pushing down on the chest of the victim while Father Thaddeus knelt on the other side of the body. As the priest intoned prayers and leaned over to anoint the forehead, hands, and lips with oil, the spear end of his crucifix dangled only inches from Johnny Bonino's neck. Isabella remained on her knees next to him during the rite, weeping.

Father Thaddeus packed up his Last Rites kit, and Martha heard sirens growing louder. Moments later, police and ambulance personnel swarmed in and took over.

Martha moved away, sat down at a table, and nibbled at the scallops on her plate, ashamed that she still had an appetite. Dr. Ianelli and Father Seamus supported Isabella back to a table near Martha's. It was a touching scene, worthy of an Instagram shot. Isabella gazed at Father Seamus with soulful eyes, her dark hair mussed, her make-up unsmudged. Luca, her son, came over, and she draped her arms around him.

The police came over to the table.

"I'm sorry, Mrs. Bonino, but we have to ask you some questions." Isabella nodded.

"Was your husband allergic to anything? Dr. Ianelli says it's anaphylactic shock. An allergic reaction, he says."

*"Per amor del Cielo! O Dio mio. O Dio mio."*

The policeman looked at Father Seamus. "Does she speak English?"

"Yes. Very well. The stress, I guess…" He turned to Isabella. "Can you try to speak in English, Isabella?"

She took in a deep, shaky breath. *"Sì.* Yes. He was allergic. Crab and penicillin. *È tutto.* That's it. He wears a medical bracelet."

"Yeah, I saw that. Covered in diamonds. Hard to miss," the policeman said.

Isabella nodded. "He always said everyone would notice it even if he was unconscious. And he never eats crab. Everyone knows that."

"Where's his plate?" the police officer asked.

"*Qui.* Here. He was sitting right next to me. He left to go to the bathroom. He was gone for a while. I thought he must have started talking to someone." Isabella pointed to the plate. "*O dio mio.* Is that...*penso di si*...but he would never..."

"What's that, Mrs. Bonino?"

"*Granchio! Mio dio. Granchio. Dio no.*"

"Granchio?"

"That's crab in Italian," Dr. Ianelli translated.

"I don't see any crab."

Father Seamus looked closely. "She's right. It's the crab eggs benedict. There's crab salad sort of hidden underneath the egg. I had some myself."

The police officer inspected the plate. "I see. And it's partially eaten."

"Johnny would not eat that. *Sono sicuro.*"

Luca added, "Dad would not eat that. He *did not* eat that," as though saying it would make it so.

Father Seamus motioned toward the catering trays. "They're all labeled. He would have checked. We all knew he was careful not to eat crab."

"Let's see the trays," the policeman said. Father Seamus led him to the buffet table and gestured toward the tray with the missing card.

What a tragic train of mistakes had led to Johnny Bonino's death.

"Hello, my dear." Martha had been so caught up in the drama unfolding at Isabella's table that she had not noticed Marya sitting next to her. "I hope you are well. It must have been quite a shock for Mr. Bonino to collapse so near you like that."

Martha recalled the last time Marya had expressed her concern, which had been due to the discovery of a body buried in her back-yard. She turned to the old woman. "At least this time it it isn't murder."

"Perhaps," Marya said.

# CHAPTER 4

30th Week in Ordinary Time
Monday, October 24

MARTHA DROVE PAST HARRIMAN ACRES, KNOWN AS
Skeeter Flats to the locals, a gated community filled with McMansions
that sold at the going rate of three million plus. Main Street then narrowed to a causeway, which led to Pequot Island, home to successful
bankers, city lawyers, doctors, and financiers who lived in fifty dis-
tinctive, custom waterfront homes.

As she drove over the causeway onto Center Street, the only public road on Pequot Island, she kept her eyes focused, tunnel vision,
on the road ahead, trying to avoid memories of her former life, her
childhood as a Pequot Islander. Martha recalled the embarrassment
she had suffered at her parents' estate sale. All of Pequot Bays had
shown up, it seemed, including her wealthy neighbors, who had no
need to buy used lawn equipment at a discount. Her face still got hot
when she remembered the whispers and stares. By mutual inclination, she and those whom she had formerly called friends had steered
clear of each other ever since. Martha had gained back a measure of
respect as a stalwart presence in the church and former civilian police
commissioner, and had even come to terms with being Martha the
Uber driver. She kept the past in the past and people at a distance—
she had acquaintances rather than friends. Quincy was more loyal
than any human.

It had not been difficult to keep to herself. Pequot Bays was home to only a few who, like Martha, fell into the middle-class niche, and she had little in common with either the wealthy or those who served them. The wealthy resided in Skeeter Flats, Pequot Island, or Middle Point. The cooks, maids, chauffeurs, and gardeners lived in public housing, like Marya, or rented ramshackle homes quite unlike their counterparts nearer to Main Street, which had been renovated to appear exactly as they would have when constructed in the 1890s, painted in the original colors, not a shingle or awning out of place. As Martha drove past the private access road that had once led to her childhood home, she heard a still, small voice in her mind. A question. Was she treating Marya like her friends had treated her?

*Of course not. I'm just busy.*

Center Street ended at a second causeway broken by a picturesque cast-iron bridge, which led to a long, wooded, S-shaped island that stretched for a mile into the bay. At the end of the bridge, she passed a small, shingled police substation with a large stop sign. It was hardly ever manned, but strangers wouldn't know that. This was Middle Point, and here the road split at a fork. Gertrude Avenue, named after a Vanderbilt child, rose to the left, and Nelson Avenue, named after a grandchild of another former resident, curved to the right. She drove past a half-dozen paved private drives on either side, which led down to the water. At one time, Middle Point had been home to three vast estates, but property taxes had struck even the rich, and now seventeen residences held the island's population. For the most part, the old homes had been demolished and replaced with even larger structures built to more modern tastes. Gone were the third floor attics occupied by scores of domestics. Gatehouses, stables, and boat houses had been torn down or converted and modernized into mansions in their own right. Martha had little reason to come here, even before her parents' fall from grace. The Middle Pointers had as little in common with the Pequot Islanders as the Pequot Islanders had with the servant class.

A winding road bordered on both sides by towering red oaks

led to Winthrop Lane. A narrow allée of trees ended at a small brick gatehouse almost swallowed by overgrown bushes and vines. Just beyond, however, rose an ornate cast-iron gate with the words *Lazarus Oaks* scrolled in gold in an arc at the top. Martha pushed a button on an intercom post, announced herself, and the heavy gates creaked open. Immediately, the road changed into a brilliant white surface with hints of pink, which she realized were crushed oyster shells, often used before asphalt became common. She drove past paddocks empty of horses and a show ring, carefully raked, with freshly painted jumps lacking only a mounted rider. To her right, a wall of squared box hedges closed off what appeared to be a lawn set up for croquet. To her left, a tennis court with smooth red clay, and, just beyond, a changing cottage painted in lavender and hunter green had a small patio with chairs and green striped umbrellas open, as if ready for spectators wearing straw bowlers and holding gin and tonics, waiting for white-clad tennis players to begin their game. A few steps below, she glimpsed the pool, which ended at elephantine boulders presided over by a bronze Nepture astride a spewing dolphin. Hadn't she seen something similar at the Pitti Palace in Florence?

She approached a brick building rising behind a limestone porte cochere. On the first floor, a row of elegant French doors opened onto a terrace. Large windows looked out from the second floor, and a dozen gables poked through the slate roof. Martha pulled to a stop as the drive curved around a limestone pool with a marble fountain of an alluring Venus surrounded by cavorting cupids and seahorses. All was silent except the soothing splash and gurgle. The house had survived, seemingly untouched, from the Gilded Age. She felt she had stepped back in time.

Her reverie was broken by a man with patchy white hair, his shoulders and back bent with the bony alterations of time, his fingers knotted onto a wooden cane. He yelled, "Dad, your Uber's here."

She heard a sound like a mixture of hens cackling and a grizzly growling. "Tell her to come and get me."

"He's around the back," the old man said to Martha.

Martha drove to the side of the house and got out of the car. An even older man sat in a cast-iron chair, covered by a blanket. His faded parchment features were oddly wrinkleless, mummified, an impression highlighted by his bald, pale head. A table was set out in front of him with sumptuous fruits and meats. He held a bunch of large red grapes and plucked one with fingers that appeared to be permanently clawed, then moved his head down rather than raising his arm up and took the grape into his mouth. He picked up a large linen napkin with the same grasping fingers and wiped some juice from his chin. "Don't just stand there gawking, come and get me."

Martha walked over as the man shook off the blanket. He wore a fine linen suit and a royal purple tie. He also wore one of the Dies Irae crucifixes. Was he a member too? She looked around at the magnificent mansion and grounds. Did he hope that leaving 10% of his vast wealth to Dies Irae would buy his way into heaven?

"The walker's over there."

Martha retrieved the walker, passing a sweaty gardener, who stood up to stretch near a border of hydrangeas. He eyed the delicacies on the table.

"Don't just stand there gawking. Get back to work."

That appeared to be one of the old man's favorite phrases.

The gardener knelt back down in the dirt and weeds. The old man took a slice of meat from the table and fed it to a sleek gray Weimaraner at his feet. He looked up at Martha. "I have five brothers, and they are all coming to visit this weekend. I want the grounds in tip-top shape."

Martha hauled the rich old man up out of the chair, positioned the walker in front of him, and followed behind, ready to catch him if he fell. She folded the old man into the rear seat of the car and then folded the walker into the trunk.

*By the stones of Saint Eskil, this is a lot of work for a lousy tip.* Martha couldn't recall the man's name although she had come here once before. Only *Lazarus Oaks* had shown up on her Uber phone. His chauffeur had died, and he couldn't find a suitable replacement. They all wanted too much money, he said. He had given Martha a 2% tip.

Martha drove back the way she'd come, remaining silent as the old man cackled about his visit to the doctor the week before. "Told me I was in great shape. Said my heart was as healthy as someone half my age."

She checked out the old man in her rearview mirror. *So that must mean he has the heart of a fifty-five year old.* Martha had often been regaled with such stories of health and well being as she drove old people to wakes and funerals.

They arrived at McMurray's Funeral Home, where her fare was attending Johnny Bonino's wake. She drove up the driveway, unfolded the walker, and followed the old man through the double doors into the foyer. She parked the car, then decided to stay and pay her own respects. Kill two birds with one stone, as Marya might say.

She hesitated to approach the open casket, recalling the tortured face and body she had seen at the brunch. But when she glanced up from the kneeler after making the sign of the cross, she saw that McMurray's Funeral Home had done its magic. He looked, if not like Johnny Bonino had looked in life, at least not like the hideous, swollen monster that he had in death. He appeared peaceful. His hands, clenched and taut when she had seen him struggling for breath, were folded on his chest, a rosary woven between his fingers. The Dies Irae spear-like crucifix she had seen him grasping was still around his neck, now with another charm on the chain, a delicate cylinder made of interlaced metal wire. It looked familiar.

After a quick Our Father, Hail Mary, and Glory Be at the casket, Martha joined the long line to offer condolences to Isabella Bonino. Isabella wore a chic little black dress, sleeveless and tight in all the right places, as she chatted away, lively gestures accompanying her words.

Michael Ward sat nearby, his one unruly black curl falling onto his forehead, with no lines of grief from his own recent loss disturbing his handsome features. Aldo Todi sat next to him, pallid and coughing. Michael was talking to several people about his favorite topic, fishing. Martha had heard him pontificate about its beneficial effects on more than one occasion.

"...better than meditation. It reduced my blood pressure. Ask Dr. Ianelli. You should try it. Come along with me any time. If you're upset, fish for bass. Sit in a boat all alone in the middle of the bay. Puts everything in perspective. I recommend eel fishing if you're mad or frustrated. By the time I've whacked one a few times with my eel hammer, all my frustrations are gone. Interesting fact. Did you know eel hammers are called priests? They administer last rites to a fish." He laughed. Several people on the receiving line looked over at him with disapproval. He gave a quick glance at Isabella. "Maybe I'd better talk about something else."

By then, Martha had reached Isabella. She mumbled, "I am so sorry," squeezed Isabella's hand, and moved on, stopping to add her card to a six-foot-high Mass card holder. It took some searching to find a free clip.

"Oh, Gertie," Martha said. "Almost didn't see you. Hi."

Gertie Doppeldecker stood behind the Mass card holder. With her beige hair and beige sweater, she was almost indistinguishable from the beige flocked wallpaper of the funeral parlor. Gertie nodded, but then looked away and gave a little wave. Martha turned and saw that unpleasant man, Aldo Todi, in the line nearing the casket, give an almost indiscernible answering nod. Two mourners behind Aldo stood Marya Cook. Martha waved at Marya and sat down in one of the scarlet-cushioned folding chairs in the reception room. The talk, of course, was about how careful one must be about allergies, and to always carry an EpiPen. Martha watched as Marya made the sign of the cross and knelt down at the casket.

Father Thaddeus strode into the room. He exchanged a nod with the rich old man Martha had driven to the wake. Luz Flores followed after him, almost running in her effort to keep up with his long-legged strides. She carried the same briefcase that the priest had used when giving Last Rites to Johnny Bonino, and she wore a different version of her makeshift nun's habit, a black skirt and vest with a white blouse. Luz seemed to be getting skinnier by the day. Ken and Barbara Vance followed, Ken holding onto Barbara's pale wrist, the veins of his thick forearm bulging. When he neared the rich old man, Ken ran over and spoke a few words to him, lowering his head repeatedly as though bowing, before running back to follow in the wake of the Dies Irae priest. The guests made way as Father Thaddeus proceeded to the front of the room with the same gravitas as if he were processing down the aisle at a papal coronation. He cut in front of Dr. Ianelli, who had reached the front of the line, and began speaking to the widow. Bitsy Ianelli stepped on the priest's toe with a stiletto heel and said in her Brahmin tones, "So sorry, Father. Someone pushed me."

A boom, an explosion, a blast. What was it? A gunshot? A bomb? It echoed deafeningly in the confines of the room. The pungent smell of gunpowder filled Martha's lungs. Her ears rang. A confusion of people scrambled toward the exit. Before Martha could join them, the owner of the funeral home ran in against the tide of people running for the door. His deep voice carried over the commotion. "It's all right. It's okay. Calm down, everyone. Just an accident. Everything's okay." The chaos subsided under his continued reassurance. When a semblance of quiet came over the scene, he explained it had only been a nasty prank. A boy had set off a firecracker and then run away.

Martha looked around, trying to spot Marya. The old woman, unstable even with her cane, might have fallen in the melee of people rushing to the door. But there she was, unfazed, still near the front, talking to Gertie Doppeldecker.

Martha's rich old man approached her and grumbled that the explosion had given him a shock. "Young people these days. I need to get home and have a bit of brandy to calm down."

Martha glanced one more time at the body, again impressed at the transformation of the agonized death mask she had seen at the golf outing. Something was different, though. Something missing.

The necklace with the crucifix and charm that had been around Johnny Bonino's neck—it was gone.

M&M

## Tuesday, October 25

The next morning, Martha drove the rich old man from Lazarus Oaks to Saint John's for the funeral. All these deaths were good for business. Even though she was feeling churched out, she decided to stay.

Following the old man into the church, arms extended to catch him if he toppled over—he was particularly wobbly today—she glanced at the large window on her left to check her reflection. She gave her blunt-cut, glossy, straight brown hair a shake, then smoothed it down. It was her best feature, and she regretted the white hairs that had begun to appear. At forty-one, she was nearly as old as her parents had been at the time of their sudden deaths. Had their hair begun to turn gray? She could not remember. The window mirrored the stocky, strong body she had inherited from her father. As a teen, she had bemoaned not having her mother's graceful, slender frame. But she had also inherited her father's common sense, which had proved extremely helpful when she had been orphaned at nineteen.

Driving on Pequot Island had dredged up memories she preferred to keep buried, and her mind continued to wander down a road she rarely allowed it to travel. Her parents' lifestyle and the mansion where she grew up had placed her family among the most prosperous in Pequot Bays. That was saying a lot, since Pequot Bays was one of the most expensive zip codes in the US. But once the bubble burst, her years of traveling around the globe had been reduced to driving to an upstate home in Cooperstown, New York, her hideaway, which she often rented out to cover expenses. She had never returned to college. The cost deterred her, and she felt safe and secure in her little apartment. And safety, security, and routine had meant everything to her after the shock of her parents' car crash. How different her life could have been.

She pulled a dog-eared index card with neat purple script out of her cross-body bag.

> *Just one thing: forgetting what lies behind but strain-*
> *ing forward to what lies ahead,*
> *I continue my pursuit toward the goal.*
> *Philippians 3:13-14*

She could not fathom why Marya Cook had chosen to give her that particular card out of the heaps of index cards she created, laminated, and carried around to dole out to anyone who stopped to talk to her, but for some reason, Martha carried it with her.

Straightening her bulky, chocolate-brown cable-knit sweater and brushing off the matching wool slacks, she felt satisfied that none of Quincy's hairs would show. She evened the ends of the paisley scarf draped around her neck. After depositing the old man in the front pew on the Saint Joseph side of the church, she moved away to the side chapel and looked around the nave.

Another poor turnout. Mostly the same mourners as at Lisa Ward's funeral. Probably the weather. They were predicting gale force winds. Dark clouds from the approaching storm prevented the stained-glass saints from cheering up the sad proceedings as they had at Lisa's funeral.

A rumble of thunder in the distance joined the organ as it thundered the opening chords of "Precious Lord, Take My Hand."

Isabella Bonino proceeded down the aisle in front of her husband's coffin in a manner more suited to a wedding than a funeral.

She wore a longer little black dress than she had at the wake, but it too emphasized her prominent curves, with high heels that accented her well-muscled legs. Her eyes were hidden by large, chic sunglasses. A black lace mantilla covered her luxuriant dark hair, a quaint salute to her Italian roots.

The wind blew the bushes and trees to a fury so that they brushed and knocked against the windows.

Dr. Ianelli was here in his three piece suit, white oxford button down shirt, and striped tie. He exhibited no more than his usual professional sadness at the funeral of one of his patients. His wife Bitsy sat next to him, dressed to kill as usual.

Ken Vance and his wife Barbara were both on their knees, palms together, she with a rosary, he without. Luz Flores knelt next to Barbara, likewise fingering a rosary. The three sat in the first row, on the side opposite the pews for the family, a cheering section for their adored leader, Father Thaddeus, who was to be the celebrant at the Mass.

Thunder rumbled again, closer.

As Isabella passed Michael Ward, she inched close enough to brush against his elbow where it rested on the end of the pew. He looked up, and a lock of his thick hair tumbled onto his forehead. Michael sat next to Aldo Todi. Like a borzoi and a bulldog, the good looks of one highlighted the homeliness of the other.

Martha jumped as someone touched her arm. She had not heard anyone approach. Gertie Doppeldecker, always appearing and disappearing. Martha nodded at her and turned back to the funeral procession.

Isabella Bonino reached the front pew on the Mary side of the church and sat down, her legs crossed, hiking her short dress up even higher.

On the altar, Father Seamus, dressed as usual in a simple, unassuming chasuble, faded into the background, outshone by the magnificent vestments of Father Thaddeus next to him. Father Seamus sat with his arms crossed, staring away from his fellow priest.

A bright bolt of lightning dazzled the interior of the dark church, illuminating the faces as if with a strobe. A clap of thunder followed, and pelting rain pummeled the saints standing guard in the windows.

Father Thaddeus stood up, looked down his sharp nose at Father Seamus and, with a similar gaze at the entire congregation, crossed himself. "In the name of the Father, and of the Son, and of the Holy Spirit. Amen."

No one was in the side chapel, so Martha sat down in its front pew. Midway through the funeral, she heard the church door creak open, followed by a tap-tap-tap and then the fussy noise of Marya depositing her ever-present bags on the pew behind Martha.

With Father Thaddeus presiding, the funeral became a long, drawn-out, rite-filled, incense-laden affair. Martha couldn't help herself—she spent much of it watching Father Seamus grow more and more agitated, crossing and recrossing his arms and legs, and pressing his lips together into a white slash every time Father Thaddeus referred to, "The blessed departed, a faithful servant of Dies Irae."

The end finally neared and the congregation intoned the final commendation. "Eternal rest grant unto him, O Lord, and let perpetual light shine upon him. May the souls of all the faithful departed, through the mercy of God, rest in peace. Amen."

Father Thaddeus continued, "Into your hands, Father of mercies, we commend our brother, John Anthony Bonino, in the sure and certain hope that, together with all who have died in Christ, he will rise with him on the last day."

Martha rose from the pew as the pall bearers recessed with the coffin. Marya also stood up and blocked the aisle, one bag on her shoulder while she bent over to collect the other one. Martha waited, and Marya gave a cheerful smile and a wave with her cane, which caused the lilac bag to slide down her arm, so she had to restart the slow process of rearranging each bag to her satisfaction, and then tap-tap-tap-tapping her way to the door.

"Hello, my dear," Marya said. "Goodness, it's been quite a while since I've spoken to you. I do so hope you are feeling well. When I woke up this morning, my knees were quite achy and I said to myself, it will surely rain today. And it most certainly did, did it not? What a storm we had during the funeral, and it is threatening to start again now." Marya struggled in her effort to tie the belt around her lavender raincoat. "Perhaps I should not have put on this sweater before I left the apartment." Martha looked at the heavy lilac and eggplant plaid sweater. "After all, I already had on my cardigan." A deep purple cardigan with pink stripes peeked from underneath the bottom of the lilac and eggplant sweater. "And also this turtleneck—" a white one dotted with tiny violet rabbits. The belt of the lavender raincoat was not long enough to tie over all the layers.

"But as I may have mentioned to you before, my mother, God rest her soul, always told my sister and me to dress in layers." Marya darted a glance at something behind Martha's back.

Martha began, "Nice to see you, Marya, but I have an Uber—"

Marya began to speak very loudly, "Yes, it is very suspicious, my dear. We must investigate. But people are coming out now, so we must keep our voices down or they will hear us." Then, even louder, "Murder! We must get to the bottom of this!"

Martha looked around, mortified. Yes. The mourners were now within earshot, and they stood, openmouthed, around her and Marya.

"I saw it myself, my dear. Perhaps we should tell the police. Or should we just investigate the matter ourselves, like we did before? Yes. I think that might be better. The police might not believe us." Marya studied the group gathered around them and gave a sharp glance at someone standing behind Martha. "But we must not speak about this matter any further right now, my dear. Perhaps you could give me a call tomorrow so we can discuss the murder some more."

Martha mumbled something like, "Uber. Got to go." And looking down at the ground to avoid the stares of her fellow parishioners, she made a beeline for her car, so embarrassed that she did not even feel the rain that had started to come down in torrents again. She drove to the curb near the portico to pick up her old gentleman. She took an umbrella and held it over him as he tottered with his walker to the car.

"Well, that was quite a scene there, with you and your friend," he cackled.

"She's not—she's lonely. I help her out sometimes." Martha opened the door and folded his walker as he settled himself into the back seat.

"She certainly is a looney. Don't they call her the Purple Pest?"

"She's getting up in years. And old people," she looked at the man, who had several years on Marya, "don't get the respect they deserve."

"You're as looney as she is. Murder!" The old man cackled again.

Martha slammed the car door shut.

She drove in silence. Everyone thought Marya was just a kook. If only they knew what a brilliant—if somewhat quirky—detective Marya was. She had solved a murder! With Martha's help, of course. But Lieutenant O'Hara, the creep, had taken all the credit for it, and Marya, true to form, had preferred it that way. "After all," Marya had said, "any good that I do is for God's glory, not mine." She had asked Martha and the small circle of acquitted suspects to keep quiet about her role in the investigation. And Father Jim, the former associate pastor of Saint John's and Marya's biggest fan, had been reassigned to a flock that required him to shuttle between three lonely parishes, miles apart. Martha figured it was to teach him a little humility. Only a few people appreciated the brains hidden under Marya's purple plumed hats. But now, it seemed that maybe Marya was losing it a bit.

# CHAPTER 5

Wednesday, October 26

THE PHONE RANG AT THE SAME TIME THE ALARM WENT off at 6:00 a.m. Martha grabbed her cell, saw it was Marya calling, and let it go to voicemail. Marya had called her three times, counting this one, since the debacle at the funeral and had left long voicemails after each call. Martha, busy with her Uber driving, had not had an opportunity to call Marya back or even listen to the voicemails. If she was being honest with herself, she was upset at Marya for bringing her into that embarassing scene. But she would definitely call her today. Check in on her. See that she was okay. She just needed her morning coffee first.

Quincy, sleeping on the chocolate brown quilt atop Martha's bed, looked up balefully. Martha was much more of a morning person than Quincy. By the time she had dressed and finished an easy Wednesday *New York Times* crossword puzzle with her first cup of coffee, Quincy was waiting by the door, leash in mouth.

She would call Marya after she took Quincy for some exercise.

After a brisk walk, she dropped off Quincy at the apartment. "See you in about an hour, Quince, I'm a eucharistic minister this morning." She'd call Marya right after church.

The sunny day matched her mood, and she drove over to church, mapping out her day—the Uber fares, the Quincy walks, the errands she would complete in between.

Her planning continued after she arrived at Saint John's, so her attention was not on Mass but on when she could fit in her kickboxing routine. She had once asked Marya, who seemed so collected during Mass, never fidgeting or looking around, whether it was even worth it for Martha to go, since her mind always wandered. Marya had said that of course she must go. A person should not stop visiting their mother or father even if they could not concentrate on or even care about what their parents were talking about.

Martha glanced at her watch. 8:50. And Mass was nearly over. She nodded approvingly.

"The Lord be with you," said Father Peanuts.

The congregation replied, "And with your spirit."

Father Peanuts gave the final blessing. "May almighty God bless you, the Father, and the Son, and the Holy Spirit. Amen. Go in peace to love and serve the Lord."

All responded, "Thanks be to God."

The priest proceeded out, and the thirty or so congregants straggled after him, blocking the aisles as they stopped in groups of two or three to greet one another. Martha genuflected and approached the altar, snuffed out the candles, turned off the amplifier for the priest's mic, and moved the cruets with the water and wine to the small fridge in the sacristy. She shut off all the lights in the church except the spotlights on the tabernacle and the statues of Joseph and Mary, then switched off the light in the sacristy and walked into the side chapel.

She nearly knocked over Gertie Doppeldecker, who stood just outside the sacristy door and was, as usual, almost indistinguishable from her surroundings. Gertie was talking to Aldo Todi. He had an unlit cigarette hanging out of his mouth while he coughed. He quickly stuffed some bills into his wallet, then turned and walked out to the parking lot. Gertie was gone by the time Martha turned back around.

She was now alone in the church.

She sat in a pew and read through the fourteen items on her to-do list. Not so bad, but she'd better get moving. She'd call Marya from the car.

As she walked though the parking lot, the bright sun glittered on the broken pieces of glass mixed into the asphalt. Martha turned the ignition key, but as soon as she put her foot on the gas pedal, the car pulled awkwardly to the right. She got out and saw a flat tire. She sighed. The day had started off so well.

Martha called for road assistance. As she leaned over the hood of her car to write down the confirmation number, she heard the roar of an engine so loud and so close that she dropped her phone. She looked around and then froze as she saw a car hurtling directly at her. She dove to her left, feeling the air rush by as the car missed her by inches. She felt the shock wave as it smashed into her own car, and crouched into a ball with her arms over her head as metal and glass debris rained to the ground.

She heard the squeal of tires backing away and dared to look up— but her stomach sickened with terror as the car made a U-turn and raced back toward her again. She tried to push herself off the pavement to get out of the way, but her ankle shrieked with pain, and she collapsed back down. Martha had not seen the crash that killed her parents, but she had visualized it many times, and the imaginary scene flashed into her mind. She scrabbled across the ground, trying to move away. She heard doors open as people began to scurry out of the rectory, the school, and the parish buildings. The car abruptly changed direction and squealed out of the parking lot.

Moments later, Martha was surrounded by onlookers.

"Pick her up."

"Don't touch her."

"Call an ambulance."

"Are you ok?"

"What happened?"

What *had* happened? The car had come straight at her. Like it was aiming for her. But that was crazy. No one wanted to kill her… or maybe…could it be?

That weird priest, Father Thaddeus. Had he heard she'd complained about him to the bishop? Maybe he figured she was one of the devil's minions in his spiritual war. And maybe the war wasn't so spiritual. That would be crazy. But he *was* crazy. Or maybe one of his followers did it. Her head started to spin.

The sacristan, a short, gray-haired man bent over from age, known by all as Old Jerome, took charge of the scene. He cleared the area near Martha, brought an embroidered pillow for her head, and covered her with a large, ornate brocade cloth. He knelt down next to her on the ground, his expressive eyes calming her. He took her hand and assured her, "It's all right, Martha. You'll be fine." The wail of sirens grew louder. She turned her head to the side and closed her eyes, but opened them when the imagined scene of her parents' car crash flashed into her mind. She turned to seek the gentle calm of the sacristan, but instead she saw instead a pair of spike heels. They were occupied by Bitsy Ianelli, who looked tall from this vantage point. Then the EMTs took over. She felt dazed but was able to sit up, and then stand. She took a few steps with a very painful ankle and then sat on a folding chair that the sacristan had produced. She smiled at Old Jerome and, again, his kind eyes calmed her.

She saw Marya trying unsuccessfully to break through the crowd and the EMTs. Martha waved to her.

"Can you let my friend through?" Martha asked one of the EMTs.

"In a minute. How do you feel?"

"It's my ankle. Can you let her through, please?" Martha was surprised how much she wanted Marya at her side.

"Just a few more questions." After Martha answered their questions, the EMT examined her, then asked, "Do you want to go to the hospital?"

"The hospital? You think I need to?"

Bitsy Ianelli, who had been standing close by, approached. "You know, you always have to wait for hours in the ER. I'll just call Steven and tell him I'm driving you over. I'm sure he'll see you right away."

"That'd be great, Bitsy. Thanks."

Bitsy stepped away, had a short, hushed phone conversation, and then returned to Martha. "Steven's so caring. He had to rush out on an emergency. But he'll be back by the time we get to the office."

The EMTs left, making room for the Pequot Bays police. A short, balding cop with a beer gut approached, and he and Martha exchanged hostile glances. The very sight of Lieutenant Michael O'Hara drove her blood pressure up, but she forced herself to stay composed. He turned his back on her and spoke to the tall, fit young police officer behind him. Henry Milton. Martha had been his babysitter. What a shy, sweet, gentle baby he had been. And he had grown up to be a shy, sweet, gentle young man. She could understand why he could not find a job in his chosen field after he had graduated with a masters in medieval studies, but she would never comprehend his decision to become a police officer.

"Oh, it's *her.* I'm not gonna waste *my* time. You handle this," O'Hara said to Henry Milton. "And *you*," O'Hara spat to a third officer, a woman Martha did not know, "just watch and listen and try to learn how to be a police*man*. I've been training Milton myself. He's coming along. Pretty soon he'll be a real cop." He looked toward Bitsy Ianelli, who stood close by, her purebred superiority on display, and nodded. She inclined her head in return. He strode over to the sidelines.

"Hello, Henry." Martha said.

"Hank. Please, Ms. Collins, call me Hank." He glanced at the female officer next to him. "They all know me as Hank, not Henry."

Officer Henry/Hank Milton pulled out a small notepad and asked Martha to describe what happened.

"I was bending over my car and looked up and saw it coming right at me. The driver was deliberately aiming for me. I know it. Right at me. I barely got out of the way."

"Deliberately?" Henry Milton asked.

"Deliberately," Martha answered.

O'Hara looked up. "Deliberately!" he sneered.

Martha looked back at Henry. "The first *and* second attempts were both deliberate," she continued. "He swerved around and would have tried to slam into me again, except people started coming out of the buildings, so he took off."

"Did anyone else see this," Henry hesitated, "*deliberate* attempt?"

Martha shook her head.

"Can you describe the driver?"

Martha shook her head again. "Actually, I don't even know if it was a man or a woman."

"How about the car?"

Martha thought for a couple of moments and said, "Maybe a light color? I'm really not sure. I just remember the bumper slamming inches from my head."

Henry looked at the bystanders. "Did anyone see a car leaving the parking lot?"

They responded, "Yeah, a black Grand Cherokee."

"It was a brown SUV, a BMW."

Bitsy said, "White. Maybe a Land Rover. Like one of Steven's patients has."

"No, it was a grey Ford Explorer."

"I think it was red, no, blue. Not sure what kind of car it was, though, maybe a Mini Cooper."

Henry turned away without taking any notes. He asked Martha a few more questions until Bitsy interrupted, "I don't believe you're going to get much more from her. You can see that she's very upset and needs to see a doctor. May we go?"

"Yes, ma'am. Whatever you say, ma'am." Henry gave Bitsy the same little bow that his boss had. "We'll take care of the car. If we need anything else, we'll call." Henry sounded relieved he did not have to deal with Martha anymore. The female officer had not said a word, and the expression on her face had never changed.

Bitsy helped Martha stand up. She was strong for someone of her petite build. Even with four-inch stiletto heels, Bitsy's casual shoe wear, she was still short, which made it awkward for Martha to put her arm around Bitsy's shoulders and hop toward the car. She saw Marya wave and start to hobble toward her. Martha waved back, but Bitsy had already helped Martha settle into the soft leather seat of the Lexus sedan and closed the door before Marya arrived.

As they drove away, Bitsy peppered Martha with questions. Her half-lidded eyes contrasted with her sweet, heart-shaped lips that looked entirely natural, although Martha suspected they might be the product of a few Botox injections by her husband. Wavy ash blond curls, platinum at the ends, surrounded Bitsy's face and fell to her shoulder blades. Even this close up, Martha could not detect any wrinkles in the flawless skin of her cover-girl features. She really could have been a model.

"What happened? You said it was deliberate? What makes you say that?" She paused, but Martha just stared back, her energy draining away now that she was out of O'Hara's presence. "How could that be? Who do you think it was?" Bitsy paused again.

Martha tried to focus, but the breeze from the open window blew Bitsy's curls so that they looked like snakes on Medusa's head. Martha shook her head.

Bitsy continued in her aristocratic tones, "Maybe it was a drunk driver. Or drugs. There's a lot of that in town." She shook her head. "The Fairchild boy was arrested for drunk driving a few months ago. He went onto a curb, hit a stop sign, backed up, and hit the car behind him. One would have thought he would have gotten away with it. The Fairchilds are very connected. But it was Judge Albernathy behind him, in his new silver Mercedes S 500, and he's not afraid of anyone. Then there's the young Samuelson boy. He's still in the hospital after an accident driving around high on drugs." She gazed at Martha in a confidential manner, as if they were members of the same exclusive club. "It was most likely a child of a parishioner. Why else would he be in the church parking lot? Are you quite sure you didn't see who it was?"

Bitsy seemed ready to start a rumor at the nod of a head. Martha leaned back on the headrest with her eyes closed for the rest of the ride.

As Martha put her foot down to get out of the car, she realized her ankle hurt more than she'd realized. Bitsy helped her through a door with the sign *Steven Ianelli, MD, Internal Medicine*, ushered her into the waiting room, and pushed her down into an empty chair. "Sit here while I go talk to Steven." She moved past the receptionist without so much as a greeting and through the door that led to the back rooms.

The waiting room was spacious. Two rows of modern, low-slung chairs were arranged near one wall, facing another two rows along the opposite wall. Three paintings of orange and brown rectangles hung behind the chairs. The furniture and art were simple, orderly, almost Zen-like. The room, however, was anything but meditative. It was filled with loud, complaining patients. An agitated woman next to Martha leaned over and said, "I've been waiting here for an hour and a half. And a woman over there has been here since 8:00. It's outrageous. The doctor just got here. They said he had an emergency. It's always 'an emergency.'"

About two minutes later, Bitsy strode into the waiting area, stiletto heels clicking on the shiny wooden floor. She grabbed Martha's arm and pulled her into the hall leading to the examination rooms, past all the resentful heads shaking in protest.

Bitsy told her to go into the room that Dr. Ianelli used as his office while she walked the opposite direction down the hall.

Martha limped in. The room was less modern, more traditional, than the waiting room. The sizeable office contained an executive desk of burled wood and a full wall of matching built-in bookcases filled with medical texts. Dr. Ianelli's diplomas featured conspicuously on the wall opposite the door. Large windows lined a third wall. An imposing oil painting of a woman hung on the fourth, her eyes staring straight ahead, the nose on the side of the face. A brass plate noted in big black letters, *Picasso, Seated Woman with Hat, 1939.* It looked to Martha like the real thing, not a print. Martha had heard that Dr. Ianelli had made big bucks by inventing some sort of a medical device. *That must have been a pretty expensive medical device!*

Dr. Ianelli jumped up from his black leather executive chair and helped Martha ease into a seat. Then he sat down behind his desk, leaned back, put his thumbs in his vest pockets, and looked over his tortoise shell glasses at her. "Martha. What happened?"

She told him the whole story. Dr. Ianelli listened, as always, with his full attention, not interrupting or hurrying her along. "No one believes that it was deliberate, but it was."

"But who would have done such a crazy thing, Martha?"

She looked back at him, considering. Could she trust him with her suspicions? Or would he think she was crazy, just like everyone else? Martha took a deep breath. "The priest that lives in the convent."

"A priest in a convent?" Dr. Ianelli raised one eyebrow.

"You know. Father Thaddeus. The priest living in the Parish Center. On the second floor. Where the nuns used to live."

Dr. Ianelli's expression cleared. "Oh, yes. Father Thaddeus." He smiled. "For a minute there, I thought I'd have to test you for a brain injury."

"I think it was him."

"Why?"

Martha told him about the priest's attempt to coerce her into joining Dies Irae, and how she had complained about him to the bishop.

"Hmm. He tried to get us to join too. Bitsy would have none of him, though. She thinks he's nuts. All that talk about him and his soldiers battling the legions of the devil… I don't like this one bit, Martha. You better be careful. Is there anything I can do to help?"

"Just believing me is enough, Doc. Everyone else thinks I'm the crazy one. Wish I could've seen the driver, or at least the car. No one really saw anything. Everyone had a different description. Bitsy said it looked like a white Land Rover."

Dr. Ianelli chuckled. "Bitsy wouldn't know a Volkswagen van from a Rolls Royce." He leaned back in his chair and took a deep breath. "Well, we've both had quite a morning. I received a call about a patient. Heart attack. Rushed over to Saint Francis to meet her in the emergency room. Had to stay till she was stable. My patients must be getting impatient!"

"Um. Maybe a little, Doc."

He rose from his chair and started issuing orders via the intercom. "Joan, start calling the patients in. Beatrice, get ready to take the first one into room number two. Martha, you go into exam room one across the hall."

After a short but painful examination, Dr. Ianelli sent Martha down the street for an X-ray and told her to come back to his office immediately afterward. The X-ray did not show any fractures, so he gave her an ankle brace, advised elevation and conservative treatment, and they would see whether it improved at the next visit. She made a follow up appointment, then called an Uber so she could pick up the prescription for pain medication and buy the cane he had suggested she use for a while.

Limping out of the drug store with cane in hand, Martha was reminded of Marya. She would call her when she got home. Marya would believe her. But as soon as she got home, she took one of the pain pills, lay down on her bed, and went to sleep.

# CHAPTER 6

Thursday, October 27

MARTHA WOKE UP TO QUINCY'S NUZZLES. IT WAS already 8:30 in the morning, and Martha could not remember when she had last slept so long and so late. Those little orange pills were strong. She gingerly tried her ankle. It had become even more swollen and painful than the day before.

She glanced at her cell phone, which had been placed on silent, and saw that Marya had called her three times, twice yesterday and once already this morning. She would call her back in a bit. Martha wanted to discuss her theory about Father Thaddeus with Marya.

Martha hobbled downstairs and watched Quincy run out of the doggie door into the back yard and start sniffing around. The yard was enclosed by a six-foot stockade fence tall enough to provide visual privacy, although not auditory privacy, from the neighboring apartment. She knew far more about the young man who lived next to her than she wanted to from his lively telephone conversations on the patio. She had planted a low hedge of boxwood on two sides of her square brick patio, and a tall, slim arborvitae in each of the corners. Pink and purple tulips lined the fence in early spring, which gave way to pink and purple irises for late spring, pink and purple verbena in the summer, and pink and purple asters in the fall. She'd added the purple in with the pinks after she had met Marya. The flowers were protected by a mini picket fence, but Quincy had the run of the rest of the yard, which showed the marks of her passion for digging. Martha opened the patio door and breathed in the loamy, wet odor of a fresh October morning. The star asters twinkled in the morning dew. She took the scissors lying on the metal patio table and limped over to trim some stray leaves that disturbed the level top and sides of the square boxwood hedge.

Quincy's big brown eyes looked up at Martha, her head cocked.

"Sorry, Quince. Maybe I can take you out for a little walk later."

After taking a hot shower and wrapping the ankle with an ace bandage, Martha felt much improved. She sat on the brown sectional, her legs extended on the chaise, and patted the chocolate brown blanket. Quincy jumped up and settled next to her. "You know, Quince, I think I feel better. Let's go out for a walk." Quincy jumped off the couch and trotted to the front door. Martha had a moment of empathy for Marya as her ankle barked in pain with each step.

Her cell phone buzzed.

"Hello, Seamus."

"Good morning, Martha. And how are you feeling this fine morning? I heard the terrible news when I returned from a deanery meeting last night."

"Much better now that I'm moving around a bit. Going for a walk with Quince right now."

"Well now, that is grand. Do you think that after your walk you could drop by the rectory?"

"Well, got to go pick up a loaner till my car's fixed. But maybe 2:00 or so. What's up?"

"Oh, nothing important, just some…church issues."

"Sure." Martha figured it had to do with her request that the Saint Vincent de Paul Society have their collection the week before Thanksgiving. Maybe Father Seamus didn't want it to be so close to the holidays because it might eat into his own Christmas collection plate profits.

Martha's attempt at a walk failed, and she ended up calling a cab to take Quincy to a dog run where she could sit on a bench. She then called for another car to go pick up the loaner, and dropped off Quincy at home before her meeting with Father Seamus.

Father Seamus looked up from behind the desk as she limped into the room. "Well now, Martha, I didn't realize you had been so sorely hurt. I'm sorry I dragged you over here."

Martha pondered whether she should tell Father Seamus her suspicion that Father Thaddeus was behind the attack, though she thought it might make him feel guilty, since he had asked her to complain to the bishop.

"Seamus, I have something to tell you. But before I say anything, I want you to know that I don't hold you responsible at all."

He gazed back at her, forehead wrinkled. "And what could I be responsible for, Martha?"

By the time she was finished explaining her theory, he had a wide grin on his face.

"What are you so happy about, Seamus? It was all your fault for asking me to complain to the bishop!"

"Don't you see, Martha? Now the bishop *has* to take Thaddeus out of here. You must let him know about this."

"So you believe me? You agree it was Father Thaddeus?"

"Well...I wouldn't go so far as to say yes to that. But it would be good for His Nibs, the bishop, to hear a parishioner's suspicions."

"No."

"Please."

"But there's no proof."

"Well, that's never stopped you before." Father Seamus laughed. Martha didn't.

"Just joking, Martha. What I meant to say is that you're such a natural detective—perspicacious, as Marya would say—that you'll be able to find the proof necessary to show the bishop."

Martha considered. She had helped solve stickier crimes than this. And she'd better get to the bottom of this before Father Thaddeus or one of his minions tried again. "Okay, Seamus. I'll try. But what did you need to see me for, anyway?"

"Um. How're you doing?" He gestured at the cane.

"Well, I've been better, but I'm managing."

"That's good to hear, good to hear. Have a nice walk with your dog?"

"More or less. What's this all about, Seamus?"

"Well."

"Yes?"

He just looked at her.

She felt sorry for the poor guy. "Listen, don't worry about the collection. We'll move it to a different date so it won't be too close to Christmas."

Father Seamus's expression brightened. "Well, thanks for that offer, Martha. The first Sunday in January is open." He made a note on what appeared to be a baptismal certificate lying on his desk. "Done! Nice of you to understand. But that's not why I asked you over here."

"Oh." Martha regretted that she had given up her opportunity to have the collection at a more lucrative time. "Well, why *did* you ask me over here?"

The priest took a long breath. "Well then, could you just follow me now?"

Martha eyed him doubtfully, and, in Father Seamus-like fashion, raised one eyebrow.

The priest stood up from his chair, and Martha limped behind him down the hall to a windowless office that was mostly used for storing Christmas decorations. He opened the door and waved Martha in first.

Behind a small desk, wedged in by large artificial Christmas wreaths and a mound of red bows on one side, and a three-foot creche with an upside-down camel on the other, sat Marya Cook. The violet sequined bow in the brim of Marya's bright fuchsia straw hat looked right at home amid the Christmas decorations. Martha would have laughed out loud had she not been so irritated at Father Seamus's ploy. He had done this once before. Why did he think she needed to be tricked into seeing Marya? Martha had planned to call her as soon as she returned home. She turned and glared at him as she considered the possibilities of torture available for a priest in the affluent community of Pequot Bays. Maybe suffocation in a steam bath like Saint Cecilia.

"Please have a seat, my dear. Thank you so very much for coming. With all your injuries from yesterday, it must have been trying. I have been calling, but it seems your phone may have been broken in that terrifying accident yesterday. I have never understood those little phones everyone is using these days. They are very unreliable. So many of my calls go unanswered. I highly recommend using an old-fashioned telephone. Mine is attached to a wall. You always know exactly where to find it, and it never breaks down. I understand it is now called a land line, which is…"

Out of the corner of her eye, Martha saw Father Seamus slink out the door and close it.

"Sit down, my dear, sit down. I am afraid there is no ottoman, but here is a box for you to rest your foot upon so you can be as comfortable as possible. I asked Father to find us a place to talk where no one could overhear. This is a very merry office, but perhaps a bit…"

Martha sat on the folding chair but did not bother to elevate her foot on the plastic box filled with silver tinsel garlands.

"That was a very near miss you had yesterday, my dear. I suppose they did not catch the person driving the car?"

"No, but—"

"I stopped and thanked the Blessed Mother for protecting you from more serious injuries. I was sitting in church when I heard that terrible crash so, unfortunately, I did not see it. Your car appears to have been damaged quite severely."

Martha's heart warmed toward Marya as she pictured her stopping at the Mary grotto in the parking lot and praying to the Holy Mother for her.

"I'm really fine, Marya. Bitsy Ianelli drove me to her husband's office."

"How very nice of her, my dear. What exactly did she say? You know I love to hear about the 'little things.'"

Boy, did Martha know about the "little things." She proceeded to tell about the drive to Dr. Ianelli's office, shaking invisible Medusa curls as she imitated Bitsy's Boston accent. She related the entire conversation up to the point that she fell asleep in the car. "Dr. Ianelli saw me as soon as I arrived. Recommended a cane." She nodded at the cane, identical to the one Marya had placed at the end of the desk. "Prescribed some pain medication."

"Ahh. What exactly did he say, my dear?"

"Said the X-ray didn't show a fracture, and it would take some time for the ankle to mend. I have to go back for a follow up visit, and he'll check if it's healing okay."

"It sounds like he is taking adequate care of you."

"Adequate? He's an excellent doctor."

"I am sure he is. But my dear Dr. Stokes is the best. These days it is difficult to get an appointment in less than a month, but with Dr. Stokes I only have to call the office and—"

"Dr. Ianelli is great. My appointment's only three weeks away. November 20."

"Ah. But Dr. Stokes would have given me an appointment within a week, at the longest. Why, the other day, I felt a twinge on my left side and…"

After Maya had given the details of her visit to "dear Dr. Stokes," Martha said, "Someone is trying to kill me, Marya."

"Of course, my dear. I know that."

"I knew you'd believe me. And you'll understand better after I tell you what I told Dr. Ianelli." Martha adopted the doctor's mannerisms, and, looking over imaginary tortoise shell glasses, she related the conversation in detail, bringing Marya up to speed on her complaint to the bishop about Dies Irae.

"Thank you, my dear, that was very helpful."

"Father Seamus wants me to prove it was Father Thaddeus or one of his helpers who tried to run me over. Got a list of suspects here. Could we go over it together?"

"Ahh. One of your suspect lists. Very good, my dear."

Martha took out Father Seamus's list of the Dies Irae followers from her cross-body bag and handed it to Marya.

"This does not look like one of your lists. Yours are much more… organized."

"Right you are, Marya. This is a list of the Dies Irae members that Father Seamus knows of from Saint John's."

Marya perused it for a few moments and then handed it back to Martha. "Perhaps we should add a few names to the list."

"Sure. You know some secret Dies Irae groupies?" She removed a pen from her purse. "Shoot."

"Shoot?"

"I mean, go ahead."

"I do hope you have been applying ice to the injury, my dear. My mother, God rest her soul, had trouble remembering whether to apply ice or heat when my sister and I hurt ourselves, and so she told us that she would say to herself, 'I is for Injuries.' I thought that was very clever of her. The I in ice matches the I in…"

Martha hadn't talked to Marya in so long, she had forgotten how difficult it was to keep her focused on the topic at hand. She gave a little cough. Sometimes that worked.

Marya smiled. "But, perhaps, my dear, I am not getting to the point. As a young girl, I was prone to silly fancies, and my imagination often wandered. Sister Elizabeth Mary often told me that I must be concise and to the point. Perhaps I did not learn that lesson as well as I should have. I believe you yourself may have made the same comment to me as…"

Martha tried a little groan of pain.

"Oh my. I am so sorry about your ankle injury. And it is all my fault. I thought it would be me, of course, although I knew it was possible that it might be you. I tried to call and warn you, but those cell phones..." She shook her head. "I do not know why they are called smart phones. They are really quite stupid. Pardon my use of such a strong word, my dear, but you could have been killed. And all because of a cell phone. Of course, it was not the fault of the cell phone. It was entirely my fault. Well, of course it was not entirely my fault either. One must place a good deal of the blame on the murderer."

"You mean the attempted murderer. They didn't succeed."

"Very perspicacious of you, my dear. Thank God, the killer did not succeed in the attempt to kill you. One attempted murder...and one murder. I do not know who the murderer is, but I do know that there has been at least one murder. You see, the killer believed you knew about the murder and tried to stop you from investigating."

The only person Martha had been investigating was Father Thaddeus. Did Marya think Father Thaddeus had killed someone? Maybe Lisa Ward? Seamus would be happy to hear that! Martha's attempts to make sense of Marya's ramblings were making her dizzy. And Martha had put off taking her pain pill so that she could drive. A groan escaped her lips.

"Oh, my dear. You are in such pain. Can you ever forgive me for putting you in so much danger by making such a loud fuss after the funeral of poor Mr. Bonino? But you see, there was simply no other way."

Martha shook her head in an attempt to clear her mind. Had Marya just said... "Are you saying that you cooked up that 'loud fuss' after Johnny Bonino's funeral on purpose?"

"Of course, my dear."

"But why would you do that? It was so embarrassing."

"My dear, embarrassment does not compare to permitting a murderer to run free."

"But who was murdered, Marya?"

"Mr. Bonino, of course."

"Johnny Bonino?"

"Yes, my dear."

"And how do you know that Johnny Bonino was murdered?"

"Of course, I did not know for sure until after the attempt on your life, my dear, but I suspected. You see, so many allergies arise when one is an adult. I myself became allergic to milk when I was in my fifties. It was only milk I became allergic to, not any other milk products, which was fortunate, because I do so enjoy my yogurt as snack in the afternoon. Peach yogurt is my favorite, but I often try banana or apple cinnamon. When we were young, my sister and I…"

*By the freezing pond, wooden press, and saw of Saint Jonas. What do allergies, peach yogurt, and milk have to do with murder?* Martha's dizziness turned into a full, swirling head spin. "I'm sorry, Marya, but I have to go. Too much activity today. I need my pills. Do you want a ride home?"

"No, my dear. I believe I will stay and speak to Mary. I am quite relieved that we finally had this talk. We can speak more about this tomorrow. Go home and take good care of yourself. You must be very careful though. Trust no one!"

As Martha left the rectory, she scanned the parking lot to see if there were any automobiles with their engines on. She hurried over to her loaner car as quickly as her painful limp allowed. She let out a deep breath as it started up and she drove away. Martha kept glancing into her rearview mirror all the way home, checking to see if anyone was following her.

# CHAPTER 7

## Friday, October 28

THE NEXT MORNING, MARTHA FELT MUCH BETTER, IN mind at least if not in body. Her ankle was still painful and swollen and was starting to look purplish-yellow. But in the light of a new day—and another of those orange tablets Dr. Ianelli had prescribed—she felt like her old self. Even better than her old self! Martha thought about her conversation with Marya. Johnny Bonino murdered! And Martha nearly killed by his murderer. That seemed farfetched. Maybe Marya *had* lost a little of her perspicaciousness. If anyone had been murdered, it was more likely Lisa Ward. But Martha still favored her own theory that, whoever had been killed, it was Father Thaddeus who had tried to run her down. She added an item to her to-do list for the day. *#18. Confirm that the bishop told Father Thaddeus I complained about him.*

Martha began the first item on her to-do list. *#1. DO RÉSUMÉ.* Once Martha had realized she couldn't work for Uber using a loaner, she had to admit to herself that there would always be something to upset her careful budget calculations. If it wasn't the boiler breaking, it would be a problem with her car. She'd have to apply for a regular nine-to-five job. She brought her résumé up to date, wishing, as always, she had completed college. And the Uber driving wouldn't exactly wow potential employers. But at least she had her years as civilian police commissioner.

She went onto the next item on her to-do list. *#2. SEND OUT*

*RÉSUMÉ*. As she perused the online listings, she noticed that none of them had civilian police commissioner as a job qualification. As a matter of fact, none of her previous employment qualified her for a job on any listing that interested her. And they all required a college education. She slammed down the lid on her computer, then quickly opened it up and made sure it still worked. *Buy new computer* was the last thing she needed to add to her list. She glanced at Quincy flopped over on her side on the couch and smiled, remembering that Marya was scared to death of sweet, gentle Quincy. She decided to skip to #18. She'd send out her résumé tomorrow.

A straight line being the most direct way between two points, Martha decided the quickest way to find out if the bishop had told Father Thaddeus that she had complained about him was to call him and ask. Bishop Ruiz was a man of the people, not one to stand on formality. And she had succeeded in almost doubling the Bishop's Annual Appeal pledges from last year.

"Hello, this is Martha Collins, Diocesan Liaison for the Bishop's Annual Appeal. May I speak to Bishop Ruiz? It's important."

"Hold on a moment, please, Ms. Collins." Martha separated the black pens from the blue pens in her desk drawer while she waited, and checked off item #7 on her list.

"Hello, Martha? This is Bishop Ruiz."

"Hello, Your Excellency. Quick question. Did you tell Father Thaddeus that I complained about him?"

"Father Thaddeus? The Dies Irae fellow? No, sorry, Martha. Haven't spoken to anyone about that yet. Anything else I can help you with? You said it was important. Everything all right with the appeal?"

*Well, I would like to ask why you don't like Father Seamus...* But aloud she just said, "Everything's great with the appeal. Pledges keep rolling in. Sorry to bother you, Your Excellency."

"Any time, Martha."

Martha hung up. But if Father Thaddeus didn't know she'd complained about him, he had no reason to get her out of the way. Could Marya be right? Martha checked her phone. She was surprised Marya hadn't called yet.

She phoned Marya. No answer.

Martha started to clean her refrigerator. She emptied out the food-stuffs arranged by color, size, and shape, wiped every surface, and put everything back in its place. But her perfectly-ordered shelves failed to gratify her as they usually did. She grabbed some scissors to cut off the stray leaves and dead flowers from the two blue pots of chrysan-themums placed equidistant on either side of her front door. After admiring the now-symmetrical mounds of flowers, she went inside and dialed Marya's number. Still no answer. She left another message asking Marya to call her back.

Thirty-two minutes and seventeen seconds went by. Still no call back. After twelve minutes more, she called again. Still no answer.

Martha bundled up against the damp October day and went into the backyard. "Get the *giveitheck*," she said to Quincy, who opened the outdoor toy box with her nose and pulled out a crushed plastic yellow football. Martha threw it in the air and yelled, "Give it heck." Quincy caught it in her mouth, twisting and turning in the air. The giveitheck occupied her for twenty-seven minutes and three seconds. She then switched to the green squeaky frog, then the rope toy, and eventually, the pink and blue bouncy ball.

No call back from Marya.

Martha called again. No answer. She left another message.

Martha decided to stop by Marya's apartment. Driving past the large fence which hid the low-income housing from the street, Martha made a left turn into the parking lot, and stopped in front of number thirty-seven.

She rang the doorbell. Nothing. She rang it again, longer. Still nothing. What if Marya was right about the murder? What if Marya was lying upstairs dead because someone had silenced her? What if—Martha looked around nervously—the murderer was outside and watching her at this very moment? She heard a thumping sound behind the door. It was coming closer and closer. Maybe the murderer was still in the apartment. Maybe he would drag her inside and whack her over the head.

The apartment door opened.

"Oh my goodness, look who it is. Is everything all right, my dear? You look rather upset. Come in, come in. It's chilly outside. You will catch your death. Oh my, of course I don't mean you will die, but as my mother..."

Martha followed Marya upstairs, their two canes tapping a percussive rhythm on the dozen steps to the apartment. Marya bent over the faded sofa and pushed away a small pile of laundry to clear a space. She then flattened out a purple grape-patterned dish towel over a small hole in the sofa and motioned for Martha to sit down.

"Why didn't you answer my calls, Marya?" Martha asked. "Must have tried you at least ten times."

Marya pulled over a cardboard box. "If you wish, you may elevate your foot on this. Walking up all those stairs must have been quite painful." Marya seated herself on one of the folding metal chairs near a Formica kitchen table that encroached so far into the living space that the chairs were equally handy in the dining or living room. She smoothed out her lavender floral housedress and then clasped her hands on her lap. Marya waited, quiet for once.

"Well, why didn't you call me?"

"Because I had tried calling you many times before, my dear, and it seemed your phone was not working."

"It's working now."

Marya nodded. "Then I will make sure that mine is working now too, my dear."

*Touché.*

Martha leaned back, crossed her arms, tilted her head to the side, and eyed Marya. Marya met her gaze, but again remained in un-

Marya-like silence. After a moment, a slow grin crept across Martha's features. Marya began to titter.

"Oh, my dear. So nice to see you again. I have missed you."

"Me too, Marya." And she meant it. "Wanted to talk to you about your idea that there has been a murder, Mar. Makes sense it was the Dies Irae bunch, but the bishop says he never told Father Thaddeus that I complained about him. Maybe someone overheard Seamus and me talking and told him about it?"

"Well, that is a theory, my dear." Marya tipped her head to one side and pressed her lips together. "And a good theory. One that should be considered." Marya nodded. "Indeed, it should be *considered*." She hesitated a moment before adding, "But perhaps it does not take into account all of the—"

Martha lip synched along with Marya as she said, "Little things."

Martha leaned back on the sofa and put her foot up on the cardboard box. She would be here a while.

"I am sure that elevating your foot will be helpful, my dear. May I get you an ice bag? I myself prefer hot water, but that is because my pain is not due to an injury but due to arthritis. As I mentioned to you before, I is for—"

"No, no, I don't need an ice bag." Martha tried not to look at her watch but didn't succeed. "Why do you think there was a murder?"

"Very well, my dear, I will tell you." Marya took a deep breath, her eyebrows furrowing. "I must start at the beginning."

Martha nodded. She recognized and appreciated the outward signs of Marya's inward attempt to concentrate. It must require a lot of effort for Marya to relate a story in an orderly fashion.

"Well, my dear, I believe it all began with a conversation with Gertrude Doppeldecker. You are familiar with her, I am sure."

Martha nodded.

"We were speaking after Mass and she mentioned that the bereavement committee had been quite busy lately. More deaths than usual, I suppose. My mother, God rest her soul, would often say that death comes in threes. And I suppose it is true. My mother, my sister, and my sister's daughter all died before me, but of course that was over a period of many years, so it did not particularly overwork the Saint John's Bereavement Committee. Why, Gertrude was not even on the committee for any of those funerals. As a matter of fact, there was no bereavement committee at the time of my mother's death."

Perhaps Martha's impatience showed in her face, or maybe it was the drumming of her fingers, because Marya said, "Oh, but I am digressing. Oh yes, my conversation with Gertrude. I decided I would try to attend all the funerals and help out in any way I could. I do like a good funeral! Gertrude told me about the funeral of poor Lisa Ward."

"Ah. Lisa Ward. I agree, Marya, that *was* a suspicious death. Suicide. Humph."

"I knew Lisa when she was young. As I may have mentioned, my dear, I was born, brought up, and have always lived in Pequot Bays. After my mother died, I lived with my sister and her daughter in the same house we had grown up in. It was on Tide Pond."

Martha took a deep breath. Might as well let Marya chatter away. It had probably been a while since anyone had visited her.

"Lisa Ward's father was a bayman, a clammer, and when Lisa was only five, both of her parents died. She was brought up by her grandfather. He lived down the street from us. Frank Guardino was his name. I recall her grandfather very well. He was the handyman for everyone in the neighborhood. And handy he was! He was ten years older than me, but my science teacher, Sister Maria Regina, still talked about him. A legend. When he was in fifth grade, the intercom system broke, and he took it apart and put it back together—and it worked! He made toys for all the children in the neighborhood, and although we knew he was not a young man and had a heart problem, we were all quite sad at his sudden demise. The entire neighborhood turned out for his funeral. One of the toys he made was a moving dog that barked, and it followed behind his casket to the hearse. I am still moved to tears when I think of that sad procession."

A moving, barking robot dog! And here they were with an attempted murder, and maybe even a murder on their hands. Try as she might, Martha was unable to restrain herself. "That's interesting, Marya, but what were you saying about Lisa Ward's death?"

"To get back to Lisa Ward. She was about twenty or twenty-one years old when her grandfather died. She was a lovely young woman, and Dr. Ianelli took her on as his receptionist."

"I remember that. Lots of gossip about why he took on such a cute young woman as a receptionist. All his other receptionists had been models of efficiency, but she mixed up appointments, pulled the wrong records, put you on hold and never picked up again."

"I believe her grandfather had been Dr. Ianelli's handyman and even repaired some of his medical equipment. After his death, she was left penniless."

"Ah. That was the connection. Nice of him to hire her. And then he couldn't fire her, under the circumstances. I remember she quit when she married Michael Ward. But now *I'm* getting off topic, Mar. Why would anyone kill Lisa Ward?"

"We are not talking about the death of Lisa Ward, my dear. We are talking about the death of Mr. Bonino."

"I was thinking about that, Marya. Seems to me it's more likely that it was Lisa who was killed." Martha held up her fingers and ticked them off as she said, "She was rich, a devoted Catholic, had a handsome husband, and had just put down $7,000 to go on pilgrimage. And I checked. It was non-refundable!"

"Indeed, my dear, it is possible that Lisa was killed. But there are possibilities and there are probabilities. I recall in twelfth grade that Sister Thomas More said it would be a miracle if I passed Latin and logic. When I did, I reminded her of that statement, and she said that what she had meant was it was possible that I would pass but not probable. Ever since then, I have believed that miracles are indeed possible."

Martha smiled. "And is it possible that you're getting off topic now, Marya?"

"No, my dear, it is not. You see, it is possible that Lisa was murdered. But it is highly probable that Mr. Bonino was murdered."

"Why is that?"

"Lisa Ward's father was a bayman. They lived in shacks on the bay. We lived a bit nearer to town, but we were a close knit community. All the families knew each other, and my sister would help out Mrs. Bonino. She had so many little Boninos running around the house. Johnny was the oldest. You see, my dear, I knew several little things about Mr. Bonino from his childhood that convinced me that he had been murdered."

"From his childhood? What little things?"

"As my mother, God rest her soul, often said, little things are so very important. Why, just the other day I was walking down Main Street and a gentleman was standing—"

"What little things?" Martha repeated.

"So sorry, my dear. Where was I?"

"The little things that made you believe that Johnny Bonino had been murdered."

"Oh yes. The crab, of course."

"The crab?"

"Not to leave an incorrect impression, my dear, you must understand that baymen not only clammed, but also fished, laid out lobster pots, and crabbed. They worked very hard, but did not earn—"

"What about the crab made you believe that Johnny Bonino had been murdered?"

"As I was saying, my dear, before you interrupted me, the baymen worked very hard, but did not earn much money, so they ate what they caught. Johnny Bonino's father was a crabber, so his family would eat crab soup, crab cakes, crab salad, crab for breakfast, lunch, and dinner. I believe there was even a crab dessert among the crabber wives. My sister told me a secret that little Johnny had told her. He whispered that he hated crab so much, he told his parents he was allergic to it. That he broke out into hives, the same as he had done after he was once given penicillin. And so he never had to eat crab ever again. I remember this because my sister and I once tried to tell my mother we were allergic to spinach and broccoli. It did not fool her though. She would leave us sitting at the dinner table for however long it took us to clean our plates. My sister would sneak to the trash can though and throw away our vegetables. Years later, my mother told me that she knew that we did this. She was not an easy one to fool. My mother, God rest her—"

"Marya, please."

"Oh, so sorry, my dear." Marya clasped her hands together as though she was reciting in front of a classroom. "That is why, when I heard that Mr. Bonino had died from an allergic reaction to crab, I knew he had been murdered. To be more precise, I thought it probable that it was murder, because there was a possibility that he had developed an allergy late in life as I have with milk. I thought and thought the night after the wake about how to prove, at least to my own satisfaction, that it was murder, but could not come up with any ideas. I am sorry to say that I sat through the funeral not praying for the repose of the soul of poor Mr. Bonino, but trying to figure out a way to determine the truth of my own logical proposition that he had been killed. When I saw you, I remembered our last adventure together, and an idea popped into my head that if Mr. Bonino had in fact been 'done in,' as they say, and whoever 'did him in' thought that I was on to him…or her…or them, why, they would try to silence me!"

"But there's a flaw in your deductive reasoning, Marya."

"What is that, my dear?"

"Anyone at the party could have killed Johnny. Even if they weren't at the funeral."

Marya clapped her hands. "How very perspicacious of you, my dear."

Martha smiled and bowed her head. She felt rather perspicacious.

"It is true that anyone at the party could have known about Mr. Bonino's alleged allergy, but several little things led me to a probable suspect. And that suspect was at the funeral, along with several others who could have had a motive for killing Mr. Bonino. So, I decided to test my theory on the limited number of persons at the funeral. The idea of a loud conversation with you, my dear, about having seen something suspicious was the best idea I could come up with on such short notice. My test worked, so we now know the murderer was at the funeral. I assumed that the murderer would try to kill *me*, because I was the one who saw 'something suspicious.' To my surprise, he went after you. I am so very sorry I involved you, my dear, but I assumed that I would be able to warn you to be careful."

Martha thought she could understand why a murderer, if there were a murderer, would go after her instead of Marya. They would realize that no one would believe the "Purple Pest." If only Marya had let people know that *she* had been the brains behind Pequot Bays' last murder investigation, then she would have gained some respect. But Marya didn't care about that. Word had spread, though, that Martha had helped in the investigation, so an accusation from her would be taken seriously.

"Who do you think did it?"

"That, my dear, I cannot say. I have no proof. I would not think of harming someone's reputation with no proof."

"But, whoever the murderer is, they could have thought that I was investigating Lisa's murder, and that's why they came after me."

"Indeed, as I said, that is possible, my dear. Now, may I get you a cup of tea? When my sister and I hurt ourselves, my mother would make a lovely tea of cinnamon, ginger, peppermint, and lavender. I only have cinnamon, but perhaps I could put a pinch of cinnamon in a cup of my regular black tea and that would help. I believe in trying the old fashioned remedies first, before taking prescription medicines. Oh, not that I would not heed the advice of dear Dr. Stokes. He is such a nice young man and…"

As Marya prattled on, Martha pondered what Marya had told her. Martha still felt that although it was possible Johnny Bonino had been killed, it was highly probable that Lisa Ward had been the murder victim. Then again, recalling the tête-à-tête at the Bay Fest Brunch between Michael Ward and Isabella Bonino, it was possible that both of their spouses had been killed. But it was also possible that someone had overheard Martha planning with Father Seamus to complain to the bishop about Father Thaddeus and had told the priest.

Too many possibilities. It was making Martha dizzy again.

"We need to make a list, Mar, organize all the possibilities and probabilities. Make a plan."

"An excellent idea, my dear."

Martha lowered her leg from the box and pushed herself up from the creaky springs of the sofa. "Can't do it now though. Feeling a little tired."

"Certainly, my dear. Tomorrow, perhaps. But please be very careful. The murderer is still on the loose!"

# CHAPTER 8

## Saturday, October 29

LEANING ON HER CANE, MARTHA PASSED THROUGH the metal double doors, under the trellis arch threaded with white feather boas, and into the school gym. She wondered how they had managed to set up the white Christmas lights that twinkled on the forty-five foot high ceiling. White helium balloons strung together in large, bulbous masses hung down from the rafters at different heights throughout the room and were clumped together on the walls and floor. It took her a long moment to figure out that they represented clouds. The theme of Father Seamus's 70th birthday party was, "Heaven can wait. We need Father Seamus for a few more years." Drinks, the non-alcoholic ones, were being carried around on trays by fourth and fifth graders dressed up in glittery white masks, angel wings, and halos. Adorable, but messy. And Martha was always in charge of clean up after these parties.

The gym was crowded. It looked like just about the whole parish was here. Martha could not help but notice that everyone who had witnessed Marya's "loud fuss" after Johnny Bonino's funeral, including the Dies Irae gang, had turned out to wish Father Seamus a happy birthday. She'd make sure to avoid them all.

The new widow, Isabella Bonino, brushed her lush tresses from her face as she spoke to the new widower, Michael Ward, his one stray, dark curl falling onto his forehead. They stood in the middle of the gym, seemingly oblivious to the masses of people surrounding them. Gertie Doppeldecker stood very near them, wearing a light-colored cardigan. With her fluffy hair, she was almost invisible in front of a balloon cloud.

Bitsy and Dr. Ianelli strolled in through the boa-laden trellis near the door.

On the other side of the gym lurked the Dies Irae suspects. The figures of bulky Ken Vance and tall, gaunt Father Thaddeus rose above the mingling masses. Barbara Vance kept her eyes on Ken, and Luz Flores's pale eyes followed every move of the priest. Luz carried a briefcase, the one Father Thaddeus had used to give Johnny Bonino the Last Rites. Why did he always go about with an Extreme Unction kit anyway? Was he planning another murder?

Martha felt a tug on her sweater. She looked down and saw an angel pulling on her sleeve with one hand and offering a cup with the other. Martha smiled, took the cup, and watched as the shy little girl disappeared into the mass of towering adults. Martha heard her name called and looked up to see Marya waving her cane and shouting something as she tried to make her way in Martha's direction.

Martha's phone buzzed. She looked at the screen. Christopher! She was surprised to feel a tingly warmth radiating through her body. Too noisy to talk right here. She gulped down the drink and made a face. It tasted sour. She set the cup on the table and did a speedy limp-walk toward one of the exits as she answered the phone.

"Hi, Christopher."

"Hi, Martha. Can you talk?"

"Um, well no. Not right this sec. I'm—"

"Oh, okay."

"What I mean is—"

"I'll call back later then."

"Oh, okay."

"Bye."

"Bye." She stared at the phone for a moment. Not a satisfying conversation.

Martha snaked her way through the crowd toward the food tables. She put three halves of crustless egg salad sandwich onto the paper plate she held in her cane hand and wondered who made the tasty egg salad for these parties. She didn't have much of an appetite though. Had a little headache. Maybe she would wrap these up and take them home. She then aimed herself in the direction of old Mrs. Meyers's potato salad, another favorite, to add to her take home platter. She stopped to talk to a member of the Saint Vincent de Paul Society. Her headache was getting worse, but she would not miss out on those little thumbprint cookies with a chocolate drop on top donated by La Petite Tarte Patisserie.

Weaving through the crowd toward the dessert table, she felt a stinging in the middle of her chest. As she continued walking, the sting turned into a full-blown wildfire. She gasped, but no air came into her lungs. She tried to scream for help, but no sound came out. She could not hear over the sound of her heartbeat pounding in her ears. She braced herself on one of the dessert tables, but it collapsed, and she fell to the floor with it. Her eyes darted around the room, and she caught sight of Ken Vance pulling out his police radio and running toward her, but Marya got in the way. He tripped over her cane and stumbled to his knees. Bitsy Ianelli's Medusa curls entered her field of vision. Martha gasped, "Doctor."

"Steven left. I'll call him."

An unfamiliar female face came into focus and said, "I'm a doctor. Everyone get back." The woman took Martha's pulse.

She heard sirens and saw EMTs come toward her. A medic shouted, "Hypertensive emergency. Twenty milligrams labetolol. Stat." Lieutenant O'Hara, looming over her, popped a thumbprint cookie into his mouth. She broke out in a clammy sweat, and a pit at the top of her stomach churned and lurched upwards. She turned her head to stop from vomiting all over herself as the EMS crew lifted her onto a stretcher and wheeled her to an ambulance. Her eyes latched onto Old Jerome, held back by the police line, who was watching her with his compassionate eyes. She wished he could come with her in the ambulance to calm her as he had after the car crash.

*First the car crash. Now this.*

That was her last thought before the scene grew blurry and she lost consciousness.

Martha woke up in the emergency room to an insistent beeping. The headache and the chest pain were gone, but she felt weak. She opened her eyes and saw Dr. Ianelli standing over her. She had an IV in her arm and monitoring devices attached to her body.

Dr. Ianelli said, "Martha, you're awake."

"I guess I am."

"How are you feeling?"

"So much better. Thanks, Doc, for coming over."

"Let's see—"

The curtain separating her cubicle from the emergency room swished open, and a serious young female doctor with several even younger doctors in tow walked in. They did not close the curtain behind them. Dr. Ianelli stepped back.

The doctor asked, "Do you have high blood pressure, ma'am?"

"No. It's always low."

"Do you take any drugs? Ms…" She looked down at the chart in front of her. "Collins."

"Cholesterol medication."

"I mean illegal drugs."

"No."

"How about amphetamines?"

"No."

The doctor squinted at her. "It is important, Ms…" She looked down at the chart again. "Ms. Collins, that you be entirely honest. Your symptoms were those of an amphetamine overdose, and we have sent your blood for a toxicology screening." She turned away from Martha and addressed the young interns gathered around the foot of the bed. "A classic presentation."

Martha shook her head. "I do not take amphetamines."

After a brief examination in which the doctor spoke not to Martha but to the other doctors in the room, she told Martha that she did not have to be admitted to the hospital, that she had had a hypertensive emergency which had been dealt with through IV blood pressure medication. They would monitor her for a few more hours, and then she'd be discharged.

After the pack of doctors left, Martha turned to Dr. Ianelli. "Could you close the curtain, Doc? I do *not* take amphetamines."

Dr. Ianelli closed the curtain. He checked the IV medications and then gazed at her with professional concern. "How are you, Martha?"

"Fine. I do *not* take amphetamines."

"Of course not. I know you. Don't worry about those residents and interns. They're just out of medical school."

"Thanks, Doc. Just having you believe I'm not a closet drug addict lowers my blood pressure!"

He smiled. "Take it very easy for the rest of the day, Martha. You have an appointment coming up for your ankle, right? When you come in, we'll look into this also."

The curtain swished open, revealing a man with a clipboard. "Hello, Ms. Collins, my name is John. I'm a social worker. Before your discharge, we would like to speak to you about the dangers of amphetamines…"

Dr. Ianelli winked at Martha behind the back of the social worker and then left. She tried to explain that she didn't use amphetamines, but the social worker just nodded. "I understand, Ms. Collins. Many people say that. But it is useful for us to learn about the dangers of drug abuse even if we say…"

She stared at the wall for ten minutes while the social worker delivered his spiel and left a pile of brochures on the bedside table. Martha continued staring at the booklets, listening to the beeping, and trying to stop her blood pressure from rising so she could leave.

The curtain rustled open, and Martha was astonished to see Marya

Cook. Marya smiled. "I told them I was your grandmother, and they let me in—just a venial sin under the circumstances. I hope you don't mind. I wanted to keep an eye on you. How are you, my dear?"

Martha was surprised at the comfort she felt in Marya's presence. She sighed. "Oh, Mar. They say it was an amphetamine overdose. But I've never ever taken amphetamines. Well, maybe a couple of times in college to cram for a final. But not in the last twenty years."

"Amphetamines. So that's what it was."

"I do *not* take amphetamines."

"Of course not, my dear. May I ask you a question? The lemonade, my dear. At the party. How did it taste?"

"A little bitter, sour. I was thinking I'd mention at the next planning meeting that everyone has to check the 'use by' dates of the food and drink. I always do. Don't think a reaction to old lemonade caused this though."

"Of course not, my dear. You were poisoned."

"Poisoned?"

"Indeed."

"Why do you think I was poisoned?"

"I have been secretly following you, my dear, trying to protect you. I believe that it is called 'tailing.' Yes, I was tailing you. What a very appropriate word. Like the tail of an animal. Although the tail is attached to the animal, so of course the animal would know it was behind—"

"Mar."

"Yes, my dear?"

"Why do you think I was poisoned?"

"Why, that was precisely what I was telling you before you interrupted me. It was just a…"

Their eyes met, and they both said at the same time, "Little thing."

Marya tittered. "Yes, a little angel that served you your drink. She was holding the glass in her hand, but all the other cherubim used trays. And she went up to you directly, while the others wandered around until someone took a drink from them. I regret I was unable to see who sent her over to you, but I was sure someone had. I tried to catch your attention to stop you from drinking it, but you did not see me. I tried to warn you to be careful what you ate or drank at the party, but my goodness how you scoot around. I could never get close enough to talk to you." Marya shook her head. "This is the second attempt on your life that I have failed to stop."

"Hmm. I did begin to feel lightheaded a few minutes after the little angel gave me the lemonade. Then got a headache, and then… well, you know the rest." All the pieces clicked together in Martha's brain. "You're right, Marya. This was another murder attempt. Someone's trying to kill me! But no one will ever believe us."

Marya dug around in her lilac-adorned handbag and removed a paper bag, which she unfolded to reveal a plastic bag, which she untied, from which she took out an aluminum foil- wrapped object, which she unwrapped and held up for Martha's inspection: a plastic happy birthday cup with a lid, covered in plastic wrap.

"What's that?"

"I noticed where you left the cup and was able to retrieve it. I was very careful with it, my dear. I even used a napkin to pick it up so I would not smudge any fingerprints."

"That was good thinking, Marya. May I see the cup?" Marya brought it over to her. There was some liquid left in the bottom. "You haven't failed. We've got proof now that someone is trying to kill me."

Martha looked around the little curtained area and shook her head. "I've wasted too much time. We've got to get busy. What can we do? Call the police, I guess. Got to get the liquid in the cup analyzed. They'll have to believe someone is out to kill me now. They can get a list of the little angels who served the drinks at the party."

"Perhaps we should not present this to the police as a murder attempt, my dear. For some reason, they tend to think that we are a bit…loony."

Martha gazed at the old woman. Her hat, a sort of tam covered in royal purple sequins with a furry plum pom pom on top, was perched at a forty-five degree angle on the top of her head. A violet and magenta striped scarf was tied around her neck. Martha could not see the rest of the outfit because Marya still had on her lavender raincoat with a hospital blanket thrown over her shoulders like a shawl against the chill of the emergency room.

*Yes, the police might indeed think we are a bit loony.* She recalled the doubting faces when she had tried to explain that the car crash had been deliberate. "Well, what would you suggest, Marya?"

"Perhaps instead we should present this as a very bad practical joke. That someone spiked your drink as a prank. 'Spiking.' Now I wonder where that word comes from? It makes no sense at all. Perhaps it…"

Martha agreed, and while Marya nattered on, she called the Pequot Bays Police Department. A recording answered. "This is the Pequot Bays Police Department." Pause. Sing-song voice saying, "Remember, stay alive, don't drink and drive. If you know the extension…"

Martha recalled the days when she had been one of the civilian police commissioners and could dial the private line of the police chief. She'd loved that job. It was interesting. She was respected. It came with great benefits and a little salary that was all she needed to keep herself going. Until she had reported O'Hara to the police chief for planting evidence on a suspect. To get back at her, O'Hara had recruited Arlo Bennett, an ex-district attorney, to run against her, and he made sure all the police and their relatives voted for him. When Marya heard the story, she had given Martha one of her lavender note cards.

> *Blessed are you when people insult you, persecute you,*
> *and falsely say all kinds of evil against you because of me.*
> Matthew 5:11

But Martha did not feel blessed when she had to start working as an Uber driver after losing the election. Martha had evened things up a bit, though, when she and Marya had cleared Father Jim, the associate pastor at Saint John's, of murder after O'Hara had promised the DA he could get a conviction.

Finally, a live human voice said, "Pequot Bays Police Department. May I help you?"

Martha asked to speak to Henry Milton. He owed her. In her days as police commissioner, she had put in a good word for him when he applied for a job.

Luck was with her. Henry was there.

"What can I do for you, Ms. Collins?"

"I'm calling from the hospital, Henry. I've been poisoned."

"Please, Ms. Collins, call me Hank. Poisoned?"

"Yes, and I can prove it."

"Prove it?"

"Yes. I need you to come over to the Saint Barnabas emergency room, and I'll tell you all about it."

There was a pause. Then Henry said, "Hold on."

Martha held on. After a few minutes, Henry returned. "Someone will be right over."

"But I want *you* to—"

Henry hung up.

About half an hour later, a police officer pushed back the hospital curtains like they were swinging saloon doors and walked in. She was short and built too solidly to be called slim. Mid-length brown hair, no highlights, pulled back. No makeup. Plain, but too angular to be called a wallflower. Her piercing eyes made for a memorable face, Martha thought, and then realized that she *did* recall seeing that face before. Where was it? Oh yes! The *Pequot Bays Journal.*

"Congratulations on your appointment to the PBPD. Saw the writeup on you in the paper," Martha said.

The officer nodded.

"Quite an accomplishment."

The officer pulled out a memo pad.

"So now there are two female officers out of forty in the PBPD."

"One."

"What happened to Ashley?'

"She retired last year."

"Was that you with O'Hara and Henry when I nearly got run over by a car?"

She nodded. "I'm Officer Sarah Chonkin. You called the department?"

"Yes, I did, Sarah."

"Officer Chonkin, please. What is it you want to report, Ms. Collins?"

Martha presented the story as planned, a nasty practical joke gone wrong, someone spiking a drink at a church gathering with amphetamines. Officer Chonkin listened impassively. "Before you leave the hospital, make sure you sign a consent form so we can access your record to check on the blood toxicology results. Thank you, Ms. Collins and Ms. Cook." She nodded briefly at each. "Your statements will be typed up, and you will have to come to the station to sign them. I'll take the cup with me and log it in."

Martha handed it over but felt that Officer Chonkin did not hold onto it as carefully as she should. "You can pick up a receipt for it at the station when you come to sign your statements."

She left. A woman of few words. A nurse came by shortly afterwards and told Martha that the doctor had signed the discharge papers. Martha called a cab to take her and Marya home. The nurse brought her downstairs in a wheelchair, and then the two women tap-tap-tapped their way into the Uber.

Once in the car, Marya said, "This is becoming too dangerous. We must stop the murder attempts. You will tell all the suspects that you had nothing to do with my little scene after the funeral, and you must try to make it sound believable. You will have to call me a crazy old lady and say you had no idea what I was talking about. If you blame it entirely on me, no one will take it seriously." She tittered. "You will find this hard to believe, my dear, but some people call me the Purple Pest."

Martha tried to keep a straight face. "Is that so?"

"Yes indeed. So, will you do it? For me. I am quite worried."

"Sure. For you, Mar. I'll do it."

"Good. Now, my dear, until you let everyone know you had nothing do with my little scene, you are still in danger. I think it would be best if you did not remain in your own apartment at present. You must stay over with me. I will sleep on the sofa, and you can stay in the bedroom."

"Thank you for your kind offer, Mar, but I will be careful. I promise. Plus, I must take care of Quincy. Unless you wouldn't mind her staying in your apartment also."

A momentary look of terror came over Marya's features. "Oh my. Of course. Perhaps it would be best for you to stay at your own home. You would be more comfortable, I am sure. But we will drop you off first and wait while you go inside to make sure you are all right. Please turn the lights on and off when you are safely inside."

Martha had to admit as she unlocked the door to her apartment that she was a bit nervous. What if a killer lurked just inside? But her only greeting came from dear, dear Quincy. She checked the locks on the doors and the windows and then gave the all-clear signal to Marya. She collapsed on the bed, and Quincy jumped up next to her and lay down. Martha fell asleep, secure in the knowledge that she was safe. At least until tomorrow.

# CHAPTER 9

MARTHA ATTENDED HER REGULAR SUNDAY MASS, GOing early and staying afterward. She was the center of attention, with parishioners expressing concern about her wellbeing, and she used the opportunity well.

"I'm much better. Much better. Just fainted. Don't know why." She caught a glimpse of Michael and Isabella in the aisle. Ken and Barbara Vance and Luz were right behind. Gertie, of course, lurked nearby, and Aldo Todi stood next to her. The stage was set. Martha began her act. "By the way, did you see the crazy old lady at the party yesterday? The one they call the Purple Pest?" She waved at Isabella. "I've been meaning to talk to you about that ridiculous scene after your husband's funeral, Isabella. Wanted you to know I had nothing to do with it. No idea what she was talking about. Batty as they come."

Isabella smiled. "Martha, *sono sicura* you had nothing to do with it. *È pazza.* The purple lady, she's a bit…odd."

"Odd is putting it mildly," Martha said, feeling guilty that she was enjoying this a bit. "A nut case is more like it."

People chuckled all around. Someone said, "Did you see the contraption she had on her head a couple of Sundays ago? It looked like a bird's nest." More chuckles.

"Yeah, but—" Martha said.

"Last week she caused a traffic jam a mile long when she stopped in the middle of Main Street to look through her purse. My Braden was late for soccer practice!"

"It wasn't a mile—"

"Has she given you one of her silly cards yet? What a wacko!"

"Yeah, but—"

The laughing group headed toward the exit. Martha smiled, but inside she was boiling. How dare they! But then...hadn't she herself...

*Ah well. So who am I to judge?*

Martha drove home. The rest of the day, she slept and played with Quincy, feeling more relaxed than she had since the car crash.

On Monday, Martha called Officer Chonkin to see if the contents of the cup had been analyzed. She wasn't in, so Martha left a message. Officer Chonkin did not return the call.

Martha called the following day and left another message. When there was no response by the afternoon, she called again. And then again. There was a murderer out there, and there was no reason to think that the killer would be as unrushed as the local police force.

Officer Chonkin finally called. "Hello, Ms. Collins. Sorry I couldn't call yesterday. I was on patrol."

"That's all right. Can we come down to sign our statements?"

"They aren't ready yet. Maybe tomorrow."

"How about the punch? Has it been sent out for testing? Are there any fingerprints on the cup?"

"My report is sitting on the boss's desk. Maybe tomorrow he'll review it and okay the request to send it out to the lab."

"The boss?"

"Lieutenant O'Hara."

"Oh." Martha bit her tongue to stop from yelling that someone had tried to kill her, and instead said, "I will call tomorrow...first thing."

The following day, Officer Chonkin called. But it was not to report on fingerprints or a lab analysis of the punch. "Hello, Ms. Collins. Chonkin here. Officer Milton asked me to call you. They found a white Range Rover with a damaged front bumper in the grocery store parking lot. It had been sitting there a while, so they called to have it towed. Officer Milton mentioned it might be the car that nearly hit you in the parking lot. It's owned by an old man, a very old man, who lives near the store. Doesn't drive any more. His aide figured the son borrowed the car. He does that sometimes. We called the son, who didn't know anything about it. The old man is bedbound and gets a lot of visits from physical therapists and nurses, and the key is kept on a hook by the door. The aide thought maybe one of them took it. The son figured it might be the aide, though, and fired him."

"What's the name of the old man?"

"George McAdams."

"I know him. He went to Saint John's. 5:00, though, not 10:00."

"Huh?"

"I mean he went to 5:00 Mass, not my usual Mass at 10:00. Haven't seen him lately though."

"Oh."

"Any news on the poisoning?"

"Poisoning?"

"I mean the spiking of my drink."

"No."

Martha hung up. That report was never going to move from O'Hara's desk.

Martha called Marya. "I'm coming over."

"How nice. It would be lovely to see you."

"I'll make the list."

"The list, my dear?"

"The list of suspects."

"Ah, yes. The list. Very good."

Martha left for Marya's apartment. Police cars, blue lights flashing, were parked on Main Street partially blocking the roadway. As she slowed to navigate the muddle of cars, she saw Isabella Bonino and Michael Ward standing on the lawn in front of one of the Victorian homes that had been renovated into modern offices, speaking with the police, a burglar alarm *whoop whoop whoop*-ing in the background. The sign hanging from a post in front read, *The Law Offices of John Bonino, Esq.*

Martha continued on to Marya's apartment, wondering what that was all about.

Sitting on the grape-patterned dish towel with her foot propped up on the cardboard box, she told Marya about her conversation with Officer Chonkin. "We've got to do something ourselves, Marya. The police aren't taking us seriously. There were ten cars outside of Johnny Bonino's office just now. Don't you think they could spare one officer to investigate a poisoning? If I was police commissioner…"

"What an excellent idea, my dear. Yes, you must run for police commissioner."

"I didn't mean I'd run again. Arlo would wallop me. No, I'm going to apply for regular jobs, nine to five. But let's get back to business. We have to catch a murderer. We'll start like we did the last time. A list of suspects. Do you have a piece of paper and a pen?"

Marya shuffled around the apartment, shifting papers and laundry. "I know I have a pen around here somewhere." She held up a purple fountain pen. "We cannot use this one. It is only for my Bible quotes. Now where was I when I last used a regular pen? I find that I can remember where I put things if I…"

Martha thought of a quote she had once seen on a refrigerator magnet. "Patience is not the ability to wait, but the ability to have a good attitude while waiting." Ever since she met Marya, she had begun to think in platitudes.

She looked at her watch. Twice.

Finally, Marya brought over a long green pen with a purple fabric flower fastened to the top and a lavender memo pad with, *Trust in the Lord with all your heart. Proverbs 3:5-6,* imprinted on the bottom of each page.

Martha wrote *List of Suspects* on the top of the first page. "We'll start with the mourners at Johnny Bonino's funeral, since the murder attempts started after your 'little fuss.' And your prime murder suspect was at the funeral. Now who did you say that was, Mar?"

"I didn't, my dear. I have not ruled out anyone as of yet."

"Luckily, not too many people came to the funeral. And they're mostly the same ones who were at Lisa Ward's funeral. Let's start with the spouses of the victims. It's usually the husband or wife that does it.

"Number one, Isabella Bonino." Martha wrote the name on the memo pad in big capital letters. "Isabella has a son, Luca, fourteen years old. He's the same age as she was when she first met Johnny Bonino. It was quite a scandal when Johnny brought her back as his wife. Everyone was talking about it. Went to visit the village his parents came from in Calabria. About twenty years ago now. When he first saw Isabella there, she was fourteen, he was fifty. He returned every year until she was eighteen and then asked her parents if he could marry her. They said it would be all right if Isabella agreed. He was a rich lawyer, and she was a poor kid from a tiny village in Italy. She agreed. I heard Gertie say she's been having an affair with Michael Ward. Can't blame her, I guess. Johnny Bonino was an old guy when she married him. For his money, I'm sure."

"Perhaps we should be careful not to come to any conclusions before we have evidence to support them, my dear. I shall never forget the penguins."

"The penguins?"

"Yes. Though it happened many years ago, I still feel quite sad when I think of the penguins. You see, a group of us had been laughing at a man in the playground. He had three children jumping all over him and fighting and yelling at each other while he just sat there, doing nothing. What a bad father he was! Sister Thomas More caught us making fun of him and became quite angry. She said he was a good father but was very sad because his wife had died, and he was here to arrange the funeral. That day in class, she warned us to never…now what did she say? Oh yes. I remember. She made us memorize it. 'Never assume the truth of a general rule without considering the circumstances of a particular individual. It is a logical fallacy.' The example she gave was, 'Most birds fly. A penguin is a bird. Therefore, penguins fly.' We had to write, 100 times, 'Penguins do not fly.' That was Sister's favorite punishment because she said you were learning something at the same time you were being punished. We all wished she would try to convince Sister Elizabeth Mary to use that method of punishment instead of…"

That *was* a sad story about the father. Martha continued with a less critical commentary about Isabella Bonino. "There's a meeting coming up to plan a retirement party for Father Peanuts. Isabella will be there. She's always in charge of bringing the plastic and paperware to the parties. I'm always in charge of clean up. Maybe I'll ask her a few questions at the meeting.

"Next, there's the husband of the late Lisa Ward. Number two, Michael Ward, mid-forties maybe? Handsome guy. Lisa was his high school sweetheart, and they married when he came home from college. Seems to have recovered from the shock of his poor wife's 'suicide' as fast as Isabella got over her husband's death."

Marya gave her a pointed look. Martha thought of the penguins and steered her comments toward a more factual, less judgmental path. "Loves fishing. Had a conversation with him once when we were both waiting in Dr. Ianelli's office. Told me he started in the mailroom of a pharmaceutical company and worked his way up. Now he's CEO. Lives on Pequot Island, so he's made a fortune. I remember he said he moved here because a friend from college told him what a great place it was. I bet that buddy was Aldo Todi.

"He's generous. Gives scads of money to the Bishop's Annual Appeal. I have to say, whether or not he and Isabella are having an affair, they make a perfect couple. Much better than Michael and poor, mousy Lisa. That marriage was like breeding a Saluki with an Old English sheepdog." Martha paused as she pondered the result of such a crossbreed. "Luckily, their son takes after Michael.

"Let's go with the Dies Irae gang next. Number three, Ken and Barbara Vance." Martha noted the names on the memo pad. "Ken and Barbara, as in Barbie and Ken dolls. He's about fifty. Kind of scary, with his devil beard and those muscles. Never misses Sunday Mass though. 10:00. Sits in the same seat, right in front of me. Always on time. Says all the prayers without looking at the missal. Never catch him yawning or looking around. But you heard what Gertie said about him having an affair with Lisa Ward."

"Remember the penguins, my dear."

Martha smiled. "I think I'll need to go to confession after I finish this list."

"That is always a fine idea, my dear. Saint John's next confession is not scheduled until Saturday, but perhaps you could run over to Saint Mary by the Sea. They will schedule confession on request at any time and they have some particularly fine—"

"Marya, it was just a joke."

"Confession is not a joke, my dear."

"Well, not really a joke, but... Never mind. Let's keep focused here. I've chatted with Ken a few times after Mass. He works at Saint Clare's Hospital. Some low-level administrative job. He's a certified medic and volunteers on the ambulance corp. Always standing outside church with his radio receiver squawking, monitoring police frequencies."

"Oh yes, my dear. I wondered why he carried one of those devices. I have noticed that he and his wife are very devout indeed."

"They live in Skeeter Flats. Don't know how he can afford it. Those mansions go for three million and up. And let's see, Marya, what about his devoted wife, Barbara? Hangs on his every word. She makes sure everyone calls her Barbara. No nicknames. Sick of the

Barbie and Ken doll jokes, I guess. I guess Ken won't let her go to the gym with him. And she'll do anything he says. Like a cocker spaniel with a PhD from doggie training school.

"The third member of the Dies Irae commando squad is number five, Luz Flores. The one who dresses like a nun. Remember?"

"Yes, my dear, I know her."

"Me too. I used to bump into her and her husband with Merrie."

"Mary?"

"No, Merrie. Her Bassett Hound. Quincy and I would meet them. Luz was happy and lively back then. She and her husband used to ski and sail all over the place. But about five years ago, he died and she joined Dies Irae. Dropped out of Saint Vincent de Paul. Stopped sports and socializing. Now it's nothing but Dies Irae this and Thaddeus that. I don't even see her walking Merrie anymore. Nice dog for a Basset Hound. Quincy misses her."

"Excuse me, my dear, may I ask you one little thing?"

"Always, Mar."

"How did her husband die?"

"He drowned. His sailboat was found adrift and his body washed ashore a few days later. Kind of odd. They were both such good swimmers."

"One other little thing, please. Did Luz join Dies Irae before or after her husband passed on?"

"Not sure. No. Yes, I am. I remember a conversation with Luz when she was trying to get me to join. She said that she wasn't very good at getting new members since she couldn't even convince her husband. So, I guess she must have joined first and then her husband died. But it wasn't until after he died that she became such a fanatic. Hmm. Do you think...?"

"It is necessary to get all the facts, my dear. I recall an incident when one of the students in our class was accused of stealing another classmate's *Howdy Doody* lunchbox because the day after the lunchbox was missing, the student showed up with one just like it. We all believed it had been stolen until another student found the missing one in the gym behind a heater. Perhaps the dog fallacy is most appropriate here. 'If cats and dogs both have tails, then cats are dogs.' Or the furry cat fallacy. 'Cats are furry, dogs are not cats, so dogs are not furry.' I still get confused between the…"

Martha took a deep breath. She wondered if she could get Marya to write "short and to the point" 100 times. That might work.

"Stay with me here, Mar. Luz is an ER nurse at Saint Clare's Hospital. Works the overnight shift, and I believe she goes to daily Mass religiously after she gets off work at 7:00 AM. I mean religiously every single morning, not religiously religiously, although she also goes religiously religiously, if you know what I mean."

Martha waited for but did not receive an appreciative smile for the clever aside. "She arrives a half hour early on Sundays and stays a half hour afterward to pray. Can you imagine that! She once said that she saw me walking to the car after Mass and told me that I looked so focused that she thought I was doing a prayer of thankfulness. Marya, I don't even know what the prayer of thankfulness is."

"There are five basic forms of prayer, my dear. Blessing and adoration, petition, intercession, thanksgiving—"

Martha simply talked over her. "We can't forget their fearless leader. Number six, Father Thaddeus Martin." She wrote his name on the memo pad. "He's a creepy kind of guy. Wouldn't have any qualms about eliminating someone he thought was a minion of the devil whether they were one of his followers—or me!"

"*Howdy Doody*, my dear."

"*Howdy Doody?*"

"Yes. *Howdy Doody.*"

"Oh right. *Howdy Doody*. Well, next is number seven, Gertie Doppeldecker. Hard to tell how old Gertie is. Maybe in her sixties?"

"I would have guessed nearer forty, my dear."

"But her hair is pure white."

"I believe it is blond."

"So, she's somewhere between forty and sixty, with either white or blond hair. Our Gertie is sure hard to pin down. She blabs about everyone else but never herself. I don't know where she's from, what family she has, or even where she lives. Don't know anything about her."

"Not knowing anything is knowing a great deal, my dear."

"Uh, sure, Mar. I heard she's a pharmacist. Don't know where she works, but I've never seen her in the drug stores around here. Turned up in town maybe five years ago, but it's like she's been here forever. Always popping up around church. Seems to know everything about everyone. I've seen her whispering with Aldo Todi a couple of times. Saw her give him cash once…lots of it. I figure Aldo is blackmailing her."

"What an interesting theory, my dear. Perhaps you could describe what you saw?"

"I saw Gertie give Aldo some money."

"No, no, my dear. The little things. When was this? Where they were? How did they look? Little things are so—"

"Okay, okay." What was that saying about patience she had seen on the refrigerator magnet? "Well, it was the day after Johnny Bonino's funeral. I had substituted for the regular eucharistic minister and was closing up the sacristy. I nearly knocked Gertie over as I left because she was standing right outside the door. She was with Aldo. And well, I saw him put the money into his wallet."

"Was the church dark?"

"Yes."

"Did you see her give him the money?"

"He was stuffing it into his wallet."

"Were they startled to see you?"

"Yes. Gertie especially."

"Did you see him put the money in his wallet before or after they saw you?"

"After."

"Thank you, my dear. You do have an excellent memory. That was certainly helpful."

"Sure, sure. Well, let's get on with it. Next is number eight, Dr. Steven Ianelli. Most of the Saint John's parishioners use him as their GP. I'd guess he's about sixty, maybe a little older. Went to Harvard. Really smart. Has a large practice. So nice to me after the car crash. I wouldn't seriously consider him a suspect. He's patient with his patients." Martha took a quick glance but again observed no appreciative smile from Marya. A sense of humor was not one of Marya's strong points.

"Did you know, my dear, that when he was just out of medical school, he and Bitsy lived in my neighborhood? He had his office there. Bitsy was his receptionist. I don't believe they remember me though. Neither of them has ever said hello."

"Well, that's sure changed," Martha said. "Although sometimes Bitsy still fills in if the receptionist is sick. But now they live on Middle Point. That's rich even for a doctor. Most of them are Pequot Islanders or live in Skeeter Flats. I hear he made a bunch of money on some sort of medical device. But he's still a caring, compassionate guy. He even makes house calls. Goes to the funerals of all his patients. Never misses Sunday Mass. He's a listener, not a talker.

"Number nine, Elizabeth 'Bitsy' Ianelli. Elizabeth is her real name, but everyone calls her Bitsy. Like itsy bitsy, I guess. And she is itsy bitsy."

"Yes, she is petite, and so very pretty."

"Looks like a model, even though she's at least in her fifties. Can't imagine how much she spends on clothes. And her shoes! Surprising she never twisted *her* ankle in a fall from those stilettos. What a highfalutin accent she has! I think it gets heavier every year. I hear endless gossip about her."

"Do you, my dear? It is bad to speak poorly of others."

Was there an accusatory tone in Marya's voice? Martha tried a more positive note. "Well, she and Dr. Ianelli seem devoted to each other. I see them holding hands in church. And they kiss during the sign of peace. I actually don't know too much about her. Her accent sure isn't from around here. Someone told me that she was a Talmadge, from the Boston Talmadges. They once owned half of Beacon Hill. I have to admit, though, that Bitsy doesn't brag about her pedigree. Never heard her even mention it.

"Next we have number ten, Aldo Todi. He's sickly, that's for sure. Coughs all the time. I feel sorry for him, I guess, but I'd still peg him as the murderer. Well, him or Ken Vance or one of the Dies Irae gang or...well, anyway. Aldo's got those beady eyes. I bet he has his share of secrets, and he'd kill to keep them hidden. He's blackmailing Gertie—"

"Penguins and furry cats, my dear."

"Sure, sure. Okay...Aldo's a townie. Brought up in Pequot Bays, an Islander, then moved away. Returned maybe five years ago and moved back onto Pequot Island. Don't know what he does for a living, but he lives well. And like I said, he's a pal of Michael Ward's. Well, that's it. Ten suspects."

"Very good, my dear. There are also the funeral committee members, Father Seamus, the rich man you brought to Mr. Bonino's funeral, and Old Jerome, to name a few more. But the list is a good place to start. And it does contain my prime suspect."

"Which is?"

Marya just shook her head and smiled.

"You don't seriously suspect Father Seamus, do you? Or Old Jerome? And my rich old guy is about ready to keel over and die himself."

"Everyone is a suspect until proven otherwise, my dear. Perhaps this will help explain it." Marya rooted around in her purse and pulled out one of her laminated note cards.

> *Whoever is not against us is for us.*
> *Mark 9:38*

"Oh, no, my dear, you are reading the wrong side. Turn it over."
Martha turned it over.

*Whoever is not with me is against me.*
*Luke 11:23*

Martha looked at the two sides of the card again. She opened her mouth to say something but then closed it. Luckily, Marya had already wandered down a different road.

"...although I keep thinking that I have missed something, something little, but something very important. I shall have to—"

"No more thinking, Mar! We have to take action. We have to do something."

"Of course. You are so very good at taking action. What do you suggest?"

"Interrogate them." Martha perused the list. "We can get Gertie at church anytime. I'll see Isabella at the meeting to plan Father Peanuts's retirement party. The Ianellis, Aldo, Michael, Ken, and Barbara we just have to waylay at Sunday Mass. And then we'll have to figure out something with Father Thaddeus. Maybe go to one of his Dies Irae meetings."

"Very good, my dear. We shall interrogate them."

"We can start tomorrow with Gertie at daily Mass. I'm going shopping now. To Sam's. Want to come?"

"Thank you for the kind offer. It would be lovely to go out for a drive, and I believe that Sam's is having a sale on lettuce."

Martha had a long list of grocery items and Marya only needed lettuce, but it took each the same amount of time to complete her shopping at Sam's Farm and Fish Store. They chose different checkout lines, one next to the other, but Marya's moved rapidly while Martha's did not. Martha listened while Marya spoke to the cashier.

"Young man, let us go over this one more time. It appears that you do not understand me."

"I got it, lady, I got it. Listen, I ain't got time for this. There's a line… I do what I'm told and…"

"Then I must speak to your supervisor."

"He's not here, lady. Pay for it or leave it. It's just a head of lettuce."

"That would not be right, young man. It is important that—"

An overweight, balding man whose stained white apron barely covered his expansive belly approached the scene. He shook his head, mouthed to the cashier, "The Purple Pest," and then said, "I'll deal with this, Joe. Step over here, lady."

Marya moved away from the checkout counter to a more open area by the potato chip display. "Thank you, sir. My name is Marya Cook."

"Okay, Myra…"

"Not Myra, Marya. M-A-R-Y-A."

The man stared at her. "So, what's your problem *now*, Myra?"

She drew a breath and straightened her body as best she could. Still, she had to twist her head a bit to look him in the eyes. "Your sign says 'two for $5.00.' I took one and your cashier charged me $2.99. That is not correct. One half of $5.00 is $2.50, not $2.99."

"I know half of five bucks is $2.50, Myra."

"Then why are you charging me $2.99, sir?"

"You gotta buy two to get the sale price, Myra. That's how it always is."

"Well, sir, the sign did not say 'one for $2.99,' it said, 'two for $5.00.' Perhaps you should consider changing the sign so that it explains that if one purchases only one item, he will be charged more. Otherwise, you are misleading the public, and that is not…"

"Aw, geez, I don't have time for this. Just take the darn lettuce and leave."

She reached in her bag and fumbled around. "Thank you, sir, but that would not be right either. One should pay for what one needs."

"I got no time for this," the grocery man repeated as he tried to squeeze between Marya and the potato chips, no small feat for a man of his size. But he stopped in his tracks when he heard:

"Now you just wait one moment, young man. Here is the two dollars and fifty cents." Marya carefully counted out two one dollar bills, one quarter, one dime, and three nickels. She handed him the money and a laminated index card, then stepped aside so that he could walk away. He did, shaking his head and mumbling to himself. He let the index card drop.

Marya placed the lettuce into her lavender and neon orange plaid bag and resettled her belongings, purse on one shoulder and tote bag on the other, carefully balancing her burdens so that she did not list to one side. She said to Martha, "I shall wait for you outside, my dear."

Martha noticed that Gertie Doppeldecker had slipped in front of her and was loading her groceries onto the grocery belt. What luck. She would not have to waste her time going to morning Mass to interrogate Gertie. She could do it right here. "Gertie!"

Gertie looked up as she removed the last of her items from the cart. "Why, Martha. I didn't realize that you were the person I... Well, never mind that. You know I was just thinking about you, and here you are! I heard—"

Martha interrupted. "Hey, Gertie, what was the name of that man I saw you talking to outside the sacristy the other day?"

Gertie hesitated. "I have no idea who you're talking about."

"I nearly knocked you two flat running out the door of the sacristy after morning Mass, remember?"

"You must be mistaken."

"He's a short guy. Coughs a lot."

"I don't know anyone like that." Without a pause to allow another question, Gertie continued, "But remember, a few days later? When I was talking about Lisa Ward...?"

*A few days later*, Martha thought. Gertie knew exactly what she was talking about.

"The one who had the affair with you know who." Gertie motioned with her head. Martha followed the gesture and saw Ken Vance waiting in another line. "Well, a little later that day, I was putting out new altar cloths, and I couldn't help but overhear someone say that there was an argument between you know who and Lisa's husband Michael. Michael punched him. And Ken started crying!"

Gossip was like a snowball, Martha thought. He had not cried. Just looked like he wanted to.

"Ma'am, are you buying anything else?" the price checker interjected. Gertie shook her head, still looking at Martha.

The price checker's patience gave out. "Please, ma'am, the line. You got to pay for the groceries."

Martha made herself busy taking her groceries out of the cart while Gertie paid.

When Martha was leaving the store, she spied the index card Marya had given the grocery man lying on the floor. She picked it up.

*The person who is trustworthy in very small matters*
*is also trustworthy in great ones; and the person who*
*is dishonest in very small matters is also dishonest in*
*great ones.*
*Luke 16:10.*

She had to smile.

Martha limped toward her car, the cane in one hand and the bag in the other. Maybe she would hang around a bit to interrogate Ken Vance. Kill two birds with one stone.

Marya was waiting by the car, and Martha unlocked the door so Marya could settle herself into the front seat. As Martha began loading her bags into the back of the car, a hand clapped down on her shoulder. She heard a booming, "Martha," in her ear. She turned around and saw Ken Vance. Her suspect had come to her. Martha stepped back so that he was outside her personal space, and his hand dropped off her shoulder. With not a stray hair in his eyebrows, his brown hair slicked back with a part as straight as a railroad track, and a perfectly shaped and trimmed goatee that appeared painted onto his chin, he did look like a Ken doll. His bulked-up body was clad in clean and ironed blue warm-up pants and a matching jacket. The pants even had a crease. But his perfect appearance was marred by a large bruise peeking out from under a bandage on the left side of his face.

"Wow, that looks terrible, Ken." Martha touched the side of her own face to mirror his swollen cheek.

His lips tightened. "It's nothing. I fell down while running."

"You keep in such good shape. I hope this won't set your workout routine back. Nice jogging outfit you're wearing." Maybe a little flattery would smooth out her interrogation.

It did not work.

"Martha." Her name came out in a squeak. He cleared his throat. "Martha," he repeated in more manly tones. "I overheard you and Gertie. I know what people are saying about Lisa Ward and me. It's not true. Barbara and I have a perfect marriage. That time in the coffee shop, Lisa just needed someone to talk to because her husband was cheating on her." He glared. "Gossip is a sin, so stop spreading rumors about me. I'm warning you. Let the dead lie." Then he stomped away.

As Martha drove off, she said to Marya, "I guess you heard what Ken just said."

"Yes indeed. I do like his yellow outfit though."

"It's blue, not yellow."

"Of course, it would be yellow."

"It's blue."

"Yes, my dear, I understand it is actually blue."

Martha shook her head and changed the subject. "I ran into Gertie."

"Yes, I noticed that Gertrude managed to get in front of you in line."

Martha told Marya about her conversation with Gertie. "She's not a very good liar. They know each other. I saw them talking together at the party for Father Seamus too."

"Did you, my dear?"

"Wasn't it a coincidence, Marya, to run into two of our suspects in the store? And just when we needed to interrogate them."

"My mother, God rest her soul, would often quote Albert Einstein. 'Coincidence is God's way of staying anonymous.' Mr. Einstein was a scientist of some repute when I was a girl and—"

"Ken Vance," Martha interrupted. "It's Ken Vance. He's a bad one. He's the murderer. Maybe he tried to break off the affair with Lisa Ward. Maybe she wanted to marry him, but he wouldn't go along with it. So he killed her. Then Johnny Bonino found out that Ken murdered Lisa, so Johnny Bonino had to be killed. Ken has access to lethal drugs. He's a medic. It all ties together."

"My dear, please remember that smoking cigarettes can kill you because cigarettes are deadly."

"Huh? I don't smoke. Neither does Ken. Only Aldo. You think Aldo did it? He's another bad one. I wouldn't be surprised if—"

"We must not forget the cigarette fallacy, my dear. I do not recall the Latin phrase, but I believe it is referred to as 'begging the question.' What an odd phrase that is. A question cannot beg. When I raised this with Sister Thomas More, she became frustrated with me, saying that I should concentrate on the matter at hand and perhaps then I would become a more logical thinker and..."

Marya nattered on about her twelfth grade Latin and logic class all the way to her apartment. As she dropped her off, Martha reminded her that the meeting to plan Father Peanuts's retirement party, where they could interview Isabella Bonino, was scheduled for the following day at 10:00. "I'll pick you up at 9:30. Sharp!"

Cigarettes. Begging the question. What did any of that have to do with murder? How could Martha get Marya to focus if Sister Thomas More, Sister Elizabeth Mary, and all the other sisters had failed so many years ago? There was a murderer out there. And they had to stop him…or her…or them.

# CHAPTER 10

## Wednesday, November 2

MARTHA HAD NOT SLEPT WELL. SHE HAD WOKEN UP IN the middle of the night, perseverating not about the murder but about her dwindling savings. She would send out her résumé this morning. She looked through the listings and applied for several interesting jobs related to law enforcement. Her qualifications did not match the job requirements, but she hoped her years as civilian police commissioner would be enough. That had been a great job. Darn that O'Hara.

At half past nine, Martha sat in her car, idling out front of Marya's apartment. No Marya. At 9:37, the apartment door opened. Three minutes and thirty-two seconds later, Marya had hobbled to the car, arranged herself and her two bags in the front seat, and snapped the seatbelt closed. Then, realizing that she had forgotten to shut the door and could not reach it with her seatbelt fastened, she began to disarrange herself.

Martha reached for her own door. "I've got it, Marya."

"That is very kind of you to offer, my dear, but I will do it myself. You must keep off your ankle as much as possible."

Once they arrived at church, with the seven minutes and twenty-one seconds required for Marya to exit the car, place the lavender and neon orange plaid tote on her right shoulder and her lilac-adorned imitation leather handbag on her left, and hobble over to the parish center, the meeting was already in full swing.

Martha felt the curious glances when people observed Marya enter the room. Being around Marya so often, Martha had become less aware of what an odd appearance the tattered, beflowered, proudly purple Marya made. Most of the seats were taken, but there was an open one next to Isabella that Martha claimed as her own.

The meeting was held in the kitchen/dining room of the parish center, a large, open space with institutional appliances and austere metal tables and chairs, suited for feeding twenty-five hungry nuns who had taken a vow of poverty but very spartan for an upscale crowd used to dining with celebrity chefs.

The old guard committee heads had claimed the first table, farthest away from the door, where they argued about the main issue: What would be the theme of the party? Martha waved at Bitsy Ianelli, who was seated across the room. Bitsy was always in charge of beverages at these types of functions. Martha noted with approval that Marya was busy arranging herself and her bags in an open seat near Bitsy. But her new companions, including Bitsy, scooched their seats away from Marya's and aimed their backs at her.

Isabella wore impeccably tailored, close-fitting jeans and a tight-but-not-too-tight navy blue striped T-shirt that showed off curves only partially hidden by a sweater draped over her shoulders. A ray of sunlight graced her dark, wavy hair and soft-lipped features, framing her like an actress in a spotlight. As Martha scrutinized her suspect, she noticed several white hairs among the luxurious tresses. Were those crow's feet forming around her eyes? Isabella's beauty would not carry her very much longer.

Martha whispered, "Hi, Isabella. I was wondering if you'd be interested in volunteering for Saint Vincent de Paul. We need people. There are maybe four of us under the age of eighty-five."

Isabella looked up. "*Ciao*, Martha, I would love to, but I'm sooo busy. But if you would like a donation..."

Even though her real motive for talking to Isabella had nothing to do with the Saint Vincent de Paul Society, Martha bridled at the excuse. Too busy doing what? Getting her nails and hair done? Martha shot a glance at Marya. If she had known Martha's thoughts, she would have mentioned penguins or furry cats and advised a visit to the confessional.

"How thoughtful! A donation would be great. You can put it in one of the poor boxes." She paused before adding, "So sorry about your recent loss, Isabella."

Isabella lowered her gaze and wiped away an unseen tear. "*Grazie*, Martha. I saw you at the funeral. So kind of you to come."

"No problem. Hey, what was that commotion in front of Johnny's office yesterday?"

"A break-in. The lock on the door was broken and the alarm went off. The computers were still there, but Johnny's law clerk is checking to see if anything else is missing. I wouldn't know. I never went to his office."

Angry voices at the front table drowned out any further conversation.

"It's got to be all about Lucy."

"No, Lucy is too mean. Linus, definitely Linus."

"But Schroeder plays the piano!"

"Excuse me, my dear. Excuse me, excuse me." Marya had left her chair and was working her way over to Martha. The tall, violet, daisy-like flower on Marya's hat bobbed as she tottered over and stopped behind Isabella. "I am pleased to see you here, my dear. It is always best, after such a loss as yours, to try to get out and live as normal a life as possible. My mother, God rest her soul, always said a busy person never has time to be unhappy. When…"

A Linus supporter on the other side of Isabella cleared her throat and shushed Marya. But Marya continued in a soothing tone, "When my mother passed on, we were unprepared for her death, although she was quite old and had several medical conditions. She had a little box that I would fill with her pills. I had to be very careful because there were two morning pills, one afternoon pill, and three in the evening…"

The woman cleared her throat again, scowled at Marya, and moved closer to the debate at the front of the room. "If it's *Peanuts*, then it's got to be Charlie Brown, or, at the very least, Snoopy."

Marya sat down in the vacated chair.

"Johnny was old too. *Un vecchio uomo.*" Isabella shook her head. "He had angina and had to have a stent. Since then, he took an aspirin every day, cholesterol medication, sleeping pills, and then some other drug I don't know the name of." She tossed back her dark hair. "I don't take any medication."

Marya patted Isabella's arm. "It takes time to get over such a sudden, unexpected loss such as yours, my dear. Very difficult."

"*Si*, it takes time. Very difficult." Isabella checked out a scratch in the nail polish on the pinky of her right hand.

"The funeral was lovely."

"*Grazie.*"

"And the wake also. Such an unusual crucifix Mr. Bonino was wearing."

"It was from Dies Irae. So the members could recognize each other. I had one I never wore. Johnny never left the house without his. Someone stole that, you know. At the wake."

"And the charm that was on the chain with the crucifix. That was very unusual. Do you mind if I ask what it was?"

"The charm? Oh, yes. I don't know what it was. He only recently began carrying it around in his pocket. Called it his lucky charm. But he never wore it on the chain with the crucifix."

"Do you know, my dear, the priest at your husband's funeral reminded me of Father George, one of the priests at Saint John's while I was in the third grade. His homilies made my sister and me so fearful of going to hell that we attended confession twice a week. We had a difficult time thinking of sins to confess, so we would ask our friends for suggestions. My goodness, he must have thought the two of us were scoundrels."

Isabella smiled. "*Davvero*. That is Father Thaddeus. I don't like him, but Johnny insisted we join Dies Irae. It's like a private club. He said it gave him access to powerful people and big clients. We were planning to quit though. A few days before he died, Johnny said he'd come into a big annuity and didn't need Dies Irae anymore. *Che peccato*, he hadn't gotten around to changing his will."

"Martha," a screechy voice rang out, "do you have your committee ready to clean?"

"I do," Martha said. Her part of the meeting now being done, she stood up and made her way to the door. She waited for Marya to gather her belongings and follow. As they reached the stair landing, Martha heard a swish and the patter of feet. She turned and saw the coarsely-woven brown fabric of a monk's robe sweeping up the stairs to the second floor.

M&M

*By the hot coals, pepper, and iron rakes of Saint Dulas, what am I doing here?*

For once, Martha trailed Marya as they both hobbled with their canes through the parking lot toward the side chapel of Saint John's. How had she allowed Marya to persuade her to go to confession?

Martha stopped at the stone grotto with the pure white marble statue of Mary as Our Lady of Grace, hands outstretched. She removed the garland of bright, multicolored plastic flowers that someone had placed on the head of the statue and threw it in the garbage. Since she was going to confession, she might as well do whatever unkind things she felt like. No other reasons to drag her feet came to mind, so she walked under the simple red-tiled roof of the church portico and into the side chapel of Saint John's.

It was a small chapel with ten pews at right angles to the main church, usually used by parishioners who did not want the priest to see them arriving late to Mass. The pews faced a large stained-glass window depicting the Judgment Day in the far side of the nave. Christ sat on his throne draped in a flowing white robe, Mary on His right in blue with a compassionate look on her face, and John the Baptist on His left, dressed in a rough camel's hair tunic tied with a leather belt, his expression as severe as Mary's was gentle. At Christ's feet, an open-winged, red-garbed Angel Gabriel blew his horn to announce the Judgment Day. It was an appropriate subject to ponder for those who came to celebrate the Sacrament of Penance and Reconciliation.

Behind the pews was a large window on the wall of a confessional room with a shade drawn over it, allowing dark shadows and shapes to show through but not the identities of the penitents. A light above the window showed green when the priest was present and alone. When Martha walked into the chapel, it was red. Marya had preceded her and sat in a pew next to a man kneeling with his face hidden in his hands. Martha sat down in the last pew, furthest away from the confessional, hoping more penitents would come and the priest would have no time for her.

A loud, acrimonious voice issued from the reconciliation room, but Martha, try as she might, could not make out the individual words. The kneeling man looked over at Marya, smiled, and shrugged his shoulders. Martha saw the green eyes, strong features, and tousled dark hair of Michael Ward. How interesting that one of her prime suspects was going to confession.

She moved up and knelt in the pew right behind Marya. She had a good view of Michael's profile as he sat forward and gazed at the stained-glass window. After a few moments, he let out a deep sigh, almost a groan, and slumped back in the pew. He glanced at Marya, whose eyes were aimed straight ahead at the Judgment Day scene, looked away, then turned back, this time staring at her. She seemed unaware of his gaze.

"Excuse me," he said to Marya. "I know it's not right to interrupt, but may I ask you a question?"

"Of course, my dear."

"I've seen you in church. You stay after Mass. You pray."

"Yes. I do pray."

"My grandmother prayed after Mass. My father's mother. She never missed a Sunday and made sure my father and our whole family went too. When my father died, I was the oldest boy, so she put me in charge of hauling my two brothers to church. On time. Dressed in their best." He smiled. "I kept coming, even after she died, even after my mother died. I don't know why. Habit, maybe. Then I married Lisa. Now she's dead too. But I still come." He drew in a long breath. "Do you go to confession often?"

"I try to come every week, my dear."

"Every week!"

"Yes. Sometimes I think that God gets bored with me, but the Holy Father says that God never tires of forgiving, though we sometimes tire of asking Him to forgive us. I find that frequent confession lifts the darkness that can come over one in the world."

"The darkness?"

"Yes, my dear."

"You feel the darkness?"

Marya gazed into his eyes and nodded. "We all must fight against it. Even the saints."

Michael turned to the stained glass Judgment scene and was silent for a moment, then took a deep breath and turned back to Marya with feverish, over-bright eyes. "I am stuck in the darkness, and I have been for a very long time. Tell me, is there any sin that cannot be forgiven?"

"I believe that is something you should talk to the priest about in confession. But *I* think," Marya leaned toward him, her eyes shining, "why, I think He is just like my mother was, God rest her soul, when my sister or I did something wrong. She would punish us of course, my mother was very strict, but as long as we were sorry for what we did, she would forgive us and never bring it up again. I think that God is the same. He waits for us, His arms wide open, just wanting us to turn back to Him so that he can forgive us and make us feel better. No matter how bad one thinks his sin is, God has heard worse."

Michael smiled. Some of the joy and enthusiasm seemed to be transferred from Marya's eyes to his. "Thanks. It—"

The door to the confessional banged open and hit the wall. The heads of the three waiting penitents snapped toward the noise. Ken Vance strode out the door.

Ken glanced at Michael as he walked by. He raised his hand to cover the left side of his face, then jerked his arm down and continued out of the chapel, not stopping to pray. Michael's posture grew rigid, and the softness that had entered his features moments before changed to a stiffened jaw and a hard, cold glare locked on Ken's retreating figure.

Marya said to Michael, "Go on, young man. It's your turn."

He shook his head. "No, you go ahead. I'm not ready yet."

She nodded, stood up, crossed herself, and entered the confessional. Just few minutes later, she emerged and walked to one of the back pews. Martha looked over at Michael, who motioned that she should go ahead of him.

No avoiding it now. As Martha shuffled toward the reconciliation room, she realized she had been so focused on her suspect that she hadn't prepared for confession. She usually had a list of sins written out to read to the priest. What was she going to say?

She chose to use the kneeler behind the screen rather than the chair that brought her face to face with the priest. "Forgive me, Father, for I have sinned. It has been two years since I last went to confession."

"And how have you sinned in that period of time, my daughter?"

She recognized the voice of Father Peanuts. She wondered if he recognized hers. Martha had a hard time imagining, as she always tried to, that she was confessing to Jesus instead of a priest.

A vision of Marya popped into her head. *Dear Marya.* "I have not been as nice as I should be to a good friend of mine."

"Anything else, my child?"

"I'm envious, Father, when I see what other people have. Money, a big house, friends, a good job…" Wow, where did that come from? "I don't pray enough." That one was always on her list. "I enjoy gossip." So was that. "I volunteer a lot, but not with love." That one wasn't. "I'm impatient…very impatient." She thought about the penguins. "I'm judgmental." That didn't quite capture the penguin problem, but it was the best she could come up with on short notice.

Oh, the furry cats. "I jump to conclusions about people without really knowing them." Or was that the penguins? Or the dog tails? She'd have to talk to Marya about this.

"Anything else, my child?"

*Isn't that enough? It's way more than I meant to say.* Aloud, she said, "No, Father. That's all…that I can remember right now."

"Very well. Please remember, my child, that you are to celebrate the sacrament at least once every year."

After she received absolution, Martha stood up from the kneeler and felt…she felt like smiling. How strange. Why would she feel happy after admitting all the things she'd done wrong? Maybe she'd talk to Marya about that too.

Leaving the reconciliation room, she nodded to Michael to go in after her, but he did not move. Martha entered a back pew and started the prayers Father Peanuts had assigned her for penance.

Marya put a coin in the box in front of the statue of Joseph, clicked on the candle light, and stood, head down, for a moment. She then walked over to Michael Ward and sat next to him. After she spoke to him, he stood up and walked over to the confessional. He stopped when he got to the door and looked over to Marya, who nodded her encouragement. He opened the door and walked in.

# CHAPTER 11

32nd Week in Ordinary Time
Sunday, November 6

AS SOON AS MARTHA WOKE UP, SHE CHECKED, AS SHE had every morning since she sent out her résumés, for responses to her job applications. Not a one, which she guessed was not surprising since she had sent her first round of applications to jobs requiring master's degrees, hoping her experience as police commissioner would overcome that obstacle. She would not let that get her down. She checked the listings and sent out more résumés, this time for law enforcement jobs requiring undergraduate degrees. After about an hour, she closed her computer, not slamming it down as she had before, but with a bit too much force. She took a deep breath. She would *not* let this get her down.

When Martha picked up Marya for Mass, she was shocked to find her already waiting outside in her lilac, mauve, and lavender Sunday best. As she settled herself into the car, Marya said, "Come, my dear, you are late. My mother, God rest her soul, often said, 'When you are early, you are on time. When you are on time, you are late.' You see, when I was young, my dear, I am afraid that I might have dawdled occasionally, and my mother would…"

Martha had a difficult time keeping a straight face as Marya regaled her with old adages about punctuality. As she turned into the Saint John's parking lot, she saw that Henry was on crossing guard duty.

"I'm going to ask Henry to help us get the test results, Marya. You go ahead and go inside."

"Good idea, my dear. But remember, do not be late for Mass!"

Martha parked the car and walked to the church side of the crosswalk. Henry stood in the middle of the street, gesturing with his left hand to let through the expensive cars from the wealthy areas east of town that were turning left into the parking lot. He held up his right hand to stop the right-turning cars of the Pequot Bays townies.

She was pretty sure that Henry had caught sight of her, but when the light turned red for the cars and green for pedestrians, he did not walk over to accompany her as per proper Pequot Bays Police protocol. Instead, he skulked over to the opposite side of the street, glancing around as if looking to make a break for it. But she had him now. She limped across the street, leaning on her cane more than she needed to and wincing at each step. She stopped in front of him.

"Hi, Henry."

"It's Hank, Ms. Collins. I didn't know you walked to church."

"I don't. Came over to talk to you."

"Oh."

"I need your help."

"Oh."

"The report about the fingerprints and drink analysis. Officer Chonkin put it on O'Hara's desk, and he's sitting on it. I need you to get it to the lab."

"Got to go. The light is about to turn." Henry left Martha, again holding up a hand to motion the left-turning cars into the parking lot. Then he walked to the opposite side of the street. Martha limped over, wincing with every step.

Henry sighed. "You want me to tell Lieutenant O'Hara that he should do a favor for you?"

"You could tell him to do his job, but no, Henry. I want *you* to do a favor for me. Somehow get it to a lab."

The conversation was interrupted as an elderly lady approached the crosswalk from the other side of the street, and Henry went to walk her across. Martha followed him.

"I can't do that, Ms. Collins. I helped you out once and nearly got fired. I know you got me this job, but I think we're even now."

Martha searched her mind, trying to come up with a threat. "Well then, Henry Milton, you had just better be careful about getting so close to O'Hara. I'm…I'm going to run for civilian police commissioner again. And when I win, and I will win, O'Hara will be history. And where will you be then?" She glared at him and stomped away as well as she could with her limp and a cane, crossing the street against the light.

As she entered church, she checked out her suspects. Michael Ward was in the first pew in front of the Saint Joseph statue. Isabella Bonino was on the other side, in the first pew in front of the statue of Mary as Undoer of Knots, the Blessed Mother gently fingering a knotted cord. Aldo Todi sat a few pews in back of Michael, directly behind Luz Flores, who sat on the aisle next to Barbara and Ken Vance. Gertie Doppeldecker was in the same pew as Aldo Todi. Dr. Ianelli and Bitsy sat on the Mary side of the church, toward the front.

Noting with approval that Marya had settled herself behind Dr. Ianelli and Bitsy, Martha squished together a family of four to make a space for herself on the aisle, right behind Aldo.

She glanced at her watch. Father Seamus was presiding today, so she was not surprised when Mass started late, at 10:04. Still, his homilies were reasonably short, so she figured Mass would be over by 11:00.

She succeeded in paying proper attention through the first two readings. Then Father Seamus read the Gospel.

"Beware of the scribes, who like to go around in long robes and accept greetings in the marketplaces, seats of honor in synagogues, and places of honor at banquets. They devour the houses of widows and, as a pretext, recite lengthy prayers. They will receive a very severe condemnation."

A stir and murmuring rose from the back of the church. Father Seamus glanced up from his reading, paused for a moment, and then continued.

"He sat down opposite the treasury and observed how the crowd put money into the treasury. Many rich people put in large sums."

The hubbub grew louder. Martha turned around to see a figure in a dirty jacket left open over a filthy sweatshirt and sweatpants. He had long, matted grey hair, and his beard—if that was what the unshaven, unkempt patches of hair on his face could be called—had bits of…of…something caught in it. His shoes were untied over swollen feet. Martha recognized him as one of the homeless men who regularly appeared on the streets of Pequot Bays, no matter how often the residents complained and the police tried to eject them from the area. He shuffled down the center aisle, looking around and nodding at all the faces turned toward him. As he neared, Martha caught the ripe smell of unwashed human. When he arrived near Luz Flores, he clamped a dirty hand on her shoulder and gave her a big smile. He continued on and sat in the front pew.

Father Seamus read on through the murmuring. "A poor widow also came and put in two small coins worth a few cents. Calling his disciples to himself, he said to them, 'Amen, I say to you, this poor widow put in more than all the other contributors to the treasury. For they have all contributed from their surplus wealth, but she, from her poverty, has contributed all she had, her whole livelihood.'"

Father Seamus did not seem to take note of the homeless man, who grunted and muttered and shuffled till he left midway through the homily. It *was* a particularly boring homily.

At the sign of peace, Martha refocused on her suspects. Everything you needed to know about a person, you could learn from how they acted as they exchanged greetings at that moment in the Mass.

Isabella Bonino gazed with her smoky eyes at Michael Ward as she extended her graceful arm in his direction, her lips slowly mouthing,

"Peace." Michael, however, stared only at the painting of Christ the King on the dome above the altar, his expression the same as when he had stared at the stained glass window of the Last Judgment before walking into the confessional.

The Dies Irae group exchanged the sign of peace among themselves. Ken Vance bent toward his wife, Barbara, and offered his cheek without looking at her. She had been watching and waiting for this moment. She had to stand on tiptoes to peck at the proffered cheek. She then turned to Luz, and they exchanged a long hug, Barbara's soft, pudgy body enveloping Luz's skinny frame.

Aldo Todi, not coughing for once, kept his beady eyes straight ahead, aimed at the white streak down the middle of Luz's short, dark hair. After she emerged from her hug with Barbara Vance, Aldo touched Luz's shoulder, and she turned around. They shook hands.

Gertie Doppeldecker kept her eyes locked on Aldo the whole time. They did not exchange the sign of peace. He never turned to meet her gaze.

After Mass, Martha followed the Dies Irae crew. Ken ranted the entire way. "Did you see that fellow? Disgusting. He stunk! Walked right in front of Father Seamus and the altar. No respect. Didn't even genuflect. Just plopped down in the front pew."

Luz dropped back from the conversation and let Ken and Barbara walk ahead. Martha followed Luz toward the Mary grotto where Marya sat on a bench chatting with the unwashed, unexpected visitor at Mass.

By the time Luz made it to the grotto, the man had ambled away. Martha moved closer. Aldo was skulking around behind her. Why was he following her? What was he plotting?

"Hello, Ms. Cook," Luz said.

"On your way to return your empties, my dear?"

Luz smiled.

"Oh, but my friend Martha must be confused about what we are talking about. Perhaps you could explain it to her."

Luz turned to Martha. "You've heard there have been complaints about some homeless men living in the woods. I live in Harborview Park, near a lovely preserve where the homeless men gather. I have walked there almost every day for twenty years and have become friends with them. They're gentle men. Maybe not gentlemen, but gentle men. I give them cans and bottles to return for the deposit money. And I talk to them about Jesus. I saw Marya doing the same thing one day." Marya and Luz exchanged conspiratorial glances. "One of the men showed me a card that she had given him with a Bible verse on it. 'Blessed are you who are poor, for yours is the kingdom of God.' Wasn't that it, Ms. Cook?"

"Indeed it was, my dear."

"My neighbors are angry at me for giving them my empties because it encourages them to stay, but I was rewarded today. John came to church. That's his name. John. Did you see him, Ms. Cook? He gave me a great big grin." She gave a great big grin herself. "I do wish that Father Seamus's homily had been a bit more interesting though. I wonder if John would be interested in joining Dies Irae. Perhaps I should invite him to our next meeting."

"It is a wonderful thing that you are doing, my dear. But perhaps one step at a time."

"I guess you're right, Ms. Cook. Everyone wasn't as happy as we were to see John at church. And I don't know how welcoming Ken would be to him if he joined Dies Irae."

"Yes, my dear. However, one must not be affected by what others think of someone we like."

Martha felt a pang of…what?

Luz stood up from the bench and nodded at Aldo. "Now, Aldo, let us go for a walk. I must speak to you about something very important."

"Ready to go home, Marya?" Martha asked.

"In a—"

"Michael!" Isabella ran past the two women toward Michael

Ward, who stood with Father Thaddeus in the parking lot. Michael abruptly turned and walked toward his car. As Isabella ran past Father Thaddeus, the priest caught hold of her arm and said a few words. She shook him off, snapped something at him in Italian, and continued running toward Michael, calling out his name again.

Michael opened the car door, started the engine, and sped off.

Isabella looked back at Father Thaddeus and rotated a fist with pinky and index finger extended.

Martha turned to Marya. "Don't think I'd want to be an enemy of hers. What a temper! Ready to go home?"

"Not quite yet, my dear. Would you mind if we rest here a bit longer? By the way, I like your violet sweater, my dear."

"It's not violet, it's brown, Marya."

"Oh, so it is."

Martha sat down next to her on the bench and told her about the talk with Henry.

"That is a fine idea, my dear, about running for police commissioner."

"Oh, I didn't mean it. It was just the best I could think of as a threat to get something moving."

"Perhaps you should consider it seriously, my dear."

"Nah, I don't have anyone to support me, and O'Hara has the whole police department and their families, and the PBA."

"Oh, my dear, that is not so." She ruffled around in her bag and came out with one of her laminated note cards with purple script and handed it to Martha.

> *We are surrounded by so great a cloud of witnesses, let*
> *us persevere in running the race.*
> *Hebrews12:1*

"A cloud of witnesses?"

"The saints, my dear, the saints. And all of the other witnesses to the faith that have preceded us into the Kingdom of God. My mother for example. They will intercede for us. We only have to ask. And they far outnumber police and their families. Perhaps we should—"

"I think it's against the law for dead people to vote, Marya." Martha shoved the card in her pocket. "Anyway, I told you, I've started applying for jobs online. Let's go."

"Do you mind if we stop for one more moment so that I can offer a prayer for Johnny Bonino's soul?"

"Sure, Mar." Martha, impatient as she was, recalled the man's contorted face and offered one of her own. But it seemed to Martha that Marya's prayer was particularly long.

"Let's go, Marya."

Marya took even more care than usual gathering her belongings. "Excuse me, my dear, one moment. My purse keeps slipping down my arm. It is getting quite heavy. I must clean it out one of these days. But I am afraid that if I throw anything out, I will need it the next day. I often find that is the case. Perhaps there is something I can take out…"

Marya rummaged through the lavender and neon orange plaid tote, removed a piece of paper, read one side, turned it over, and read the other. "I must keep this. Dear Dr. Stokes gave it to me at my last visit, and it may come in handy quite soon." She put it back in her bag and removed another piece of paper. "Now this one, perhaps I can throw away. It is only—"

Trying to keep her voice even, Martha said, "Marya, I have to walk Quincy. Can't you wait till you get home to clean out your bags?"

"So sorry, my dear, of course you are correct. Your dog must be walked. She does seem to be a friendly dog. I am not very familiar with canines. The only other dog I have come in any extended contact with was owned by my mother's employer. When I helped my mother, God rest her soul, clean the house, it would follow us around, snarling. I believe the breed of the dog was called a Doberman Pinscher.

Pincher. What a funny name for a dog. Why, they have paws, not fingers to pinch with…"

"Quincy doesn't even know how to snarl, Marya. But can we get going?"

"Certainly, my dear, certainly." Marya readjusted the lilac-adorned imitation leather handbag on her left shoulder, and the lavender and neon orange plaid tote on her right shoulder, and started shuffling toward the parking lot.

As they passed a bench on the other side of the Mary grotto, Marya said, "I seem to be a little out of breath, my dear. Let us sit for a bit. You can rest your ankle."

Martha screamed…to herself. "I'll go get the car and bring it over."

"Oh no, my dear. That is not necessary."

"Oh yes, it is."

When she drove up, Marya was still sitting, but Gertie had joined her.

"Oh, hello, my dear. Thank you for getting the car. Gertrude and I were just having a lovely chat. I was thanking her for the excellent job she does every Sunday after Mass. People are so very careless. Leaving their bulletins in the pews and placing the prayer books back upside down. She is always the last to leave."

"And the Cheerios. I'm down on my hands and knees picking up the Cheerios."

"I was telling Gertrude all about the history of our town. She has only lived here for five years and had no idea how the baymen in the old days supplied New York City with their oysters and clams. Why, it was Pequot Bays oysters that were used in the first oysters Rockefeller. She has invited us to come over for tea at her home right now. I have taken the liberty of accepting the invitation for both of us, my dear."

Gertie looked at Martha. "Oh, I didn't know that she was with you."

Marya rose from the bench. "Yes indeed, my dear friend Martha took me to church, and it is so kind of you to invite us both to tea. You go along and get your car, my dear, and we will follow you to your home. Martha is a very good driver, so you need not worry about her bumping into the back of your car. When I drove a car many, many years ago…"

Gertie walked over to her own car, an old Toyota.

As they drove away, Martha said, "Is that why you took so long to leave church, Marya? You're always slow but… I mean you were even slower than… I mean… Anyway, I don't think that Gertie wanted me to join the two of you for tea."

"Yes, she seems a very private person. But perhaps a bit lonely because of it. I was telling her about the Pequot Bays I knew as a young girl. It was the same but different. The rich were a great deal richer, if you can imagine that, my dear, and there were fewer of them. The servants and the baymen, there were more of us and we were poorer, but I think we were happier. Ours was a very close-knit community, you know…"

Martha let Marya drone on as she followed Gertie's car. She had expected Gertie to turn left onto Main Street, but she turned right. She followed the car past the fountain decorated with cherubs that fronted the entrance to an exclusive gated community. Its name was proclaimed in curlicued letters on a brass plaque attached to stately columns: Harriman Acres. Gertie did not turn at the gatehouse. Maybe she wasn't a pharmacist. Probably a housekeeper for a family on Pequot Island or Middle Point.

They drove over the causeway onto Pequot Island. Martha kept her eyes straight ahead, as she always did, trying to avoid the familiar sights of her childhood. But even the smell of the damp earth and the sound of the wind blowing through the trees brought back memories.

Martha became aware of something odd. Marya was silent. She looked over and saw Marya watching her.

"Are you all right, my dear? I recall you once lived here."

Sometimes it seemed like Marya could read a person's mind. "I'm fine, Marya. It was a long time ago. No sense thinking about the past." Martha fumbled for the tissue box attached to the car's sun visor and blew her nose.

"When you reach my age, my dear, you find that things that happened long ago are perhaps more real than the present. We can learn a great deal from the past."

Martha drew the car to a stop at the private access road that led from Center Street to what was once her childhood home. She turned toward Marya, not wanting to meet her eyes. "Oh, Mar, I'm so sorry. How I've treated you. Can you ever forgive me?"

When Martha raised her eyes, she found the kindest, most accepting, most loving gaze she had experienced since she had been the apple of her parents' eyes. A pain at the base of her throat worked its way up to her head, and she burst out sobbing, barely able to catch her breath. A pair of arms enveloped her, and she laid her cheek on a shoulder layered with sweaters and shawls so that it was soft as a pillow. She wept and wept and wept until the pain was gone. She raised her head and, although her eyes were almost swollen shut from crying, she saw her surroundings clearly for the first time since she had left the island and moved into her condo. She recognized trees along the road that she had climbed, a gazebo barely visible through the evergreens where she would meet a friend…

Martha took another tissue and blew her nose. "There's a pond over there, Mar. Just beyond that stand of trees." She pointed to a majestic group of pines in the distance. "It froze over in the winter. Winters were colder then. I used to sneak there with a friend, and we would ice skate for hours on end. Once we were caught by the owner of the house, and we thought that we'd get into big trouble. But she just invited us inside for hot chocolate and told us that she used to skate there when she was young, and we could skate there any time we wanted." She smiled. "You know, once we had her permission, it wasn't nearly as much fun as it had been before."

"I know exactly what you mean, my dear."

"You do? I could never imagine you doing anything wrong."

Marya tittered. "Yes indeed. I recall that my sister and I would go to the Main Street Community Center to play checkers with our friends, even though our mother told us to come home immediately after school. When we were old enough that we were allowed to go, why, we stopped going altogether. I still enjoy a good game of checkers though."

"I am shocked that you could be so disobedient, Mar."

"Oh, there is much about me that you do not know, my dear."

"I believe you are right, Mar."

Martha jumped at a loud rap on her window. It was Gertie.

"What in heaven's name are you two doing here! I drove all the way home and waited and…" She gave Martha a sharp glance. "What's wrong with you?"

Martha's brain was still fogged from crying, so she just shook her head.

"Allergies," Marya said. "My dear friend Martha has very bad allergies. So sorry you had to come all the way back, Gertie. We were just admiring the view."

"Well, come on. Let's go." Gertie got back in her car and pulled away down Center Street, and Martha followed close behind.

Martha chuckled. "Allergies? I don't have any allergies, Mar."

"Just a venial sin, my dear, under the circumstances." They grinned at each other.

Gertie put on her blinker to turn left, but Martha could not see where she planned to turn until Gertie pulled onto a small, overgrown lane with just enough room for a car to drive without being scratched by the thicket surrounding it. She followed Gertie down a bumpy dirt road until it ended. Gertie stopped, and Martha stopped behind her. They got out of the car, but there was no house to be seen, just more overgrown bushes and weeds.

"Here we are," Gertie said.

"But where's the—"

"What lovely, naturalized grounds you have, my dear," Marya interjected. "I know that some people prefer formal gardens, but I am partial to natural landscapes. Like God Himself created. We cannot match their beauty, and when we try, we must use all kinds of dangerous chemicals and make such loud noises to control nature. There is a word for this type of gardening, my dear. Perhaps you know it. I believe it is called zero gardening or perhaps zero planting or zero—"

"Thank you, Ms. Cook. But the neighbors don't agree." Gertie turned down a barely visible path, pushing branches away so Marya could pass and then letting them go so they snapped back in Martha's face. Gertie held Marya's elbow to steady her as they walked. Martha leaned heavily on her cane so that she would not reinjure her ankle.

"My closest neighbors are the Evanses. They have very formal gardens and a lawn with sprinklers that pop up from the ground every day. Have you ever heard of them? Robert and Roslyn Evans. Mr. Evans owns a manufacturing firm, one of the largest in the US. They have two children, Brittany and Taylor. Taylor's been married three times and is now living in France with someone who claims to be a count or maybe a prince and is in the middle of another divorce. This way." Gertie motioned toward a rusty gate, permanently open and covered in ivy.

"You know, I couldn't help but notice that there were several visitors to Mrs. Evans when her husband was away on business. One of them was the second ex-husband of their daughter, Taylor. Before he was an ex-husband. When I first moved here, Mrs. Evans complained that I didn't care for the grounds properly. Since Mr. Evans wasn't ever home, I don't think he cared one way or another. But Mrs. Evans did. Watch your step here," Gertie added as they passed over a particularly uneven, rocky patch of ground. "Mrs. Evans went to town hall and lodged a complaint, and I got a ticket, a violation that said I had to show up in Village Court and threatened a fine unless I fixed up my property. But I had a conversation with Mrs. Evans about that and about…about the things I had noticed. Shortly after we talked, I got a letter that said the complaint had been withdrawn." Gertie glanced at Martha through narrowed eyes. "I notice things sometimes."

By the feet of Saint Apphian, Gertie was almost as bad as another busybody Martha and Marya had known—Enid Mayhew. She'd better watch out or she could end up like Enid!

Martha caught a view of a house through the overgrown bushes and trees. The "zero gardening" thinned somewhat as they approached, and they began to walk on the remnants of a driveway which encircled an elaborate white marble fountain that was now filled with fetid green rainwater. Behind it, shrouded by ancient rhododendrons and burning bushes, was a massive, decrepit hulk of a Victorian mansion—three stories high, covered in shingles of different shapes and pierced by long windows, only a few of which were unbroken. Above it all were three towers, one flat-topped with a widow's walk looking out to the sea, the second with a slate mansard and an elaborate weathervane hanging at a perilous angle, and the third, towering above the others, a bulbous, steeple-like structure, now open to the elements. Most of the shutters tilted away from the house on their rusty hinges, but a few were still closed in place. Plywood-covered windows on the first floor had once looked out on the large, dilapidated wraparound porch the three women now traversed, avoiding the rotted portions of the plank flooring. The house had been painted battleship gray many years before, but where it had peeled, the garish colors of the Victorian era—marigold, lime, and puce—peeked though.

"Well, here we are, Ms. Cook," Gertie said as they approached the door.

Martha shivered as Gertie unlocked the padlock and the door creaked open on rusty hinges.

"My, how very nice, my dear. Why, it is exactly as it was when it was first built. They do not build houses like they used to. Nowadays, no one respects old buildings. They are just torn down and replaced by very large buildings that all look alike. Pequot Bays looks so different than it did when I was young. My sister and I used to go to Al's Soda and Pharmacy, but now it's been replaced by Star—"

"Thank you, Ms. Cook. I'm glad you appreciate it. I have to admit that I was nervous about inviting you here. I don't have many visitors. My neighbors on the other side, the Wentworths, came over once. Have you heard of the Wentworths?"

Gertie held the door open for Marya and walked in behind her. "Watch your step, Ms. Cook." The door slammed shut, and Martha had to use all her strength to reopen it. Gertie was a lot stronger than she looked. A musky, damp odor surrounded Martha as she entered the old house.

"...don't know what Mr. Wentworth does, but Mrs. Wentworth, Lisa is her name, is a vice president of a financial concern. They're young, maybe in their thirties. No children. They have big parties, and she came over once to apologize for the noise. I told her I didn't mind. I feel sorry for her. I can't help but hear the arguments they have, usually about his drinking. I once found him lying against a tree on my property, and he kept repeating, 'Don't tell Lisa, don't tell Lisa.' I told him that I wouldn't if..."

Martha followed Gertie and Marya past a gloomy, rickety staircase, down a hallway lit by only one dim, flickering bulb. Gertie looked ghostly as she glided down the corridor, her pale hair and clothing bathed in the faint light. They passed several doors with the paint peeling off, all closed, one nailed shut with a wooden plank across it. Martha thought she heard footsteps—or was it just the window shutters rattling? Was that whispering or the rustle of leaves? She sneezed several times from the dust.

"God bless you, my dear."

"It's the dus—"

"Yes, indeed, my dear, it is your allergies acting up again. I believe in November there is leaf mold outside. Perhaps that is the problem." Marya turned back to Gertie, and the two proceeded down the hall, Gertie chatting away.

They walked into a kitchen that had not been updated since the 1940s, with worn out linoleum, painted metal cabinets, a short refrigerator, and faded gingham curtains on the windows. Yet it was brightly lit with the walls freshly painted canary yellow and as clean as Martha's own kitchen. With the eerie effect of the dilapidated dwelling dispelled, Gertie no longer appeared wraithlike, but—even this close in this bright light—Martha still could not tell whether she was forty or sixty years old, or whether her hair was white or blond.

Marya said, "Goodness, my dear, you have the same kitchen table as I do. I obtained mine from—"

"Do you? That's nice. I found mine on the street. You can't imagine the things I have found on the street. Why, I found a desk in front of the Sanders. They live four houses away. The Sanders, that is Megan and Brandon, are from California. They threw away a desk once. I didn't take it because it was too heavy, but I couldn't help but notice some papers in one of the drawers, and…"

Martha's attention drifted as they walked through the kitchen into the only room with an open door, an office with a desk and computer workstation. It was also Gertie's library, with a comfortable chair, small table, and lamp near a window, surrounded by neat piles of hardcover books. It must have been her work room too because it housed a table filled with old-fashioned devices and bottles that reminded Martha of a pharmacy. It was also her den because a small TV faced a bright chintz sofa and two wooden rocking chairs arranged in a conversational grouping.

"You two sit here while I go make some tea." Gertie spoke for the first time to Martha. "I suppose you want coffee. I can't help but notice that you drink coffee at the church functions."

Was there anything Gertie did not notice? "Tea will be fine."

Martha walked around the room after Gertie left. She lifted a surprisingly heavy brass mortar and pestle and admired its intricate floral carving, then set it down and picked up a hand-blown apothecary bottle from a collection on the wooden table. The glass-stoppered bottle was partially filled with a reddish liquid. Martha turned it around and saw a skull and crossbones embossed on the back. She replaced it among the other bottles and jars, then noticed a stack of unopened letters addressed to Marilyn Q Turner on the desk.

"Psst. Mar. Look here. Who's Marilyn Turner?"

"Turner. Turner. My goodness, that name reminds me of something I haven't thought of in years. Perhaps it is this old house, my dear. It is a bit creaky and spooky. I remember that when I was a young girl, my mother, God rest her soul, would tell my sister and me that if we misbehaved, 'the Turnerman' would come and take us away. The Turnerman could turn into all kinds of scary monsters, and my sister and I were quite frightened. I have since learned that 'the boogeyman' is the correct terminology. I wonder why—"

"Mar, you have to focus now. Marilyn Turner. Why is Gertie receiving mail for Marilyn Turner? When I get home, I'll Google it. It's a common name, but I can figure out—"

"Perhaps you can drop me off at the library when we leave here and I will do some research also, my dear."

"The library! It would be much faster to—"

"I think," Marya interrupted, glancing over Martha's shoulder, "it would be an interesting contest, my dear, to compare results from a library search with a goggle search. It would be rather like the tale of John Henry, the steel driving man. When my sister and I were young, my mother, God rest her soul, would read us stories every night. Tall tales were my—"

"What are you two doing over here? I told you to sit down," Gertie said from behind Martha's back.

"We were having a discussion about the internet, my dear. Martha believes that one can rely on goggling computers to obtain whatever information one needs. I believe that the library is much more informative and certainly much more pleasant—"

Gertie slid a manila folder over the letters. "Ah, computers. The wife of one of my neighbors caught her husband cheating when she saw his emails to his mistress. Charlie Simpson. He was rich but not too smart." Gertie, speaking only to Marya, relayed the details of the divorce while they drank their tea.

Martha, employing her interrupting skills that had been fine-tuned during her acquaintance with Marya, waited for Gertie to take a breath, then inserted, "Does Michael Ward live on Pequot Island, Gertie?"

"Michael Ward. Yes, he does. Not near me though. But speaking of him, the other day in church I overheard Ken Vance say to Barbara that God would have vengeance on Michael Ward for killing his own wife."

"Killing his wife?" Martha gave Marya a quick look. Her phone buzzed, and she glanced down at it. Christopher! But she couldn't talk now. She had a murder to solve.

"Who says he killed his wife?" Martha asked.

"If he didn't, he might as well have. Cheating on her with Isabella Bonino drove her to suicide. And Isabella is as much at fault as Michael. They're both Islanders, you know. They live right next door to each other. But then Ken Vance is no angel either. He and Lisa Ward…" Gertie shook her head. "Poor Barbara Vance. The only loyal spouse of the bunch. But maybe only for lack of opportunity. I wouldn't be surprised if she was the next one to die. Ken beats her, you know. You must have noticed the bruises on her arms. I saw Barbara crying like a baby just last week with Luz Flores. I couldn't help but notice Luz take out a little pink bag filled with pills. She gave one to Barbara and said it would make her feel better. Luz is a nurse, so she has access to all kinds of medication—prescribed or not. I understand that some of the most unexpected people take drugs these days."

Gertie took a quick glance at Martha as she said this.

*She knows about the amphetamines!* Was Loose Lips O'Hara telling people about her overdose? Saying she was a user? Of course he was. Well, she would take care of him! She would start filling out the forms to run for commissioner tomorrow. And once she was elected…

But first, to the business at hand. Martha went over the list of suspects in her mind. Gertie was sure to know something about everyone. "Do Dr. Ianelli and Bitsy live on the island?"

"No. Middle Point. La di da. How he gets the money to live there, I don't know. He makes a nice living as a doctor, but most of the professionals live in Skeeter Flats, or some of them here on Pequot Island. Middle Point…well, that's for the kabillionaires. Bitsy came from money, you know. Old money. Lots of old money. They say she gave it all up to marry Dr. Ianelli when he was a medical student. Her family didn't approve. They came over on the Mayflower. Ianelli didn't. His family came over in a ship, all right, but below decks in steerage. Immigrants. Bitsy's relatives refused to go to the wedding. Once he started raking in the dough, though, they warmed up to him, but he, and she, wouldn't have anything to do with them. Bitsy never forgives or forgets a slight. I have to say that they're one of the few happy marriages in Pequot Bays. She adores the ground he walks on, and he'd do anything for her."

"How about Aldo Todi? Does he live here?"

"Aldo Todi? Hmm. Can't place the name. More tea?"

Aldo was the only human being on the planet that Gertie would not gossip about. He was blackmailing her for sure. But about what?

"No thanks."

Martha could not think of a way to interject her last suspect, Father Thaddeus, into the conversation. He definitely did not live on Pequot Island. So she just said, "What do you think of Father Thaddeus?"

"Father Darth Vader, that's what I call him. He's from the dark side. Everything's the devil this and the devil that. He says that

Johnny Bonino and Lisa Ward were possessed by the devil, and they were punished for their sins. He says that we'd all better be careful because the end time is nearing, and God will destroy the unworthy."

Nothing new there.

"Gertrude, my dear, you are so very sociable," Marya interjected. "I was born here but do not know nearly as much as you do about our fellow Pequoters. How did you come to move to Pequot Bays?"

"It's a nice town."

"And do you have any relatives here, my dear?"

"No relatives."

"Where are you from?"

"Around abouts. More tea, Marya?"

"No thank you, my dear. It is time for us to go. As it says in Proverbs 25:17, 'Don't wear out your welcome by staying too long at the home of your friends.' I was thinking of perhaps using that quote on one of my notecards, but then I thought that I might never have a chance to give it to anyone, as I rarely have visitors, and if I did, it would be quite rude to present it to a guest, would it not? Thank you for this lovely get-together, Gertrude. It reminded me of the old days. Every Saturday, my mother, God rest her soul, my sister, and I would drop by the Jacksons, and every Sunday the Jacksons would visit us. Perhaps you would like to come to tea at my little apartment one day. It is not so grand as your own home, but—"

"Oh, I don't mind. I'm not like other people who live around here. Why, the other day, I said hello to one of my neighbors on the street, and she ignored me. It was Samantha Green, who lives not three houses away from me. And I thought to myself that she had a lot of nerve being so snobby because I heard that she…"

Martha tried to tune out the story of Samantha cheating on her husband with Robert Jordan, yes, *the* Robert Jordan, the one who starred in the TV show Gertie could not remember the name of, but it was the latest hit crime drama, and her husband had found them together in bed and beat up Robert Jordan so badly that he could not shoot a scene for over a month, and Robert Jordan sued Samantha's husband, whose name Gertie couldn't remember but who was very rich from investing in a product that cured cold sores...

Marya arranged her bags on her shoulders, tottered out of the house, and Gertie led the two women back to Martha's car with many warnings directed toward Marya to watch her step.

Martha glanced at her phone. Christopher hadn't left a voicemail.

Once settled into the front seat to her satisfaction, Marya said, "That was an extremely interesting visit. I learned one or two things that I must follow up on. Would you mind dropping me off at the library, please?"

"I don't mind. But why don't you just let me Google Marilyn Q Turner for you? Much faster and much more information online."

"Thank you, my dear. You are always so thoughtful. But I prefer to do it my way. Going slowly is the fastest way to arrive at a destination. Trying to find the answer to a problem is the problem to finding the answer, you see."

Martha shook her head. "Sure, Mar, sure."

"When I let my mind alone, my dear, it works on the problem without me. And it is not only when I am in the peace and quiet of a church, or the library, or a park bench. In the most unexpected places, my mind comes up with an answer, even without my help. Why, I was in Tony's Stationery last week to buy some note cards and was looking at pens when..."

Martha let Marya drone on. She could find out all about Marilyn Turner in half an hour on the computer.

She dropped off Marya at the library, went home, and sat on the deck with her foot elevated, listening to her young neighbor's phone conversation about his most recent online dating experience. She threw the giveitheck out into the yard and watched Quincy's contortions as she caught and tortured the ball. She knew she should call Christopher back but had to work up the nerve. It had been a lot of years since...

She took the giveitheck and threw it so hard, it flew into the neighboring yard. Her neighbor said, "Hold on a sec and I'll tell you about the goodbye kiss," and the giveitheck sailed back over the fence.

Having no interest in the goodbye kiss, Martha went inside. She fixed herself and Quincy some lunch, then sat down at the computer. Within minutes, she had the answer to her question. Marilyn Q Turner was a licensed pharmacist—the same as Gertie. There were two possibilities. First, that Gertie had killed Marilyn Turner or was keeping her prisoner and had taken over her identity, or, second, she *was* Marilyn Turner. Martha favored the first possibility. No one would ever choose to change her name to Gertie Doppeldecker.

She called Marya. No answer. Probably still dillydallying around the library. She was surprised to receive a call from the auto repair shop on a Sunday, but it was open, and her car was ready. Martha immediately called a cab to take her there. As soon as she was back in her own vehicle, she put her regular phone on silent in the glove box, placed her Uber phone into the car mount, and breathed a sigh of relief to be back into her regular routine. She drove two Uber fares and then tried Marya again.

"Hello, hello? This is the Cook residence. How may I help you?"

"Hi, Mar."

"Oh, hello, my dear."

"You've been gone for a while. How long were you at the library?"

"Why, I just arrived home this minute, my dear. It took several hours to find what I was looking for."

"It took me five minutes to get my answer. Marilyn Q Turner is a pharmacist. Same as Gertie. I figure that Gertie is Marilyn Turner or has taken over her identity."

"Very good, my dear. How perspicacious of you."

"Thanks. How about you? Do they even keep pharmacy license records in the library?"

"Oh, that I don't know."

"Well, what did you do all that time in the library?"

"I do love going to the library, my dear. Our town has a particularly nice one, don't you think? I often wander around the shelves and come up with a book that I never would have thought to read. When I arrived at the library today, I saw the book *Rebecca* by Daphne DuMaurier lying on a return cart and picked it up. Have you read it, my dear?"

"No. What did you find out at the library, Mar?"

"What a shame you have never read it. The book is about an old mansion called Manderly whose inhabitants have many secrets. The heroine, a young woman who is never named in the book, marries, and is brought back to her new husband's ancestral estate. It is run by a housekeeper who had been devoted to the owner's first wife, Rebecca, who drowned the previous year."

"Not what did you find out about the book, Mar. What did you find out about Marilyn Turner?"

"The sinister housekeeper convinces the heroine that the husband still loves Rebecca—"

"But what did you find out at the library about Marilyn Turner?"

"—but the truth is revealed after a costume ball."

Martha figured it was a waste of time to try get Marya back on track. She would just have to let her finish rambling.

"It is revealed that Rebecca was murdered. It is so very atmospheric. I do love a good gothic novel."

"I don't."

"As I was perusing *Rebecca*, I thought of dear Gertrude's old house. It reminded me of Manderly. Did you not find it rather atmospheric? Perhaps that is why I recollected the Turnerman who so frightened my sister and me when we were young. I began to wonder why our bogeyman was called the Turnerman. You may recall that I mentioned the story of John Henry while we were at Gertrude's. My mother, God rest her soul, often read that story to my sister and me."

*By the house of Saint Pelagia, now Marya is going to tell me the story of John Henry. I'll have to keep Marya away from the library.*

"I already know that story, Marya."

"Do you, my dear? It is one of my favorites. Did you know that although it is a tall tale, it was based on a real person?"

"Marya, please. Gertie. Marilyn Turner."

"That is exactly what I was talking about, my dear. I wondered whether the Turnerman was perhaps also based on a real person. There is a microfilm reader in the basement of the library that I have used from time to time to look up old editions of the *Pequot Bays Journal*, and so I decided to look up very old editions, from before my time, to see if there was a crime associated with a man named Turner. I found that in 1890 there was a series of murders of domestics in Pequot Bays. A local man named William Turner was convicted and hanged. He had a son who left Pequot Bays, married, and had a son who could be just the right age to be Gertrude's grandfather. He moved back into the house where old William Turner had lived and had a son who would be just the right age to be Gertrude's father. They lived there quietly until he was discovered to be the grandson of the Turnerman, and he and his son were hounded out of town. An article in the *Pequot Times* had a picture of Gertrude's grandfather, whom she strongly resembles, and the very house we visited today. When Gertrude moved back into her own ancestral home, she must have changed her name so that no one would discover her past."

Martha shivered. "So Gertie's great-great-grandfather was a serial killer? That explains why she was giving Aldo the money. He must have found out somehow and is blackmailing her. But why would she change her name to Gertie Doppeldecker?"

"Why, to cover up the fact that she was the great-great-granddaughter of a serial murderer, my dear."

"No, I mean, why Gertie Doppeldecker? Why would anyone choose that name out of all the names in the world?"

"Why, I suppose it is because no one would suspect that anyone would ever change their name to Gertrude Doppeldecker."

# CHAPTER 12

Monday, November 7

THE FOLLOWING MORNING, MARTHA CHECKED whether she had received any responses to her applications. She had not. She perused the listings for law enforcement jobs without college degrees, which mostly consisted of security guard positions. She filled out several applications, her spirits dampening with each send icon she clicked.

She went into the yard and threw Quincy the giveitheck. As she watched the dog twisting and fighting with the crushed football, a little of Martha's own fighting spirit returned. Should she try? Could she win? Quincy trotted over to Martha, dropped the giveitheck at her feet, and looked into her eyes. It sometimes seemed that Quincy, just like Marya, could read her mind.

Martha grinned. "Oh, why not, Quince. I'll give it a try."

At 10:00 sharp, Martha turned into the parking lot of the Pequot Bays Police Department. She parked and sat for a moment. The two-story white brick structure, a square on top of a rectangle, had been built to be a precinct house, jail, holding facility, and gym for the police. The blue and white no-nonsense *Police Dept.* sign proclaimed its functionality. It did not, however, meld with the overall Victorian sensibility of Pequot Bays, and was therefore situated a proper distance away, on the edge of town, where it served as a greeting, or a warning, to anyone entering the village.

Martha remained in the car, hesitant to take the first step to run for police commissioner. The front door of the station opened and O'Hara's belly, followed by the rest of him, came into view. She knew Marya would not approve of her thoughts as she watched him strut over to his squad car and drive away, but they worked to propel Martha out of her car and toward the station. She would show O'Hara.

Martha walked into the lobby, which was ill-lit and contained five molded plastic orange seats. Even though smoking had not been allowed inside for years, the room gave the impression of being filled with smoke and stained with nicotine. Martha knew from her previous stint as commissioner that it was not much better inside.

Martha went to the bulletproof window. She knew the receptionist, who was looking down at her cell phone. But even after Martha said, "Hello, Jeannie, how are you doing these days," the woman gave no sign of recognition. Jeannie had always been an O'Hara groupie.

"I'm here to pick up the packet to run for commissioner."

Jeannie's blank eyes showed some interest. "You're running again?"

"Yes."

"You think you can win this time?"

"Yes."

"How come?"

Martha just stared back at Jeannie.

"You know, Arlo Bennett is running for a second term. You didn't win last time. How come you think you can win this time? You're an Uber driver now. He's still a former DA."

Martha tried to keep her face from reddening.

"But hold on. I'll go get the packet." Jeannie left her desk. Martha heard her say, before the door leading to the back of the police station closed, "Hey guys. You'll never guess who—"

As she waited, Martha realized that Jeannie was right. It was crazy to think she could beat anyone, much less Arlo Bennett. She decided to forget the whole thing. It was a stupid idea. No use bothering about the forms. She turned to leave, but outside, she heard the low rumbling of thunder. Dark clouds were forming in the east. As she watched the powerful clouds coalesce into shapes like anvils, she thought of Marya's cloud of witnesses—the dead who were going to push Martha to victory in the election—and had to smile. Well, maybe she'd just stick around and pick up the papers. It wouldn't hurt to have them. Just in case.

She waited until Jeannie reappeared with a thin envelope and a smirk on her face. As she pushed the envelope through the space at the bottom of the bulletproof glass window, a clap of thunder exploded, and the lights went out. Jeannie flinched and gasped, her hand flying to her throat. With only one small window opening to a dark sky, the room was pitch black.

Martha smiled and said that she hoped that Jeannie had a nice day. The pelting rain did not start until after Martha had reached home. Her lights were still working.

Two hours later, Officer Chonkin called.

"Hello, Ms. Collins. Wanted you to know that I just sent the cup of punch out to the lab. Lieutenant O'Hara read the report and said that he would be personally supervising the case. He said I should have sent it out for testing immediately and I was to tell the lab to get the results stat. The statements will be ready for signature later this afternoon. Lieutenant O'Hara said to come by at 2:00 sharp to sign them. He took the cup over for fingerprint testing himself. He said that there were no detectable fingerprints on the cup, just a bunch of dirty smudges. Oh, and we got the toxicology results from the hospital and spoke to the emergency room doctor about it. They showed high levels of methamphetamine in your blood. Very high. High enough to cause your hypertensive episode. He said you told him your blood pressure is normally very low. That was lucky. He said it saved your life."

Well, things were finally moving! Furious as she was about the delay and the "smudges" on the evidence, Martha would have to thank Henry. Somehow, he had pushed O'Hara into action.

She called Marya and told her she'd be by after lunch to take her to the police station so they could sign their statements. Marya was ready and waiting on the curb when Martha drove up.

The police station had returned to normal after the storm, with the lights back on and Jeannie staring at her cell phone. She glanced up at Martha. "Twice in one day? To what do we owe this honor?"

"We're here to see Officer Chonkin," Martha said.

"Oh. Right. Have a seat."

Martha had time to read the PBPD newsletters for the last six months before Jeannie returned and led the two women through a metal door with a thick glass window into a small, windowless conference room. Martha heard the sarcastic tones of O'Hara's voice from down the hall. "Hey, Chonkin. So how come you're always following Hank Milton around anyway?"

"You told me—" Chonkin said.

"You think he's hot?"

There was laughing, and one of the other officers said, "Better watch out, Milton, she might tackle you." More laughing.

"You gonna report her for sexual harassment, Milton?" O'Hara asked. More laughing.

"You told me—"

"Why don't you leave Milton alone for once and get me those statements you waited so long to show me?".

"You told—"

"Now, Chonkin! Get them now."

Moments later, Henry Milton walked past the open conference room door carrying a briefcase. He did not respond to Martha's hello, but walked on, head down, through the metal door that led into the lobby and to the parking lot outside. Martha and Marya continued waiting. And waiting.

After a few minutes, Martha saw Henry walk past the conference room the opposite way and called out to him. "Hey, Henry, could you tell Officer Chonkin to hurry with the statements? We don't have all day."

Henry stopped and gazed at her for a moment. "Please call me Hank, Ms. Collins. I'm sure everything's ready now." He mumbled something in what seemed to Martha to be Italian and walked on.

Martha laughed. "You know he studied medieval poetry in college. He's tried to fit in here, but I guess he can't help himself sometimes. Wonder what that that meant?"

Marya did not laugh. "He said, '*Lasciate ogne speranza, voi ch'entrate.*' That is the inscription on the gate to hell in Dante's *Inferno*. 'Abandon all hope, ye who enter here.'"

The door slammed open, and Lieutenant O'Hara barged into the conference room.

Martha was not happy at all that O'Hara was handling this. But she took pleasure in how bad he looked. He had gained weight and lost hair since she had last seen him. His shirt strained so hard to cover his belly that one of the buttons had slipped out, and skin peeked out between the remaining buttons. There were only a few strands of hair left in his attempt at a comb-over.

They glared at each other.

"Gained some weight, O'Hara?"

"How's the Uber business going these days, Collins?"

"I thought Officer Chonkin was handling this."

"You're going to have to deal with me, Collins. So, I hear you're going to run for police commissioner next year."

She met his sneer with one of her own. "Yes, I am."

"We'll see. So, you got your best buddy with you again." He turned toward Marya. "Myra, isn't it?"

"It's Marya. M-A-R-Y-A. I find that many people get quite confused with the—"

"Okay, Myra, here's your statement. And here's yours." O'Hara tossed the papers down on the conference room table. He sat down, crossed his arms, and leaned back on the chair.

The two women read over the statements and signed them. He took the papers, looked first at the signatures, then at Martha. "And you really think anyone is going to believe someone spiked your drink with amphetamines, and that this loony over here knew that someone had spiked your drink and ran over to pick up your cup to save it?" He shook his head. "Next time you try to come up with a cover story for your drug overdose, you better think of a better one. You know there's a law against filing a false police report." He left, snickering.

Martha said to his back, "You know there's a law against tampering with evidence." She stormed out of the police station. "That pompous, nasty, stupid son of a—"

"My dear, you just went to confession. Perhaps we should say a prayer for Lieutenant O'Hara. It is impossible to be angry at someone you are praying for."

"No. It's impossible to pray for someone you're angry at."

"Well then perhaps you should say a prayer that you will feel inclined to say a prayer for the lieutenant."

"No way."

"Well then, say a prayer for the inclination to say a prayer that you will feel inclined to say a prayer for the lieutenant?"

Martha thought for a minute, trying to figure out what Marya was saying, and then said, "Nope."

"How about—"

"No, Marya. You can give it up. I will never pray for that...that..."

"Well, my dear, you know that I do not give up on anything. So *I* will pray that you will be inclined to say a prayer that you will be inclined to say a prayer for the lieutenant."

Martha had to smile.

Marya opened the car door before Martha had a chance to get to her key fob and unlock it. "That's odd, Mar. I always lock it."

When they were two blocks from the police station, she heard a siren and saw a police car with lights on behind her signaling for her to pull over. "I wonder what this is all about. They must have forgotten something."

She pulled over to the side of the road and rolled down her window. Henry came over to her, followed by O'Hara, who lumbered to the other side of the car and motioned for Marya to roll down her window.

"Hi, Henry. What's up?"

"Um. Er."

Henry seemed tongue-tied. Didn't even tell her to call him Hank.

"What's the problem?"

Henry did not look at Martha but across at O'Hara. "I have to give you a ticket, Ms. Collins."

"A ticket?"

"Yes, a ticket."

"For what?"

Henry continued looking at O'Hara. "The air freshener."

"What are you talking about, Henry?"

"The air freshener," O'Hara pointed at the pine tree-shaped air freshener hanging from the rearview mirror.

"The air freshener?" Martha repeated.

Henry took a deep breath. "There's a law against having objects near the windshield that can obstruct motorists' views. May I see your registration please, Ms. Collins."

Martha was speechless. As she opened the glove compartment to get her registration, a small pink organza drawstring bag fell out right into Marya's lap. O'Hara reached into the car and grabbed it. He held it up and shook it. "Well, well, well, what have we here?"

"I have no idea," Martha said.

"That's what they all say. I'm confiscating this."

"Huh?"

"Give her an appearance ticket for possession of a controlled substance," O'Hara said to Henry.

"Huh? What's going on here?"

"Buying from the local dealer, Collins. Just like all the other rich suburban housewives," O'Hara sneered. "I don't know how many people are going to vote for a known drug user to be police commissioner."

Henry gave Martha the two tickets.

"This is crazy. I've never seen that before in my life."

"Tell it to the judge." O'Hara smirked and strutted away. Henry followed, head down.

Martha turned to Marya. "Don't you dare pray for him. You know what he just did to me, right?"

"I'm afraid I do, my dear. He had poor Henry plant the drugs in your car while we were in the police station."

"Exactly. He's not getting away with this."

"No, my dear, he will not."

Martha drove Marya home in silent fury. Marya rummaged though her purse, and as Martha stopped in front of her apartment, she pulled out one of her laminated, purple-scripted cards and gave it to Martha.

> My peace I give you. I do not give to you as the world
> gives. Do not let your hearts be troubled and do not be
> afraid.
> John 14:27.

Martha tried to smile. "Thanks, Mar." Her heart, though, was troubled.

When she arrived home, Martha checked the key fob to make sure it worked. It did. She went online to look up how to break into locked cars and learned about relay devices that could hack into keyless entry systems. So that's how they'd done it. She felt her muscles tense and a pounding in her ears. She called a lawyer she knew, who referred her to a criminal lawyer, and she phoned to make an appointment.

"Hello, Ms. Collins. What can I do to help you?"

"I need a police lieutenant arrested."

"I beg your pardon?"

"Michael O'Hara, PBPD. He's a lying, double-crossing, un-derhanded—" Martha's voice rose with each insult, and her hands shook. She clenched the phone in one hand and a pencil in the other to control them.

"I think you'd better take a deep breath, Ms. Collins."

Martha took a deep breath. "Deceitful, evil son of a—" The pencil snapped.

"Maybe several deep breaths."

She took several deep breaths. The red mist clouding her vision slowly cleared. She continued in more normal tones, "He planted drugs in my car."

"Hmm."

"It's true!"

"Oh, I believe you. What drug?"

"Don't know. He confiscated it."

"Were you arrested?"

"No. Got a ticket."

"For what?"

Martha looked at the ticket. "Possession of a controlled substance in the fourth degree."

"I see. Well, Ms. Collins, at worst, it'll be a misdemeanor, and we can probably get it reduced to a violation or dismissed. We'll talk about it in detail when we meet, but try to forget about it for now."

"Forget about it! Not a chance. Don't want it dismissed. I'll go to trial if I have to. O'Hara can't get away with this."

"We'll see."

# CHAPTER 13

Wednesday, November 9

MARTHA WOKE UP AT FIRST LIGHT. YESTERDAY'S RUN-in with O'Hara seized her thoughts, and her stomach knotted up at the memory. She woke Quincy, who rose and stretched grudgingly. Despite her bad ankle, she drove to their favorite park and tried to take a short walk, but her black mood did not lift. If anything, her agitation infected Quincy, who growled at a cocker spaniel. Martha dropped off Quincy at home and went to morning Mass. It was her day to serve as eucharistic minister, and she could now manage the short walk to the altar without her cane. Marya often said she went to church when she felt troubled. Maybe it would help.

Walking through the parking lot, she glanced around nervously, as was now her habit. Great. She had one person trying to kill her and another trying to ruin her reputation.

She had arrived so early that the church was empty. After a few moments, she gave up on her attempt to pray, and instead fell to thinking—plotting, really—how to get back at O'Hara. She would go to trial. She would testify. She would persuade the jury of her innocence, and they would come back with a verdict exonerating her and demanding the arrest of O'Hara.

A bell dinged, startling Martha out of her imaginings, and the priest processed from the sacristy into the church. Only then did she become aware that about thirty fellow churchgoers, including several of her suspects, had filled the pews in front of her. She decided to distract herself by interrogating them.

She moved forward and sat behind Aldo Todi, whose slumped shoulders shook in an effort to silence his hacking cough. Only two of the Dies Irae gang were here, Luz Flores and Barbara Vance. The postures of the two women were more relaxed than usual, with no Ken or Father Thaddeus around to require their rapt attention. Aldo sat behind Luz. Isabella Bonino, definitely not a regular at morning Mass, sat in the first pew, right in front of the statue of Mary.

When Barbara Vance came up to receive Communion, Martha was shocked by a swollen purple bruise around her cheekbone and eye socket that was visible despite a heavy application of makeup.

Returning to her pew, Martha fell back into perseverating about the drug bust and almost forgot to follow her suspects out of church after Mass. She noticed Marya sitting near the Mary grotto, mostly hidden by the foliage. Too late for Mass again, she was saying a rosary.

Isabella and Luz were talking together under the portico, Isabella's gestures even more animated than usual. Barbara Vance and Aldo stood nearby. Martha stopped next to Barbara and said, "Hi," as though to rest her ankle and have a friendly after-Mass chat. Barbara nodded and then turned her attention back to the conversation between Isabella and Luz. Martha did the same.

"I'm leaving Dies Irae, Luz. Your little organization is losing another member. We're all either dying or dropping out. *Certo*, you don't mind if we die, you get rich. You stole 10% of my money when Johnny died, and 10% of Michael's when Lisa died. But you're not going to get any more of mine." Isabella flicked the back of her hand under her chin. "I'm leaving and changing my will, and I'll get Michael to do the same. So's Aldo." Isabella's hazel eyes flashed at Aldo. "That's about the only thing Aldo and I agree on."

"Yes, I know Aldo has issues with Dies Irae," Luz said. "But I hope to convince him otherwise. And I hope to convince you and Michael also."

Isabella shook her dark hair. "*Quel prete pazzo, Padre* Thaddeus and Ken. They are putting pressure on Michael. I had convinced him to quit." Her eyes narrowed, and she flipped her hand from palm down to palm up. "*È combiato.* He changed his mind. Lately, *Padre* Thaddeus has made him change his mind about many things. But I won't give up. And I can be as persuasive as that priest and his *compadre* Ken combined…in my own way." She put her hands on her hips and arched her back, displaying her persuasive attributes. "Michael only joined as a favor to Aldo, and he only stayed for the business connections. *Sua moglie,* Lisa, she was the believer. Ken Vance, what is the expression, held sway over, yes, dominated Lisa." She eyed Barbara Vance. "So tell me, what happened to you, Barbara?"

"A running injury," she said.

"I didn't know you ran."

Barbara turned so that only the unblemished side of her face was in view as she spoke. "You mustn't do that, Isabella. You mustn't quit, and you mustn't try to convince Michael to quit. Please."

Barbara sounded desperate. Isabella looked at her. "Why not?"

"It will save your life."

"Save my life?"

"I mean your eternal life."

Isabella shrugged. "*Basta.* Your eternal damnation threats don't scare me. Michael and I, we won't give away our inheritances. I will protect what's left for Luca, and Michael must think of Justin." Isabella smiled, but not with her eyes, and sashayed away.

Barbara and Luz exchanged glances, walked away, and stopped near the Mary grotto to talk. Marya was no longer fingering her rosary beads. Maybe she would, for once, put her investigation before her prayers.

The two women paused for only a moment and then walked on. Martha went over, sat down next to Marya, and related to her, hand gestures and all, what Isabella had said.

Marya looked worried. "Thank you, my dear. I am afraid that explains it very well."

"Explains what?"

"Why, what Barbara and Luz said."

"Ah, good, you did hear something. What did they say?"

"Barbara said, 'Must we tell them?' And Luz said, 'You know we must. We have to tell them everything.'"

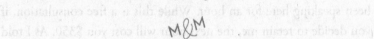

That afternoon, Martha went to the criminal lawyer and gave her a full history, beginning with the feud between Martha and O'Hara that started when Martha, in her former duties as civilian police commissioner, had reported O'Hara for planting drugs on a suspect. O'Hara had retaliated by finding a candidate to run against her in the next election and making sure he had the support of the PBA, the rank and file members, and their family and friends, which was more than enough to carry the small town of Pequot Bays. The feud had been reignited last year after the murder of a Saint John's parishioner. O'Hara had believed she was killed by a local priest. Despite evidence of his innocence, O'Hara had persuaded the DA to keep the priest in jail. Martha, with some help from a friend, had uncovered the real murderer. The DA had been unhappy with O'Hara and let him know it.

Then Martha recounted to the lawyer her visit to the police station, when she and her friend were kept in a windowless room while Henry used a relay device to hack into her key fob and plant the amphetamines in her car, through the traffic stop, with Henry on one side of the car asking for her registration and O'Hara at the passenger window poised to grab the packet of pills as it fell from the glove compartment. Martha left out the part about the amphetamine-laced lemonade at the party for fear that the lawyer might think she was paranoid…or a druggie. "So I wondered whether, after

I'm found innocent at trial, juries can make recommendations that someone—O'Hara in this case—could be arrested."

The lawyer gazed down at her desk for a moment before she looked back up at Martha. "That's quite a story, Martha. By the way, you are an amazing mimic. I felt like I was with you in the car while Lieutenant O'Hara and Henry made their traffic stop. As your lawyer, I'm sure you want me to tell you my honest opinion. We have been speaking here for an hour. While this is a free consultation, if you decide to retain me, the next hour will cost you $350. As I told you on the phone, you have been charged with a misdemeanor. Since you have had no other run-ins with the law, I am sure I can get it dismissed with no fine and merely a promise that you will not break the law for the next ninety days. I would charge you a flat fee of $3500 for that. But if you want to go to trial, I'll charge by the hour, and it could cost thousands, at least ten to fifteen thousand dollars, plus expenses. I am willing to do that, but I would highly recommend the former. There is no guarantee that you would win the trial. You have no direct proof, and juries tend to believe the police. And no, there is no hope that a jury would recommend that Lieutenant O'Hara be arrested. Think about it and let me know what you want to do."

Martha left the lawyer's office, her hopes dashed. She looked at her watch. She had promised to drive Marya to the doctor and then wanted to take Quincy to a nice dog run. She put Quincy in the back seat and drove over to Marya's apartment. When Marya caught sight of the dog, she came to an abrupt halt.

"My goodness. Perhaps I should take the bus, my dear."

"Don't worry, Mar. You know Quincy goes right to sleep when the motor starts running. She'd never hurt anyone. Gentlest dog ever, aren't you, girl?"

Marya entered the car even more slowly than usual. Once she was belted in, Quincy put her paws on either side of the back of Marya's seat and nuzzled her head. Marya sat, motionless, eyes wide open.

"Go on, sit down in the back, Quince." Martha scratched the

back of Quincy's neck. "That's a good girl, that's a good girl. See what a good girl she is, Marya. She likes you." Quincy kept pawing and nuzzling Marya. "What a good dog you are, Quince."

Marya did not respond. She sat, silent, clutching her bags. Martha remembered that Quincy had been a very useful tool once when she wanted Marya to stop rambling and focus on a murder.

Martha started the car. Quincy immediately lay down in down in the back seat and went to sleep. "Quincy really likes you, Mar."

Martha told Marya about her visit to the lawyer. "I don't have the money to pay for a trial. I guess I'll just have to get it dismissed. O'Hara's right, you know. No one will believe someone spiked my lemonade with amphetamines at the party. I didn't even tell the lawyer about it because I was afraid she'd think I was crazy, or a drug addict...or both. O'Hara's already started talking about how I take amphetamines. I'll never be able to run for police commissioner. O'Hara's won. It's hopeless."

"Do not despair, my dear. Have faith." Marya smiled, and Martha saw compassion, understanding, and shared hurt, but none of the doubt or hopelessness that was dragging her down. Maybe she would hold off calling the lawyer.

"Well then, you're going to have to put in a good word for me in your prayers, Marya. I need a miracle."

"We shall see."

They arrived at the office of Marya's doctor.

"Thank you, my dear, for the ride to town. I'll do my errands and take the bus home."

"Why are you going to the doctor, anyway, Marya? Are you okay?"

"I am quite all right. Just some questions about medications, my dear."

Martha watched Marya totter over to the doctor's office. Aldo Todi and another man were leaving a men's clothing store next door. Marya said something to Aldo's companion, but Aldo grabbed the man's arm and pulled him away before he could answer. Martha thought that the guy with Aldo looked vaguely familiar.

Driving home with nothing to distract her, the memory of yesterday's drug frame-up cast its pall over Martha. *By Saint Apolonia's teeth, can things get any worse?*

As she passed by Café Gourmand, she caught a glimpse of Christopher holding the door open for Amanda Lombardi. She pressed her hand to her abdomen to stop her heart from sinking any lower. Apparently they could.

# CHAPTER 15

### Saturday, November 12

MARTHA FELT NO BETTER THE FOLLOWING DAY. ONLY two weeks till she had to appear in court, and she still had not decided what to do. She decided to call Marya and ask if she wanted to take a short walk on the waterfront in the afternoon. Martha's ankle still throbbed, so Marya's pace would be a nice change from Quincy's eager romping, and her chatter would be a pleasant distraction from Martha's brooding thoughts.

Martha picked up her friend, and they drove down to Harborview Park. As Martha put on her blinker to turn into the parking lot, Marya said, "My dear, I have an idea. There is a nature preserve quite nearby. The one that Luz mentioned. It is quite hidden from view, but I know it from my youth. Might we go there? I can no longer manage the gravel road to get to the preserve, but with your car, why, we could drive right there."

"Sure, Mar."

Martha followed Marya's directions and turned onto a road she had never noticed. They bumped along a dirt lane—really two dirt tire tracks with wildflowers in the middle—for a short distance until they arrived at a sandy, open space. There were no other cars.

"This nature preserve, my dear, is for the birds. You see that boardwalk. It goes down to the bay side of the beach. It was known as Millionaire's Lane when I was a child. I believe it is now known as Billionaire's Lane. Sea planes used to land near here, but I heard that now there is a paved spot for helicopters to land at the end of the lane."

Martha turned toward a rustling sound nearby and saw someone scurrying off into the bushes. "It must be one of the homeless guys wandering in here from Harborview Park. Like Luz mentioned."

They walked on the boardwalk toward the beach, Marya chattering about her sister, her sister's daughter, and her sister's daughter's son, who was Marya's beloved grandnephew and her only remaining relative. Martha could manage the slow stroll along the boardwalk with the assistance of her cane, but she was concerned about Marya's difficulty walking on the uneven boards and suggested that they go back. But Marya looked up at her with shining eyes and said, "I have not felt this young for years, my dear. Let's push forward. Ever onward!"

The two walked on, with Martha at the ready to catch Marya should she stumble. The meandering boardwalk led them over a salt marsh in a tidal creek to the edge of Pequot Bay. Benches dotted the boardwalk, and Martha and Marya took advantage of several of them on the way to the beach. During these breaks, they watched piping plovers advance and recede at the foamy edge of the waves, as though reluctant to wet their feet. Terns hovered and then divebombed like miniature warplanes. A great white heron did a high step march in the water with raptor-like clawed toes, its razor-sharp yellow beak ready to strike at any unwary minnow.

A man sat on one of the benches. Head slumped down, he looked to be asleep, with a straw hat covering his head. A large tackle box sat next to him, along with a fishing rod and an ice chest. They approached quietly so as not to disturb the peaceful scene. As they neared the bench, Marya stopped so abruptly that Martha bumped into her, and Marya almost tumbled over.

Marya pointed to a dark red puddle underneath the bench. "What is that, my dear?"

"Maybe he was gutting some fish?"

"I do not think so. This is too thick and dark for fish blood."

They took a few steps closer. The man did not stir.

"Excuse me, sir," Marya said, "are you all right?"

There was no response.

Martha touched his shoulder. The body fell over on its side onto the bench, the straw hat falling off the head. The features, now visible in profile, were those of Michael Ward. His face appeared peaceful. But from back of his head…or what had been his head…spilled blood, bone fragments, and…Martha looked away. That must be his brain. He was quite dead.

Martha called the police. As soon as she hung up, Marya said, "My dear, we must be quick. Very quick. Before the police get here. Take out your phone please. I have heard that these phones have cameras, my dear. It that so?"

"Yes."

"Perhaps then, they are smart after all. I need you to take pictures for me. Before the police get here."

Martha took out her phone, glad to be doing something other than staring at the once-handsome head.

"Take pictures of the entire scene please. Now the face. A close up of the face. You do not need to take a picture of the back of the head. Now, the glove that is right over there. I believe it is a mitten, not a glove. The tackle box please. And the ice chest. Please take a picture of that. Very good. Now, most important of all. You must run, very quickly, to the parking lot. Do not move your car, but take a picture of the entire parking area with your car in it. Then take as many pictures of the ground as you can before the police arrive."

Martha ran, her stride lopsided from the brace and her ankle protesting every step. She had just finished taking pictures when the police roared into the parking area, lights and sirens blasting. There were eight police cars and two ambulances. O'Hara was there and snarled at her. Henry and Chonkin acknowledged her with a nod. Ken Vance was one of the six EMTs who poured out of the ambulances. Martha led the long line of emergency personnel down the winding boardwalk to the body. Marya stepped away from the bench as the police and EMTs took over the scene.

"Do you want to go and sit down on a bench, Mar?" Martha asked.

"No, my dear, I'm not tired in the least. I would prefer to watch. I have made my own deductions, and I am curious to know if the investigating officers will agree with me."

"What deductions?"

"In a moment, my dear, perhaps we can discuss it in depth."

The police fanned out over the boardwalk. O'Hara and another plainclothes police officer took the lead. A photographer came, and they ordered her to take pictures of the glove. Then O'Hara picked it up, smelled it, and made a face. He handed it to his colleague, who did the same. The two men nodded at each other.

O'Hara barked orders at the group. "Milton, Chen, Pierce, follow us to Harborview Park. We're going to raid Hobo Town. Pereira, Elliot, Gomez, guard the scene. Chonkin, stop standing around doing nothing. Go get a statement from the old ditz in purple and her little buddy over there."

Officer Chonkin went over to the two women. Marya said, "Do you mind if we sit on one of the benches away from all of this, my dear? I am very tired. So much excitement and upset, you know. And I am not a young as I used to be."

Marya did not look at all tired to Martha.

"Of course, ma'am."

They moved down the boardwalk to the next bench, out of sight of the commotion around the body. Marya and Martha gave their statements, and Officer Chonkin was putting away her pad when Marya said, "So, my dear, I suppose they believe that a homeless person was responsible for the murder?"

"Can't discuss police business, ma'am. Thanks for your help."

"But you know, that would be quite impossible. It does not take into account all of the little things. My friend Martha laughs when I talk about the little things, but they are very important."

"Thanks for your help, ma'am," Chonkin repeated as she tried to step around Marya, who had risen from the bench and was blocking the narrow path of the boardwalk.

"Very important. Especially little things that do not fit in. Sister Thomas More, my twelfth grade logic and Latin teacher, would not stand for any logical fallacies. One of my favorites was the red herring fallacy. Sister explained that the name is a reference to the fact that people fleeing from trackers with bloodhounds would sometimes wipe a smoked herring, which is red and strong smelling, across their path to throw the dogs off their trail. I once ate a…"

"I'd better get back now. They'll be wondering where I am." Chonkin stepped off the boardwalk into the sand and prickly brush to get around Marya.

But Marya went on, in a louder voice, "The mitten, you see. That has led the police to believe that a homeless person was responsible for the crime. But that does not take into account the other person who was with poor Mr. Ward while he was fishing."

Chonkin stopped, stepped back onto the boardwalk, and removed her pad from her pocket. "Who was the person you saw with the victim when he was fishing, Ms. Cook?"

"Of course, I did not see the other person, officer. If I had, the murder would not have taken place. The murderer would have known that he had been seen. Such a shame we did not come earlier—"

Chonkin turned to Martha. "Did you see anyone fishing with the victim?"

"When we first arrived, I thought I saw someone take off into the bushes. Definitely didn't see anyone fishing with Michael though. He was dead by the time we got here."

Chonkin asked a few questions about the person Martha had seen run into the bushes, but she was not even able to describe the color of the clothes on the back of whoever it was. Chonkin put away her pad again.

Martha said, "I didn't remember that guy till you mentioned him, Marya. Scary to think we were that close to the killer."

"No, no, no, my dear, that certainly could not have been the killer. That was a homeless person. And a homeless person could not have been the killer. Automobiles are so expensive these days. And then one must pay for car insurance. It is not surprising that—"

Chonkin shook her head and stepped off into the bushes again.

"Why couldn't a homeless person have done it, Mar?"

"Think, my dear, what did I have you take pictures of?"

Chonkin paused, her back still to the two women.

"Well, the tackle box, the ice chest, and the empty parking lot, mostly, and then Michael's face and the glove, well, the mitten."

"Very good. And so...think, my dear, think."

Martha thought.

"I will give you a hint, my dear. It's the tackle box. And the ice chest. And the parking lot. As Sister Mary Joseph, my sixth grade English teacher would..."

Martha had developed a talent for shutting out Marya's chatter, so she was able to think as Marya nattered on, but could not come up with any connection between the murder and the pictures she had taken. "But we didn't even open the tackle box or the ice chest. And there was nothing in the parking lot. No other cars but mine."

Chonkin turned around. "The parking lot was empty? There were no other cars but yours?"

"Yes, and I've got pictures."

"You have pictures of the parking lot?"

"Yes. Marya told me to take them before the police arrived."

Chonkin eyed Marya for a long moment. "That was a very good idea, Ms. Cook."

Marya met the police officer's gaze. "Thank you, my dear."

Martha looked from Marya to Chonkin and then back to Marya.

"Anyone care to tell me why an empty parking lot is so important?"

Marya inclined her head toward Chonkin. "Go ahead, my dear. Please explain."

Chonkin said, "Well, you see, Ms. Collins, the tackle box and the ice chest. They were too big for the deceased to carry from his home to the preserve, so if his own car wasn't in the parking lot, that means that someone drove him there. And the question is, where is that person?"

"Very good, my dear, very good. But actually the question is, *who* is that person," said Marya.

Chonkin gave a quick nod. "Thank you for your statements. I'll be in touch."

# CHAPTER 16

33rd Week in Ordinary Time
Sunday, November 13

THE NEXT MORNING, MARTHA'S CELL PHONE RANG. IT was Marya.

"Hello."

"Hello, hello. May I speak to Martha Collins please?"

In her most formal tone, she said, "This is Martha Collins speaking."

"Hello, Martha, my dear. This is Marya Cook."

"I know, Mar. I know."

"I received a telephone call from Officer Chonkin. Our statements have been typed up. She would like copies of the photographs. Perhaps you could take the film in to be developed."

"Sure, Mar. The film. To be developed. Will do." Sometimes it was easier and faster to just go along with Marya's old-fashioned notions.

"It will not even be necessary to go to the station to sign the statements. Officer Chonkin asked if she could drop by my apartment and bring them over. She could be here at about 3:00. Would it be possible for you to come here at that time? And please bring your list of suspects with you."

Martha arrived at Marya's apartment at 2:30. Marya opened the door wearing a lavender straw hat sprinkled generously with glitter, sequins, and tiny iridescent stars twinkling in various shades of purple. Martha had never seen that one before. Marya sported her most cherished keepsake, her mother's large turtle broach with the green rhinestone shell and one missing blue rhinestone eye, perched on the shoulder of a white blouse bedecked with bright purple irises. She was dressed to the nines. Once upstairs, Marya scurried around making piles of the papers that were scattered around the apartment and dusting the flat surfaces as she tidied.

"It has been so long since I have had a visitor for afternoon tea, my dear. Except you, of course, and that was quite a long time ago. Would you mind putting on the kettle and rinsing off three cups and saucers from the cabinet? I believe I have three matching ones. And I may even have three teaspoons. I am afraid they may be a bit dusty. Those were my mother's teacups, God rest her soul. She…"

Martha found the cups, teaspoons, and a chipped sugar bowl and creamer. She washed and dried them, filled the sugar bowl and the creamer, and placed them on the counter next to the sink.

At 3:00 on the dot, the doorbell rang. Marya tap-tapped down the flight of stairs from her living area to the front door and led in Officer Chonkin. "Come in, come in, my dear. So nice to see you again. How very considerate of you to bring the statements here instead of having us go to the station. This is very good service indeed. Ah, here we are. Please sit down and make yourself comfortable."

For once, no papers covered half the sofa. Chonkin sat on the grape-patterned dish towel that covered the small hole, so Martha took a seat on the royal purple afghan on the other end.

"May I get you some tea, my dear?"

"No, thank you, ma'am," Chonkin said.

"Oh, but I have set it up quite in your honor." Marya motioned toward the linoleum kitchen table that took up a quarter of the living area and was piled high with newspapers, magazines, and unopened mail, topped with the papers that had been swept up from the sofa. There was one small, open space, freshly dusted, where Marya had placed a white doily, the sugar and creamer set, three teaspoons, and three cups with saucers, their teabags already in place.

"Well then, I guess... Okay."

The tea kettle whistled, and Marya poured the hot water into each cup. Chonkin opened the briefcase on her knees, pulled out a manila envelope, and removed two statements. She gave one to Martha just as Marya offered Martha tea. Martha took the cup and saucer in one hand and the statement in the other. Chonkin looked quite out of place holding the delicate flowered teacup and saucer. Marya offered everyone sugar and cream, which they refused, and then sat down in a folding chair next to the kitchen table looking quite pleased with herself.

"I recall when I was a little girl, my mother, God rest her soul, would bring out the good teapot and teacups and saucers on Sundays after Mass. We would sit in our very best clothes and have tea and cookies. These are the same teacups that we used then. The one I am holding has a very small chip, but the other two are perfect. I am so sorry I have no cookies to offer, but—"

"Ms. Cook, I'm on a break and I have to get back to the station before they miss me, so could you look at the statement and sign it."

"Oh, my goodness, certainly. That was so thoughtful of you to take time from your coffee break to bring these to us. Although I suppose this is a tea break, not a coffee break. These days everyone drinks so much more coffee than—"

"Mar, sign the statement so Officer Chonkin can get back to work."

"Of course, of course. So sorry, Officer."

Martha and Marya read the statements and signed them while Chonkin gulped down her tea. Chonkin rose from the sofa, grabbed the briefcase, put the teacup on the kitchen table, and collected the papers from the two women. She started toward the stairs, then stopped and turned around. "I forgot to tell you. They got the results back from the lab. There was enough methamphetamine in the paper cup to kill someone. O'Hara says that's just proof you set it up yourself, Ms. Collins. After all, you didn't die."

"Humph," said Martha.

Chonkin did not turn around to leave but stood there.

"Are you quite certain that you would not like some more tea, my dear?"

Chonkin hesitated, took in a deep breath, then slowly released it. "Well, maybe one more cup." She walked back to the sofa and sat down.

"Certainly, my dear." Marya went to get the kettle. Chonkin sat in silence while Marya chattered away as she re-tea-bagged and refilled the cups, re-offered cream and sugar, which was re-refused by her guests, and then sat back down in her folding chair. She stopped her chatter and looked at Chonkin. "Now, my dear, I believe you have something to discuss with us."

Chonkin studied Marya for a long moment, her eyes resting first on the glittering, sequined hat, then on the bejeweled turtle. With a barely perceptible shake of the head, she pulled out her pad from her pocket and flipped through the pages. Finally, she spoke.

"O'Hara's arrested one of the homeless people for the murder of Michael Ward. They raided Hobo Town. I guess that's what they call the area in Harborview Park near the site of the murder where some of the homeless sleep. They found a bloody hammer buried there that they figure is the murder weapon. The deceased's wallet was in the pocket of one of the homeless guys. His name's John. No last name yet. He was dressed better than the other homeless guys. They figure he robbed the deceased and ended up killing him. Then bought new clothes with the money he stole. I told O'Hara about no car in the parking lot and the ice chest and the tackle box, but he told me... Well, he didn't appreciate the suggestion. On my own, I asked around. The deceased liked to go fishing. He'd invite anyone who wanted to go along with him. Mostly, a close friend named," she glanced down at her pad, "Aldo Todi. I spoke to Mr. Todi, who said that he wasn't with him yesterday. He was at home. Alone."

It was the longest speech Martha had ever heard from Chonkin.

Chonkin took out a pencil and tapped it against her notepad. She eyed the two women.

"Yes, my dear? I believe you have a question?" Marya prompted.

"I was wondering…" Chonkin took a deep breath. "Do you know the names of anyone else that might have a reason to kill Michael Ward?"

"Well, my dear, we do happen to have a little list here that might help. Martha, if you would?"

Martha brought out her list of suspects and gave it to Chonkin.

Chonkin looked down at the list, then back up at Martha, her head tilted to the side. "You seem very well prepared." She read the list, took some notes, and gave it back to Martha. "I don't know why I told you all this. Please don't tell anyone else about it. I really must go now. If O'Hara sees I'm late…" She shook her head, pushed herself up from the creaky sofa, and went down the stairs and out the door.

Martha looked at Marya. "Looks like O'Hara's arrested the wrong guy again."

"Yes indeed, my dear."

"What are we going to do, Marya? The murderer's struck again, and I might be next."

"You need not worry about another attempt on your life, my dear. Not yet."

"What do you mean, 'Not yet?'"

Marya just smiled. "Would you like some more tea?"

# CHAPTER 17

Monday, November 14

"WE HAVE TO DO SOMETHING, MAR."

Martha, who always passed out the minute her head hit the pillow, had woken at 3:33 a.m. and been unable to fall back to sleep. She waited till 6:00 a.m. and then called Marya.

"My dear, we must think before we act. As Proverbs 13:16 says, 'Wise people think before they act; fools don't.' Oh my, I am not saying that you are a fool, my dear. You are very perspicacious. But as my mother, God rest—"

"Oh, never mind, Mar. Let's just go to morning Mass." At least they could spy on whichever suspects came to pray.

"What an excellent idea, my dear. I have found that it is more important to pray before you act than to think before you act. But I still keep thinking that I have missed a little something that is very important…"

After Marya settled herself in the car, she handed Martha a laminated, purple-inscribed index card that said:

*The less I pray, the harder it gets; the more I pray, the better it goes.*
*Martin Luther.*

"Martin Luther again." Martha shook her head disapprovingly. Marya had quoted him in the past.

"Many years ago, my dear, I overheard a song on what I believe was referred to as a 'boom box.' 'Boom box' is certainly a good description of the large object this youngster carried on his shoulder as he walked down Main Street. I have never forgotten the lyrics to that song. 'Your worst enemy could be your best friend.'"

Martha could not help but smile. "Mar, that's a Bob Marley song. He's...well...he's not Catholic *or* Protestant. He's something else."

Entering the church, they walked past O'Hara, who was speaking to Father Seamus under the portico. Martha looked in the opposite direction.

During the sign of peace, Martha scrutinized the suspects. Isabella, in front of the Mary statue, wore oversized cat-eye sunglasses. Her hair was tousled, and she was dressed in a loose sweater and jeans, though she still looked elegant. At the sign of peace, she did not look around or acknowledge anyone.

Ken Vance sat to the left of his wife Barbara, who was next to Luz. At the sign of peace, Barbara turned right and gave a long hug to Luz, leaving Ken without the usual peck on the cheek. Aldo, behind Luz, looked more pallid and sickly than usual, his lips almost blue. He did not exchange the sign of peace with his neighbors until Luz turned around and shook his hand. Gertie stood several rows behind, her eyes on Aldo.

O'Hara, true to his nickname, "Loose Lips," must have filled in Father Seamus about Michael's death because during the eucharistic prayer, Father said, "Remember those who have died in the peace of Christ, especially Michael Ward, who passed away last night." Martha could not hear him continue with, "And all the dead whose faith You alone have known," over the buzzing reaction from the pews.

After the final blessing, everyone jumped up and circled around Gertie so fast that Martha could barely get close enough to hear her say, "Well, I couldn't help but overhear Lieutenant O'Hara when he was speaking with Father Seamus before Mass. The police think it was a homeless person."

The surrounding parishioners murmured, "Oh yes, of course."

"Dangerous."

"And the smell."

"Maybe now they'll get them off the streets."

"That's exactly what Lieutenant O'Hara said to Father Seamus. He said if it was up to him, he'd just lock them all up. He said he tried that once, but then had to release them a couple of hours later. Why, just the other day, I was minding my own business right on Main Street, and one of them made me walk off the sidewalk into the street because he had a big grocery cart filled with empty cans and bottles." She darted a glance at Luz.

"Gertie, what else did Loose Lips say to Father?" someone asked.

"They arrested one of them. He had Michael's wallet."

Gertie looked gratified at the "oh my goodnesses," "oohs," and "ahhs," that followed.

Luz left the group. Marya followed her, so Martha followed Marya. Aldo trailed behind them with his ever-present cough, lighting a cigarette. Martha caught up with Marya and whispered, "Did you notice? Aldo's been following us lately."

"I don't think it is us he is following, my dear." Marya stopped, turned around to face Aldo, and said, "How generous of you, Mr. Todi, to have purchased those nice clothes for that homeless man who was in church with us the other day. And a haircut. He looked so handsome when I saw you together in Jack's Menswear."

Of course. That's why the fellow looked so familiar—it had been the homeless guy with Aldo at the clothing store next to Marya's doctor's office. But why did Aldo buy him clothes? Chonkin had said the guy they arrested was better dressed than the others. So he must be the one. Aldo must have hired him to murder Michael Ward.

Luz turned to Aldo, a smile on her face. "Why, how nice of you, Aldo."

Aldo glared at Marya, jammed his hands in his pockets, and tromped away without saying a word.

Luz smiled at Marya. "So, Aldo is helping out our favorite church-goer, Ms. Cook. What a good man he is."

Aldo, a good man? Humph.

Luz gazed after Aldo as he walked toward the car, her features relaxing. "You know, Aldo and I went to elementary school together at Saint John's, and high school too. After college, I married, and he left Pequot Bays for work. Then his family moved back to Sicily, and we lost touch. He returned after my husband died, and we reconnected when he joined Dies Irae. What a character! He loved to joke around at meetings about his 'Sicilian connections,' playing the tough guy, saying he was in 'the family business,' asking whether there was any-one that needed 'to be taken care of.'"

Martha wasn't so sure it was just a joke. She threw a pointed look at Marya, but Marya and Luz were exchanging smiles.

"Do you know what Mr. Todi really does for a living, my dear?"

"No, I don't. He won't talk about it. You know, he doesn't like Dies Irae now, but he was enthusiastic about it at first. I asked if he knew anyone else who would be interested, and he brought in poor Michael and Lisa Ward. I think Michael brought in Johnny Bonino. Johnny was Michael's lawyer." She shook her head. "Only Isabella is left. And she may not be with us very long."

Luz's brow furrowed, and the intensity returned to her features. "Aldo wants me to quit and join the Columbiettes instead. He just doesn't understand, you know. He says Father Thaddeus is too controlling. I have tried to explain that by obeying Father Thaddeus, we are showing God that we are willing to obey whatever He asks of us. Father says Satan has blinded Aldo from seeing the light of God shining on him through Dies Irae."

"Dies Irae is certainly an interesting organization, my dear," said Marya.

Luz leaned forward. "Would you like to join?"

"Before I could consider that, I would have to learn a great deal more about it. My only knowledge of the organization is from a conversation I had with Father Thaddeus on one occasion. As a matter of fact, Father Thaddeus inspired me to create two new cards. Let me see." Marya shifted around objects in her bag and came up with one plasticized note card with neat purple handwriting and handed it to Luz. She read it aloud.

> *Men do not fear a powerful hostile army as the powers*
> *of hell fear the name and protection of Mary.*
> *Saint Bonaventure*

"My mother, God rest her soul, often said to my sister and me when she did not approve of the children we were playing with that our friends were a reflection of ourselves. I suppose one can also tell a great deal about an organization by the persons who run it. I understand that Ken Vance is very involved in the organization."

"Ken Vance. Yes. He likes to sit at Father Thaddeus's right hand. He's our treasurer. The financial part is all him. Ken has come up with several creative ways to increase our income. But I don't mean to imply that you must have a lot of money to join, Ms. Cook. We are doing fine financially. We have recently had large inputs of money through…various sources. What I am trying to say is that we really don't need money from you, Ms. Cook. I am sure Ken is just concentrating on raising more because…because… Well, I really don't know why he is doing that. But Father would never be concerned with how much money a person had if they wanted to join. He is only concerned with souls."

"Yes, my dear, Father Thaddeus appears to be very devoted. These days it is difficult to distinguish a priest from his parishioners except when they are performing religious functions. When I was a young girl, no priest would be seen in public without his proper clerical dress, but now Father Thaddeus stands out. I've never seen him in anything except his formal cassock."

"Yes, Ms. Cook. You know, he is never off duty, day or night. But I am sorry, I have to go now. I'm off work today, so I have to update the Dies Irae website, clean Father Thaddeus's rooms, and arrange for this week's Evening Prayer service. Hopefully I will see you there. It's Thursday night. It's open to everyone."

"Perhaps you shall, my dear."

As Luz turned to leave, Marya again peered into her bag. "Ah, one moment, my dear. Here it is. The other card." She held it out to Luz, who took it and read it aloud.

> But even if we or an angel from heaven should pro-
> claim to you a gospel contrary to what we proclaimed
> to you, let that one be accursed!
> Galatians 1:8

Luz looked at the card for a moment, then at Marya, then back down at the card. She opened her mouth as if to say something but then closed it and walked away.

Driving to Marya's apartment, Martha said, "I've been thinking, Mar. Aldo definitely killed all three of them."

"Why do you think that, my dear?"

"First, why should he buy those clothes for the homeless guy? Because he hired him to murder Michael or set him up as a patsy. Second, Aldo was the friend that usually went fishing with Michael. Third, he has no alibi."

"But what was his motivation, my dear? Motivation is so important."

"I got that too. He kills Lisa Ward and Johnny Bonino so his pal Michael can get together with Isabella. Michael feels bad about the murders and the affair, so he goes to confession. Michael repents, breaks up with Isabella, and tells Aldo he's going to confess to the police, not a priest. That, of course, would doom Aldo too. So Aldo silences Michael…forever."

"My goodness, that is very intriguing, my dear."

Once in the apartment, Marya bustled around to prepare the tea. The doorbell rang—two long and one short buzzes. Marya said, "I believe that is Tom Baker. Would you mind opening the door, my dear?"

Martha went downstairs and let in a tall, skinny kid, with blond hair that was shaved on half his head and hung down to his shoulders on the other half. She had not seen him since O'Hara had arrested him, wrongly of course, for breaking into Marya's apartment in connection with the murder she and Marya had solved. Other than the tattoos covering his entire left arm, he had not changed a bit. He was followed by a short, chubby boy with his hair gelled straight up who had not yet entered the throes of adolescence, and then by a handful of others tumbling in in such a confusion of arms, legs, and heads that Martha was not able to tell one from the other.

That tall kid, the leader of the gang, was a troublemaker. She had better warn Marya to stay away from him.

The group tromped up the stairs, one behind the other, and Martha followed. Marya greeted them with a big smile. "Hello, my dears. Hello, Tom. So nice to see all of you. Would you like some tea?"

There were mumbled "no"s and "uh uh"s all around. The boys started sniggering, but stopped at one sharp look from their tall, skinny leader.

"It is just as well because I do not have enough cups for everyone. Well then, perhaps a Werther's." Marya fumbled around in an eggplant-decorated jar and drew out a handful of Werther's Original caramel hard candies. She held them out and, following Tom Baker's lead, each of the boys stepped forward to take one.

Marya said to Tom, "Well my dear, have you and your…shall we call them deputies…discovered anything in your investigations?"

"H–yeah, I mean, yes ma'am, we did. A local pusher. He's called Pink Panther or Pink. Muddy knows him." Tom nodded at the dirtiest in the line of dirty boys. The boy stepped forward, nodded at Marya, and then stepped back.

"Muddy's mom buys jellybeans from him."

"Jellybeans? But Easter is not for months. Where does he find them? But we are not interested in candy. We—"

"Jellybeans, amps, you know, speed. Amphetamines. Just like Ms. Collins here got busted for."

Martha flinched, and she felt her cheeks turn hot. Marya had told these hoodlums about her drug bust!

"Pink peddles amps to the local rich crowd, so he fancies up his products. Sells 'em in those little pink sacks you described to me. He got popped about three months ago."

"Popped? My dear, you must—"

"Busted. Arrested. The pigs—"

"Tom!"

"Sorry, the cops confiscated a bunch of amps and a bunch of those little pink sacks. You asked about the fat p—"

"Tom." Marya shook her head.

"You asked about O'Hara. But he had nothing to do with the bust. It was another...cop that copped Pink. Pink's locked up. Awaiting trial."

"Thank you, my dears. I do believe that deserves a second Werther's." She held out the plastic bag, and each of the boys took one, Tom Baker last of all. Then they tumbled out of the room and down the stairs.

Marya looked after them, a fond smile on her face. "I call them Tom Baker's Street Boys. I asked them to find out about amphetamines that are being sold on the streets, and especially about that little pink bag in which your amphetamines were found."

"But, Mar, I still don't know what to do. And I have an appointment in a week with the lawyer to discuss it."

"That should be just enough time to decide, my dear. Would you mind calling Officer Chonkin and asking if she has another moment during one of her breaks to visit us?"

Martha obliged. "Hello, Officer Chonkin please. Not in today? No, I'd prefer not to leave a message. When will she next be in?"

Martha hung up. "Wouldn't tell me when she'd be in. Not 'police protocol.' If I were police commissioner…"

"You mean, when you *are* police commissioner."

Martha smiled at her friend. "Wish I were as sure as you are. Oh well. I'll call Chonkin tomorrow. Why do you want to talk to her? What are you thinking?"

"Oh, my dear. You know me. Right now my thoughts are all jumbled up in my head. I must organize them. Let us wait until we meet with Officer Chonkin."

# CHAPTER 18

Tuesday, November 15

"MY GOODNESS, YOU ARE BECOMING SO PRAYERFUL! I am glad you are taking Martin Luther's advice to heart, my dear."

Martha just nodded to Marya as they walked into church. She had decided that until they could come up with some other idea, they'd continue going to morning Mass to observe and interrogate whichever suspects attended. At least they would be doing *something*.

They spied Gertie holding court near the front of the nave. "… always wandering around church even after he's finished putting everything in order. And he's the sort of person who can't keep anything to himself." Gertie paused for a moment. "I wonder if they have female sacristans. Old Jerome's getting up in years, you know. Does anyone know if sacristans get paid? Anyway, I couldn't help but overhear him talking to Father Seamus. He said that the homeless person they arrested for killing Michael Ward was the same one who walked into church in the middle of Mass last Sunday! Can you imagine? We were all sitting in church with a murderer!"

The gasps were interrupted by the ding of the bell that announced the start of Mass and Father Peanuts's entry into the nave. The group around Gertie scattered to their seats.

As Ken walked to his regular pew, he announced for all to hear, "He desecrated God's house. I could sense his evil spirit when he walked by me in church."

The only suspects at church this morning were the Dies Irae crew,

Ken and Barbara Vance and Luz Flores, so Martha steered Marya to the pew behind them. The parishioners who had been attentive enough to open their missals and find the entrance antiphon intoned, "For the LORD watches over the way of the righteous, but the way of the wicked leads to destruction."

At the sign of peace, Barbara turned to Ken. Whatever had disturbed her so much that she'd refused her husband his usual cheek peck at the last Mass had blown over. Barbara then turned to Luz, but Luz could only manage a half smile and a nod.

Luz remained in church as everyone was leaving, so Martha told Marya to stick with her while she tailed Barbara and Ken. Ken held onto Barbara's forearm as they walked to their car, not saying a word, and drove away. Martha returned to church.

Luz had moved to the pew in front of the statue of Mary. Marya remained in her own pew. Both women knelt quietly, Marya with her eyes on the crucifix above the tabernacle, Luz with her eyes on Mary.

Martha sat down next to Marya. She noticed that the flowers on either side of the altar did not quite match, three white chrysanthemums in one vase, four in the other. The tabernacle cover was crooked, but she refrained from rearranging it, feeling it would interrupt the prayerful mood. Someone had left a bulletin on the pew in front of her. A Cheerio lay on the floor. She turned around to check the clock at the back of the church, compared it to her watch, and was pleased to see that the clock was no longer four minutes slow. She decided to say a prayer to Mary as Undoer of Knots to untie her knotty problem with the amphetamine stop. She couldn't remember the whole thing, only the part that said:

*Holy Mother, Mother of God and our Mother, to you who untie with a motherly heart the knots of our life, we pray to you to receive in your hands today this knot. I beg you to undo it for the glory of God, once and for all. You are my hope.*

She lost track of time as she discussed the problem with Mary. When she checked her watch again, five minutes and twenty-nine seconds had passed. No solution had come to mind, but somehow she felt more hopeful.

After fourteen minutes and seventeen seconds, Martha could no longer keep still. She left the pew, got the key from the sacristy, emptied the Saint Vincent de Paul poor boxes, counted the money, and then neatened up the already neat sacristy. She could not imagine how Marya and Luz could sit there doing nothing for—she looked at her watch—thirty-seven minutes and twenty-two seconds! Martha sat in the side chapel near the door to the parking lot and read, first the church bulletin—which she had already read on Sunday—and then the Bishop's Annual Appeal brochure which she herself had put on the table near the door. Luz and Marya were still just sitting there! As Martha circled the word "Advent" in the hidden word game placed in the bulletin to keep children occupied during Mass, she finally heard Luz stir. Luz walked toward the door, but Marya just sat, completely still. Enough was enough.

"Marya, I have to go." Martha thought her own voice sounded harsh and loud as it echoed through the church.

Luz looked over to see the source of the noise. There were tears on her face. Then Luz gazed at Marya, who still sat motionless in the pew as if she had not heard Martha.

Luz walked over and sat down next to Marya.

*Oh no, surely they aren't going to pray some more, are they?*

"Hello, Ms. Cook. I hadn't noticed that you were here."

"Why, hello, Luz. My goodness, you startled me. How are you, my dear?"

"I'm so sorry to have interrupted you. Do you have a moment?"

"Of course I do." She turned to Martha. "We are not in a hurry, are we, my dear?"

"Oh no, no. No rush at all. Just sitting here praying. After Mass. Prayers of thanksgiving. Stuff like that."

Marya smiled and turned back to Luz. "I was just talking over a few things with Jesus. He is such a good friend."

"Yes, he is. I was beseeching Mary's aid, and then when I got up, well, I heard your name. I feel somehow that you must be the answer to my prayers."

"Perhaps."

Luz's eyes filled with tears that trickled down her cheeks. "I don't know why I am so upset. I shouldn't be so upset. Do you know Aldo Todi?"

"Why yes, my dear, I do."

"Well, Aldo was admitted yesterday to the hospital because his emphysema has become worse. You know I'm an emergency room nurse there, so I visited him whenever I had time."

"That is very charitable of you, my dear. One of the corporal works of mercy is to visit the sick."

"Father Thaddeus wouldn't agree with you. He's directed me to stop checking in on Aldo." An impish smile lightened her features. "But I refused to heed him. During one of my visits, Aldo confessed that he's had a crush on me since elementary school." She blushed.

Luz looked...lovely. Like she had five years ago, when Martha used to see her walking hand in hand with her husband, laughing as their Basset Hound tugged at her leash trying to get to Quincy. Her husband's death had been hard on her, and her efforts to cope with the grief by throwing herself into Dies Irae did not seem to have brought any happiness back into her life.

"Aldo said he'd decided to move back to Pequot Bays as soon as he heard my husband died. He became a eucharistic minister and arranged to be assigned to the same Masses as me." She laughed. "I'd actually wondered about that because usually the assignments are alphabetical."

*When was the last time Luz had laughed?*

"He confessed that he'd joined Dies Irae only to see me. And became very involved when he saw how important it would be to me. Aldo said he wasn't allowed to tell me all the things he'd done for Father. But," she said with the same fleeting grin, "you know, I think

**187**

he'd have told me everything if I hadn't insisted he not break his vow. That's Aldo for you!" She laughed. "He hoped if Father Thaddeus liked him, then maybe I'd like him too. But he became furious and quit when he came to believe Father Thaddeus was taking advantage of me. Aldo said he wouldn't let anything or anybody harm me. And he said he'd do anything to get us together."

"Aldo thought that you and he could get together!" Martha said. "But that's impossible."

Luz turned toward Martha. "Why is that so impossible?"

"You and him? He's so...so...short."

Luz's eyes narrowed. "Yes, he is not a tall man."

"And well...not so good looking."

Luz crossed her arms.

"Beauty is in the eye of the beholder," Marya interjected.

"And...unpleasant."

Luz pressed her lips together and turned her back on Martha to face Marya.

"Martha, my dear, you are meandering from the topic at hand. I recall that Sister Anne Marie, my mathematics teacher in sixth grade, once said that the shortest distance between two points is a straight line. It did not have to do with mathematics though. She always spoke in mathematical terms even when it had nothing to do with mathematics. In this case, I was trying to explain why I had not done my homework and somehow found myself speaking about a cloud I had seen that quite reminded me of—"

"Meandering? Me?"

"Exactly. Always remember, short and to the point." Marya turned back to Luz. "So, my dear. What were you were saying about our generous friend Aldo?"

"After I got off work, I brought Father Thaddeus to give Aldo the sacraments. Father is such a saint. So good of him to go even though Aldo is speaking against Dies Irae. He even brought Aldo homemade chocolate chip cookies someone had given him. I returned after I took Father Thaddeus home." Luz gave a lopsided grin. "I visited him again even though Father told me to polish the candlesticks for the evening service. I bumped into Dr. Ianelli—you know, he's Aldo's doctor—as he was leaving the room. Dr. Ianelli told me it's good Aldo finally quit smoking, but…but…it may be too late. Aldo had taken a turn for the worse by the time I returned." Luz burst into tears. "In the hospital…" She took a gasping breath to control her crying. "Aldo told me that he thanked God for his emphysema. Because in the hospital he could see me every day."

"Mr. Todi's suffering has brought him great wisdom, my dear. As Saint Paul said to the Thessalonians, 'Give thanks in all circumstances.'"

Her eyes filled with tears again. "Ken is driving Father to the hospital today so that he can give Aldo Last Rites."

"I will keep him in my prayers, my dear."

"Thank you, Ms. Cook. I am sure your prayers will help." Luz took a deep breath and pulled herself upright. "But I don't know how I got to talking about Aldo. That is not what I wanted to speak to you about."

"What did you want to speak to me about, my dear?"

"It's our mutual friend, John. Did you know he's been arrested for the murder of poor Michael Ward?"

"Yes, my dear, I did."

"Everyone in church today seemed happy, relieved almost, to hear that poor John has been arrested. Ken certainly was. I'm sure he'll say the same thing about John as he did about Aldo. At evening prayer last night, Ken said it was God's judgement that Aldo is so sick. That he was being punished for talking against Dies Irae." Luz shook her head. "Oh, here I am, talking about Aldo again. What I wanted to say was that I know John didn't murder Michael Ward."

"And how do you know that?"

"He just couldn't have. He has kind eyes."

"I do not believe he did it either. Although for other reasons."

"I knew you'd agree. But, you know, there's nothing we can do about it. It's hopeless."

"Young lady," Marya said in such steely tones that both Martha's and Luz's heads shot up in attention. "Never, never lose hope. Perhaps you and I alone can do nothing, but with God all things are possible. Or as my mother, God rest her soul, would say, 'It ain't over till it's over.'"

"I think that's a quote from Yogi Berra," Martha said.

"Yogi Berra? No, my dear. My mother never spoke of a Yogi Berra, and I am sure she would not have used a Hindu or Buddhist quote. Mother was always careful to adhere to the Christian tradition."

Luz touched Marya's arm and said, "Thank you for your wise words, Ms. Cook. I shall not lose hope." She gave Martha a brusque nod and left the church.

M&M

When she arrived home, Martha called the police station. Chonkin was in.

"Marya asked me to call and see if you could come over some time today."

There was a pause before Chonkin said softly, "I will come over on my lunch break. That's from 12:00 to 1:00."

Martha called Marya. "Officer Chonkin is coming over at noon."

"Perfect, my dear. Would you mind very much picking up some up some McVitie's digestive biscuits on your way here?"

Martha arrived at 11:30. When Marya opened the door, she said, "Thank you my dear, for getting these delicious biscuits. Here is the three dollars and twenty five cents." She held the money ready in her hand.

"Oh, not necessary, Marya."

"It *is* necessary." She again held out the three dollars and one quarter. Martha took it, and Marya nodded. "Thank you, my dear."

Marya scurried around as she had the last time Chonkin came over, and Martha pitched in by getting the tea service ready. Marya positioned the biscuits in a circle on a china plate. Then she tottered over to a large box she had placed in front of the sofa, covered it with a hydrangea-decorated apron, and placed the cookie plate on the box. She stood back to admire the effect. "That will do quite nicely, don't you think, my dear?"

"Very nice, Marya. The biscuits are a good idea. I'm impressed that Chonkin is giving up her lunch hour for us."

"Indeed, my dear."

The doorbell rang, and Marya insisted on going down the stairs to answer it herself. "After all, she is my guest, and it is only proper. My mother, God rest her soul…" The clunk of Marya's cane as she negotiated the stairs drowned out the rest of her remarks.

After Marya performed her tea ceremony, she picked up the plate and held it out to Martha and Chonkin, seated in their respective places on the sofa.

"Thank you for the cookie, Ms. Cook."

"It is a McVitie's digestive biscuit, my dear, not a cookie. They are more substantial than cookies, and since you were good enough to come over on your lunch hour, I did not want you to be hungry. My sister and I used to bake biscuits on—"

"Ms. Cook, what did you want to see me about?"

"So sorry, my dear. Yes. I will be," she glanced at Martha, "short and to the point." Marya walked over to the table and picked up several index cards that she had placed next to the sugar and creamer. "I received poor grades in extemporaneous speaking in eighth grade, and the nuns suggested I use note cards when giving a speech in front of the class. I found that quite helpful."

Marya stood up as straight as she could, fighting against her aging posture. She looked quite like she was reciting in front of a class of eighth graders.

Marya read the title of the first card out loud. "The Drug Stop."

Martha cringed. She had thought this meeting was going to be about the murders.

"Officer Milton left the police station with a briefcase while Martha and I waited in a windowless conference room. When he returned, he said, '*Lasciate agne Speranza, vol ch'entate,*' which means—"

"Abandon all hope ye who enter here," Chonkin supplied.

"Quite correct, my dear." Marya looked back down at the card. "Lieutenant O'Hara brought in our statements as soon as Henry returned. Only moments after we left the station, Martha was stopped for the air freshener violation. Lieutenant O'Hara, who just happened to be with Officer Milton, approached the passenger side, requested I roll down my window, watched as I opened the glove compartment, and grabbed the pink sack as it fell out." She turned to Martha. "Please tell our guest what happened next."

"Well, O'Hara told Henry to give me two summonses."

"And then?" Marya said.

"He just handed them to me. Right away."

"Did he write them out in front of you?"

"No. He had them ready before the stop."

"You see, Officer Chonkin," Marya said, "those summonses had already been prepared."

Marya put down *The Drug Stop* card, picked up the *Tom Baker's Street Boys* card, and explained about the Pink Panther amphetamine drug bust and the pink sacks he used.

When she was through, Marya walked to her chair and sat down. She looked so pleased with herself that Martha could not help but say, "You did an excellent job, Marya," in a tone not unlike her own eighth grade teacher's, Sister Victoire, the only nun remaining at Sacred Heart Academy when she had received her own Catholic school education.

Martha and Marya both looked at Chonkin, who sat impassively. Then she said, "So what you're saying is that Lieutenant O'Hara planted some of the amphetamines and one of the pink sacks from the drug bust of the Pink Panther on Ms. Collins."

"Exactly," Marya said.

Chonkin looked at her watch. "I have to go. Thank you for the tea and the biscuit, Ms. Cook."

# CHAPTER 19

Wednesday, November 16

THE NEXT DAY, WHILE MARTHA SAT ON A BENCH watching Quincy play with the other dogs at the dog run, her cell phone rang. She hoped it was Christopher, but it was Marya.

"Hello, hello, may I speak to Martha Collins please."

"This is Martha Collins. Hello, Mar. Have you heard from Chonkin?"

"No, my dear. So sorry. They have posted the date for Mr. Ward's funeral. It is tomorrow. I must speak to you before then."

"We're speaking now, Marya."

"Oh, you are so funny, my dear. Of course, you are right, we are speaking right now. But I am not so very comfortable speaking on the telephone as I am in person. Would it be possible for you to come over here today?"

"Sure. I'll be over in half an hour."

She dropped Quincy at home and went to Marya's. As the two women limped up the stairs together, Marya said, "Thank you so much for rushing over here. How is your ankle, my dear? You seem to be doing a bit better on the stairs."

"It's coming along. Thinking of cancelling my appointment with Dr. Ianelli."

"Oh no, my dear, you must not do that. It is important to make sure the ankle is healed properly. And then there may be some physical therapy or lotion that he may recommend. My mother, God rest her soul, prepared arnica flowers in oil to treat the bruises of my sister and me. There are some preparations I have seen in Myles Pharmacy that still use arnica. Perhaps I will get that for you. And then you could use my hot water bottle also. I have a compression stocking, my dear, that—"

"No, no, that won't be necessary, Marya. I'll go to my appointment."

Martha smoothed out the grape-patterned dish towel on the sofa and sat down, noticing that she had not been granted the honor of a tea party, but she kept this observation to herself. Marya sat as usual on the folding chair by the table.

"What's this all about, Mar?"

"Oh, my dear, you now know that you must be vigilant, and I shall also take great care that you are not placed in any real danger. Certainly, I would never want that. Why, I would miss you very much if anything should happen to you. I have so enjoyed becoming friends with—"

"Mar, I feel pretty sure that you don't want me dead. What are you talking about?" But Martha had an inkling of what Marya was up to. *No, never, no way.*

"Quite so, my dear. Let me explain. You were so very successful in persuading the killer you had nothing to do with the scene outside the church after Mr. Bonino's funeral and that you had no suspicions about murder that he or she felt comfortable enough to kill again. You and I must go to poor Mr. Ward's funeral, my dear."

"Sure, Marya. I'll take you to the funeral." But that was all she would do.

"And, my dear, I must present another 'scene.'"

Well then, it would have to be a monologue. "You're not talking about a scene like last time, are you?" Martha would have nothing to do with it. She had almost died—twice.

"Exactly, just as at Mr. Bonino's funeral."

"Oh, Marya. I…I…"

"And to think I was concerned you would not agree to my little scheme. We can leave the funeral a bit early and then, when everyone else is leaving, we will have our scene. I do hope that all of our suspects will be present, but if not, we can reenact it for the absentees at another time. Mr. Todi of course will not be there, since he, poor man, is in the hospital and very sick, so he poses no threat at the present time. Now, my dear, shall we start writing our script? I have always been interested in the theater. When my sister and I were young, we were both involved in plays at school. She would star in the musicals, of course. Such a lovely voice, like an angel. I myself, however, was not gifted with a talent for musicianship. You may have noticed that in church I sing very softly."

Martha had not noticed Marya singing softly but had noticed her singing off key.

"So instead of musicals, my dear, I would try out for plays. The height of my theatrical career was when I played the part of Emily in *Our Town*."

Martha was barely listening. *By the hair of Saint Glyceria. A scene.* Martha thought for a moment about Saint Glyceria. Beaten, starved, and roasted. And all Marya wanted from Martha was enough faith to take part in an embarrassing scene so that they could catch a murderer.

"So shall we plan our little drama, my dear? As they say in Hollywood, 'Lights, camera, action.' And you do so like action."

"In front of everyone?"

"Of course, my dear. That is the point of the scene."

"That would include, most likely, my doctor, the respected and beloved Dr. Ianelli, his wife Bitsy, who is the center of social life at Saint John's, Ken and Barbara Vance, and Luz, who know all the same eucharistic ministers and lectors at Saint John's that I do, and Gertie, who 'can't help but overhear' and tell everyone about everything? And all the rest of the suspects, the funeral committee, the priests, the undertaker, and anyone else who cares to come to the funeral?"

"Yes, my dear. We must rehearse very well. Thespians always hope for a large audience," Marya tittered.

Martha paused and took a deep breath. "What possible objection could I have to such a plan, Marya?" Gazing at Marya's bright eyes and merry upturned lips, Martha began to grin, and then laugh. Marya joined in.

"But this time, my dear, we will make sure that you are protected from any murder attempts."

"And you too, Mar."

"Yes, I will take care, but for some reason it appears that they do not consider me a serious threat. I cannot imagine why." Marya picked up a purple feather boa lying on the table next to her and wound it twice around her neck. "It's a bit cool in here, is it not? My mother, God rest her soul, always told my sister and me that we must keep our throats and our heads covered against any chill." From the pocket of her sweater, Marya removed a violet wool knit cap festooned with lavender bows and pulled it down over her ears.

"No. Can't imagine why they don't take you seriously, Mar."

"Now, my dear, what can we do to keep you from harm?"

"Well…I've got Quincy to protect me." Martha thought about sweet, friendly Quincy who slept through fireworks on the Fourth of July and greeted all strangers—dogs or humans—with ferocious tail-wagging. The only thing she attacked was the giveitheck.

"And I've got a gun too."

Marya's eyes widened. "A gun, my dear?"

"Yup. Haven't thought of it in a long time. It's locked in a safety box in my closet. As police commissioner, it's easy to get approved for a license to carry a concealed handgun. So I applied for one. Practiced a bunch at the PBPD shooting range. I became a pretty good shot. Glock 19. Won't fit in this," Martha motioned at her cross-body bag, "so I used to carry a bigger purse."

"That will do very well, my dear."

After the two of them worked out their respective parts for the scene, Martha left. She had just stepped into the door to her apartment when her cell phone buzzed.

"Hello, hello. May I please speak to Martha Collins?"

"Hi, Mar. It's Martha."

"I just received a telephone call from Officer Chonkin. She has a break in thirty minutes and would like to come over to talk to us. Is it possible for you to interrupt your busy day to come back over and meet with her?"

Martha limped to her car as fast as her bad ankle and cane would allow and raced right back to Marya's apartment. Ten minutes after she arrived, the buzzer rang, and Martha hobbled downstairs to let in Officer Chonkin. Her face gave nothing away.

After Chonkin and Martha were settled on the sofa, and after Marya made her prolonged apologies for not having enough time to make tea, Chonkin said, "That's all right, Ms. Cook. I'm not thirsty." After an awkward pause, she continued, "What you said about Ms. Collins's drug bust made sense. It explained how Lieutenant O'Hara treated me when you were in the conference room that day to sign your statements. He made sure I didn't follow Milton—and the lieutenant had ordered me to follow him everywhere—so Milton was free to go out, jimmy the lock on your car, and plant the amphetamines. It explained why he took such an interest in the case and brought the statements to you himself, something that a lieutenant doesn't normally do. It explained why he was riding with Milton. He never goes out on patrol. I also remember Lieutenant O'Hara saying to the guys after you were busted that this would put the kibosh on your plans to run for police commissioner again."

Martha nodded. She'd always known that was the reason for the bust.

"I decided I'd poke around. I'm a newbie here, so it wouldn't be unusual to ask some general questions about the procedures around the station house. But I had to be careful. O'Hara can be a dangerous enemy."

"That's for sure."

Chonkin continued, "I'd heard about Pink. It was before my time, and I didn't know the details. Lieutenant Lopez made the bust. He's a good guy and happy to talk about it. He told me exactly how many sacks were confiscated. You know, the captain's retiring and both lieutenants, Lopez and O'Hara, are vying for the promotion. Lopez hopes the bust put him in the lead."

Martha shuddered at the thought of Captain O'Hara.

"The confiscated drugs in their little pink sacks are kept in the evidence room at the police station. There are strict protocols to get into the evidence room. Only lieutenants and up can get the keys, and two police officers have to go in at a time. They sign for a key to the evidence room, and then there's a separate key for the particular evidence drawer they're interested in. I checked the sign-in sheet. The day before Ms. Collins's bust, O'Hara signed for the key to the evidence room and for a key to another drawer, not for the Pink evidence, but the one right next to it. Milton signed in to go with him. Once they sign in, they go get the drawer keys themselves, so it would be easy to take the key to whatever drawer they wanted. There's a video camera recording everything that goes on in the room."

"A video camera! That's it! We've got him!" Martha said.

"Wouldn't be so sure of that, Ms. Collins. Lieutenant O'Hara is not a stupid man. He'd never let himself be captured on video stealing something from an evidence drawer."

"Well, did you see it? What did it show?"

"I can't ask to review the video. It would be a highly unusual request. The lieutenant would hear about it."

"Then why don't you tell Lopez about it? He'll check and see that the amphetamines are missing, and then he'll get the tape."

"I thought of that, but what if no amphetamines are missing? Lieutenant O'Hara would have my head."

"Well, how about if I tell my lawyer? Maybe she can get the tape."

"We have no proof. It's all conjecture. The chance of convincing a judge to order a police station to turn over the tape to a criminal defense lawyer is zero. Anything I find out about this, I need to handle my way."

Martha's heart sank. "Then we have nothing."

Chonkin looked at her watch. "Got to go."

# CHAPTER 20

## Thursday, November 17

THE FUNERAL OF MICHAEL WARD WAS SUCH A HEART-rending affair that Martha was too caught up to watch her suspects during the sign of peace. Uncontrollable sobbing from Justin, so suddenly an orphan, echoed in the nave during the entire Mass. His beloved mother lost to him just months ago, and now his father. He was only a year older than Martha had been when she was orphaned at nineteen, and she had shared his inability to be consoled by the promise that he would meet his parents in heaven.

Father Thaddeus intoned, "To you, O Lord, we commend the soul of Michael Ward, your servant. In the sight of this world he is now dead; in your sight may he live forever. Forgive whatever sins he committed through human weakness, and in your goodness, grant him everlasting peace. We ask this through Christ our Lord. Amen.

"In peace let us take our brother to his place of rest. May choirs of angels welcome you and lead you to the bosom of Abraham; and where Lazarus is poor no longer may you find eternal rest."

The organ thundered with the opening chords of "Dies Irae" as the coffin was rolled down the center aisle. It seemed to Martha that even the saints in the stained-glass windows were shaken by the heavy bass notes.

Martha prayed. She prayed that the solemnity of the occasion, the dramatic music, and the weeping of the bereaved young man would stir the heart of the killer, that his remorse would cause him to reveal his awful guilt to the gathered mourners, and justice would have its way—and the mortifying "scene" Marya had planned would not be necessary.

She scanned the suspects in the pews in front of her to see if a guilty expression would betray one of them.

Barbara Vance sat huddled with Luz Flores, leaving a large space between herself and her husband. Ken made a comment to Barbara, who ignored him and continued speaking to Luz. Seemingly unaffected by his wife's snub, Ken turned his gaze toward Father Thaddeus, who looked back at him, both with unyielding expressions, as if they were the instruments of God's judgment prepared to lead the damned to their eternal punishment.

Isabella Bonino sat alone, her mascara unsmeared by tears. She wore a simple black dress, not as skin-baring or close-fitting as the one she'd worn at her husband's funeral. Martha could not make out the emotion behind her icy stare. Dr. Ianelli, present as always at the funerals of his patients, wore his customary solicitous expression and three-piece suit. He sat next to his wife Bitsy, who looked down her nose at the gathered mourners as though she herself sat in judgment of her inferiors. Gertie Doppeldecker peeked out from the sacristy door, the expression on her face hidden in the shadows.

Justin walked behind the coffin as the pallbearers wheeled it toward the rear doors and the final stop in Michael's earthly journey. His eyes scanned the church as he continued crying like a little boy who suddenly found himself alone in a strange place. Martha could not tear her eyes from him as she relived her own walk down the same aisle following two caskets toward two waiting hearses.

The gathered mourners stirred and began to rise from their pews, calling Martha back to her senses. She recalled with an unpleasant jolt that she and Marya had a scene to enact now. They had not left the funeral Mass early to set up for it, as they had planned. She looked over at Marya, who was watching her with concern. "Are you all right, my dear? This must be difficult for you."

Tears welled up in Martha's eyes. "I'm fine, Mar." She stood up and took a deep breath. "Now, we'd better get moving."

Marya gathered her belongings, quickly for once, and tap-tap-tapped down the side aisle. Martha followed behind, her cane echoing after Marya's. A young couple smirked at the old woman. A child poked his mother and pointed at her. Marya had on the hat she always wore to funerals, a felt cloche covered with purple grapes hanging rakishly over one side almost down to her shoulder, with a purple net covering her face like a bridal veil. She wore a dark violet and black striped sweater over black pants, which surprised Martha until she realized that a purple ribbon ran down either leg. Her ever-present lilac raincoat was covered with a deep purple macrame fringed shawl. Oh well, at least she looked a little more subdued than usual.

They passed Isabella Bonino who was standing, arms folded over her chest, unmoving, glaring at Father Thaddeus as he walked toward the sacristy. Martha had no trouble reading the emotion behind that expression. Pure, unadulterated hate.

Martha and Marya situated themselves facing each other under the portico, and Martha removed two note cards from her pocket. The first was laminated with purple handwriting. Marya had given it to her after their "rehearsal" the previous night.

> *Pray, hope, and don't worry.*
> *Saint Pio*

Martha prayed and hoped but could not stop worrying.

The second notecard was in her own handwriting and contained the lines for the scene they were about to enact.

Martha took a deep breath. She had made a commitment, and she always kept her commitments.

People began to exit the church. At the appearance of the first suspect, Isabella Bonino, they began Marya's "little drama." Martha had the first line. "But Marya, how can we be sure it was not the homeless person who committed the murder?" Even to her own ears, Martha sounded wooden and unbelievable.

"You are an interfering monster. *Tu sei il diavolo.*" Martha froze as she heard Isabella Bonino shrieking, then slowly turned.

Isabella's back was to her. She had not screamed at Martha but at Father Thaddeus, who had emerged from the sacristy. Ken Vance was with him.

"*È tutta colpa tua.* How dare you interfere with us. We were meant for each other." She looked around wildly at the group that had gathered around her. "*Non capisci.* You don't understand, God created us to be together."

Ken grabbed the priest's arm and pulled him toward the parking lot. Isabella continued her rant. "*E tu*, Ken. You brute. What are you going to do with his money? Buy an even bigger house? Maybe on Pequot Island this time."

Ken Vance stopped, just steps from Martha and Marya, keeping his back to Isabella.

"Johnny always said you're not the saint you pretend to be. He knew you put all our money to good use. For yourself! He called it 'funny business.'"

Ken turned and slowly folded his arms across his chest. His huge biceps looked to be the size of Isabella's waist. He took a threatening step toward Isabella, but then stumbled and fell. Over Marya's cane.

Ken said, "How dare you!" Martha was not sure whether he was speaking to Isabella or Marya.

Isabella's skin grew mottled. Her hands shook. She began to laugh. Luz Flores walked over and took her arm.

The emotion drained from Isabella's face, and it took a moment before she could focus on Luz. "Luz. You get away while you can. Before it's too late. Go with your Aldo."

Luz's eyes widened. She gave a quick glance at Father Thaddeus and then looked away.

The priest took a step toward Luz, glancing down to make sure that there was nothing in his way. "Luz," he said in a low, command-ing voice.

She looked at him, and this time she did not look away. Her hand dropped from Isabella's arm.

He nodded at her. "Good. Now come."

Isabella moved between Luz and Father Thaddeus. "Don't listen to him, Luz. He'll ruin everything for you like he did for me." Isabella laughed and shook her head bitterly. "That I should help Aldo. *Mi disapprovava*. He disapproved of me. He's as much to blame as the *padre* here. And Michael left him even more money than he left those two thieves."

Ken's voice cracked as he said, "That idiot left…" He cleared his throat and started again in a deeper voice, "That idiot left Todi mon-ey? How do you know that?"

"*Si*. Johnny was Michael's lawyer. And Johnny told me every-thing. *Tutto!*" Isabella turned and strode away, hips swaying, back toward the church.

Luz stood, her eyes darting back and forth between Isabella and Father Thaddeus.

Father Thaddeus grasped Ken's arm and whispered to him. The priest then regarded Luz, his eyes narrowed to slits, and with a quick jerk of the head, motioned that she should come to him. Father Thaddeus and Ken strode toward the building that housed the parish center and Father Thaddeus. The priest did not even bother to turn around and make sure that Luz followed.

She did, head down, shoulders stooped.

Marya poked Martha with her cane. "What was it that you were saying about the murder?"

Martha had hoped and prayed that the interruption would make it impossible for them to carry on with their little drama, but that was not to be.

*Thanks a bunch, Saint Pio.*

Martha looked down at her card and started over. "But Marya, how can we be sure it was not the homeless person who committed the murder?"

Marya peered dramatically from left to right and then said very loudly, "Shh. We cannot let anyone hear us. We have solved one crime before, my dear. We have captured one murderer. What we saw today will surely help us catch another one."

The onlookers' heads snapped from Isabella to Marya. Ken, Father Thaddeus, and Isabella all stopped in their tracks. Martha forgot to say her next line. Marya stood expectantly, and poked Martha with her cane.

Martha said, "Yes, what we saw today will surely help us catch the true murderer."

"I'm sorry, my dear, I can't quite hear you. Could you speak louder?"

"Yes, what we saw today will surely help us find the true murderer."

"I am sorry, I still cannot hear you."

Martha yelled, "Yes, what we saw today will surely help us find the true murderer," and then stomped off into the parking lot, her embarrassment overcoming the pain in her ankle.

She waited for Marya in the safety of her car. But Marya did not follow her.

The parking lot was now almost empty, but Marya had still not tap-tap-tapped over to the car. Martha rechecked her watch. She had been waiting five minutes and forty-two seconds. Even Marya should have made it by now.

Martha froze. What if their little scene had already worked? What if the murderer had attacked Marya? What if she was lying on the ground somewhere right now? Martha threw open the car door and did a cane-assisted limp/run across the parking lot to the portico, but Marya was nowhere to be seen. She rushed into the side chapel that led to the main church, now dimmed, incense from the funeral leaving its mysterious fragrance. She heard moaning. Martha dashed into the nave. With a rush of relief, she saw Marya and Isabella seated together in front of the statue of Mary. Isabella was weeping.

Martha sat down a few rows behind them.

Marya patted Isabella's hand. "Now, now, my dear."

Isabella raised a mascara-streaked face to Marya. "I was fourteen when I first met Johnny. *Una bambina*. Living in a dying village. Everyone who could leave, left. I was eighteen when he asked my parents for my hand. I said okay. Anything to get out of that place. Johnny was fifty-three. An old man. He brought me here. Then I met Michael. I knew we were meant to be together. *Era il destino*. Lisa and Johnny, they were just…they were just in the way. And then, after they were gone, we could get married…" Her sobbing interrupted her story. "But nothing turned out like it was supposed to after Johnny and Lisa died."

"You are young, my dear. One day you will learn that we are not in control, God is."

"Then I am mad at Father Thaddeus *and* God."

"My dear, God is good. It is a blessing that Mr. Ward died so soon after going to confession, cleansed of his sins. Perhaps you might want to go to confession as well, my dear."

Isabella shook her head. "No, *Signora* Cook. *Grazie per la tua simpatia*. But I will never apologize to God. I want an apology from *Him*." Isabella stood up and stomped out of church.

Marya turned to Martha. "You did an excellent job on our little drama, my dear."

"That's it, Marya. That's the last one. No more scenes."

"No more shall be necessary, my dear. I am preparing for the final act. Today is a very busy day. I must go to the library and Maguire's funeral home."

Martha did not ask about the visit to Maguire's. They had just baited a cold-blooded killer, and it would be just like Marya to plan her funeral in advance. There would be no one to make the arrangements after she died and, anyway, Marya liked funerals.

Martha was quiet the rest of the way to Main Street. She realized there would be no one to plan her own funeral either.

Before getting out of the car, Marya turned to Martha. "You must take great care, my dear. Keep your phone near you and let me know if any one of our suspects approaches you. Carry your pistol with you always. It will not be long now before I have all the pieces to the puzzle."

On her way home, Martha stopped at Sam's Farm and Fish Store. As she tugged on one of the nesting grocery carts, Isabella walked in and stopped in front of the Italian parsley. She looked like she had recovered from her outburst after the funeral. Her eye makeup was immaculate again. She started walking toward Martha. Why hadn't she gone home to get her gun first! Martha glanced around. There were lots of other people in the store, and all the men had their eyes locked on Isabella. Way too public for a murder attempt.

"Ah, hello, Isabella."

"Sorry I was so upset after the funeral. I don't know what came over me."

"That's all right. Funerals are tough."

"I heard what you said to *Signora* Cook. How do you know that the homeless man didn't kill Michael?"

"Um. I'd rather not talk about it right now." She and Marya had not discussed how to answer that question.

Isabella looked down at the wilted bunch of Italian parsley in her hand. "Well, I'm finished with my shopping. Could you come to my home for *caffe* so we could talk about it?"

"No, sorry. Busy. Very busy. Maybe tomorrow." Martha turned her grocery cart around and wheeled to the cheese section, for once happy to be surrounded by pushing and shoving patrons with their carts as they vied for the odiferous cheeses in the narrow aisles.

Once she saw Isabella leave, she went to the checkout line, loaded up her car, and drove home. No one in sight. She let out a sigh of relief as she locked the door.

Her cell phone rang. Local, but she did not recognize the number. "Hello?"

"Hello, Martha, this is Bitsy Ianelli."

"Oh. Bitsy."

"Steven's receptionist is out, so he asked me to call and reschedule your Monday appointment. I need him at home to talk to a contractor. We're redoing the master bath. How's tomorrow instead? He usually does his dictation for a few hours on Saturdays, but he'll take a break to see you. How's 3:00?"

"Aw, that's nice of him, but he doesn't need to do that. My ankle is doing really well. I probably don't need to see him at all."

"No, I'm sure Steven wouldn't agree with that. He's concerned about your hypertensive episode. And he's already upset at me for taking him away from work. He'll really be mad if I can't reschedule his appointments. You know Steven. He's so devoted."

"That he is. Well, okay. I'll see him Saturday at 3:00."

"Great, Martha. I'll mark you down. Bye."

The cell rang again as soon as Martha hung up. "Hello?"

"Hi, Martha, it's Luz Flores."

"Hi, Luz. What's up?"

"Father Thaddeus wants to invite you to a meeting this afternoon."

"A meeting?"

"Yes. He'd like to speak to you personally about joining Dies Irae. You see, Father has the spiritual gift of the ability to read souls. And he sees great potential in you."

"Great potential? For what?"

There was a pause and murmuring in the background before Luz said, "He sees strength in you. Strength that can be harnessed for good."

"Well, thanks, but no thanks. I'm busy today."

More murmuring. "How about tomorrow?"

"I'll see. Bye." Martha hung up before Luz could say anything else.

She spent the rest of the day cleaning her already spotless apartment, with the first order of business cleaning and oiling her gun and transferring the contents of her small bag to a larger tote. Martha was in the process of making her pre-dinner cosmo when the phone rang. Was it Christopher?

"Hello, hello. May I speak to Martha Collins?"

"This *is* Martha Collins."

"Oh, hello, my dear. This is Marya Cook."

"I know."

"I am so sorry to bother you, but would it be possible for you to come over? I would like to show you something."

Martha looked at her bottles of vodka, triple sec, cranberry juice, and lime set out in a line on her kitchen counter and sighed. "Sure. Be right there." She grabbed her tote and left the condo. On the way to the car, she kept her hand on the gun in the tote and rotated her head from side to side, checking for possible assailants.

No one tailed her, shot at her, or crashed into her on her way to Marya's apartment. Marya greeted her at the door. Martha stepped inside and closed the door behind her.

"Hello, my dear. Thank you for coming."

"Needed to talk to you anyway. Our plan is working, Mar. I've become extremely popular since we put on our little drama after the funeral. Isabella invited me for coffee, Luz invited me to a meeting with the whole Dies Irae gang, and I even got a call from Bitsy changing my appointment to Saturday at three, when Dr. Ianelli usually does his dictation. That just leaves Gertie and Aldo, and Aldo's in the hospital. We have to figure out a plan. How we're going to trap them."

"Very good, my dear. We shall arrange our meetings with the suspects."

Once upstairs, Martha sat on the sofa while Marya cleared away several piles of papers on the table and uncovered a jigsaw puzzle of a purple unicorn. "My dear grandnephew gave me this jigsaw puzzle. I wanted to show it to you."

"You brought me over here to show me a jigsaw puzzle?"

"Although I prefer crossword puzzles, I find a good jigsaw puzzle stimulating also. I must have started this one months ago. It is almost complete but is missing two pieces. I am sure they are around here somewhere. I certainly did not throw them away."

Martha looked around the apartment. Yes, Marya was not one to throw things away.

Marya set her jaw. "And I will not take this puzzle apart until I have found them! You see, my dear, like the two missing pieces of my puzzle, there were two little things that needed to be explained about the circumstances surrounding our murders. And, as you know, it is the little things that are important. I had been thinking all along that I had missed something. A clue to the murder. Fortunately, at the funeral yesterday, I did not miss missing it again."

"You did not miss missing what again?"

"You look puzzled, my dear. Ah, another delightful turn of phrase. 'Puzzled.' You don't look like a puzzle, but you look like you are looking at a particularly difficult puzzle. I do love—"

"Mar. The very important thing you missed. Please."

"Ah, yes. Let me be clearer, so that you will no longer be 'puzzled.'" She tittered. "Do you play checkers, my dear?"

Crossword puzzles, jigsaw puzzles, and now checkers. Would Marya ever stop playing games and get to the point?

"No. I don't play checkers."

"That is a shame. One day I will teach you. A few days ago, I was playing checkers with a friend. I was not concentrating because I was thinking about how I could prove who the murderer was, so I did not see a double jump right in front of me. My friend, who is a very competitive person, did not inform me about my mistake until I removed my hand from the checker and he had begun his own turn. I did not allow that mistake to happen again, and later on in the game, I double jumped him and won. Now do you understand, my dear?"

"No."

"At the funeral yesterday, even though the clue was right in front of me, I almost missed missing it again. But I didn't. And it led me to one of the missing pieces of the puzzle."

"What did you not miss missing?"

Marya began to shuffle through her lilac-covered bag. She brought out, however, not one of her laminated notecards, but a laminated, grainy copy of a part of a blown up photograph of…of…some sort of an object.

"What is this, Marya?"

"A close-up photograph of the charm that was removed from Mr. Bonino's neck at the wake."

Martha examined the photograph more closely. "So it is. I'd forgotten about that. How did you get this?"

"Why, at the library, my dear. Pequot Bays has such a lovely library. So much more pleasant than goggling."

"So, the charm is one of your little pieces. Is it important?"

"Perhaps. That depends on the second little thing that—"

The doorbell rang. Two long buzzes and one short.

"Ah. Here are my guests. They are right on time. Would you mind answering the door for me, my dear? My knees are acting up today. I hope you brought an umbrella with you. I am sure it is going to…"

Martha went downstairs and opened the door. Tom Baker strolled by her without a word, the half of his head with the long hair toward her so she could not see his face. He was holding a little boy by the arm who looked to be about nine or ten. His mousy, curly hair was rumpled and dirty and too long. His clothes were rumpled and dirty and too small. Tom hoisted him up the stairs by the arm.

"Hello, my dears. So nice of you to come. How are you, Tom? I hope you have been attending school more regularly and doing your homework as we discussed."

Tom said, "This is the kid. Take off your hat, Socks."

"Oh no, my dear, you certainly don't have to take off your socks."

Martha looked down at the kid's socks, yellow with green dinosaurs and clearly visible under his jeans, which were three inches too short.

"Only your hat, my dear."

"His name's Socks."

"Oh, that is quite funny, Tom. Have you ever heard of Abbot and Costello? Perhaps that was a bit before your time, but my mother told my sister and me about them. They were comedians and had a very funny routine. Abbot, or was it Costello, begins by saying, 'Who's on first?' Then Costello, or was it Abbot, says, 'Who's on first?' And then Abbot, or maybe Costello, says, 'What's the name of the person on first.' And then Costello or Abbot says, 'What's on second. I Don't Know who's on third.'" Marya paused. "I cannot recall the name of the person on fourth base, or I would go through the whole routine for you. Perhaps his name was 'I cannot recall.'" Marya tittered.

The two boys looked mystified.

Marya removed her Werther's Original caramel candies from her lilac bag and held them out to the boys. Tom took one and then elbowed the little boy, who reached in and took his own.

"Socks set off the firecracker in the funeral home, Ms. Cook."

"Young man, that is a very dangerous thing to do. I knew a boy who played with firecrackers during school hours at Saint John's, and one went off in his hand. Two of his fingers were blown away. He learned to write left-handed, but the sisters did not find that an adequate excuse for his illegible handwriting. I recall that Sister Michael Gabriel made him write a three-page essay five times before she would accept it. He said an older student had given him the firecracker and told him to set it off, but the sisters would not accept that as an excuse either. Sister Marie Therese made him stay after class and write 100 times on the blackboard, 'I will not set off firecrackers.' So, you see, there can be severe consequences to playing with fireworks. How about you, young man? Did anyone give you the firecracker?"

"Nah. I know a kid who sells 'em. Five for a dollar." He looked down at his hands. "I'm left-handed anyway."

"Why at the wake, young man?"

"You know, everyone's so gloomy when somebody dies. I figured it'd be killer."

"Killer?"

"He means dope," Tom said.

"Dope?"

"He means fun," Martha said.

Marya smiled. "Ah, yes. We would say 'a gas' in my day." Her stern expression returned. "But it was not a gas, young man. Do you still have any of those firecrackers left?"

His right hand went into his pocket. He looked away from Marya, said, "No," and started skulking toward the stairs.

"Young man," Marya said in her steely tones.

He stopped, and his head shot up.

"Give me the firecrackers."

He glared at Marya but took a scrawny fist out of his pocket and dropped three firecrackers into Marya's outstretched hand.

"All of them."

He removed four more and gave them to Marya.

"Thank you. You may go now." Marya picked up the bag of Werther's and held it out to Tom Baker, who took one. The little boy reached out to take his, but Marya snatched the bag away. "No, my dear, you may not have another one. You must learn that there are severe consequences to bad behavior."

The little boy looked as if he was going to cry. Tom grabbed him by the arm and left.

"So, the second little piece was the explosion at the wake. Why is that important, Mar?"

"Think, my dear, think."

Martha thought. "Well…if the explosion was set up as a diversion so that the murderer could steal the charm, then that would mean that the charm was an important clue. But it wasn't, Mar. The kid did it on his own. So, I guess the charm isn't important after all."

"That is true, my dear, but it is also entirely false. I am not sure what Sister Thomas More would think about your conclusion. Perhaps the wish fallacy. 'If you say your wish out loud, it won't come true. Your wish came true. Therefore, you didn't say your wish out loud.' But let us stick to the facts, my dear. It is a fact that there was an explosion, and it is a fact that the necklace went missing. But the two events were not related. Therefore, I—"

Marya abruptly stopped talking and stared down at the floor. "My dear, could you just reach under the sofa and pick up the objects near your left foot?"

Martha leaned over and saw two purple puzzle pieces. She picked them up and gave them to Marya, who placed them in the remaining empty spots of the unicorn puzzle.

"Thank you, my dear. You are always so much help to me. I am now almost certain who the murderer is."

"Well, who is it?"

"As you know, I prefer to keep my conclusions to myself until I have all the answers. I cannot be 100% certain until I know the motivation for the murder, and that eludes me. Our investigation is now more like a crossword puzzle, my dear, rather than a jigsaw puzzle. With a crossword puzzle, one clue leads to another. If I am correct about who the murderer is, it will lead us to the answers to my remaining questions. I promise that you will be among the first to know, and I always keep my promises. My sister and I used to pinky swear until my mother, God rest her soul, told us that it once meant that the person who broke the promise had to cut off their pinky finger. My mother, God rest her soul, then told us about what Jesus said, let your yes be yes and your no be no, and told us that swearing is not necessary. So my sister and I—"

"Marya, what can we do to find the other pieces? I mean, the answers to your empty squares? We can't just sit here. If our scene worked, now the murderer's after *us*. What can we do?"

"Why, go to church, of course."

# CHAPTER 21

## Friday November 18

MARTHA WOKE UP TIRED. SHE HAD TOSSED AND turned all night, trying to figure out what Marya was thinking. She'd finally dozed off, but then woke up in a sweat from a dream in which she was unable to move as a car came roaring toward her.

She picked up Marya for morning Mass, and once Marya was situated and belted in the car, Martha figured she would try again. "So, Marya, who was it you said was the murderer?"

"I did not say who the murderer was. Did you bring your gun, my dear? Did you load it?"

"Yup." Martha tried another way. "I was thinking last night that the scene you made us act after Michael's funeral didn't do any good. No murder attempts on either of our lives yesterday. Are you sure you're right about the murderer?"

"Don't you worry, my dear. There will be another murder attempt."

"Oh. Great." Martha drove in silence the rest of the way to church. Maybe pouting would work.

Pouting did not work. Marya took advantage of Martha's silence to explain several examples that Sister Thomas More had used to differentiate the wish fallacy and the barking dog fallacy. "If it barks, it is a dog. It does not bark…"

A thundering voice rang out as they entered church. "What are you doing here?"

It wasn't a murder attempt, but at least someone was upset about their investigation! Martha put her hand inside the tote and held onto the grip of the gun.

The voice continued, "How dare you go into my personal drawer?" Martha, who was limping less and able to walk with her cane at a more rapid pace, hurried over to the sacristy, not waiting for Marya. Gertie stood in front of on open drawer marked "Father Thaddeus," with the priest of that name towering over her, hands on hips.

Gertie muttered, "Just neatening the drawers." One of her hands was closed as if clutching something behind her back. Father Thaddeus glowered and slammed the drawer shut. Gertie backed out of the sacristy. She bumped into Martha and almost jumped right out of her skin.

"Oh, it's you. What are you doing here this early?" Gertie shoved the hand into the pocket of her jacket.

"What was going on in there, Gertie?" Martha asked.

"Oh, you know Father Thaddeus."

"No, actually I don't. Do you?"

"No, I don't know him either."

"You don't seem to know anyone around here, Gertie. You didn't know Aldo Todi either."

Gertie gave Martha a sharp look. "I was going to look for you this morning. I wanted to invite you two over to have tea again after Mass."

"We—"

Marya stepped in front of Martha. "Hello, Gertrude, dear. So sorry, but we cannot have tea today."

"How about tomorrow?"

"No, I am sorry, we cannot."

"Sunday?"

"Yes, I believe that would work for us."

Gertie shrugged her shoulders. "You two have a busy social life."

"And you, my dear, are busy with your church tasks. You are so very helpful. Cleaning, watering the plants, helping the sacristan and the priests set up for Mass."

"Thank you, Marya. At least someone appreciates my efforts."

"Yes, my dear, I certainly do. I try to help a bit myself, you know. If there are any leftover bulletins after Mass in my pew, I will pick them up. Sometimes, I find a glove, or a piece of jewelry someone has lost. That reminds me, my dear. There is a lost charm that I am very concerned about, and I was wondering if you could tell me whether you have seen it. Perhaps it was dropped in church." Marya rustled through her bag and brought out the grainy photograph she had shown Martha the day before.

Gertie scrutinized the photograph and then scrutinized Marya. "I'll be sure to keep an eye out for it."

Gertie looked with alarm at something looming over Marya's head. "Got to go." Martha followed her glance and saw Father Thaddeus approaching them in full liturgical regalia as Gertie scampered away.

"What were you talking to that busybody about? Her tongue is evil. She is a minion of the devil and doomed to the netherworld."

"Yes, Father," Marya said. "It is true that we will have to give account on the Day of Judgment for every careless word we have spoken. Even those spoken behind a person's back."

"I have not said anything behind Gertrude's back that I have not said to her face."

"I have never understood why, Father, if one criticizes a person to their face, it is permissible to repeat it behind their back. And then, would the opposite apply also? I mean, if one speaks ill of someone behind their back, would the sin be forgiven if one repeated it to—"

"I have no time for such nonsensical—"

"We were just speaking to Gertrude about how very helpful she was cleaning up after Mass and how much everyone appreciates her. As a matter of fact, I inquired whether she had found a lost charm. Perhaps I could ask you as well." Marya showed him the photo.

Father Thaddeus peered at it. "I advise against wearing any adornment other than a crucifix or a religious medal." He looked at Martha with the full force of his intense gaze. She could not look away. "Are you meeting with us today?"

Marya stepped in front of Martha. "No, Father, I am afraid we are very busy today."

He continued looking at Martha. "Tomorrow?"

Marya answered, "No, Father, not tomorrow either."

"I was not talking to you. Martha, we will speak when this one is not around. She does not understand." He strode back into the sacristy.

Ken and Barbara Vance walked in. Ken said, "Hello, Martha. Coming to the meeting today?"

Marya said, "I'm sorry. We are so very busy today."

"I wasn't talking to you."

"Martha, please reconsider," Barbara said. "It could save your… your eternal life."

"In that case," Marya said, "perhaps Monday would work. Excuse me, may I ask you a question?" Ken glanced over and would have kept on walking, but Marya placed herself and her cane directly in his path. "I am so sorry to bother you, but one gets attached to things, even if they do not have any monetary value. Why, when I was a little girl, I found a rock that seemed to me to be shaped in the form of an 'M,' although my mother and my sister did not agree and were always after me to throw it away. But I valued it and kept it in my sock drawer. Why, I haven't thought of that in years. I wonder what became of that rock. I recall one day I was removing a pair of socks, and it fell out and landed quite hard on my foot. Then I moved it. Now, where did I move it?"

Ken tried unsuccessfully to step over her cane.

"Oh, but here I am meandering, and Mass is about to start. What I wanted to ask was whether either of you have seen a charm that, perhaps, may have been lost in church. I am very concerned about its loss." She held out the photo at them.

Ken grabbed the photograph from her, perused it, and said, "Why are you bothering us with this?"

Barbara said, "I can't really say. It's blurry."

Ken thrust the photo back at Marya, grasped Barbara's arm, and stared at the cane blocking his way. "Can we get by now?"

"Of course, of course, my dear. Thank you for stopping for a moment to help me. I find that that these days, people rush around so, that they do not have enough time to…" As she continued babbling, her purple and neon orange plaid bag slid from her shoulder, and as she tried to lift it back, the lilac bag also slid down. So, she placed both bags and herself in the aisle, blocking Ken's way. Ken looked around, seeking an alternate route, but Barbara stood behind him, and Martha positioned herself—legs apart, arms akimbo—behind them both. About three or four other parishioners were now clogging the aisle behind Martha. Martha understood Ken's frustration but could not stop herself from enjoying the scene.

Eventually, Marya reorganized herself and withdrew her cane so that Ken and Barbara were able to squeeze past her. Martha overheard Ken mutter, not very quietly, "Purple Pest," as he moved on.

A few more parishioners passed the slow-moving Marya, and Martha overheard mention of "Lavender Looney" with a guffaw and "Lilac Loser" followed by giggles.

Martha said loudly, "Now what was it that Father Thaddeus was just saying to us about an evil tongue, Marya?"

The two limped on, their canes tapping a catchy beat. Marya stopped in front of Luz, who was seated in front of the Saint Joseph statue at the front of the church, her head down, displaying the white streak in her black hair. Marya patted her hand as they passed. "May I ask you a question, my dear?"

Luz looked up, tears streaming down her face.

"Oh my. What is wrong?"

"It's Aldo. His condition has worsened since he received Last Rites from Father Thaddeus. He is very near death."

"It is good that you are praying to Saint Joseph, my dear. I believe that he had the happiest death of all, with Mary and Jesus by his side."

"Oh, Ms. Cook. I will miss him so. I never knew how much he meant to me until now, until I am about to lose him. Father Thaddeus says I must forget about Aldo. That he is being punished by God for speaking against Dies Irae. But I can't help it. I... I..." She started sobbing.

"I will pray for Mr. Todi, my dear. And for you also."

Luz took a deep breath. "Thank you. I feel that your prayers go straight to heaven. Did you have something to ask me?"

"Oh yes, I did. Thank you for reminding me, my dear." Marya showed her the photograph. "This charm is lost, and I was wondering if you recall seeing it. Perhaps it was lost in church."

Luz studied the photo. "Sorry, I can't help you."

Father Thaddeus presided at Mass. His homily was all about the sins of speech, which he divided into reviling, calumny, detraction, tale-bearing, derision, and cursing. Martha had no idea that gossip could be so complicated.

After Mass, Marya took longer than usual getting her belongings balanced on her arms. By the time they had left the pew, church was empty but for Isabella Bonino sitting in front of the statue of Mary.

"Hello, my dear. I am so glad to see you here."

"I don't know why I came, *Signora* Cook. Habit, I guess. *Sono arrabiata*. I'm so angry at God. And Mary too."

"Ah, my dear, I myself have been mad at God before. My sister died, and then shortly afterwards my niece died. I was angry, and I told Him so. To be close to someone means that you have to communicate your true feelings. A good relationship is based on honesty. In the end, after a long time, we reached an understanding, and the anger left me. I forgave Him and slowly learned to trust that whatever he had in mind was for the good. And, my dear, after all, who was the anger hurting, me or God?" Marya hesitated. "Actually, it probably hurt us both."

"No, I will never forgive God." Isabella's eyes glittered in anger.

"Well, perhaps you can ask God for the grace to forgive Him."

Isabella shook her head. "*Mai.* Never."

"Well, perhaps you can ask God for the grace to ask Him for the grace to forgive Him."

"No."

"Perhaps you can ask God for the grace to ask Him for the grace to ask Him for the grace to forgive Him."

Isabella stared back at Marya, brows furrowed. Martha understood her confusion.

Marya said, "I imagine that Justin Ward is feeling much the same way you do, my dear. I have not seen him in church since his father died."

"*Triste. Doloroso.* He is not eating or sleeping and will not leave his room. An aunt is staying with him. I visited a few times. Did you know that the Wards live right next door to me?"

"I wonder, my dear, if you could give me Justin's address. I have a Mass card to give him."

Isabella studied Martha and Marya for a moment before she spoke. "I have an idea, *Signora* Cook. How would you like to give it to him in person? I could drive you two there myself. His aunt has been asking everyone to visit Justin, to shake him out of his depression. I've been visiting, and a few friends also. *E probabile* a visit from you would shock, I mean, help him out of his depression. It couldn't hurt."

"Well, thank you very much, my dear. We would love that. I had planned to visit him myself. But you need not drive us. Martha will follow you in her car."

"*Va bene.* We will park at my house and walk over. There is a path between Michael's house and mine."

In the car, Martha asked, "Is this safe, Mar?"

"'Fortune favors the bold.' That is a quote that Sister Thomas More taught us in Latin class. It was said by an ancient Roman philosopher as he set out to investigate the eruption of Mount Vesuvius at Pompeii. Unfortunately, he died on the expedition when—"

"Why do you want to see Justin Ward, Mar? Should we add him to our list? Never considered him. But money is a great motive for murder, and he *is* going to inherit a lot of it. That is, assuming his father was more prudent than my…I mean, I think his father was a good businessman."

"Justin and I had a lovely conversation at the funeral of his mother. I told him I knew her father and her grandfather from the old neighborhood, and I knew Lisa herself. I would like to speak to him some more about his mother."

Of course. Marya wanted to speak to Justin about Lisa Ward's suspicious "suicide."

They followed Isabella's Maserati as she crossed the bridge to Pequot Island and then turned down one of the private roads leading to her home. Martha had guessed that Isabella was an Islander. The Skeeters flaunted their wealth, the Islanders merely displayed it, and the Middle Pointers were so rich that they could feign indifference.

A tall wrought-iron fence surrounded Isabella's property. A gate opened as Isabella drove up, and remained open long enough for Martha to follow. The gate bore a polished brass nameplate with *Hilltop* inscribed in black, and there did seem to be a slight rise to justify the name as they ascended the long driveway to the house—a hacienda with stucco walls, an arched entranceway, and a red-tiled roof.

Isabella pulled around the back and into the only open door of a five-car garage. Martha stopped in an area off to the side.

"My house. *La mia casa.*" She tossed her dark mane of hair back and gazed at the two women.

"What a lovely home, my dear. I have never been fortunate

enough to visit Italy, but I would imagine this is exactly what an Italian villa looks like," offered Marya.

"Big," said Martha.

"*Grazie, grazie.*" Isabella watched Marya as she rustled around getting her bags in order on her left and right shoulders and then stepped forward with her cane. "I brought you around the back way, Signora Cook, so we can walk through my grounds to the Wards. Can the two of you manage?" She looked at their canes.

"Yes indeed, my dear," Marya said before Martha could respond. "We both enjoy walking very much, and it would be a delight to see your garden. Dear Dr. Stokes says that walking is the best exercise for me, and I must keep it up."

"*Va bene.* I just have to get something from the house, and I'll be right back. You might want to leave your bags in the car, Ms. Cook. It's quite safe here."

Marya clutched her bags. "Oh no, my dear, I could never do that. At any time, one may need a handkerchief, a safety pin, needle and thread, paper and pen, or so many other things. One never knows what the future holds. My mother, God rest her soul, always said, 'Sometimes life takes an unexpected wrong turn in the right direction.' Why, suppose we are in…"

Martha slid her hand into her own bag and touched the cold metal of the Glock.

Isabella returned from the house with a bag over her shoulder. She led them past a pool and tennis court and opened a locked iron gate, which slammed shut behind them. They proceeded down a winding flagstone path through a wooded lot onto a trail defined only by the trampling of feet on the soft mossy undergrowth and leaves. Why were they going so far out of the way? Into such an overgrown area?

Martha turned to Marya. "Can you manage this, Mar? Maybe we should go back."

"I certainly can, my dear. I am enjoying it tremendously."

Martha slowed down so that she was behind the other two women and kept her gaze on Isabella, watching her every move as they twisted and turned along a barely-visible path hemmed in by tall bushes. Martha had lost her bearings. Her hand clutched the butt of her gun. Isabella and Marya disappeared behind two tall bushes. Martha darted around the bushes, but still couldn't see them. There were only more bushes and shrubs. She had reached the stockade fence surrounding the property. A dead end. She looked to the right and left but couldn't see the two women. They had vanished. Then she saw a break in the fence, a hidden gate that opened into the neighboring grounds. She rushed through it, ignoring the scratches and scrapes from the underbrush.

On the other side were two more tall bushes surrounded by shrubbery, but no Marya. She scrambled around the bushes. There stood Isabella and Marya, waiting. Martha took a shaky, deep breath. She would not let them out of her sight again.

They followed Isabella into a deeply forested area, like a wilderness, not a garden. Isabella stopped and reached into her bag. Martha's index finger touched the trigger on her gun.

Isabella pulled out a water bottle and stared back at Martha. "*Stai bene?* Are you all right? You look like you just saw *un fantasma*."

"I'm fine. Just fine."

"You want some water? I brought us each a bottle."

"No, I'm fine."

They continued on. The trees opened up onto a manicured lawn, where they passed a tennis court and pool, and arrived at a small side door to a large house. The door appeared to have been the original front door. The old house—a stately Georgian home—was still there in its entirety but was now dwarfed by a monumental addition. The brick matched, but little else corresponded between the gracious old house and the new, square, multi-windowed structure.

Isabella rang the doorbell, which was soon answered by a gray-haired woman in a nondescript black dress and oxford shoes. "*Come va*, Teresa?" These are two friends of Michael's from church, Martha and Marya. This is Teresa Corsia, Michael's sister who has come over from Italy to stay with Justin. Michael changed his name from Corsia to Ward because he thought it would help him in the business world. Corsia means ward in *Italiano*. Teresa, how is Justin? I thought it might help if they spoke to him." Isabella and Teresa continued their conversation in Italian.

Martha could not connect this dour older woman with her handsome, vigorous brother. With a heavy accent, Teresa said to her guests, "I take breakfast, but he not open door. Is locked. He becomes worse, not better. *Ti sono grato per* these two persons." She looked at Marya and raised an eyebrow. "*Penso di sì.*"

She led the women into a large wood-paneled salon, which was furnished with an upholstered formal sofa not chosen with comfort in mind. Matching chairs and carved wooden tables stood around the faded antique Persian rug in the center of the room. Landscapes, dark from age, hung at regular intervals on the walls. An oil painting of remarkable quality hung above the fireplace. It depicted a group of ornately dressed men with bright satin, velvet, and fur-trimmed cloaks drinking wine as they sat at a banquet table laden with meat and fowl and fish. On the floor next to them were dogs being given scraps from the table and a beggar who was given nothing. The Biblical scene of Lazarus and the rich man.

Teresa and Isabella continued speaking in Italian. Isabella turned to Martha and Marya. "Teresa wants you to know that Michael was proud of this house. Their parents were poor, peasants, and Michael worked hard for many years to get the best *per la famiglia*. He liked the old house, but Lisa wanted something more modern, so Michael built the addition. When he moved his parents to America, they lived here in the old wing. After they died, he moved his private den and office here. He kept it for himself. Not even Lisa and Justin came in."

Isabella flicked open an old fashioned hook-and-eye lock on the interior of the door and passed through into the new addition. The sun from a cloudless sky shone through windows lining two walls of a spacious, high-ceilinged room and through tall, single-paned doors that opened onto a patio. The sun illuminated the already bright, spotless all-white furniture, rug, and walls. The only colors in the room came from the bright blues and yellows in the cushions scattered around the sofas and chairs and in the floral paintings on the one windowless wall. Although she would have liked to organize the pillows in a more orderly fashion, Martha preferred the new addition.

They followed Teresa up a wide, curving set of stairs to a generous landing with hallways leading left and right. Teresa led them right to the third door, where a tray with congealed eggs, bacon, and toast sat untouched on the floor. Teresa shook her head as she picked it up. "This is Justin's room." She knocked on the door and was answered with a grunt. "Justin, friends here to visit." She turned, and Isabella followed her down the stairs.

No sound came from inside the room. Martha knocked but received no response. Marya took her cane and rapped the door, hard, and followed with a commanding, "Young man, open this door immediately."

The door opened, and an unshaven, pajamaed Justin faced them. His gaze stopped at Marya, and his eyes filled with tears. "Ms. Cook."

"May we come in, my dear?"

Justin nodded and opened the door wider.

The shades on the four windows had been drawn. The bed was rumpled, the sheets and blankets flung on the floor, pillows squashed and strewn. A television flashed and droned in the background. Justin led them through the bedroom into a connecting room furnished with two high-backed leather chairs and a desk with a huge computer screen, then into a living area with a comfortable sofa and chairs and an even bigger screen. Justin's "room" was larger than Marya's whole apartment.

The women sat down on the chairs. Justin walked to the desk and picked up a card—laminated and inscribed with neat purple handwriting. "Thank you for this, Ms. Cook. It helps." Justin plopped onto the sofa and stared down at the card clutched in his hand.

"I need your help to find your father's murderer."

Justin lifted his head, a blank expression on his features. "They already got him. He's just a stupid, homeless drunk."

"No, my dear. That man is innocent. The killer is a respected member of our community and will go unpunished unless you help us."

Justin's eyes regained their focus as he met Marya's gaze. "What do you mean?"

"You must promise to tell no one what I have said. The murderer is someone you know, and if you put the killer on alert, the consequences will be swift and devastating."

Justin's eyes widened. "Someone I know...I promise. Who is it?"

"Do they still teach logic in school today, my dear?"

"Huh? I don't think so."

"Such a shame. If the police had Sister Thomas More for a teacher, they most certainly would not have arrested the wrong person." She paused for a moment. "I believe the librarian would be the correct one."

"Ms. Noonan killed my dad?"

"Oh, my goodness, no. I am referring to the correct logical fallacy, 'All librarians are smart and shy.' Although our Ms. Noonan does fit the stereotype, in fact, all librarians are not smart and shy. Certainly, Sister Cecilia was not shy at all. Although she was quite smart."

Marya regarded Justin as though expecting approval for her explanation but received the more common reaction.

"Please, Ms. Cook, could you get to the point? Why do you say the homeless guy didn't murder my dad? They found the bloody hammer in the homeless camp, and my dad's wallet was in his pocket."

"He has been, as they say, 'framed' by the real murderer. 'Framed' is certainly an unusual term for—"

"Then who murdered my father?"

"That I will not say until I understand the murderer's motivation and have proof enough to guarantee a conviction. But I will tell you this. I need your help to stop another murder."

"My help?"

"Yes. I have something to show you."

"Okay, what is it?"

"I will show it to you once you take a shower, get dressed in some clean clothes, and eat breakfast. Come, Martha. We will wait downstairs."

She rose from the chair, and Martha followed her downstairs.

Fifteen minutes later, Justin, dressed in jeans and a T-shirt with his hair still dripping wet, came into the kitchen and wolfed down the fresh plate of scrambled eggs and bacon his aunt had fixed.

"Okay, I ate. What do you have to show me?"

Marya shuffled through her bag and brought out the grainy picture of the charm.

Justin looked at the photo and smiled. "Yes, I remember that. Mom showed that charm to me. It was her grandfather's. She was going through a big cardboard box filled with papers she said were his inventions. She said her grandfather once told her it was worth a million dollars. It was in an envelope with some papers."

"Thank you, Justin. Could you go see if you can find it?"

He jumped out of the chair and leapt up the stairs.

Teresa stood up, walked over to Marya, her eyes brimming with tears, and gave her a hug. "*Caffe? Qualcosa da mangiare?* Eat? Drink?"

"How very kind. Perhaps just a cup of tea."

Teresa started to get up, but Isabella said, "I'll do it, Teresa."

"My mother, God rest her soul, always said that eating between meals was…"

Isabella scurried around the kitchen while Marya rambled on about her mother's dietary habits, until Justin returned carrying an envelope.

"I found the envelope the charm was in. But the charm's missing. Most of the papers about the inventions are gone too."

"Who else knew about that envelope, my dear?"

"Maybe the lawyer, I don't know. Dad went through mom's papers with him after she died. He was the executor of the estate."

"May I see the envelope?"

He gave it to her. Handwritten across the front, it said, *The Guardian.*

"By the way, my dear, do you know who was the executor of the estate?"

"I think Mr. Bonino was," Justin said, nodding at Isabella. Isabella nodded back.

"Perhaps, Justin, you would contact Mr. Bonino's law office and ask if they can find your father's file for you."

"Will they give it to me? I'll try, Ms. Cook."

"And Isabella, my dear, would you check through the papers you have at home to see if there are any documents that refer to 'The Guardian?'"

"Yes, I can do that, *Signora* Cook."

Martha and Marya rose from the table to leave, Teresa plying them with handmade cannoli. Justin walked them to the side door.

"Sorry the charm was gone, Ms. Cook." He looked around to make sure that Isabella and his aunt were not following them. "Can you still catch my dad's killer?"

"With your help, my dear, I can. Please call me later today, after you speak to Mr. Bonino's office, and we can discuss this further." Marya rustled through her bag and extracted a pen and a small notebook. They exchanged phone numbers.

Isabella stopped chattering in Italian with Teresa. "I'll be right there. I must show you the way home, or you may get lost and never be—"

"No!" Martha said. "No need for you to come with us."

"Oh, yes, I think I must."

"No. We'll go out the front door and use the sidewalk. You and Teresa are having a nice talk. We'll see ourselves home."

"*Certo?*"

"Very sure."

Isabella shrugged and turned back to Teresa.

When the door closed behind them, Martha said, "Well, you certainly got Justin out of his funk, Mar. But I hope you can follow through on your promises."

Marya was quiet on the walk to the car, and during the drive over the causeway, she stared silently at the whitecaps. Finally, she said, "Could you drop me off at church, my dear?"

"Sure, Mar. I'll empty the poor boxes. You know there's someone that puts in hundred dollar bills, at least one, sometimes two, every week! One day I'm going to figure out who it is. Without that money, we'd have a hard time helping out people like—"

Martha caught herself before she said "you." Marya lived in the same housing project as many of the people the society assisted.

The two women entered the church. Marya sat down in front of Mary as Undoer of Knots. As Martha began to unlock the poor box, she heard Marya say, "Holy Mary, filled with God's presence, during your whole life you accepted the will of the Father with complete humility, and the evil one was never able to catch you in his snares. You never cease to intercede for us with your Son to solve our problems. With infinite gentleness and patience, you show me how to untangle the bundle of knots that are choking me… Holy Mary, Mother of God and my Mother, with such motherly love you are untying the knots that hinder me: I ask you to receive in your hands this knot that I present to you…"

Marya paused for a few moments before adding, "Mary Who Unties Knots, pray for me. Amen!"

Marya sat quietly as Martha pulled out the bills that had been folded so that they would fit into the small slot at the top of the poor box, and then emptied the rattling cache of coins at the bottom.

Martha had often noticed Marya put in her own few coins as she left church.

Marya stood up, stopped in front of the altar, and gazed at the stained-glass windows.

Five saints, each in his or her own window, formed a semicircle in the sanctuary apse so that they looked down on the altar and tabernacle. These windows were larger than those lining the nave, and the saints were better known.

The sun had begun its descent in the cloudless late-afternoon sky. It shone behind the Saint Stephen window, spotlighting the bloodied torso of the first martyr rather than the ecstatic expression on his face as he gazed at the heavens. A blood-red ray of light pierced the air. To Stephen's right was Saint Francis of Assisi in his brown robe, a bird perched on his shoulder and a turtle and rabbit at his feet. The setting sun shone through the blue sky surrounding him. The blue and the red rays emanating from the two windows combined into a purple glow that almost touched Marya.

Marya looked over at the statue of Mary. "Thank you, my dear." She then tap-tapped over to Martha. "We can go now."

"Great. I'm through too." Martha replaced and locked the poor box cover.

"Hurry, hurry, my dear. I must go see dear Dr. Stokes."

"Oh, I didn't know you had an appointment."

"I don't, but he will see me in an emergency."

"What's wrong, Marya? Are you ill?"

"Oh, a great deal is wrong. But I am not ill, although I have been very stupid. Fortunately, the cloud of witnesses, you know, has been busy interceding for me. Saint Stephen and Saint Francis have clarified the situation, so there is only one more question to be answered. I must visit my dear Dr. Stokes right away. By the way, that reminds me, your own visit to the doctor is tomorrow at 3:00, is it not?"

"It is. Do you have any questions you want me to ask him?"

"Yes, I will give you the photograph to show to him. Also, I must ask you to do me a favor. I recall that the last time we partnered, you obtained certain personal information on our suspects from the parish records."

"Well, I was working in the office, you know. On the silent auction and…the records were there and…no one was around, so…"

"Yes, yes, my dear. I understand. Perfectly. I am afraid I must ask you to do so again. I need the telephone numbers and, I believe that the term is email addresses, of all of our suspects. Is it possible that you could get those for me? Today? Under the circumstances, I am sure it would be only a venial sin. But we will both have to go to confession as soon as possible."

"I'll check the records as soon as I drop you off, Mar."

"Very good, my dear. And then call me as soon as you are finished. Now, enough dillydallying. Time for action! Come along, come along. I must see the doctor immediately. The early bird gets the worm. My mother, God rest her soul, woke us up two hours before school every morning. She often said to my sister and me, 'Lose an hour in the morning and you will be looking for it all day long.' I was never quite sure what she meant. I prefer the quote about the early bird getting the worm. Although…"

Martha had to admit she was impressed by the sheer number of early to bed, early to rise platitudes Marya recalled and recited on the way to the doctor's office.

The last thing Marya said, though, as she left the car, had nothing to do with waking up bright and early. "We must be very careful now, my dear. We have set the stage for a final, very dangerous scene. Trust no one. Make sure you have your gun at your side at all times."

# CHAPTER 22

Saturday, November 19

MARTHA WOKE EARLY THE NEXT MORNING, EVEN EAR-
lier than usual. Maybe Marya's early to rise platitudes had worked
their way into her subconscious. She got out of bed carefully, so as
not to disturb Quincy, although she could have jumped on the bed
like a trampoline and the only response would be a baleful stare.

The ankle felt better. She really did not need to go to Dr. Ianelli's,
but it would give her an opportunity to to show him the photograph.

As she drank her morning coffee, her thoughts drifted to Justin
Ward. That poor kid. First his mother murdered, then his father. Lisa
Ward had lost both her parents, and now her son was left an orphan.
Martha shook her head, stood up, and walked around the room to
clear the memories that threatened to invade. She noticed a yellowish
stain on the countertop near the sink. She scrubbed it, scrubbed it,
and scrubbed it until she noticed that she had scrubbed through the
finish. She wiped away a bit of wetness on her cheek. Must be from
the spray bottle.

But she would not sit around ruminating over the past. Marya
could do her praying and thinking, but Martha had to act. She sat
down at her computer. *The Guardian.* What did that mean? The
guardian of what? Was Justin's grandfather a member of a secret organization? Maybe his mom, dad, and his dad's lawyer were all members of the same organization? A criminal organization. Maybe they
all knew a secret and had to be killed. Martha Googled *The Guardian*

but came up with nothing better than a baseball team, several newspapers, charities, and home security systems.

The phone rang. "Hello, hello. May I speak to Martha Collins please?"

"Hi, Mar. It's me."

"Hello, my dear. I just received a telephone call from Officer Chonkin. She's finishing up on the night shift and asked if she could come over at 10:00 this morning to speak to us."

"Interesting. First she gives us her half-hour coffee break, then her lunch hour, and now there's no time limit. Think that means something, Mar?"

"I certainly hope so. Will you be able to be here at that time?"

"Wouldn't miss it."

"By the way, my dear, I spoke with Justin Ward, who called Johnny Bonino's law clerk. They are unable to locate the Ward file. The will was in the safe, but all the other papers are missing."

"That's too bad, Mar, I thought we had a good lead on *The Guardian*. Oh well. See you soon."

Martha, pistol in the tote at her side, arrived at 9:30. She had stopped off at La Petite Tarte Patisserie and picked up some mini cheese puffs. Those McVitie's digestive biscuits had been too dry and crumbly for her taste.

"Oh, thank you, my dear. How thoughtful. I was able to get to the grocery store today also." Marya brought out a box of Ritz crackers and a plastic container of onion dip. She made two circles of the Ritz crackers on the outside of a dinner plate, one just inside the other, and placed the open container of onion dip inside the cracker rings. She then took a smaller plate out of the cabinet and began to work on a design for the cheese puffs. The tea kettle whistled at the same moment the doorbell rang.

Martha went downstairs and opened the door. Something about Chonkin looked different. She had on the same uniform, dark blue pants and short sleeve button down shirt, on her short, strong frame.

Her brown hair was pulled back as always from her plain, angular face. But was that…it couldn't be…a slight smile on her face?

Officer Chonkin trailed Martha up the stairs with a bag in her hand. She handed it to Marya, who opened it. "Look what Officer Chonkin brought. Oh my, this is turning into quite a party." Marya reached into the bag and held up a large dried sausage for everyone to see.

"Kielbasa jałowcowa. I'm Polish." Chonkin sat down on her side of the sofa and said no more.

Martha took the other side of the couch, and both women listened to Marya chattering away as she went into the kitchen, cut the sausage, removed the inner ring of Ritz crackers, and replaced it with kielbasa slices. She brought the plates to the two women. "What a lovely brunch we have here, my dears! Cheese puffs, onion dip, and your lovely sausage!"

Martha and Officer Chonkin each swiped a cracker into the onion dip, took a slice of kielbasa and a cheese puff, and placed them on a napkin. Marya then served tea. Martha was afraid to move for fear she would either spill the tea or drop the hors d'oeuvres from their precarious place on her knees. She decided the wisest choice would be to gulp down the tea first, which she did. She heard gulping from the other side of the sofa and wondered if Chonkin had made the same choice.

Marya said, "Oh my goodness. You two must have been thirsty. Here, let me get you some more tea."

Martha and Chonkin said simultaneously, "No! Thank you." Chonkin said, "Thank you Ms. Cook," and Martha added, "Maybe later, Mar."

After the hors d'oeuvres had been eaten, with complimentary commentary on all sides, Chonkin looked at the two women. And yes, there it was again, the slight smile. Chonkin leaned back on the couch and hooked her thumbs onto her gun belt. Finally, she spoke.

"I did some investigation on my own after the last time we met. I figured Milton was the weak link, so that's where I started. We were on patrol together, and I told him I knew he'd gone with O'Hara to the evidence room and they took amphetamines from the Pink drawer and planted them on you. The minute I said it, I knew it was true. You should have seen the look on his face. Like a kid caught with his hand in the szarlotka box. Say, Ms. Cook, that reminds me. What was the name of that cookie we had at the last tea party? I want to get some."

"They are not cookies, my dear. They are biscuits. McVitie's digestive biscuits. I have some left. Let me get them for you."

"Hold on, Marya, let Officer Chonkin finish her story."

"That would be very nice of you, Ms. Cook."

Marya rustled around in the kitchen, put three McVitie's digestive biscuits on a plate, and brought them around to her guests.

"What happened next?" Martha asked.

Chonkin chomped on a biscuit and re-hooked her thumbs onto her gun belt. "Henry denied it at first. I reminded him that everything done in the evidence room was on video. Told him he'd better come clean because he was being set up as a patsy. We all know O'Hara's jealous of Lopez's big bust. If a cop stole some of the confiscated drugs, the prosecution would be jeopardized. That would be fine with O'Hara. Milton would be blamed, fired, maybe even charged with a crime. It's a plot worthy of Machiavelli. Milton didn't say anything..." She paused, looked at the two women, and added, "Then."

She reached for another biscuit. And took her time eating it.

Martha took the last biscuit and ate it herself.

"The next time we were on patrol, Henry said he'd been thinking. He said, and I quote, 'He who seeks to deceive will always find someone who will allow himself to be deceived.' I was surprised he knew the quote. Not many of the Pequot Bays police officers have read Machiavelli's *Prince*. I quoted him one back, 'The lion cannot protect himself from traps, and the fox cannot defend himself from wolves.

One must therefore be a fox to recognize traps, and a lion to frighten wolves.'" Chonkin smiled. A real smile. "I studied Renaissance literature in grad school. Couldn't get a job in that field, though, so I became a cop. Did you know Henry studied medieval literature?"

"Yes, we did," Martha said.

"His real name is Henry, not Hank, by the way." Chonkin added.

"Yes, it is," Martha said.

"He opened up then. I think the quote made him more comfortable with me. He said that he hadn't known the evidence room was on CCTV. Said that O'Hara didn't even go into the room. He told Henry he'd stand guard outside. Henry asked me what he should do. I told him his only option would be to come clean, go to Lopez and rat out O'Hara. Lopez would take it from there. I quoted Dante to him. 'The weapons of divine justice are blunted by the confession and sorrow of the offender.' He responded, 'The path to Paradise begins in hell.' Then we got in a little argument about whether Dante is a Renaissance or a medieval author. By the time we were through, he felt more relaxed. I got him to write out a statement and sign it. He gave it to me to keep because, as Dante said,

"'Thy soul is by vile fear assail'd, which oft

"So overcasts a man, that he recoils

"From noblest resolution, like a beast

"At some false semblance in the twilight gloom.'

"Henry figured he'd chicken out. Here it is." Chonkin opened her bag and pulled out two yellow, lined notebook pages with messy but legible handwriting and waved them around. "I have these originals and three copies." Martha reached for it, but Chonkin put it back into her bag. "I have to think of the best way to handle this. O'Hara is very canny, and a lot of the men are on his side. But Lieutenant Lopez has his supporters too. It's a regular political zoo over at the station. Even Machiavelli would have been impressed."

"I need it to give it to my lawyer," Martha said.

"No. I told you that if I found out anything, I would handle it my way. We'll deal with it in-office, and the charges against you will be dropped. I don't want Henry to get into trouble. We English majors have to stick together."

"Well, can't tell you how grateful I am, Officer Chonkin. That was amazing work."

Chonkin squirmed and didn't meet Martha's eyes. "Got to go."

Not one for compliments.

Chonkin nodded her goodbyes and clomped down the stairs.

"I better go now, too, Mar. My appointment with Dr. Ianelli is at 3:00, and I want to get in as many Uber fares as I can before that."

"Certainly, my dear. I also have an appointment with a doctor. My dear Dr. Stokes. He was unable to see me when you dropped me off yesterday."

"Your Dr. Stokes wouldn't see you? Thought he was always available."

"He had received a telephone call just before I arrived. One of his relatives became ill, and he rushed away. His secretary gave me an appointment for today. Would it be possible for you to drop me off?"

"Sure. Let's go."

On the way to Dr. Stokes's office, Marya said, "I must speak to you before you go to your appointment with Dr. Ianelli. I will call you immediately after I meet with dear Dr. Stokes. I hope to gain some information that will be useful for our investigations." She then began to pepper Martha with platitudes about trusting no one, starting with, "Be careful who you trust, salt and sugar look the same," which accompanied a story about her mother's difficulties with baking, and then morphed into, "Better safe than sorry," which led into her sister's adventures on an ice skating pond. As she opened the car door in front of Dr. Stokes's office, Marya said, "Remember, I will call you when I am finished here. I certainly hope your smart phone works!"

Martha grinned. "Don't worry, Mar, it will."

"Do you have your weapon?"

"Yup." Martha patted her bag. "Right here."

"Keep it with you at all times, my dear."

Martha nodded.

As she drove away, Martha was thankful that she no longer had to worry about the drug bust. Just one less concern. There had been three murders already…and she still might be the fourth.

# CHAPTER 23

Saturday afternoon, November 19

MARTHA DROVE AN UBER FARE AND THEN MADE HER
way to Dr. Ianelli's office. Marya hadn't called. She mustn't have discovered anything important from Dr. Stokes.

The office had once been a private home on the edge of town,
to which Dr. Ianelli had added parking around the back. A small
Victorian with long, gothic proportions, it boasted a steep roof, tall
windows, unpainted shingles weathered gray by the salt air, and an
ornate gable. A white picket fence surrounded the property, and
an immaculately trimmed privet hedge led up to the front door
past a gold plaque that announced, *The Office of Dr. Steven Ianelli.*
Martha drove around back and parked. She saw only one other car, a
Mercedes, which she knew was the doctor's.

Martha checked her watch. She was a half hour early, but she
wouldn't have time for another fare before the appointment. Since
Dr. Ianelli was seeing her outside of regular hours anyway, maybe
he'd see her now. She took her personal phone out of the glove box
and put her Uber phone away.

Martha opened the door to the office. The waiting room was
empty. There was no receptionist. She called out, "Doc?"

"I'm in my office. Come on back."

Martha walked into the hallway and went to his office.

Dr. Ianelli was looking out a window as she entered, and he swiveled his black leather desk chair around and gestured for her to sit

down. "Hi, Martha." He looked over his tortoise shell glasses as she sank into one of the chairs. She kept her tote bag on her shoulder. Not that she thought that Dr. Ianelli was a serious suspect, but, "Better safe than sorry."

"Hi. Thanks for seeing me today."

"No problem. I like any excuse to stop doing computer work. It's a pleasure to see you. How are you, Martha? Any more hypertensive episodes? Dizziness? Chest pain? Headaches? Nausea?"

Martha shook her head in response to each symptom. Should she tell him about the amphetamines in the drink? He was her doctor… but he was also a suspect.

"No. Feeling good."

"How's the ankle?"

"Much better. I'm still using the cane, but I don't think I really need to."

"Well, let's check you out. Go on back to examining room number four. Remove your shoe and sock. I'll be right there. I just have to get a few things."

Martha walked down the long hall to the end, past three other examining rooms, and paused. She had never gone into the last one. She looked back and saw the doctor standing outside his office, following her progress down the hall. He called to her, "You still have a limp, I see. Yes, that's the one. Go on in. Sit down. Make yourself comfortable. I'll be right there."

She entered the room. It was larger than the others. The walls were painted pure white and lined with stainless steel cabinets and drawers. A bright overhead light fixture beamed down on the examination table in the middle of the room. She sat down and placed her bag next to her. Not that she seriously thought…but just in case.

She took off her shoe and sock and waited. The white paper covering the top of the examination table crinkled as she moved. Why were doctor's offices always cold? She looked at her watch. And why, even with no other patients, did they make you wait? She heard some soft steps down the hall, but no one came in. Was it a rule that patients had to wait between the time they were sent to the examining room and the time the doctor got there? Well, she shouldn't be impatient. She would try to finish today's *New York Times* crossword puzzle. Saturdays were hard for her, and this one was no exception. She moved aside the gun to take the puzzle out of her bag, but just stared at it for several minutes without making a single entry.

She would make sure not to ask Marya whether she had finished it.

Finally, with a knock, Dr. Ianelli walked in and closed the door behind him. He was dressed more casually than usual, no suit jacket, tie, or vest.

As Martha put the crossword puzzle back into her bag, she pulled out the photograph she was supposed to show him. "Oh, Doc, may I show you something?"

"Of course." He took it from her and looked at it for several seconds. "Now why would you show this to me?"

"I have a friend who's trying to find it. She's showing it to everyone from church, not just you. Have you seen it around?"

He shook his head, put down the picture, and took hold of her ankle. He moved it to the left. And not too gently.

"Ow!"

"Sorry." He moved it to the right.

"Ow!"

"Sorry."

He walked over to one of the shiny metallic drawers. "It's not progressing as fast as I would like, Martha. That tenderness should be gone by now. I'm going to give you a shot that should help with the inflammation." He pulled open the drawer and took out a syringe.

"Can I get a prescription for this, Dr. Ianelli? I hate needles!"

Dr. Ianelli turned and smiled at Martha. "Now don't you worry. Have I ever hurt you before?" He drew out medicine from a vial into the syringe.

True enough. Martha had trusted him with her health care for more than twenty years. But Marya had warned her to trust no one, even her doctor. It would be ridiculous to make a fuss. But then, who cared about being ridiculous if he was about to inject her with poison? As she watched him fiddle around with the syringe, he looked up and gave her a grin and a friendly wink. No, Dr. Ianelli wasn't a…

As he walked toward her with the syringe, she heard a rustling in the hallway, a stomping of feet and a tap…tap…tap…? No, that couldn't be. But by the dirt of Saint Daria…

Martha's back was to the door, but she heard Marya say, in that steely voice of hers, "Steven Matthew Ianelli. Stop it right now."

Dr. Ianelli's head shot up, and he stopped in his tracks.

Martha turned toward the door. Officer Chonkin stood in the doorway with her hand on her holster, a commanding figure in her police blues.

Dr. Ianelli stared at Marya and Chonkin. Martha had to smile. They certainly did make an odd couple. "What's going on? What is this? A commando raid?" He turned toward Martha, a look of amusement in his eyes. "Is this the friend you were talking about?"

Martha looked at Marya. She was dressed less formally than usual, perhaps due to the covert nature of the operations she had planned for the day. Her hat was a purplish tweed baseball cap. No, not a baseball cap. It had two visors, one in front and one in back. And were those earflaps tied up on top? She wore lavender and maroon striped twill pants and a purple satin varsity jacket with *Viking Football* and a horned helmet on the back.

Martha met Marya's eyes. They reminded Martha of her grandmother's eyes after she had caught Martha when she fell from the top of a playground slide. Martha glanced at the syringe and then back at Dr. Ianelli. "Yes, this is the friend I was talking about. Her name is Marya Cook."

"Well, Ms. Cook, I have seen you around, but I am honored to finally be introduced to you. Now, perhaps you would be so kind as to tell me why you entered my office without permission. And brought a police officer with you. I assure you there are no lawbreakers here… other than yourselves." Dr. Ianelli walked over to the sink and pushed the syringe plunger, emptying its contents into the basin.

Officer Chonkin took a step in from the door, her hand still resting on her holster. Marya tapped over closer to the doctor, stopped, and cocked her head to meet Dr. Ianelli's gaze. Martha felt vulnerable with one of her shoes and socks off.

"Dr. Ianelli, I am so sorry to have come in unannounced and interrupted your work, and I appreciate you taking your time from your busy schedule to listen to me. I have some very important information that I have discovered, and it could not wait. But I must ask you a favor. I am not as young as I once was. I wonder if you would be able to guess my age. Doctors are usually quite good at that. However, I went to a new eye doctor several weeks ago, and he could not believe it when I told him how old I was. But the old saying is not, 'You are as old as you look.' It is, 'You are as old as you feel.' My mother, God rest her soul, often said as she was growing older, 'It's important to have a twinkle in your wrinkle.' I certainly don't feel—"

Martha started putting on her sock. "Mar, short and to the point."

"Ah, yes, my dear. Thank you. As you know, I sometimes have trouble with that. Sister Elizabeth Mary often—"

"Marya." Martha tried to sound like Sister Elizabeth Mary.

"Of course, my dear, of course. What I was trying to say is that it might be easier if we went into the reception area where there is a comfortable place for me to sit down. As I said, I am not as young as I used to be." Chattering away, Marya turned around walked out the door and down the hall.

"Where are they going now?" Dr. Ianelli shook his head at Martha. "What is going on?"

"I have no idea," Martha answered truthfully.

Officer Chonkin walked behind Marya, forming a solid barrier, and Dr. Ianelli followed. Martha shoved her foot into her shoe and limped after them. "Why didn't you call me, Mar?"

Marya stopped, causing Chonkin to bump into her and Dr. Ianelli to bump into Chonkin. She turned and eyed Martha with a look that reminded Martha of the time her grandmother had caught her using an antique china porcelain platter as a sled. "I did. Many times. When you did not answer, I was able to reach Officer Chonkin, and we have been looking all over for you."

"I didn't get any of your calls. Look..." Martha pulled out her phone. "Oh, I guess you did call. But I didn't hear..." She looked at it closer and groaned. "Oh no. I put it on silent mode while I was driving for Uber..."

Marya's features betrayed the same emotion as her grandmother's when Martha had explained that that the snow was very soft. Then she turned around and proceeded into the reception area.

Father Thaddeus, his briefcase at his side, sat in the waiting room with a black shoulder cape over his usual cassock, eyes closed and hands clasped in prayer. Luz Flores, Barbara Vance, and Ken Vance sat next to him, hands clasped, heads down.

As the group entered the reception area, Father Thaddeus opened his eyes and stood up, struggling a bit with his cassock as he extricated himself from the low chair. "Ah, Dr. Ianelli, you are precisely on time. I am sure we shall have a fruitful conversation. But what are these others," Father Thaddeus paused for a moment and looked down his nose, "doing here?"

"What are *you* doing here?" Dr. Ianelli asked.

"Why, because the Holy Spirit has—"

The door opened, and Aldo Todi walked in.

"What are *you* doing here?" Dr. Ianelli, Father Thaddeus, and Ken Vance all sang out in chorus.

"Let's start with you, Father," Dr. Ianelli said. "What are you doing here?"

"I am here because the Holy Spirit has touched you, Dr. Ianelli.

Ken received your email stating that you wished to join Dies Irae, and he immediately came to me and rearranged my schedule so we could get here by 3:30. And, as you requested, we have brought our most loyal guardians, Luz Flores and Barbara Vance, with us. I must say, though—" The priest rearranged his mussed cape— "I did not understand the rush. It would have been nice to receive more notice." He glowered at Aldo. "He did not request your presence at this meeting. What are you doing here? I thought you were in the hospital."

Aldo glared back. "I got out yesterday. They tried a new antibiotic. It cleared up the pneumonia overnight. Sorry, Doc, but I signed myself out without telling you. When I called Luz, she was out, but I got her message that she was coming here. So here I am." He looked at Luz, who gazed back at him with glowing eyes.

Father Thaddeus did not look pleased by the miraculous recovery.

Dr. Ianelli said, "I didn't send—"

As he spoke, the door opened again, and Isabella Bonino and Justin Ward walked in. Justin beamed at Marya.

Bitsy rushed in behind them, stiletto heels clicking. "Steven, what's up? Are you okay? I got your text from the phone you borrowed saying to be here at 3:30. Did you find your own phone?"

She walked over to Dr. Ianelli and took his hand.

"There is nothing to worry about, Bitsy. I'm fine."

She looked at Father Thaddeus. "What are you doing here? What is everybody doing here?"

"God has called your husband to join us in the fight against the Evil One."

Bitsy looked at her husband, who scratched his head, gaped at the people filling his reception area, and then turned back to Father Thaddeus. "I did not invite you here, Father. I do not have any interest in becoming a part of your…your…group."

The door opened once more, and everyone turned to see Gertie Doppeldecker sidle in. "So sorry I'm late, Doctor." She surveyed the others in the room.

"Late for what? What are you doing here?" Bitsy asked.

"Dr. Ianelli emailed me about a possible job proposal from one of his patients. He asked me to come over at 3:30 sharp."

Dr. Ianelli eyed the gathered group. "This is nonsense. I didn't send any of those emails, and I never sent a text to you from someone else's phone, Bitsy. What did your email say, Isabella?"

Isabella gazed at Justin. "I didn't get an email. Justin called and said he was sick and needed a ride to his 3:30 appointment with you."

All eyes turned to Justin. He smiled. "I was doing a friend a favor. I had a conversation with Ms. Cook yesterday, and she dictated to me what she wanted in each of your emails. I set up a fake account, and she called a couple of hours ago to tell me to send them out. Except for Ms. Ianelli." He nodded at Bitsy. "That's my own cell number. You see," his smile vanished, "Ms. Cook said that she wanted to get you all together because one of you killed my father, and that she would prove it."

There was silence for just a moment, until everyone started talking all at once.

Father Thaddeus rose from his chair and moved toward the door. The deep and majestic tones he used when delivering his homilies carried over the other voices. "I do not appreciate this joke at all. I will not remain here and listen to the ravings of a crazy woman. Let us leave."

Ken and Barbara jumped up from their chairs. Father Thaddeus eyed Luz, but she gazed at Aldo and remained seated. Aldo sat down next to her.

Marya nodded at Justin. "Thank you, my dear, for your help. My mother, God rest her soul, often said that people talk about the faults of those who arrive late. I wonder if the same could be said about those who leave early. You see, Dies Irae profited greatly by the death of your father, money which might not have come their way had he lived."

Her tone changed into what Martha now thought of as Marya's

Jedi mind-control trick. "Father Thaddeus, therefore, had an excellent motive to murder Mr. Ward. And you, Mr. Vance, who are in sole charge of the finances of Dies Irae, had an even better motive. But we will discuss that in detail in a moment. I am getting ahead of myself. 'Ahead of myself.' What an interesting expression. How can one get ahead of oneself? Perhaps tripping over one's own..."

Father Thaddeus and Ken exchanged glances. Father Thaddeus gave a short nod, and they walked back to their chairs.

Bitsy said, "This sounds interesting, dear. I always suspected something sinister about that cult." She looked down her Brahmin nose at Father Thaddeus, who looked down his own sharp beak at her. Bitsy took her husband's hand, and they sat down in the second row of chairs in the waiting area. The rest of the group followed suit.

"Justin, my dear, it appears that our guests will be staying. Could you perhaps help me once again? Would you pull a chair over for me? Ah, just here, that is perfect. And one of those little glass tables perhaps, right there. Yes, yes."

Justin repositioned the chair as Marya directed, so that it faced the two rows of chairs where the "guests" were seated.

Officer Chonkin stood at attention in front of the door. Martha moved one of the chairs to the side so she could have a good view of everyone while also blocking the back exit.

Marya settled the neon orange and lavender plaid tote bag on the ground and placed the lilac-bedecked imitation leather bag on the glass table in front of her. She smiled at her seated guests. "I had quite a time, you know, figuring out which one of you committed the three murders."

"Three murders?" several voices echoed.

"Yes, three murders. And I will get to them all, one at a time. I do not want to get 'ahead of myself' again." She tittered.

Martha leaned back in her chair and crossed her arms. Finally she would learn who had killed Lisa Ward, Johnny Bonino, and Michael Ward.

Marya started rifling through her handbag. "Sister Elizabeth Mary required us to practice extemporaneous speaking in seventh-grade English class. She would get quite frustrated with me, I am afraid. I was not nervous speaking in front of the class as some of the other children were, but perhaps I was not 'short and to the point' as you say, Martha dear. Sister allowed me to use index cards with notes on them so that I would not go 'off topic,' as she said."

Marya extracted her hand from the depths of her bag. She was holding a stack of non-laminated index cards bound by a rubber band. "I have brought some with me today. I believed I would have to do some explaining, and," she looked around delightedly at her listeners, "I was right!

"Three murders. I thought at first I should start chronologically, but then I decided to go backwards. Yes, backwards made more sense to me. I would start at the end, then go to the middle, and then the beginning."

"Yes, backwards would make more sense to her," Ken sneered, and chuckles arose from the seated group—all but Justin, whose brows drew together, his face tightening. Martha wished she could give him the laminated note card that Marya had once given her, "Pray, and let God worry." It was a quote that often came in handy when dealing with Marya.

Marya tittered along with everyone else. "Yes, I myself was confused. Three murders, nine suspects, and all needed motive, means, and opportunity. I was never good at mathematics, but I do know my times tables. Nine times three is twenty-seven, and twenty-seven times three equals eighty-one. So many possibilities, I found it was difficult to arrange my thoughts in an orderly fashion. It was not until I discovered the motivation for the murders that everything fell into place. Motivation was the key here. And the key was hidden until the end. And so, I will end with it. This is how I shall proceed: First the third murder, then the second, then the first, and I will address opportunity, means, and motive in that order, rather than motive, means, and opportunity."

"Well, that makes perfect sense." Ken rolled his eyes.

"As I said, three murders. Nine suspects."

Marya picked up the pile of note cards. She had a difficult time pulling out the top one from the tightly rubber-banded pile, but after a few moments' struggle, she slipped it out and placed it on the table in front of her. Martha was able to see the title,

> *The Third Murder—Michael Ward—Opportunity and Means*

in black, in Marya's meticulous script.

"Mr. Ward was the final victim. My dear Justin, I am sad for your loss, but I am happy for your father. As Jesus says, we do not know the day or the time, and I rejoice to know that Mr. Ward had the grace of forgiveness when he died. He was murdered soon after he went to confession. It is the murderer for whom I am sorrowful and whom I pray will confess and seek forgiveness for his or her sins." Marya paused and looked around as though she was waiting for one of the suspects to jump up and confess. Martha hoped that was not how Marya planned to trap the killer.

"And I too will pray for the homeless man who committed the grave and mortal sin," Father Thaddeus intoned.

Marya said, "Jesus, an innocent, was harshly judged by Pilate. Perhaps, Father, there might be a lesson in that. In fact, all of the suspects *except* Mr. Nance had opportunity and means to murder Michael Ward."

"Mar, you mean Mr. *Vance*, not Mr. Nance."

Ken Vance gazed smugly at the others gathered in the room.

"No," Luz said, "She means Nance. John Nance."

Marya nodded. "Yes, John Nance is the name of the gentleman without housing who is presently in jail. And he is the one person who could not have murdered Michael Ward."

EMILY HANLON

Ken Vance scowled as Marya continued. "You see, Mr. Ward was driven by the murderer to the remote area where he was killed. He could not have walked there on his own with a large tackle box and ice chest. He did not drive himself because his car was not in the parking area. I do not believe that Mr. Nance owns a car, as I have observed him carrying all of his possessions in a shopping cart. The most likely persons who would drive him were his fishing friend, Mr. Todi, or Isabella, another kind of friend. Anyone could have planted the wallet in Mr. Nance's pocket, although the most likely persons would be Mr. Todi, who purchased Mr. Nance's clothing for him, or Luz, who was Mr. Nance's friend."

Luz said, "Aldo would never do that."

At the same time, Aldo said, "Luz could never do that."

They turned and smiled at each other.

"But all of you do have cars and could have persuaded Mr. Ward to drive there with you. All his friends, everyone at Dies Irae, and anyone at Mr. Bonino's wake, would know that Mr. Ward's hobby was fishing. He promoted the benefits of fishing like Father Thaddeus evangelizes for Dies Irae. He tried to convince everyone to try it, and any one of you could have taken him up on his offer. Everyone had the opportunity. Officer Chonkin was so good as to check into your whereabouts that afternoon." Marya looked down at the notecard. "Father Thaddeus and the members of the executive committee of Dies Irae were interviewed together. He would not allow his followers to be questioned separately, but advised Officer Chonkin that they were together for the entire afternoon. That created alibis for them all, for what that is worth. The rest of you were alone. No one had an alibi. And the means was right there in the tackle box. The priest."

Father Thaddeus straightened up to his full, rangy height. "I did not kill Michael Ward."

Marya tittered. "I meant the eel hammer. It is called a priest. As

253

Mr. Ward was meditating, relaxing, fishing, any one of you could have walked behind him and swung it full force on top of his head."

Martha shivered, picturing the peaceful scene broken by a crashing blow to Michael's skull.

"Since everyone had opportunity and means to murder Mr. Ward, motive was the missing piece of that puzzle." Marya paused for a moment and shuffled through the cards. "Or was the puzzle missing three pieces? After all, there were three murders, and they each had a missing piece. Of course, the missing piece was the same for each murder—it was motivation. So, I wonder, mathematically, whether that would be considered three pieces or..."

"Marya," Martha said, "you can work on the puzzle later."

"Of course, my dear, you are right. For the present, let us discuss the second murder. Again, everyone had opportunity and means. Except for Mr. Nance. I do not believe I observed him at the party."

"Party? What party?" Justin said.

"Good question, Justin." Dr. Ianelli said. "And who is the second murder victim?"

Marya, again with difficulty, pulled out the next notecard from under the rubber band. It was entitled,

*The Second Murder—Johnny Bonino—Opportunity and Means.*

"Why Mr. Bonino, of course."

Isabella said, "Johnny was not murdered. He had an allergic reaction to crab."

Dr. Ianelli nodded. "Isabella's right. Johnny Bonino was not murdered. He died of anaphylactic shock." He looked around at the others. "That means he had an allergic reaction to crab. The signs were unmistakable." He glanced over at Ken Vance, who nodded. "But if you want to arrest one of us, Officer, I'll go quietly." He held out his hands as if offering them up to be handcuffed, laughing. "Maybe we should all go."

There was shuffling and scraping of chairs.

Marya placed her notecard on the desk. "Yes, Mr. Bonino died of an allergic reaction, but no, he was not allergic to crab."

"*È stato*." Isabella stopped on her way to the door. "Crab and penicillin. He spoke about it to everyone. You wouldn't know because you didn't know him. *Dai, andiamo*, Justin."

Justin did not move from his seat but continued gazing at Marya.

"But I did know Mr. Bonino, my dear. I knew him longer than any of you."

"He never mentioned that."

"He may not have recognized me as the sister of his babysitter. I had known him since he was a child. Mr. Bonino's father was a bayman, a crabber. The history of Pequot Bays is an interesting one. Perhaps someday I will write it down. There are very few of—"

"Marya," Martha said.

"Ah yes. Short and to the point. Let me see, where was I?" She looked down at the cards on the table and shuffled a few around. "Now where did I put that card? I just had it… Ah, here it is." She read over the *Second Murder—Johnny Bonino—Opportunity and Means* notecard, front and back, before looking up. Isabella had turned toward the door.

"As I said, Mr. Bonino's father was a crabber. The family had crab for breakfast, lunch, and dinner. He grew to hate it, but in those days, people ate what was placed in front of them. He began to lie to everyone, tell them he was allergic. He had broken out in hives from penicillin once and claimed that he had the same reaction to crab. I suspect his mother knew better but went along with it. Johnny was always her favorite. He was the oldest in a family of eight, and all the others were girls. My sister helped Johnny's mother take care of her children, and he told her his secret."

"So then, how did he die, Ms. Cook?" Isabella walked back to her seat.

"He died of an allergic reaction," she paused, "to penicillin. Each of you could have heard of his allergy to both crab and penicillin. He spoke of his allergy to crab often, and he wore a flashy medical bracelet announcing he was allergic to penicillin. Again, all the members, or past members, of Dies Irae knew Mr. Bonino well and could have known of his allergies. Dr. Ianelli, as his doctor, would know, and so could Bitsy, who filled in in the office when someone was sick. Gertrude, well, Gertrude often can't help but overhear conversations, and knows a great many things. My dear Dr. Stokes advised me that penicillin can be administered orally, and so any one of you could have brought him a drink that was spiked with penicillin. Spiked. There is that funny word again. Isn't—"

"Marya."

"Sorry, my dear. Where was I?"

"Penicillin."

"Thank you. When everyone was running over to see what the commotion was, any of you could have slipped a plate with crab on it where poor Mr. Bonino had been sitting. The card identifying the crab plate had been removed by the culprit, so everyone would believe Mr. Bonino had eaten it unknowingly. And all would assume that the allergic reaction was to crab. Perhaps, if the authorities are persuaded that Mr. Bonino was murdered, they will exhume the body and test it for penicillin."

Marya reread her index card. "Such a murder, of course, would have to be done by someone with some knowledge of drugs. But all of you have knowledge of and access to medications, or are close to people who do. Mr. Ward worked for a pharmaceutical company, so Isabella and he could have worked together to kill Mr. Bonino."

Justin looked at Isabella, eyes wide.

"I did not... I am not..." Isabella said.

"Mr. Vance works at a hospital and is an EMT. Barbara has access to his bag. Many people, including Mr. Vance, would do a favor for a priest who said he was feeling ill and needed antibiotics. Gertrude is a pharmacist. Luz is a nurse. Dr. Ianelli is a doctor, and Bitsy could get medicine from him. Mr. Todi has always intimated he has connections with the underworld, the mafia, a criminal element, so one could assume easy access to drugs. In any event, it is not difficult to get a prescription for penicillin. Perhaps it was just left over in someone's medicine cabinet. Everyone had the opportunity and means to kill Mr. Bonino. Again, motivation was the second...or was it the first...or...was it the only...or perhaps—"

"Marya."

Marya nodded at Martha. "Motivation. Why were both Mr. Bonino and Mr. Ward killed?" Marya picked up the pile of notecards. As she tried to remove the rubber band with her arthritic fingers, the cards went flying all over the table in front of her. Martha shuddered. Without the notecards, Marya would revert to her nattering, unorganized, run-on self. She would never be able to form a sentence that made sense, much less prove that one of these people was a murderer. Martha said a quick prayer, hoping that God would do the rest.

Marya glanced at Martha, a merry look on her face. "I know what you are thinking, my dear. You remember what happened last time we solved a crime and my cards became all jumbled, and perhaps I became a little jumbled along with them. But this time I have planned for that. I have numbered the note cards! As my mother, God rest her soul, often said, 'Your best teacher is your worst mistake.'"

Martha had to smile.

Marya easily rearranged the notecards and picked up one entitled,

*Motivation—Isabella Bonino.*

She read, "Isabella Bonino was having an affair with Mr. Ward."

With a quick movement of her head, Isabella swung her dark, wavy hair away from her face. Her expressive eyes flashed. "*Sei pazza.* I was not...I would not..."

"You deny it, my dear, but it was clear by the well-worn, winding path and hidden entrance between your property and Mr. Ward's, by your familiarity with the old house that his son and wife never used, and by the lock between his part of the house and theirs, that you were carrying on an affair while Lisa Ward and Johnny Bonino were still alive."

Martha watched Isabella's expression darken, a storm gathering in her features.

Marya looked up from the notecard. "Lisa Ward was dead. The only thing remaining between you and Michael Ward was your husband."

Isabella exploded, "*Basta*! You don't understand. You call it an affair. It was no 'affair.' It was two souls meant for each other by God. We were born to be together." She held her hands out, palms turned upward, and turned up her face to the heavens.

She slowly let her hands drop to her side, her head falling forward. She turned to Marya, the storm over. "Yes, we were having…an affair. Yes, I wanted to marry Michael. And he wanted to marry me. But no, we did not kill my husband. And why would I kill Michael? I loved him." Her voice faded as she repeated, "I loved him."

It was a shame that Isabella was not a soprano. The scene Martha had just witnessed was worthy of *Tosca*. She had never liked those melodramatic operas.

Marya looked down at the *Motivation—Isabella Bonino* card, then back up at Isabella. "Yes, my dear, you loved Mr. Ward. But there is a wide divide between human love and God's love, and only a thin line between human love and human hate. Mr. Ward experienced God's unconditional love and forgiveness when he went to confession. He told you it was over. His sins were in the past. You would not accept that. Knowing that he felt peaceful and happy while fishing, you thought that would be a good opportunity to convince him to change his mind. You asked to take him fishing, but your hopes were dashed. He refused your advances. You saw the priest hammer in the tackle box and killed him in a fit of fury. We all observed your scene after the funeral. We know you have a bad temper."

"I loved him. I did not kill him." Isabella hid her face in her hands and began to cry.

"Perhaps," Marya said.

Marya turned her gaze to Aldo Todi and then turned to her next card:

*Motivation—Aldo Todi.*

She read it over, front and back, and then looked up at the subject of the notecard, who scowled at her. Luz placed her hand on his am.

"And you, Mr. Todi. You reveal very little about yourself. You were brought up here, then moved away for many years, then returned. What happened during those years, where you obtained your money, what you did for a living, all have been shrouded in mystery. But we know enough to establish a basis for your motivation to kill Mr. Bonino and Mr. Ward. Your motive for killing Mr. Ward is simple. He bequeathed a large sum of money to you. Justin obtained a copy of the will. It is a *very* large sum of money. Why should he leave such a sum to a friend rather than to his son? We do not know whether you are in need of money, Mr. Todi, but, as Ecclesiastes tells us, 'Whoever loves money never has enough; whoever loves wealth is never satisfied with his income.' You were even observed taking money from poor Gertrude."

Gertie gasped and jumped out of her seat.

Marya looked over at Gertie. "Yes, my dear?"

Gertie glanced at Aldo. He glared back. She sat down.

Marya turned back to Aldo. "Money, the root of all evil as Saint Paul says, is motivation enough for murder."

Aldo glanced at Luz and then back at Marya. His flat, ugly features and casual sneer hardened. His face became mottled. A vein in his throat pulsed. Officer Chonkin unsnapped the safety on her holster and rested her hand on the gun barrel. Martha's hand slipped into her bag.

Marya looked directly at Aldo, meeting his cold stare. She repeated, "Money, the root of all evil, is all the motivation one needs for murder, is it not, Mr. Todi?" There was a small smile on Marya's face. It seemed almost as though she was taunting him.

Luz removed her hand from his arm. Aldo's nostrils flared, making him look even more toadlike than usual.

Marya looked down at the card. "Michael was your only friend, although it escapes me what he saw in your character so that he would befriend you." Marya looked up at Aldo with almost a sneer on her face. Martha had never seen this side of her. Aldo clenched and unclenched his fists.

Martha was enjoying this. She would see if he could take the insults as well as he could give them out.

"Or perhaps, as someone has suggested to me, you assisted your only friend Michael and his lover Isabella in their efforts to free themselves of their unhappy marriages, and then, when in his remorse he told you he was going to confess to the police, you had to kill him. You could have easily planted the evidence on Mr. Nance. He thought you were his friend. We saw you purchase clothes for him."

Martha heard Luz gasp. Her hand covered her mouth as she looked wide-eyed at Aldo and moved as far away from him as she could.

Aldo glanced at Luz. A guttural roar escaped him as he jumped out of the chair. He did not face Marya but Luz. He forced out each word as though it was being torn from him. "It was a fund for the Knights' charities." He was shaking now.

The almost-sneer on Marya's face turned into a beaming smile. She addressed Aldo, even though his back was to her. "A charitable fund, Mr. Todi. Just as I suspected. Could you tell us about it?"

"The Widow and Orphan Fund." He spoke so low, it was difficult to hear him.

"What a lovely name. Could you tell us a bit about the Widow and Orphan Fund?"

Aldo dropped back into his chair. He scowled at Marya. "It helps widows and orphans. In sub-Saharan Africa."

"Sub-Saharan Africa. How very interesting. How was it that you became interested in that area of the world?"

He turned toward Luz. "After you got married, I had to get away, far away. So I joined MSF, *Médicins Sans Frontières*, Doctors Without Borders. I was a logistician. I went all over. Sudan, Democratic Republic of Congo, Central African Republic. Areas torn by conflict. I saw true misery. When my parents died and left me money, a lot of money, I set up a donor-advised fund with the Knights of Columbus, the Widow and Orphan Fund. It funds Round Tables set up by the Knights in areas of conflict in Africa. The money Michael left me was for that fund. You can check. It's on the up and up."

Gertie popped up out of her seat. "And I never gave him money. He gave me money. He helped me even when I didn't ask him."

"Yes, my dear, I knew that. When you were seen putting money in your wallet, Mr. Todi, it was because you did not want anyone to see you helping Gertrude. 'Do not let your right hand know what your left hand is doing.' You have put on a very big show, Mr. Todi, for a very long time, so that no one would know what a charitable gentleman you are."

Luz placed her hand back on Aldo's arm, then moved it so that she was holding his hand. She looked at him. He looked at her. A gentle expression washed over him, entirely changing his features. He looked, although not exactly like a handsome prince, at least not like a frog.

"Of course," Marya added, "I could not rule out the possibility that you could have killed for the good of the fund."

Luz and Gertie both glared at Marya. *If looks could kill*, thought Martha.

Marya turned the *Motivation—Aldo Todi* card over and placed four cards all in a row on the table in front of her.

*Motivation—Luz Flores*

*Motivation—Barbara Vance*
*Motivation—Ken Vance*
*Motivation—Father Thaddeus.*

She contemplated first the notecards and then the four subjects of the notecards, seated side by side in front of her. "All of you had similar motivations. You are devoted followers of Dies Irae, guardians of the good, and would do anything to protect the organization. Each of you knew that Mr. Bonino and Mr. Ward had bequeathed ten percent of their very large estates to Dies Irae, and that both were considering quitting, which meant that they would change their wills."

Marya picked up the four notecards and splayed them out in her right hand as though playing a hand in poker. "Perhaps all of you participated in the murders together. Or perhaps only two of you did. Maybe Luz and Barbara acted together, or Ken and Barbara." As she spoke, she arranged the cards into different orders with her left hand. "Only four of you, but so many possibilities. I wonder whether this would be four to the fourth power. I recall Sister Anne Marie explaining powers in algebra. Is not that an interesting way of describing it? Why would it be called a power? I cannot—"

"Marya," Martha said, "focus."

Marya looked at Martha. "No, my dear, it is you who are off point. Focus is a geometric term, nothing to do with algebra. Although perhaps you are on point. I believe a focus is a point." She tittered at her own joke. "However—"

"I mean, concentrate, Mar. Short and to the…point."

"Ah yes, my dear. Now I understand. Perhaps I have become a bit sidetracked. Where was I?"

"Murder. Motivation. Dies Irae."

Marya plucked the *Motivation—Luz Flores* card from her hand, read it, laid it on the table, and cocked her head. "Luz Flores."

Luz gasped. "I would never…" Her eyes were so wide that in her thin, intense face, she looked like a velvet picture of a saucer-eyed waif.

"Never say never, my dear. Although, as my mother, God rest her soul said, 'Never say never say never.'"

Luz looked, as Marya would have said, puzzled.

"You have devoted your life to Dies Irae since the death of your husband and would do anything Father Thaddeus asked. Although you professed to defend Mr. Nance, your fervid devotion to Dies Irae would overcome all of your misgivings, and it would be easy for you to plant the evidence on him."

Luz combed her fingers through the white streak running down the middle of her short dark hair. "I would never…"

Marya picked out the *Motivation—Ken Vance* card, laid it on the table next to the Luz card, and contemplated it. "All four of you would kill for the cause, but it seems that one of you has a more pressing and personal motivation. Mr. Vance works as a billing clerk at the hospital, yet the Vances live in a Skeeter Flats mansion." She looked at Ken. "Where did the money come from? How can you afford to pay the taxes and maintain it? Not on your salary, surely. Do you obtain money, as Mr. Bonino told Isabella, through some 'funny business?' Is that why you are pushing to raise the tithing limit to 15%? So you can cover your personal withdrawals?"

With each question, Ken clenched his fists tighter and tighter. He wore a sleeveless T-shirt, and the veins in his arms, already engorged, stood out even more. "No," he squeaked. He cleared his throat. "No." A little lower, but still high pitched. He cleared his throat again and finally managed, a deep, booming, "No," that was so loud, it appeared to startle Ken himself.

Marya looked at Father Thaddeus. "I understand that you do not concern yourself with finances, Father, but perhaps a review by an outside accountant might be in order."

Father Thaddeus locked his gaze onto Ken, as though peering into his follower's soul. Ken looked away.

Placing the *Motivation—Barbara Vance* card next to the other two, Marya said, "Barbara is a devoted and obedient wife."

Barbara met Marya's gaze and gave a quick nod.

"But would you obey an order to kill? Perhaps you suspected the true source of your wealth and killed to protect it. Or did you believe Ken was a murderer, and you did nothing to stop him?" Marya looked up at Barbara. "A sin of omission."

Barbara's soft, pudgy face turned even more pallid than usual. Her lips trembled, and her eyes returned to their customary resting place, the face of her husband. Ken looked down at her, cracking his neck from side to side. Barbara flinched. She tore her glance from his and turned to Luz.

Marya added, "Or perhaps Barbara *and* Luz did nothing to stop Ken."

She placed the *Motivation—Father Thaddeus* card on the table above the other three. "Father Thaddeus." She nodded at him. "I do not think Father Thaddeus murdered Mr. Bonino or Mr. Ward."

Father Thaddeus, his posture straight and tall, gave a stiff-necked nod toward Marya.

"But you could have ordered any one of your followers to do so," she continued in the same agreeable tone of voice. "Or perhaps you merely expressed your displeasure, as King Henry II did of Thomas à Becket, and asked, 'Will no one rid me of these two troublemakers?' Trusting your devoted followers to carry out your unspoken wishes."

"How dare you insinuate…"

A chorus of, "He did not. We did not. I did not…" broke out from the Dies Irae group.

"Perhaps," Marya said.

She picked up the four Dies Irae notecards, placed them neatly at the bottom of the deck, removed the top card, *Gertrude Doppeldecker—Motivation*, and set it down on the table.

"Gertrude Doppeldecker."

Martha had forgotten she was in the room. Gertie sat slouched over in her chair, a beige bundle, her hair barely distinguishable from her sweater. She twisted her neck to the side and met Marya's gaze. "Yes, Marya?"

"You too were a suspect."

"Me?"

"Yes, my dear."

"But what reason would I have to kill anyone?"

"Sometimes, my dear, reason is not necessary for murder. Reason is necessary for logic, but not for motivation. Sometimes they are quite the opposite."

Ken turned to Father Thaddeus and said, "Clearly logic and reason are not necessary to accuse completely innocent people of murder." The suspects snickered—all except Gertie.

"As my dear friend Martha once pointed out to me, very perspicaciously I must add, you were always very careful never to speak about yourself. That was a very significant fact. It meant you had something to hide. But what might that be?" Marya read the front and back of the *Gertrude Doppeldecker—Motivation* card and then refocused her gaze on Gertie.

"When we went to your home for that lovely tea party, Martha noticed a pharmacist license hanging in your office under the name of Marilyn Turner. As I thought about that, my mind went off on its own, travelled down a path from long ago. It does that sometimes. I remembered that when my sister and I got into mischief, my mother, God rest her soul, would say that if we did not behave ourselves, the Turnerman would steal us away, and we would never be seen again. All the local mothers said that to their children. I later learned that the monster that scared little children was usually called the bogeyman. And so, I began to wonder, why was it that the mothers in Pequot Bays called it the Turnerman? Was there a grain of truth in our local legend? Perhaps there was once a man named Turner, a real man who really did steal little children away from their mothers. Martha dropped me off at the library, and I looked through microfilm of old issues of the *Pequot Bays Journal*. I checked backwards from the time

I was a child and discovered that there was a serial murderer in 1883. He lived on Pequot Island. On Bridle Path Road. Where you live, Gertrude. His name was…"

Gertie whispered along with Marya, "Andrew Turner."

The room was silent as Gertie continued speaking. "Yes, Andrew Turner was my great-great-grandfather. He was insane. And his insanity carried over to the generations that followed. His son, after marrying and having three children, was put in a mental institution. Two of the three children died young. One survived. That was my grandfather. He never spoke about how his brothers died. He never spoke much at all. He usually just sat in his rocking chair by the fireplace, even in the summer. My father was his only child. He was a brutal man, my father. He would beat my mother and me. He didn't kill anyone though. Except himself. He committed suicide. Hung himself five years ago, soon after Mother died. I inherited the house and moved in, the first Turner to live there since my grandfather. I'll never marry. I'm the last of the Turners. It will all end with me." She looked around the room. "But I didn't kill anyone. It skipped my generation. It wasn't me." Everyone continued staring at her. "Maybe I stole a few things now and then, just to make ends meet. But I never, never could kill anyone."

"Perhaps." Marya contemplated all the suspects. "Any one of you could have murdered Mr. Ward and Mr. Bonino. But the third murder made it completely clear. The third murder is, of course, the first murder, and it led to the second and third murders, or as I spoke about them, the third and second murders. Sister Anne Marie spoke about serial numbers as a staircase, either ascending or descending, from smallest to largest or largest to smallest. We are descending the staircase. Going down, not up. Or are we going up? 3-2-1, not 1-2–"

Bitsy said, "We are going nowhere. Not up or down, more like upside down. Let's go, dear." Bitsy picked up her purse.

There were murmurs. "She's right." "Purple Pest." "This is getting ridiculous." The others began to gather their belongings.

Marya said, "The murder, the very first murder, the murder which eventually brought about the deaths of Mr. Ward and Mr. Bonino—that murder could only have been done by one person." Martha had to strain to hear over the scraping of chairs and the murmuring of the group. "And that person was neither Isabella nor Gertrude nor Barbara nor Mr. Vance nor Luz nor Mr. Todi nor Father Thaddeus." Marya eyed each suspect as she intoned their names.

Then her eyes came to rest on Dr. Ianelli and Bitsy.

Martha froze. Oh no! Marya had forgotten that Dr. Ianelli and Bitsy were in Europe when Lisa died. They got back only the day before the funeral. They had no opportunity to kill her.

"Mar."

"The killer is…"

"Marya."

"My dear, I *am* being short and to the point. No need to interrupt. The murderer is—Dr. Ianelli."

"Mar, Dr. Ianelli was in Europe when Lisa Ward died. He couldn't be the murderer."

Dr. Ianelli slowly turned and faced Martha, his eyes cold and hard, a vein pulsating in his neck. "Thank you so very much, Martha. I should sue this…this…this Purple Pest for slander, but what would be the point? No one will believe her anyway. And she doesn't have, excuse the expression, a commode to pee in."

Bitsy attempted a shrill, tinkling laugh. "Shall we leave, Steven?"

"Yes, we shall. Come with me, Bitsy." With his eyes locked on Marya, he enunciated, "Everyone shall leave." Dr. Ianelli and Bitsy rose as one and strode toward the hallway leading to the examination rooms, holding hands. Even with her five-inch spike heels, Bitsy was still a good five inches shorter than her husband. He took off his tortoiseshell glasses and looked fondly at her. "You look lovely today, darling. But then you always have."

She did look lovely, her face made up to conceal any flaws in her complexion left by the passing years. Her simple, elegantly tailored little blue dress was draped to cover any imperfections not taken care of by the expertise of her personal trainer. Her loose blond waves were too shiny, too perfectly formed, to be natural. She reached up to smooth down a stray strand of Dr. Ianelli's salt-and-pepper hair. "We must get you ready, dear. Is your jacket in the office?"

The others began to make their way to the exit, giving a wide berth to Gertie. Father Thaddeus was first through the door, and Ken and Barbara Vance followed close behind. A moment later, they walked back in. The priest said, "There's a police car blocking the parking lot exit. Miss Chonkin, move it so that we may go."

"It's Officer Chonkin, Father. And it's not my unit."

"It's mine." Officer Henry Milton walked into the room. "And I think you should all sit down and hear what the lady has to say." His voice rang with newfound confidence and authority. They obeyed. Henry stood, hands on hips, forming a barrier to the door. He nodded brusquely at Officer Chonkin, and the smallest of small smiles crossed her lips.

The room quieted down.

Marya said, "Of course, Dr. Ianelli did not kill Lisa Ward. Lisa Ward killed herself."

"But you said there were three..." said Martha.

Dr. Ianelli stopped at the entranceway to the hall and whispered something to Bitsy. She continued down the hall while he remained, looking over his tortoise-shell glasses at Marya.

Marya looked at Martha. "I had thought, my dear, that it was possible Lisa Ward had also been a murder victim, but I did not believe it was probable for the very reason that my principal suspect, Dr. Ianelli, had no opportunity to kill her. And once I finally understood the motivation for the murders of Mr. Bonino and Mr. Ward, I knew that she had died at her own hand. She committed suicide because she was deeply depressed about Mr. Ward having an affair. She was not in her right mind." Marya turned to Gertie. "When you saw Mr. Vance at the café with poor Lisa Ward, he was being a good friend to a despairing soul. Nothing more. You are not a murderer, my dear, but as the Jewish sages have said, each time someone speaks badly of others, it is like killing three people, the speaker, those listening, and those being spoken about. There is much excellent advice in the Bible about—"

Ken Vance broke in. "Yes, Lisa was deeply depressed. She did adore her husband. He was her whole life. And he betrayed her. I didn't kill Michael Ward, but he deserved to die. He might as well have forced the pills down her throat."

Marya nodded. "Her suicide led Mr. Ward to go to confession and to break off the relationship with Isabella. God forgave him, Mr. Vance, even if you cannot. If it is any help to know, my dear," Marya said to Isabella, "with such guilt hanging over his head, your relationship with Michael was doomed from the start. It would never have worked."

Marya turned toward Justin, whose head was in his hands.

"My dear Justin, I am sorry that at such a young age you must come to terms with these harsh truths. The Bible says, 'The truth will set you free.' But I prefer another quote, from a book almost as long as the Bible, 'The truth will set you free. But only after it is finished with you.'"

Marya turned to Dr. Ianelli. "It was you. You killed Mr. Bonino."

Dr. Ianelli stood with his arms crossed, head cocked, and eyebrows raised, like he was listening to a patient explain particularly interesting symptoms. "This is absurd. Whether it was an allergic reaction to crab or penicillin, I tried to save his life, not kill him. Everyone saw that. I tried everything. EpiPens, CPR."

Marya paused for a moment as she pulled three note cards from the deck and read the front and the back of each. Martha saw they were labeled:

*Dr. Steven Ianelli—page 1,*
*Dr. Steven Ianelli—page 2,* and
*Dr. Steven Ianelli—page 3.*

"Yes, you used two EpiPens, and I noted that when you removed them from your bag, the EpiPens were not in their boxes. They had no plastic wrapping around them. I observed the one that Mr. Vance removed from his bag was in a box. My dear Dr. Stokes advised me that EpiPens should never be used unless they are in some sealed wrapping. So I knew that you had altered them so that they would be ineffective."

"Yes," Ken said. "I must have sensed something was wrong. So I tried one more."

Dr. Ianelli spoke as though explaining a complex disease to a simple minded patient. "If I used an EpiPen that was not in a wrapper, that does not make me a murderer. He died of anaphylactic shock. I tried to save him. As you said, everyone knew he was allergic to crab and penicillin, and if it wasn't the crab that set him off, anyone could have administered the penicillin by adding it to his drink. Your 'dear Dr. Stokes' is right about that."

Marya read over the front and then the back of the *Dr. Steven Ianelli—page 1* card. "The reason you were my principal suspect, what gave you away from the start, was that you knew, like me, that Mr. Bonino was not allergic to crab. As his doctor, he would have advised you about his real allergies. And yet, you told everyone at the party that he died from an allergic reaction to crab when you knew that was impossible. Officer Chonkin obtained the death certificate, which stated that he died from anaphylactic shock due to an allergy to shellfish. Why would you attest to incorrect information on an official document? I wonder, if one were to review Mr. Bonino's records, what allergies would be listed? Would they include crab, or only penicillin?"

"Ridiculous. Do you think I can remember the allergies of all of my patients? If I made a mistake, that does not make me a murderer. And he may have told someone else that he wasn't really allergic to crab."

"That was possibility I considered, but his own son thought he was allergic, so he had not told his family, and therefore I thought it unlikely he had told others."

Bitsy came back into the room, looked at her husband, and gave a barely perceptible shake of the head. She stood next to him and took one of his hands in both of hers.

"But what possible reason would I have to murder Johnny? Or Michael? Or am I just a crazy serial murderer?" He glanced at Gertie, who glared back at him.

Marya placed the *Steven Ianelli—page 1* card face down on the glass table and began reading from the *Steven Ianelli—page 2* card. "Indeed, you were the one person without any apparent motivation for the murders of Mr. Ward and Mr. Bonino. Everyone else had motive, means, and opportunity, but only you, Dr. Ianelli, had a reason to kill the third victim. And once that murder was uncovered, it was clear why it led to the murders of Mr. Bonino and Mr. Ward."

"So, who is this mysterious third murder victim?"

"Frank Guardino."

"Who the heck is Frank Guardino?" Ken Vance asked.

"That was my great-grandfather." Justin slumped back down in his chair. "Why is everybody in my family being murdered?"

The others followed Justin's lead, making their way back to their seats, leaving Dr. Ianelli and Bitsy standing alone, facing Marya.

"Yes, Justin, your great-grandfather. He took care of your mother after her parents died. You didn't know him, but everyone in the old neighborhood did. He was a brilliant fixer-upper and a handyman." She reread the *Dr. Steven Ianelli—page 2* card. "When you graduated from medical school, Dr. Ianelli, you did not have this lovely spacious office where we are now. Your office was in your home, a small house near my own neighborhood, and your only patients were the baymen and the workers. We all knew you, including me, although you do not remember me. Bitsy was your receptionist and assistant at that time. You knew Frank Guardino, of course. He was your handyman, and he even repaired some of your medical equipment. Officer

Chonkin obtained the death certificate of Mr. Guardino. You, as his doctor, certified that he died of natural causes, a heart attack."

"You are correct about that at least," Dr. Ianelli said. "He did die of natural causes. He had heart problems for many years."

"We will never know how you killed Mr. Guardino. Time has erased all traces of that. But I know why. Just like the trail of breadcrumbs that Hansel and Gretel left in the forest, there were several little things that led me to Mr. Guardino and the motivation for his murder."

Martha waited for the next comment that she knew Marya would make.

"The little things are very important. Isn't that right, my dear?" Marya nodded to Martha. "As Saint Teresa of Calcutta said, 'We cannot do great things. We can only do little things with great love.' And then there is the Little Flower. I chose Thérèse as my confirmation name. I do love the Theresas. There is also Theresa of—"

"Mar!"

"Sorry, my dear. Where was I?" Marya read both sides of *Dr. Steven Ianelli—page 2* card, both sides of the *Dr. Steven Ianelli— page 3* card, and then looked around, brows furrowed. She read them again. "Motivation. Where did I put that? The third murder? No, the first murder." She shuffled through the deck, glancing at each of the cards, murmuring to herself. "No, not means. Not opportunity. Motivation. First murder. Where would I have filed that?"

And Marya had been doing so well. Martha thought of a prayer she now knew by heart from hearing Marya repeat it.

*Saint Anthony, perfect imitator of Jesus, who received from God the special power of restoring lost things, grant that...*

Bitsy pulled at her husband's sleeve. "We really must go, Steven, or we'll be late for dinner with the Wallaces. And we've been planning this for ages. I spoke to Muffy today, and we decided to go to the new restaurant. The one on the water. It's hard to get reservations, but..."

"Ahh. Here it is." Marya pulled out a card from the clutter in front of her. It was labeled:

*Little Things.*

"Four little things. The charm, the firecracker, the change in the outfit, the incompetent receptionist." She looked up at Dr. Ianelli and repeated, "The charm, the firecracker, the change in the outfit, the incompetent receptionist."

Dr. Ianelli rolled his eyes. "The charm, the firecracker, the change in the outfit, the incompetent receptionist. Yes, Bitsy, it's time to go." He did not move though. He stood, facing Marya, while Bitsy tugged at him.

"The firecracker, of course, was the problem. Was it a diversion planned so that the charm could be stolen? If so, it could only have been planned by someone who saw the body in advance of the wake, which would be limited to the immediate family, Isabella, and her son. However, Isabella would have no reason to stage a diversion to steal the necklace at the wake. She could have done it any time before. I was confused. But then I remembered about black cats, and so I checked with Tom Baker's street boys."

There were murmurs of, "Black cats?" and "Tom Baker's street boys?"

"If a black cat crosses my path and then I get into a car accident, did the black cat cause the car accident? Of course not. So, I called Tom Baker, who found the little rapscallion who set off the firecracker, and I learned that he did it on his own, as a lark. It was, therefore, not a diversion, and the field of suspects opened up once again."

"I have no idea what you are talking about," Dr. Ianelli said. "What charm? What necklace? I do remember the firecracker though."

"Why, the charm around Mr. Bonino's neck that was stolen at the wake. Isabella had no idea what it was, so I visited my friend, Mr. McMurray Jr. I know him quite well. I knew his father also. He is the second generation McMurray to run the funeral home. Mr.

McMurray Jr. has quite a sense of humor when you get to know him. But, that aside, he is very diligent. Especially when jewelry is concerned. I recall—"

"Marya," said Martha, "the charm around Mr. Bonino's neck that was stolen at the wake."

"Oh yes, thank you, my dear. I spoke to Mr. McMurray Jr. and asked how it came to be around the neck of the deceased. He said that they had found it clutched in his hand, so the mortician put it on the necklace with the crucifix when they prepared him for the funeral. You will recall that when he died, Mr. Bonino was holding out his fist as though to show us something."

"Are you accusing me of stealing a necklace?"

"Yes indeed, either you or Bitsy or both of you together."

"Well, I suppose that being accused of larceny is better than murder."

Bitsy laughed nervously. No one else joined in.

Marya reached into her bag and promptly, for once, found the photograph of the charm. "I do not believe that I had the opportunity to show the picture to you, Bitsy. Officer Chonkin, would you be so kind?" Marya held out the photograph to Chonkin, who took it over to Bitsy, who stopped laughing.

"And why should I steal a dead man's necklace?" asked Dr. Ianelli.

"An excellent question. Had I been less distracted and more attentive to what was going on around me at Mr. Bonino's funeral, I would have figured that out sooner." Marya looked down at the *Little Things* notecard and then back up at Dr. Ianelli. "I had only seen the charm around Mr. Bonino's neck for a moment at the wake, and its removal was just another little thing that needed explaining. It was not until I missed my double jump that I remembered I had missed missing your tie tack and cufflinks, which you always wore. You did not wear them at Mr. Bonino's funeral or Mr. Ward's funeral. The very day after the wake, you began to wear oxford shirts with buttons instead of cufflinks, and a tie clip instead of a tie pin. Another little thing that needed explaining."

Dr. Ianelli glanced down at the rolled-up sleeves of his oxford shirt.

"I went to our lovely town library and checked some old editions of the *Pequot Bays Journal*. You attend so many functions around town, it was not difficult to find a picture of you wearing the tie tack and cufflinks. You stopped wearing them because—"

"Because I lost one of the cufflinks."

"—you were afraid that they would connect you to the charm. And you were correct. Your cufflinks and tie tack were reproductions, in gold, of the exact charm that had been stolen from around Mr. Bonino's neck."

Chonkin took the photograph from Bitsy and brought it back to Marya. "I showed most of you this copy of the closeup of the tie tack. Justin Ward recognized it as a charm of his great grandfather, Frank Guardino. His mother kept it in an envelope with some papers, in a box where she saved all the documents that concerned her grandfather's inventions. She told Justin that her grandfather once said it was worth a million dollars. Justin found neither the charm nor the papers, but he found an empty envelope labeled *The Guardian*. He recalled his father going through the box of documents with his lawyer, Mr. Bonino, after his mother died. Did you hear Mr. Bonino's last words, Dr. Ianelli?"

"I was too busy trying to save his life."

"He said, 'The Guardian.' When I first saw the envelope, I began thinking again of our four Dies Irae suspects, who call themselves guardians of the good. Had it not been for the witnesses, it is possible I would never have discovered its true meaning."

"The witnesses?" Dr. Ianelli asked.

"Yes, two of them."

"What did they witness?"

"Everything."

"Who are these witnesses?"

"Their names are Francis and Stephen."

"What are their last names?"

"I am afraid I don't know."

"Where are they now?"

"Why, they are here with us."

Dr. Ianelli and Bitsy looked around the room, as did the others.

Marya tittered. "Oh, my dears, you cannot see them, but they are here. They are with us always. There are clouds of them. Clouds of witnesses, as they are called by Saint Paul. The saints in heaven. I am reminded of this every time I walk into Saint John's and see our beautiful stained-glass windows. Saint Francis and Saint Stephen—"

"Marya! The Guardian."

"But that is exactly what I was speaking about, my dear. You will recall the day we stood in front of the sanctuary windows and were touched by the light from Saint Francis and Saint Stephen. The blue ray of light from Saint Francis combined with the red from Saint Stephen blended into purple. And that revealed to me the meaning of The Guardian. One must blend the names, you see. Francis and Stephen. Frank and Steven. Frank Guardino and Steven Ianelli. GUARDino and IANelli. GUARD plus IAN equals GUARDIAN. One needs only to combine the names to come up with the answer."

Marya put down the *Little Things* card down on the desk and read over the *Dr. Steven Ianelli—page 3* card.

"There was a connection between the two, but what could a physician and a skilled tinkerer have in common? The envelope with the charm was in a box holding documents concerning Mr. Guardino's inventions. So, it was some sort of an invention that connected the two, and my good friend Martha mentioned to me that you had made a great deal of money on a medical device. As you said, Mr. Guardino had heart problems for many years, so perhaps it had something to do with the heart. I took the photograph to dear Dr. Stokes, who immediately recognized it as a medical device known as a stent, a metal mesh tube that helps keep arteries unblocked. He informed me that it was immediately and hugely successful beginning in about the year 1987, which, I recall, was around the time you left our little neighborhood and moved to Middle Point. Dr. Stokes even took the time to do a bit of research on this electric device he carries with him that looks rather like an Etch-a-Sketch screen. He confirmed that you, doctor, and you alone, were credited as its creator.

"Now that I knew what The Guardian was, and your connection to it, I returned to the library and looked at the local papers around the time that Mr. Guardino died. I found a newspaper article about the invention. The inventor had refused to be interviewed and wanted to remain anonymous, which the article attributed to your modesty and humility. But the real reason you wanted to avoid publicity was because you did not want your co-inventor to know the invention had been successful. While Mr. Guardino likely would not read medical journals, he would read the local paper. The article was published just before Mr. Guardino's death. He must have confronted you, wanted his share of the credit and the money, and so you killed him."

"You are correct, I did invent The Guardian stent. I did it alone. But even if Guardino had helped, why wouldn't I have shared the money with him? There was more than enough to go around. It was phenomenally successful."

"Because of love, Dr. Ianelli. Love you had already secured. Bitsy's love. She had given up everything for you. She had been disowned by her family, lost her wealth and her prestige to marry you. You were from a poor family, mired in debt when you graduated from medical school. The two of you worked hard together to establish your medical practice, living in a small house on the wrong side of the tracks. I would imagine those were happy years. But you wanted to give Bitsy everything that she had given up for you. You wanted to be the richest man in Pequot Bays. Wealthier and more respected even than her parents. And you were willing to kill for her."

Dr. Ianelli gazed at Bitsy. "You're right, those were happy times." Bitsy smiled up at him. "But," he looked back at Marya, "wrong again about the murder. I suppose in baseball, an average of .500 is considered excellent. But this is not baseball."

"No, Dr. Ianelli. This is not a game." Marya met his gaze, then glanced at the *Little Things* card. "This explained another little thing. Why you hired young, inexperienced Lisa, although your receptionists were always very competent and Lisa was not. If I may paraphrase a quote by Machiavelli," Marya gave a nod toward Chonkin and Henry, "'Keep your friends close, keep your enemies closer.' You had to keep a close eye on Lisa after you killed her grandfather. Was she a danger to you? Did she know about the invention? She apparently did not, and must not even have recognized the tie tack and cufflinks that matched the charm her grandfather had once shown her, so you did not kill her, and she married Mr. Ward."

Marya turned over the *Little Things* card and read the back. "You were safe for many years. Until Mr. Bonino began to blackmail you. Ironically, it was Lisa's death that set in motion the actions that led you to murder Mr. Bonino and Mr. Ward."

"Murder, robbery, blackmail. This is quite a story you've come up with. Talk about inventions!" He shook his head. Bitsy laughed.

"Johnny Bonino was Michael Ward's lawyer and the executor of Lisa Ward's estate. Mr. Ward showed him the papers and the charm, which was a…" she looked down at the card, "a prototype of the stent from the box of documents about her grandfather's inventions that Lisa kept in her room. Mr. Bonino had had a stent placed in one of his arteries, so when he saw the charm, he may have recognized it. The missing papers in the envelope must have been a contract or partnership agreement signed by Mr. Guardino and Dr. Ianelli for The Guardian stent. He knew Mr. Guardino from the old neighborhood and that he was an inventor. He could goggle 'Guardian Stent' and find out, just as Dr. Stokes did, that its invention was credited only to Dr. Ianelli. And yet, he had proof in his hands that Mr. Guardino was entitled to half the profits.

"Mr. Bonino must have confronted you with the contract and threatened to tell Mr. Ward, who, as Lisa's heir, would have been entitled to half the profits from the stent. So, you began paying him hush money. Shortly before his death, Mr. Bonino told Isabella that he had come into a large annuity that would pay him for the rest of his life. You were that annuity. He also started carrying his 'lucky charm,' the prototype of the stent.

"You were the one who broke into Mr. Bonino's office to try to steal the contract. I presumed you were unsuccessful because, if you had been able to find it, you would not have been compelled to kill Mr. Ward. You knew that if the contract was located among Mr. Bonino's legal files, it would have been returned to Mr. Ward. He would give them to another lawyer, who could make the same connection between you and Mr. Guardino. I asked Isabella if she would go through her husband's personal papers to see if she could find a contract that referred to the Guardian stent. I suspect at some point Bitsy became aware of the murders, most likely before Michael Ward was killed, and began to help."

Dr. Ianelli's eyes narrowed. "Don't you dare bring Bitsy into this."

"She may not have been aware of the murder of Mr. Guardino, and perhaps not even that of Mr. Bonino, but I am quite sure that Bitsy was involved with the murder of Michael Ward. That would make her an accessory to murder. Perhaps Officer Chonkin would know more about this than I, but I believe an accessory to murder would be punished in the same manner as the actual murderer. Did you find the contract, my dear?"

Martha was confused for a moment until she realized that although Marya was still looking at Dr. Ianelli, she was speaking to Isabella.

"Yes, I did, Ms. Cook. It was in our safe. At home. I brought everything." She took out a manila envelope.

"Thank you, my dear. Since blackmail was not part of Mr. Bonino's regular legal practice, he would have taken the file home for safekeeping."

Dr. Ianelli took a quick step toward Isabella, but Officer Chonkin jumped in front of him and snatched the folder. They glared at each other a moment before Chonkin walked back to where she had been standing and Dr. Ianelli returned to Bitsy's side.

"Even if you could prove a connection between me and Guardino for the Guardian stent, that does not make me a murderer. You have no proof of that."

"Yes, no hard proof. Isn't that always the hope of every wrongdoer? How were we to prove the murderer was the murderer? And so Martha and I pretended that we knew who the murderer was in order to trap you. Unfortunately, that put my dear friend Martha in great danger three times. It was not until your last murder attempt that we finally obtained proof to connect you with the first two attempts and thus to the murder." Marya picked up and read over a card entitled:

*Murder Attempts on Dear Martha.*

"The first murder attempt. You tried to run over Martha with a car. Bitsy may not have been an accomplice in that attempt, but she most likely was for the next two." Marya eyed Dr. Ianelli.

He glowered at Marya. "I don't mind your ridiculous accusations against me, but you'd better watch what you say about Bitsy."

"It was a clumsy try, perhaps because you panicked and were in a hurry to silence her. You told Martha you were late for office hours because you met a patient in the emergency room. It will be easy to check whether you were there that morning. Bitsy said the car that nearly killed Martha was a white Range Rover, like the car of one of your patients. You said Bitsy would not know a Volkswagen from a Rolls Royce. That is not true. Bitsy described exactly the year and model of the car driven by the unfortunate young man who backed up into Judge Albernathy's car while he was drunk. That would be the young man who was drunk, not Judge Albernathy. Judge Albernathy is not a drinker. He is president of the parish council. I came to know him—the judge, not the young man—because I would often stop him in church to request that a handrail be placed near the lectern for our elderly priests. Father Peanuts, you know, is quite shaky these days. It took almost two years, but he finally agreed. I tried to thank the judge, but he scurried away from me."

"Marya. Please."

"You are quite correct, my dear, I am digressing. But I should never have thought Judge Albernathy was such a humble man that he would not want to be thanked for his efforts. Now where was I?"

"Bitsy and the Range Rover."

"Oh yes. You had to discredit Bitsy because she was right. When the car was found, it turned out that it was not *like* the car of your patient, it *was* the car of your patient. A patient who was bed-bound and to whom you made house calls. His aide will surely recall a visit by you the day I enacted my little drama after Mr. Bonino's funeral, which was the very day before the attempt on dear Martha's life. You—not a therapist, nurse, or an aide—stole the key. The aide, unfortunately, was fired, so we were not able to ask him. I am sure the police will be able to track him down. But if not the aide, the Medicare billing records will suffice."

Marya turned over the *Murder Attempts on Dear Martha* card and read the back. "The second murder attempt. You poisoned Martha at the party. You spiked—ah, there is that word again—the cup of lemonade with amphetamines and hightailed—oh you criminals have such colorful vocabularies. Hightail—I wonder—"

"Marya," Martha said.

"Yes, my dear. So sorry. Hightailed it out of there as soon as you saw the little angel walk over to Martha. Bitsy was in charge of beverages at the party—"

"Leave Bitsy out of it. I'm warning you."

"As I said, Bitsy was in charge of beverages at the party. Yes, I am quite confident that the two of you planned this together." She nodded in agreement with her own statement.

Dr. Ianelli took a step closer to Marya, who looked up at him. Martha was impressed that Marya did not seem at all intimidated by Dr. Ianelli's fierce stare.

"But still, there was no hard proof. Until today, that is, your last attempt. We stopped you just before you injected Martha with a lethal overdose of amphetamine. So now we have you. I am quite sure that although you emptied the syringe, it will still contain traces of amphetamine.

"And we also have Bitsy. She left to clean the syringe, which means she knew it contained amphetamines, not a pain killer. That will prove that Bitsy is an accomplice to a murder attempt. But she could not clean the syringe. Officer Chonkin had already taken it into her possession." Marya looked at Chonkin, who gave a slight nod.

Officer Chonkin strode over to Bitsy and Dr. Ianelli. "I am arresting you both for the attempted murder of Martha Collins. You have the right to remain silent. Anything you say will be held against you. You have the right to an attorney—"

"Bitsy had nothing to do with it. It was only me. I asked her to clean the syringe."

"Then I am arresting her for aiding and abetting the attempted murder of Martha Collins. If you cannot afford an attorney, one will be appointed for you."

"She had no idea it contained methamphetamine."

"Do you understand these rights? Do you still want to talk? Dr. Steven Ianelli? Elizabeth Ianelli?"

"Leave Bitsy out of this."

"I'm afraid I can't."

"She knows nothing about any of the murders. I did them all alone. It was me. Only me."

And there it was. No mistaking it now. A full-blown smile on the face of Officer Chonkin.

As Henry and Chonkin led the Ianellis out of the office and into the squad cars, the others began to rustle around in their chairs. Marya collected her notecards into a neat pile and placed them in her bag. Ken stomped over, scowled down at Marya, and squeaked, "You purple—" He cleared his throat and continued in a deeper voice, "You purple pain in the—"

Father Thaddeus interrupted in a voice not unlike Marya's steely tones, "I will meet you in the car."

Ken whipped around and strode toward the door, grabbing Barbara's wrist as he passed her.

Father Thaddeus did not move, but watched as Marya stood and arranged her lilac bag on her left shoulder. "Ms. Cook, it appears you have a gift for sensing evil. We can use people like you in our organization."

Marya shook her head and touched the brown cord of the scapular around her neck.

The priest pulled himself up to his full height and swept majestically out of the room. Luz and Aldo followed. Martha looked around for Gertie but, as usual, she had disappeared without anyone noticing.

Justin, who had continued staring wide-eyed at the door through which the Ianellis had been led away, gave a shake of his head and stood up. Isabella tried to talk to him, but he waved her away.

Isabella approached Marya. "I guess there are some things that can never be forgiven, Ms. Cook."

"There was another person who said something very like that to me, my dear. I will tell you what I told him: No matter how bad you may think your sin is, God has heard worse."

Isabella gazed at Marya. "It was Michael you said that to, wasn't it?"

Marya nodded.

Isabella let out a long breath. "Maybe I shouldn't be so angry at

God. Maybe it was my own fault." Head down, hair covering her face, she walked slowly out the door.

Justin came up and gave Marya a hug, causing her bag to drop and her cap to tilt sideways. "Ms. Cook, thank you so much…for everything. Can I come and see you sometime? I would love to hear more about my mother when she was young, and my great-grand-father."

"Certainly, Justin. I do so enjoy talking about the old neighborhood. Did you know that your great-grandfather was a champion checker player? He taught me how to play. Maybe I could teach you."

"And maybe I could teach you how to play computer games. I just got *Doom Eternal*. It's all about conquering demons. You'd be good at that."

"Demons! Oh my goodness."

"There's also *Hades, Halo, Divinity: Original Sin 2*…"

"Divinity, original sin. Yes, that sounds interesting, my dear. Perhaps we might start with that."

Martha had to smile.

# CHAPTER 24

## Saturday, December 10

MARTHA DUG AROUND THE DEPTHS OF THE CLOSET IN the Saint Vincent de Paul office and pulled out the files from her prior campaign for civilian police commissioner. She placed them on her desk, sat down, and stared at them. If she really planned to make a run for commissioner, she had to start now. The election was in three months. Marya had volunteered to help, but that surely would not be enough. Martha sat, thinking. Marya would have approved.

Although the drug charges had been dropped, word had already spread that she was an amphetamine abuser, and no one would vote for a pill-popping police commissioner. Arlo Bennett was a former DA, and she was...an Uber driver. Who would vote for her? The election would be humiliating. What had she been thinking?

Martha sighed, rose from her chair, and picked up one of the files. She'd just throw it out.

She heard a rap on the door.

"Come in."

"Hello, hello, my dear. I was in the neighborhood and decided to drop in to see how you were doing on your campaign drive." Marya was dressed in a casual purple outfit. Where had she found those lilac jeans with the neon violet cuffs? She had not attempted to tie the belt of her ever-present lavender raincoat around the layers of sweaters, vests, and jackets underneath. The hat was a simple plum baseball cap, but covered with campaign buttons. *Jimmy Carter for President* surrounding a grinning peanut, *I Like Ike, Humphrey-Muskie, Hoo But Hoover…*

"It's not a campaign drive, Mar. Actually, I've decided—"

Marya looked over her shoulder. "In here, my dear. This is the office."

In walked Luz Flores, rosy-cheeked and smiling, wearing jeans, a T-shirt, and a gray cardigan with a blue and gold circle patch embroidered with *COLUMBIETTES* above a large white cross with three stars underneath. She'd gained a little weight. "Hello, Martha." Luz looked over her shoulder. "Put it over there, Aldo dear, in the corner. Careful, don't overexert yourself."

Aldo Todi walked in pushing a hand truck laden with two large boxes and a long cardboard tube. He placed the hand truck in the corner. He was only slightly out of breath. "Would you open one and show Martha, Aldo dear?"

He opened one of the large boxes and pulled out a metal yard sign proclaiming, in red, white, and blue, *Martha Collins for Police Commissioner.*

"When Marya told us that you were running for police commissioner, we decided to buy these signs for you. There are 250 of them. I made them red, white, and blue in honor of the three patronesses of the Columbiettes." She smiled at Aldo. "Red is Saint Joan of Arc, white is Saint Thérèse, and blue is, of course, Mary. I have lots of ideas for your campaign." Luz turned toward Aldo, beaming. "Show Martha what else we brought her."

Aldo obediently opened the cardboard tube and pulled out a roll of plastic. Luz took one end, and Aldo had to back out of the office as he unfurled a bright red banner. The visible portion of it read: *VOTE FOR HONESTY AND INTEGRITY. VOTE FOR MART—*

"We'll hang this across Main Street," Luz said. "I made it red because, as I said, red represents our patroness Saint Joan. She fought on against all odds. With Saint Joan and the Columbiettes on your side, you can't lose, Martha."

Martha said a quick prayer to Saint Joan, who she knew was the patron saint of cowards, and put the file she had been planning to throw away back onto the desk.

Aldo refurled the banner, walked back into the office, and smiled at Martha. She could not recall ever seeing him smile. Plenty of sneers, lots of sarcasm, but no open, happy smiles. He looked different, and it was not just the smile. His bluish features were ruddier now, and he was not hunched over in his efforts to fill his lungs. He stood up straight, which added about three inches to his height.

"Thanks, Aldo. You look great."

Luz said, "Yes, doesn't he! He had pneumonia on top of emphysema. Thank God the antibiotics finally kicked in. His new doctor made some suggestions about his medications that seem to be working well too. Thanks for the recommendation, Marya." She took one of Aldo's hands in both of her own and looked at him. "And he's stopped smoking."

Aldo gazed back at Luz. "It's because I have something to live for now."

Luz blushed.

"You look great too, Luz," Martha said.

"Yeah, doesn't she look like a million dollars?" Aldo and Luz reluctantly turned their eyes away from each other toward Martha. "I make sure she's not working too hard and she's eating right."

"Aldo's a wonderful cook. He even bakes fresh bread." She laughed. "I think I've gained five pounds in the last two weeks. He takes good care of me."

Martha hesitated to raise the subject. "But what about Father Thaddeus? Who's taking care of him?"

A shadow fell over Luz's features. "This is not for public knowledge, but since you know pretty much everything anyway, Father was removed from his duties. Dies Irae sent him away to a retreat house to get some rest and calm his nerves. For at least a year, maybe longer. The priest who replaced him was horrified at all the time I spent cooking, cleaning, and doing Father Thaddeus's chores." A twinkle came into her eyes. "He ordered me to get some rest and calm my nerves too."

Barbara Vance poked her head in the door. "Oh, hi, Luz. Hi, Martha. Marya told us about the campaign drive, but we can't help out. Not today." She walked into the room. Barbara had on tight black pants with a brightly colored V-neck T-shirt displaying a bit of cleavage. That buttoned up, bow-tied blouse she always wore had covered some voluptuous curves.

Gertie Doppeldecker came in and stood next to Barbara. She wore blue pants and a fire-engine-red top with matching lipstick and fingernails. Marya had been right. Gertie was in her forties, not her sixties, and her hair was blond, not white. "Where'd you get those jeans, Marya? I'd like a pair."

"Why, thank you, my dear. But I am afraid that they are one of a kind. I bought them in our thrift shop three years ago. That is the wonderful thing about thrift shops. One knows that one will not be walking down the street and see someone wearing the same outfit. I recall my—"

Gertie looked at her watch. "I would love to help, but we have our first meeting of the Saint John's chapter of Silent No More in ten minutes. It's an abuse survivors group. We're meeting right down the hall from you."

"Good for you, Gertie," Martha said.

"Not Gertie anymore. My secret is out. I can be Marilyn Q Turner again." She shook her head. "I always hated the name Gertrude Doppeldecker, which is exactly why I used it. I figured no one would think I'd chosen that name on my own."

"What does the 'Q' stand for, Gert—I mean Marilyn."

"Nothing. My middle name is 'Q.'" She shrugged. "I don't know why. You know how…odd…my family was. It was better not to ask questions." She looked at her watch again. "I can't be late. I'm president."

"And I'm vice president," Barbara said. "Good luck, Martha. We'll vote for you." The two hooked arms and strolled off.

Luz shook her head. "Poor Barbara. That new priest from Dies Irae hired an accountant to check into Ken's bookkeeping, just like you suggested, Marya. And you were right."

Aldo nodded. "He was dipping into the till. Big time."

"How much?" Martha asked.

"Over three million dollars."

"Wow! Was he arrested?"

"Yesterday." Laughter rang out from down the hall. "And I don't think Barbara is inclined to post bail."

A tromping of boots stopped at Martha's office door. Officers Sarah Chonkin and Henry Milton walked in. "Good day, everyone," said Chonkin. "Cool hat, Ms. Cook."

Henry said, "Ms. Cook told us about the campaign drive. We're both on duty, but we wanted to stop by to wish you luck."

Chonkin nodded. "And we're not the only ones at the precinct house that'll support you. The Lopez faction doesn't want Arlo to be reelected. He's too closely tied in with O'Hara. Lopez, by the way, is now Captain Lopez. And *Sergeant* O'Hara reports directly to him."

"He's not my boss anymore," Henry said, a broad smile on his face. "He's assigned to desk duty. He's lucky he doesn't have to report to me." A beatific smile came over his face as he considered the possibility.

"Anything new on the investigation?" Martha asked.

"As Marya surmised, the syringe Dr. Ianelli planned to use on you contained traces of methamphetamine, and it matches the meth found in the paper cup. They searched his house and found both cufflinks and the tie tack. He also had a key to the Range Rover that ran you down, and they verified he never entered the hospital that morning. They located the aide, who confirmed Dr. Ianelli visited the old guy who owned the Range Rover the afternoon before." She nodded at Marya. "Everything just like you said, Ms. Cook. Forensic is going over his computers to see if there's any incriminating evidence. There usually is. They're going to exhume Johnny Bonino's body to check for traces of penicillin. Oh, and Bitsy's gone."

"Gone?"

"Yeah. We didn't have enough to hold her. She was released. Left for Montenegro. Dr. Ianelli's out on bail, but he can't leave the country. They took his passport."

"Guess she needed a vacation," Martha said.

"The DA figures it's more than a vacation. We don't have an extradition treaty with Montenegro." Chonkin shrugged, nodded at Henry, and the two turned and tromped back down the hall.

Father Seamus ambled in. "Well now, Martha, I heard you were using the Saint Vincent de Paul office for some non-church-related business. I suppose you might have a moment to discuss some church-related business?"

Of all the…but then he beamed a smile and gave her a wink. He motioned with his head that she should follow him into the hallway. "I wanted to thank you, Martha."

"For what?"

"When I asked you to put a bug in the bishop's ear about the eejit, I never hoped for such a grand outcome—a year in rehab and out of Saint John's for all eternity! Wish I could do something in return."

"Just pray I get elected commissioner."

"Well now, maybe I can do more than that."

"Don't need you to stuff envelopes, Seamus. Got plenty of help with that."

"You know I can't preach from the pulpit about your candidacy, but I might have some say-so on the street. I don't know why, but people seem to trust me."

They grinned at each other.

Marya, Luz, and Aldo were rearranging the boxes in the corner when Martha went back into the room. She sat at her desk, thinking. O'Hara would be after her worse than ever now. But at least she'd get eight votes, and maybe a couple more from some disgruntled cops. That was something. And with Luz spearheading the campaign and Father Seamus electioneering for her, well, anything was possible. She reached into the pocket of her sweater, took out one of the cards Marya had given her, and placed it on the desk.

> *We are surrounded by so great a cloud of witnesses,*
> *let us persevere in running the race.*
> *Hebrews 12:1*

She opened the file on her desk and removed a four-inch, tabbed, color-coded, indexed three ring binder labeled *Campaign for Civilian Police Commissioner* and turned to the tab labeled *First Organizational Meeting.*

Another head popped through the door, this one with a blond curly man bun. "Hi, everyone. My name's Christopher. I'm an old friend of Martha's. Ms. Cook told me about the meeting. I'm here to help." He looked at Martha. "Okay?"

Martha smiled. Maybe anything *was* possible. "Sure thing, Christopher. I need all the help I can get! Okay, everyone, grab a seat. Let's start the meeting."

# ACKNOWLEDGEMENTS

Thank you to two special organizations, the Saint Vincent de Paul Society and the Knights of Columbus.

The Saint Vincent de Paul Society, the Church's best-kept secret, helps millions living in poverty. The heart of our ministry is to visit our friends and neighbors in their homes, find our way into relationship with them, and be transformed by those whom we visit. It is a mission easier said than done, and the ups and downs of Martha's developing relationship with Marya mirror my own struggles in my Vincentian ministry.

I learned about the Columbiettes and the Knights of Columbus by doing research for my book. Charity is at the heart of their work and their faith, and they provide assistance all over the world. My thanks to those generous souls who spent so much time talking to me at the picnic and the diner.

If any of my Church Lady or Men readers are seeking to join a worthy organization, you can't go wrong with either of these.

And thanks to Karen Ullo and Rhonda Ortiz, my kind, compassionate, and patient editors, from whom I learned so much, and Roseanna White for her amazing book covers. I still have a hard time believing that anyone would spend so much time, effort, and professional expertise on my books.

And "my dear Dr. Stokes," a great internal medicine doctor with a subspecialty in murder.

And my three literati, Ned, Will, and Shane, my beta readers.

And my fourth beta reader, Mark, who read over my book almost as many times as I did. I love you.

And, finally, thanks to all my encouragers who helped me overcome my imposter syndrome and made me believe that, maybe, I am a real author after all.

# YOU MAY ALSO LIKE...

WHO AM I TO JUDGE?
(A MARTHA AND MARYA MYSTERY,
BOOK ONE)
by EMILY HANLON

When a priest confesses to the murder of a parishioner, everyone in the wealthy waterfront town of Pequot Bays is convinced of his guilt--everyone, that is, except Marya Cook, a Bible-quoting, lavender-clad octogenarian known to locals as the Purple Pest.

**"Readers will be delighted with Hanlon's deftly constructed mystery and vividly imagined world of colorful characters in this refreshing and hopeful tale of redemption."** –Susan Furlong, *New York Times* Top Ten Crime Fiction Novel of the Year

IN PIECES
(MOLLY CHASE, BOOK ONE)
by RHONDA ORTIZ

Boston, 1793 – Beautiful and artistic, the only daughter of a prominent merchant, Molly Chase cannot help but attract everyone's notice. But she carries a painful secret: her father committed suicide and she found his body. When Molly moves in with the Robb family, society assumes the worst, tempting her to take the easy way out: a marriage of convenience.

"This delightful historical romance is…as fresh and alive as Miss Austen in its treatment of really believable people in a believably real world." – Joseph Pearce, *Catholic Literary Giants*

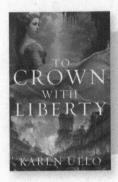

TO CROWN WITH LIBERTY
by KAREN ULLO
*Coming in May, 2024*

New Orleans, 1795 – In the wake of The Terror of the French Revolution, Alix de Morainville Carpentier—a former lady-in-waiting to Marie Antoinette, now married to her gardener—seeks peace and security in the Spanish colony of Louisiana. But her journey into the man-eating swamp called Attakapas reopens the wounds of her former life in France and forces her to reckon with the choices that saved her life at the cost of her honor—and perhaps her soul.

*Advanced Praise*: "Ullo brings us a deep and compelling look into tragedy and triumph, loss and love, desperation and determination that showcases the most beautiful and horrible facets of humanity…This is what historical fiction is meant to be." -- Roseanna M. White, bestselling, Christy Award-winning author of the Codebreakers series.

Printed in the USA
CPSIA information can be obtained
at www.ICGtesting.com
JSHW031529200224
57559JS00004B/22

Life at Saint John of the Cross Parish in Pequot Bays should have returned to normal after one of its priests was cleared of murdering a parishioner and the true killer put behind bars. But a troublesome new group called Dies Irae has moved in, led by the fire-and-brimstone Father Thaddeus. When one of its devoted followers dies under suspicious circumstances, Father Seamus enlists Martha Collins to help him oust Father Thaddeus from the parish. But when a second member of Dies Irae dies, the Purple Pest detective, Marya Cook, shuffles back into action. Can Marya unmask another murderer before he or she strikes again—or will Martha become the next victim?

In this sequel to Emily Hanlon's phenomenal debut, *Who Am I to Judge?*, the scatterbrained octogenarian sleuth, Marya, and her sensible sidekick, Martha, are back in action with new twists and turns, an assortment of scheming suspects, and of course, plenty of purple-penned notecards.

"Fans of classic whodunnits are in for a treat! This book has a complex web of enigmatic characters and labyrinth of twists and turns. Hanlon's lyrical, evocative language ensnares the reader, bringing them into her tapestry of mystery and intrigue, reminiscent of the clever storytelling in the movie *Knives Out*. Highly recommended!"

~JULIE CAROBINI,
author of Cottage Grove Mysteries and the Sea Glass Inn Novels

Emily Hanlon was raised in Texas, educated in Boston, and now lives in New York. She worked as a personal injury attorney for many years and is now an arbitrator. A life of listening to witnesses and sifting through facts has prepared her well for creating the complex entanglements of murder mysteries. She, like her sleuths in the Martha and Marya Mysteries, is active in the Saint Vincent de Paul Society, a eucharistic minister, and a card-carrying Church Lady.

CHRISM
PRESS

ISBN 979-8-88709-059-7

9 798887 090597